NANOTECH

CURE OR KILL

WAYNE E. CRISS

To order additional copies of this book, contact:
Bookwhip
1-855-339-3589
https://www.bookwhip.com

My first novel was a story of four boys who are identical quadruplets. It is titled Genetic Soul Brothers and was published in 2019. It is a story of four genetically identical boys who share a soul, have separate mothers and fathers, lead separate lives, until they find each other. Now can they die separately?

—∘∘∘❧❦∘∘∘—

A very special thank you to Dr. Nur Bilge Criss, my wife and Professor of History and International Relations, who not only contributed to the story-plots of both of these, my first two novels, but also edited my written wrongs.

Prologue

Rapid scientific advances in medical research have led to a new science called nanotechnology. It has produced substances which both cure diseases and kill healthy people. This has resulted in a clandestine war between international conservative industrial organizations and high technology scientists around the world. Nanotech molecular systems have become the weapons of choice.

A Presidential Commission, headed the U.S. Attorney General and ISAAT, a world renown security and detective company, is established to identify and pursue the leaders on both sides of this high-tech war. A second group, four boys from four different continents, call themselves the colored Musketeers, use Modified Avatar names, language, cryptographic correspondence, and extra-legal methodologies, assist in these efforts.

The war begins with simple nanotech molecular systems that turn off critical life support cells in a single person. As the rivalry advances, the nanotech 'weapons' become more sophisticated and directly interfere with the functioning of select body organs. And eventually super high-tech molecular systems are developed which have delayed initiators and can dissolve/digest body vessels within groups of people.

War had been initiated when an unknown person, calling him/herself, Korrectorizer, organized a Committee of World Conservatives composed of selected representatives from various 'fading' industrial corporations. They developed a Conservative Manifesto, and with unlimited financing are trying to stop or slow the development of high technology everywhere, all the time, and in any way possible.

As members of the CWC and their nanotech molecular system's suppliers are identified, it is learned that certain purser family members may be involved and may have become targets. Ten years previously there were 4 boys and 4 fathers. Now there are 4 boys and 0 fathers.

Curing is a private affair! Killing is an anti-private affair!
Can the 'same weapons' do both?

Dramatis Personae / Characters

<u>The Four Colored Musketeers</u>

Jamie (James) O'Reilly – Ey'tuka – small stature, light skinned, curly long dark hair, bright turquoise eyes, tense and emotional, intellectual, son of the American Czar of High Technology Theodore O'Reilly, Irish ancestry, two older sisters – Boston.

Li Jiang – Tsu'teye – very Chinese face, dark brown eyes and hair, tall and proud, careful, observant, son of Dr. Chi Jiang, Professor of Nanomedicine, deceased Irish mother, no siblings – Nanking and Los Angeles.

Kefentse Legoase – Na'via – very dark, close cut Afro hair style, dark brown eyes, skinny and athletic, hyperactive, son of work crew manager in a diamond mine, 5 older brothers and 3 older sisters - Cape Town.

Aykut Turan – Mo'ata – brown hair and almond eyes, round face with olive sun tanned skin, chunky, smiley, easy gait, most things come easy for him, computer intellectual, son of a bank vice president, one little sister, large dog - Istanbul

<u>Presidential International Commissions</u>

Mr. Jonathan O'Reilly – President of the USA, ad hoc member, lawyer, oldest brother (identical triplet).

Mr. Jackson O'Reilly – Attorney General of the USA, Chairman of the Commissions, lawyer, second brother (identical triplet).

Mr. Theodore O'Reilly – Undersecretary or Czar of High Technology, lawyer, third brother (identical triplet).

Mr. Dagda Murphy – Founder, President and CEO of the International Security Assistance and Anti-Terrorist Corp. (ISAAT) and Co-Chairman of the Commissions, Uncle of the O'Reilly brothers and Jamie – lives in Ireland, England, and USA.

Jiang Nano-control International (JNI)

Dr. Chi Jiang – oldest fraternal triplet, Professor at California Institute of Technology, President and CEO of JNI and Director of the Department of Nano-medicines at Cal Tech, Li's Father, living in Los Angeles.

Dr. Jun Jiang – younger fraternal triplet of Chi, Doctor of High Technology and Nano-chemistries and Director of Marketing in JNI, President of three import/export companies marketing in chemicals and pharmaceuticals, living in Germany, USA, and China.

Dr. Cho Jiang – youngest fraternal triplet of Chi and Jun, Doctor of Chemical Engineering and Biochemistries, Director of branches of JNI in Changzhou and Jincheng, Li's tutor uncle when he is schooling in Nanking.

Beyond the fiction of reality, there is always the reality of fiction.

Slavoj Žižek, Slovene Philosopher

1

The President of the USA

THE GREAT POTATO FAMINE OF Ireland, between 1845 and 1852, killed nearly twenty five percent of the Irish population. The famine drove thousands of Irish to leave their homeland and immigrate to the United States of America. The family of Abram and Jennifer O'Reilly, and their six children Aaron, Irene, Alfred, Mogue, Bernadette, and Harold arrived in Boston in the summer of 1846. Most immigrants came to and settled in the northeast because America, and indeed Boston encouraged this immigration as manual labor was needed for everything including transportation, construction, factory work, and farming. Mass housing was being made available for the immigrants. The O'Reilly family found a small apartment for the eight of them, settled in, and immediately started looking for jobs. Abram and the older boys, Aaron, Alfred, and Mogue quickly found dockside jobs, carrying freight back and forth between ships and warehouses. The older daughter, who was good with her hands, soon found a sewing job with a small clothing shop. While the two young ones, Bernadette and Harold, went to a neighborhood school which was taught by an educated Irish immigrant woman.

The hourly pay of each working O'Reilly was meager, but with five 'paychecks' a week, and living under one roof, they survived better than most Irish immigrants. In general, the poor immigration housing and working conditions frequently resulted in massive health care problems throughout the Boston area. Infectious diseases such as typhoid, smallpox, measles, and mumps caused death rates of nearly 30-40% of the Irish immigrants during those years. However, the youngest O'Reilly, Harold was already thirteen when they arrived, so the entire O'Reilly family escaped those deadly diseases.

This first O'Reilly family, each of whom would take any kind of blue-collar job, was typical of the basis of the manual workforce for Boston, Massachusetts, for the next hundred years. The O'Reilly children and their children's children continued to live among their 'kind' for the next several generations.

Over the years the O'Reilly men fought in American wars such as the Civil War and World War II, in Korea, Vietnam, Desert Storm, Afghanistan I and II, and Iraq, as well as the smaller-in-scale American wars such as Lebanon, Somalia, Haiti, Rwanda, Bosnia-Herzegovina, and Kosovo. They were involved in numerous areas of business, commerce, and banking in the Boston area. They had already become Irish Americans. In 1994, when the O'Reilly family's import-export firm, CELT Inc, which now owned nine container ships, five oil tankers, and two supertankers, and had offices in six countries, was listed on the *Fortune 500 List*, it did not surprise anyone.

What did surprise people was that the eldest O'Reilly son, Jonathan, at twenty years of age, bypassed business, commerce, and banking, and instead chose to study law at Harvard University. At sixteen years of age he simply declared that he planned to become President of the United States someday. And because of Jonathan's influence on his two identical brothers, Jackson, born ten minutes later, and Theodore, born ten minutes later still, all three O'Reilly sons, fifth generation from the first Abram O'Reilly immigrant family, became lawyers and entered politics.

As the O'Reilly triplets graduated and received their law degrees on the same day, Jonathan in the top ten percent and Jackson and Theodore in the upper thirty percent of their graduating class, their Father gave to each of them a multi- year rental space on one floor of one of the CELT IMPORT/ EXPORT buildings in downtown Boston. However, first, each had to intern in a highly respectable law firm for three years; then collectively they could have the lease. He simply told them they could use it at one dollar per year, but at the end of the five years they would have to find their own offices. The challenge was easily met.

At the end of three years, the O'Reilly triplets set up their law firm based on their own legal specialties: Jonathan – corporate governance, taxation, litigation, international transactions; Jackson - securities, constitutional law, structured finance, equity; Theodore – corporate law, civil legation, non-governmental organizations, corporate finance. Hence, they began with a legal team that focused on corporation related problems. Consequently, their legal firm of O'Reilly, O'Reilly, O'Reilly and Associates, started rapidly and never stopped growing.

At the age of twenty-eight Jonathan ran for the Massachusetts, District One Seat in the US House of Representatives. He won. When Jonathan turned thirty- six, he ran for one of the two Massachusetts's seats in the US Senate. He won again.

The O'Reilly triplets were of above average height and weight, with dark brown hair and eyes, light skin, and were good looking. They each had an abundance of hair that was styled to personal tastes. The only way one could tell the triplets apart is if you knew which one had which hair style at that point in time. However, Jonathan was that perfect everybody's political man.

Next, Jackson ran for the District One 'Jonathan's' Seat in the House which was now vacant. He won. When Jonathan turned forty-two, he ran for the Office of the President of the United States of America. He won and appointed his first brother, Jackson, as Attorney General and the second brother, Theodore, as Czar of High Technology.

President O'Reilly had won rather easily in 2024. The country had just suffered through many years of imperial-like decision making. The previous two governments had first decreased taxes, and then started a war in an East African country to save the people from their dictatorial president. This was in the middle of a hornet's nest, surrounded by similar hornet's nests, without taking the time to find out what a hornet, let alone a hornet's nest, was all about. Eventually America got out of that nest after borrowing ten trillion dollars, losing eight thousand young American soldiers to bullets, fifty thousand young men to bullet wounds and 'war stress', and more than one hundred thousand locals to collateral damage. The war was shared, as usual, with America's 'willing' ally, England.

In addition, these two governments had ignored twenty years of warnings by environmentalists that the earth's atmosphere and our living environment were being changed in a very negative way; the causes were related to our wasteful habits such as driving energy inefficient motor vehicles and our polluting exhaust systems, in cities, industrial plants and agricultural areas. All of this had been ignored; none of the five international environmental treaties were signed. Just like in rejecting the metric system, again Americans went at it alone. The last straw was when the importation of cheaper, better, high tech designed industrial systems, such as cars, trucks, machines, household and office appliances, electronic and personal goods sent American companies into bankruptcy, workers out of work, and brought America and the entire world into a financial meltdown for several years. The common person lost his car, house, dignity, and pride in being an American.

Where was America borrowing those billions of dollars now being used for recovery? It was China and Japan, not Saudi Arabia, who were the major winners in the export of these cheaper and better industrial products to America in the first place. Unemployment in China and Japan was five and three percent respectively; in America unemployment had reached thirteen percent just before the 2024 elections. Jonathan O'Reilly's promises for change were received positively by the American people at the level of 76% of the popular vote at that time. His promises of Two Cleanings, cleaning up of the environment and cleaning out the old technology by promoting new high technology were highly popular. His brothers and the law firm knew corporate functioning all the way down to the micro-level, so he followed up his Two Cleanings Promises immediately after taking office in 2025 and had little resistance due to his powerful election mandate. The Two Cleanings Promises continue at full speed today.

After his second election mandate of 68% of the popular vote, President O'Reilly's inauguration day began on January 15, 2029. His party and followers in most major cities throughout the United States were celebrating all day and would continue well into the evening hours. Nearly one million party workers had traveled to Washington to celebrate from every major hotel in the city, and of course they filled the Smithsonian Mall from the Lincoln Memorial to the Washington Memorial up to the fountains on the west side at the lower level of the Capitol building.

At 4:00 PM on a very cool overcast winter day, with intermittent snow flurries, President Jonathan O'Reilly was giving his second inaugural address in four years from an enclosed bulletproof platform located on the side of Capital Hill between the fountains and the Capitol. He would soon be sworn in for the second term as the forty eighth President of the USA. Most of his previous cabinet members and members of Congress were in attendance. Only his little brother, the Czar of High Technology was not there. Everything went smoothly.

The Czar, Theodore O'Reilly, had been in an automobile accident five days earlier, and he had badly hurt his hip. Each afternoon he was having physical therapy on this hip at the Walter Reed Military Hospital in Bethesda. On this inaugural afternoon, while lying on his stomach in only his shorts, and riding a hip massage machine in his private hospital room and watching his brother give his speech on television, Theodore dozed off. Then, someone placed a cold wet cloth on his face to ensure that he slept deeper and longer. When he next raised his head up, he did not remember what had happened, but the speech had finished and Jonathan was being sworn in as President, so he knew some time had elapsed for which he could not account. He stood up, examined his body carefully, did a couple of stretching exercises, and thought he felt a little soreness in his back, lower waist area near the spinal cord. But his hip also hurt when he twisted in that direction. When the slight pain sort of disappeared, he simply disregarded it. The hip hurt a lot more than a small temporary back problem.

That night the three O'Reilly brothers and their wives slipped into and out of the various hotel celebrations, gave their thanks for their supporters' hard work, and finally ended up at the White House to have one last sip of wine and congratulate one another.

The three Mr. and Mrs. O'Reilly sat around relaxing in the East Sitting Room, a family parlor on the second floor. Jon poured the wine and gave to each of his brothers and their wives a glass. He said, "Again, Morrigan was looking favorably upon us." And they all broke up laughing. Morrigan was the warrior goddess of the early Celts.

Ted responded, "Don't let Cardinal Flannigan hear you or you will be nominated for excommunication."

And again, more laughter, they had indeed carried out a successful battle to start to put the American conservative 'hold the line' mentality into the back seat. They would continue to wage war on last years' thinkers, and promote next years' thinkers. The Two Cleanings Promises would be accelerated. And America would soon be respected again around the world, have a clean and healthy environment, and be number one in technology.

Jack remarked, "So I guess we will have to stop calling Jon Presy-Pres." They again laughed but the three wives looked puzzled.

"Yes, I guess he has proven his fifty-year old promise," responded Ted. Aingeal, Jon's wife asked, "What do you mean Presy-Pres?"

And the three of them broke up in laughter at their private joke until finally Jack explained, "On our sixteenth birthday, Jon announced that he was going to become President of the United States, and that was a promise. Ted and I just thought he was kidding and we started calling him Presy-Pres." But Father thought the idea was good and he supported Jon's efforts. As time progressed, Jon, and Father, talked us into going with him. So together we all entered law school. Jon was a 'little' smarter than Ted and I, so taking the same or similar classes we could all study together. I think it did improve our grades. And then of course a law firm entitled 'triple O'Reilly', Ha, did attract a lot of attention and brought us a mass of clients just on the name. And now here we are, living Jon's promise, for a second time."

Aingeal looked at Riona, Jack's wife and Maire, Ted's wife and remarked, "This is the first time I am hearing this; how about you?"

Riona and Maire both nodded affirmatively.

And then Jon spoke up. "Well you see, Jack and Ted thought they were being smart, and they started making fun of me for shooting for the moon as a teenager. But in my opinion one can only shoot for the moon when you are a teenager. By the time you hit the mid-twenties, if you don't have your sights set upon a career, you are in trouble because other important life elements began to distract you, like a beautiful wife and lovely children."

The three wives looked at him, and Maire commented, "This is the first time that I have been called an element, but I guess a beautiful element is better than just an element."

And Aingeal said, "Don't worry, I will have a heart to heart with the new President tonight and try to obtain a more complete description of just what and what is not an element, and then we can decide if we qualify. Remember the President of the United States is just a government employee and we taxpayers pay his salary, and salaries can be changed you know."

"Are there any other neat childhood stories that we have not heard about yet?" asked Maire.

"Well, now that you ask," responded Ted. "We were about twenty, I think, and enjoying a cold beer while sitting on the boardwalk in front of Captain Jake's Tavern down in Newport Beach. It was about five o'clock in the afternoon when we heard a woman scream from the beach nearby. Well you know that Jack is our family jock. And he was immediately up and off to save the damsel in distress. Jon and I moved more slowly. By the time we were in motion the screaming had stopped and we could only see a group of people staring at someone on the ground. We hurried toward that spot; and then as the crowd dispersed, we saw a muscle-bound guy with a lovely bikini clad girl walking arm in arm toward the street. We looked at the guy on the ground. Guess who it was? Yep! It was our brother. He was unconscious. I started to yell for medics and police. But before any rescue squad could arrive, our brother slowly woke up. He had a bloody nose and a very red and shiny eye on the right side of his head. When he finally became conscious, we asked him what happened. And do you know what he said? He said that he ran into a left-handed light pole there in the middle of the beach. Of course, we looked and tried to find this pole such that we could kick it or hit it or do something to punish it for hurting our brother. But our search was in vain. And to this day we have not found that bad old left-handed light pole on the beach in front of Captain Jake's Tavern in Newport Beach."

Suddenly Ted got a pillow squarely in the side of the head and the group broke down laughing again. And the untold childhood pranks continued to be revealed for the next several minutes.

The three wives were also Irish, university educated, intelligent women from 'good' families. They were near six foot, and of moderate weight with light skin, dark hair and brown eyes, only Maire had blue eyes. They each had very calm, agreeable personalities and could lead or follow in their various women's and social club meetings. And, traditionally like some wealthy women they did not pursue careers outside the home. They had been family selected and each understood her role as a wife of a lawyer today, and a politician tomorrow. Each had one career, producing children and taking care of husband, house, children, and the company ambiance. They must show the happy healthy family unit to the world at large. They were playing their roles very successfully. All three families were comfortable winners as observed by easily chatting away the evening hours in the White House.

Because each wife was an active member of various social clubs (of all strata of the economy), one purpose was to try to feel the pulse of female voters. During these evening conversations Jon would frequently ask their opinions on certain newly implemented government policies.

Tonight, Jon asked, "Can we please get serious for a while? Concerning our new policies during the first four years, do you ladies feel any negative or special positive reactions among the American women?"

His wife, Aingeal, spoke up, "In my opinion the doubling of the government full day pre-schools has helped many single and married mothers find and hold full time jobs. It also gives the children a better start in the lower grades. I hear very positive things from social workers about such family units."

Jack said, "This has also decreased child welfare budgets of many local communities. It would appear to be good both for family and public taxes."

Jon asked, "Any other negative or very positive reactions?"

Maire spoke up, "I think people are beginning to see a difference in the pollution in many areas. The Five Great Lakes region has recognizably decreased water pollution levels. The Chesapeake Bay's jellyfish levels have dropped by 35% in the last two years. The sales of bottled water have decreased in many cities as people have new confidence in drinking tap water. Newly implemented restrictions on smoke exhaust from coal burning electric generators have helped air quality in Charlotte, St. Louis, Denver, and New York City. Because of my personal interest in anti-pollution ideas, I could list several more positive results to the anti-pollution stance that you guys have taken. I think the American women also applaud these efforts."

"And what about the extra support for high technology? Is this playing out well," Ted asked?

Aingeal responded again, "I think that there is a lag in the discovery of new technology and the availability of that technology in the market place. Am I right when I say that it was ten years or more before computers became available to everyone? And it took more than five years before cellular phones became standard purse carrying items. Solar-voltaic energy systems are many years away before they will be routinely used in single family homes."

"Now I hear you saying that we do not yet really know the effects of our supporting high technology because of the lag time between laboratory discovery and market availability," responded Jon. "Do we need to focus on ways to close this lag period? Do the rest of you think the same way?"

And the discussion of high technology, plus and minus, small support or large support, continued for several more minutes.

In this particular evening the six of them had really begun to enjoy the success from some thirty plus years of hard work and were doing what they believed in, re-integrating the USA back into a team-oriented world decision making processes, and returning the USA to the top level in high technology. The Two Cleanings Promises, environment and old technology, were the routes that they planned to use to accomplish this.

Physically, the triplets were fraternal brothers as they carried different combinations of mother's and father's genes. They were non-identical triplets. However, it was frequently difficult for others to tell them apart, as they looked identical in the face and body size and shape. In addition, they each had that confident personalities that comes with close brotherly affections, extended family support, a common goal, and success. They had a loving and giving Mother, a strong supportive Father, and a kid sister, Morri, who was six years younger.

Of course, the kid sister was the princess with three prince protectors. Morrigan was also known to be the Queen of Celtic fairies. Even though the brothers had no difficulty finding appropriate lifelong mates, and now had happy family units with several children each, the lack of a 'family agreement' of a spouse for Morri caused the little sister to finally take off and marry 'her' choice when she turned twenty-five. But she was eventually forgiven and now also lived in the Boston area with her businessman husband and three children. Indeed, the Irish were family oriented.

By having put into place a common game plan when they were teenagers, they wasted little time in outside efforts. Each brother had his own non- academic pursuits. Jon excelled in board games like chess and in card games. Jack preferred sports such as field hockey and basketball. While Ted was oriented toward electronic games and computer quizzes. But they had a serious common end-goal, and took their extra reading and academic studies seriously; they always ranked near the top in classes. Having had long term 'identical' roommates to assist in maintaining 'healthy' study patterns was not a bad thing. And having accepted the long-term game plan, they each knew what role the others would play someday. The family pecking order was sort of automatically built into the shared life pursuit, and the personal competition was always positive.

Shortly after 11:30 PM, Jack and Riona, Ted and Maire gave their kisses to Jon and Aingeal, said their goodbyes and started to leave. When Ted bent over to pick up a dropped napkin, he suddenly had a sharp pain in his back. He straightened up and rubbed it for a few seconds. The pain subsided but now his hip hurt. He just accepted the two pains as one continuous problem, said nothing and the three couples separated for the night. The gentlemen would start work immediately tomorrow after lunch and re-think their Two Cleanings Program, and the ladies would return to the White House on Friday afternoon for tea.

Each couple went directly home to bed and to sleep. Everyone was exhausted. However, the next morning one of the gentlemen did not wake up. He was already cold but his eyes were closed, a most unusual situation in death.

2

The Presidential Commission

TWO WEEKS AFTER THE SECOND inauguration of President Jonathan O'Reilly and the burial of his 'little' brother in the family Holy Gardens Cemetery in Boston, Jonathan, with his other brother, Jackson, reappointed as Attorney General, and Uncle Dagda Murphy (Dagda which is Celtic for protector of the tribe) met in the Oval Office of the White House, 1600 Pennsylvania Avenue, Washington, DC. The topic of discussion was Theodore's death and several other similar unsolved deaths over the past couple of years.

Uncle Dagda was their Mother's younger brother and a well-known international security-investigator. He was sixty-two years old and a big burly guy, nearly bald, with deep wrinkles on his forehead, brown eyes and brown – silvered streaked hair; but he had a strong sound body due to regular jogging, weight lifting, and weapons training program. He was both an English and an American citizen. Uncle Dagda had been employed for many years with the British MI6 and INTERPOL, and he also worked in association with the CIA and Military Intelligence for several of those years. He specialized in investigating international crime cartels and terrorism.

Fifteen years previously his brother in law, the O'Reilly triplet's Father, was having ship hijacking problems. So, he asked Uncle Dagda to go private and he would provide him with start-up money to establish a new international security assistance and anti-terrorist corporation, ISAAT. He offered Uncle Dagda ten million dollars plus a multi-year contract to protect the CELT ships on the high seas. Over the years Uncle Dagda and his now twenty-seven agent security- investigation company successfully completed several international security contracts with both public and private groups; they caught or assisted in the arrest, putting out of business, or the killing of three international terrorist groups: REDDS, TGFD, and KOOP. Uncle Dagda was the perfect person to assist in these deaths. He had the necessary international experience, he was private not government, and he was family.

Jackson and Uncle Dagda entered the Oval Office together. President Jonathan O'Reilly immediately stood, walked around his desk, nodded, kissed and hugged his brother. He nodded, kissed, and hugged his Uncle. He asked his secretary to bring tea and coffee. Uncle Dagda was a tea drinker. Then Jonathan spoke up, "How was your trip? Or were you in Ireland when you received my conference request?"

Uncle Dagda replied, "First my deepest sympathies for your brother. He was a very good man and accomplished a lot in just four years. And yes, my second home, the airplane, gave to me a good sleep and good meals. That is what is nice about having your own first class – true comfort. My current contracts still take me all over the world. Your Father's oil ships' contract alone requires that I regularly travel to the oil exporting countries such as Norway, Nigeria, Venezuela, and the Middle East; and his container ships' contract takes me to Southeast Asia. About the only place I do not go to is Australia. But I am training an excellent younger man and will soon make him Director for several of the contracts; therefore, I will be free for what you need me to do. And we will find them."

"I knew that you would see the same thing that we see – cooperative conspiracies," replied Jonathan.

Jackson spoke up, "I do not know how many of these medically unexplainable sudden deaths of VIPs around the world have occurred recently, but we will find out."

Dagda said, "There are thousands of unexplainable sudden deaths around the world every year. Most of them are labeled natural causes when they are older people who are not well. But yes, one must question when there are several young, healthy, and working VIPs suddenly found dead, and medical causes cannot be established for the cause of death. Two months ago, Leon Odilone, Undersecretary of High Technology for the

European Union, and now Theodore, Undersecretary of High Technology for the USA, both young people and victims of medically unexplainable sudden deaths within a very short time frame. That is why I agree with you that there is a controlled – coordinated group out there involved, and they probably have a timed agenda. We will have to find out who, why, and how they are causing these deaths."

"But where do we start when there is no real evidence of homicide or collusion," responded Jackson.

"If you will give me a free hand and maximum cooperation and leverage, I will start by trying to identify all sudden deaths of young VIPs, during the past three years in the world, which have officially been listed as medically unexplainable," answered Dagda.

"And in efforts to keep our 'little' investigation quiet, let us use MUSD for medical unexplainable sudden deaths. Is that all right?"

Jonathan spoke up, "You got it. This is not only a single unknown death of a US government cabinet official, but our little brother. Where and how will you begin?"

Dagda said, "Since I received your invitation a couple days ago, I have been thinking about that exact question. First, we must define a VIP. If a VIP is someone in government such as a President, Prime Minister, Senator, or Cabinet Official, and someone in the private sector such as Corporation or large Company President or CEO, then we can screen public coroners' reports for deaths with unknown causes for people ages fifty to eighty years, worldwide. Once we accumulate these names, we select out the VIPs. Then we start investigating them, one by one, looking for similarities and differences. This approach will allow us to identify commonness."

"How do you then want to analyze the names and investigative data," asked Jackson?

Dagda replied, "I suggest that you set up a Presidential Commission and include key Americans, Europeans, and maybe others. I currently do not know where the hunt for VIP names and the investigation data will take us. If you will allow, let me suggest several names of key people for the Commission, whom I know and have worked with in the past, give those names to you and you can make the decisions as to the final composition of the Commission. I will do that today. I will give those names to Jackson, as he should be the official Commission Secretary. We should meet in the Justice Department's conference rooms, perhaps in two months, and then as often as necessary."

'OK. I agree with this approach," said Jonathan. "What do you think, Bro?" The three brothers used to call each other bro, their special name for brother.

Bro answered, "I like the approach. And at any time that you need assistance, clearances, new contacts, special legal authorizations, or whatever, just let me know. And as Commission Secretary and Attorney General I should be able to provide almost anything you request, at least within the USA."

Jonathan added, "I will draw up a contract between the Government of the United States of America and ISAAT for your participation on the Presidential Commission on Human Trafficking. After you submit to me your recommendations for Commission members, I will contact the respective governments and request that this person be 'loaned' to us to participate on the Commission on a one year plus continuum basis. Hopefully we can solve this riddle in one year. But if not, I will be able to extend the Commission and its members at least to the end of my new four-year term."

"All agreed? - - - - All agreed!"

"Now let us talk family, as I have ten minutes before a meeting of the Environmental Council," said Jonathan. "We need to find a new Czar for Theodore's Cabinet and Council Seat. The government cannot stop. So, tell us about our Irish family. Is the new UK and IRA agreement holding up?"

Later in the day President O'Reilly received an official letter from ISAAT listing possible candidates for the new Presidential Commission on Human Trafficking. They were as follows:

Suggestions for the new Presidential Commission

The Chairperson - US Attorney General, American, Mr. Jackson O'Reilly, brother to Mr. Jonathan O'Reilly, President of the United States.

The Co-Chairperson - Mr. Dagda Murphy, Irish-British-American, President of the International Security Assistance and Anti-Terrorist Corporation (ISAAT), Uncle to the O'Reilly brothers.

Dr. Thomas Bradmier - American, Director of the Office of Science and Technology in the US Central Intelligence Agency, tall and lanky, sharp grey eyes, cowlick frontal hair, and a long narrow middle-aged face which match his lingering aspirations to be a marathon runner, doctorates in science and engineering, served 36 years in government service.

Mr. Harold Thomson - English, Director of Clandestine Operations in the British MI6, of medium build, ruddy complexion with a light grey and orange streaked beard, blue eyes, and cauliflower ears which match his beard and disappearing hair, 42 years of experience with British intelligence.

Dr. Ulda von Eulenberg - German, Assistant Secretary-General of INTERPOL and consultant to the new EUROPOL, an older large boned Austrian woman, short blondish hair, charming smile but a no-nonsense disposition, considered best criminal investigator in all of Europe.

Ms. Elizabeth Dapper - American criminal justice lawyer, slight with an almost fragile build, middle aged lady with short natural red hair and a sprinkling of freckles, green eyes, also has a serious rigid personality, 35 years of practice in New York and Washington, DC.

General Carlton Ronny - Retired NATO five-star American General, 6 foot 4 inches, young looking sixty-seven-year old, African-American Texan with short grey hair and a battle action scar on his left cheek, steel colored eyes, involved in 17 military actions overseas.

Dr. Lawrence Batley, American, Physician and Senior Forensic Pathologist from the Chief Medical Examiner's Office in New York City, intense perfectionist, 56 years old, rated the best pathologist in criminal diagnostics in the world.

At 9:30 AM, on March 7, 2029, the first meeting of the Presidential Commission on Human Trafficking began in the fourth-floor conference

room in the Department of Justice building on Pennsylvania Avenue in Washington, DC. At the head of the table was Jackson O'Reilly, US Attorney General and Commission Chairman, and on his right Dagda Murphy, President of ISAAT and Co-Chairman of the Commission. Around the table were Harold Thomson, Ulda von Eulenberg, Thomas Bradmier, Carlton Ronny, Elizabeth Dapper, Dr. Lawrence Batley, and Bryan Femer (Senior Associate in ISAAT). Mr. O'Reilly had hosted a brief cocktail party the night before where the Commission members had a chance to talk and get to know one another. So as the meeting unfolded each member knew the names and the brief background of each of the other members. This not only saved time, it allowed for a better team working relationship at the start of the first meeting.

The Attorney General, Mr. Jackson O'Reilly, and Chairman of the Commission, began, "Welcome to Washington and the Department of Justice. I want to thank you for agreeing to share your expertise and brain power with us as this task will not be easy, and may indeed be limited to only the world we call earth."

And he received appropriate smiles.

"As you understand our Presidential Commission on Human Trafficking is not related to the kidnapping, trading, or movement of people. That is simply the façade that is being given to the Commission. And there will be no reports or communications of any kind to the news media during the duration of our Commission. News reports, if any, will originate in the Office of the President of the United States. In other words, we are operating on a 100% news blackout by American laws. Any member of this Commission considered to be providing the news media with any information of the workings or results of our meetings can and will be legally prosecuted. Is this understood and acceptable?"

A general nodding of heads followed.

"Our work will focus on the medically unexplainable sudden deaths of healthy VIPs over the past couple years, and which have taken place in several countries. We will call these deaths, MUSD. We believe that these deaths are organized and coordinated by some unknown group with some unknown purpose and with a possible time schedule. And we feel that high technology is somehow involved. During the past two months Mr. Dagda Murphy, President of ISAAT, a well- known security-investigation company with a broad international platform, has begun screening all national and international coroner's data banks seeking sudden and medically unexplained deaths of VIPs between the ages of fifty and eighty years. Mr. Murphy, if you want to take over?"

Mr. Murphy, "Thank you Mr. Chairman. Yes, we have now screened coroners' data banks from North America, Europe, South America and Asia. On these four continents we identified 16,385 medically unexplained deaths of people in this age range during the past three years. If we use a definition for VIPs as high-ranking public officials, corporation presidents and CEOs, and Nobel Laureates, we can narrow the list down to about thirty-three candidates. And if we narrow it down further to those who were 'found dead' on the fifteenth of any given month, we have seven remaining candidates, but we are keeping the others on hold."

"The logic for this approach is that Mr. Leon Odilone, recent past Czar of High Technology for the European Union and Mr. Theodore O'Reilly, recent past Czar of High Technology for the United States, were 'found dead' on the fifteenth of November and the fifteenth of January, respectively. We thus have begun an investigation into each of these seven deaths occurring on the fifteenth of a month thinking there might be a linkage. Our investigations are only partially complete at this time. We will review several of these victims/candidates for MUSDs. For some of the non-America deaths I may need additional assistance. Three are in Europe, one in Mexico, and one in Brazil."

"Are there any questions about our methodology or the beginning logic in our approach?"

"Do all of these seven candidates for medically unexplainable sudden deaths, MUSD, have some type of connection to high technology?" asked Dr. Batley.

"I think they do," responded Mr. Murphy. "This is another component of our reasoning for using this logical sequence to select down from sixteen thousand victims/candidates. But we do not have enough data to say definitely, yes. As of today, we only have complete autopsy reports and homicide investigation reports on two of the candidates, Mr. Theodore O'Reilly and Mr. Dag-Fin Studheimer. We will review them this morning."

"Mr. Odilone was a citizen of Belgium, but he was employed at a senior level in the European Union government when he was killed. There are additional bureaucratic problems concerning our attempts to investigate his death."

After a pause, he continued, "Let me first review candidate number one, Mr. Theodore O'Reilly."

'Mr. O'Reilly was reported to have 'become dead' during the night of January 15, 2029. His death occurred at his Georgetown, DC home, in bed where he was sleeping with his wife. The subsequent autopsy found no medically known cause of death. The official cause of death was asphyxiation as he had stopped breathing. During the two days prior to January 15, Mr. O'Reilly assisted in the many pre-inaugural events taking place in and around Washington prior to his brother's inauguration. To our knowledge he was never alone during this time, except for one hour each afternoon, between 4:00-5:00PM, when he went to the Walter Reed Military Hospital, in Bethesda, Maryland. He had previously hurt his hip in an automobile accident and was undergoing physical therapy. Our investigation for each of these therapy days revealed no unusual problems except in the afternoon of January 15."

"On the evening of this day a hospital orderly named Bill Green was found unconscious. He had been knocked out and hidden in a closet under a pile of laundry. He was discovered at 11:00 PM when the cleaning people came to begin their rounds. All of Mr. Green's keys were missing. The missing keys included a key to the door of Mr. O'Reilly's therapy room, to a drug storage room, and the drug cabinet in that room. Several drugs, including a bottle of ether, were missing from the drug cabinet. Mr. O'Reilly's therapy room and the drug storage room were about one hundred feet apart on the same floor. No new fingerprints were found in either room. From the hallway video camera, we detected a person dressed in whites and wearing a surgical mask on the floor at 4:15 PM. He did go into and out of several rooms on this floor but we were not able to determine exactly which rooms. The hallway was quite empty as most hospital personnel were watching the Presidential swearing in ceremony on television. It is possible that someone entered Mr. O'Reilly's room and 'treated' him with a slow acting drug. But we have no proof of this; it is only a possibility. Dr. Batley would you like to add anything?"

Dr. Batley spoke up again, "There are many drugs which can cause a delayed death. But all of them also have illicit observable side effects and they leave traces of drug metabolites in the blood or urine. I performed a very careful and complete autopsy on Mr. O'Reilly. There were no marks on his body. The blood and urine analysis on the same day of the death showed no new or unusual chemicals to be present. An inventory of the drugs routinely kept in the drug cabinet on Mr. O'Reilly's floor did not show any such drug being kept there. I honestly do not know how he 'became dead'. It is extremely puzzling. And for the first time in my professional career I am at a loss to say what he died from or what killed him."

Mr. Murphy continued, "The evening of January 15, the three O'Reilly brothers had toured the various celebration sites around Washington, and talked with many of their election workers. Later they were together with their wives relaxing in the White House. Interviewing both brothers and their wives, I learned that no one noticed any 'observable side effects' or unusual behavior in their bother. Even later when Mr. Theodore O'Reilly and his wife went to bed, she said she did not notice anything unusual about her husband. They were both so exhausted from the numerous celebratory events that they were 'asleep before we hit the bed'. Does anyone have any questions?"

Ms. von Eulenberg asked, "Did you inquire about eye pupil dilation. Often drugs, as they take effect, cause the pupils of the eye to dilate. This dilation cannot be hidden. We regularly use this in seeking out drug pusher or users. The pupils will not contract when you shine a light into those eyes. Using this tool, we have legal reason to warrant an arrest and ninety nine percent of the time we find detectable levels of drugs in the blood or urine."

"I can respond to that," said Mr. Chairman. "At one point in the evening Theodore bent over to pick up a napkin and he suddenly grabbed his back as if in pain. But he rubbed his back and his hip and said nothing. I looked him carefully in the face trying to read the extent of the pain. I thought his hip was giving him more trouble than he admitted. I can say that I saw no obvious dilation of his pupils. All of the lights were on in the room so any dilation of the pupils should have been noticeable."

Mr. Murphy continued, "So you can see that we have no evidence as to how Mr. O'Reilly was killed, and I use the word killed carefully. At present there is no criminal case. As all of you know, Mr. Theodore O'Reilly, as the

US Czar of High Technology, carried out a vigorous campaign against old technology systems and assisted with every government incentive possible to promote new high technology systems. He had no known enemies, unless you consider the leaders of old technology, who are currently losing in this game of technological change."

After a few moments Mr. Chairman asked, "Are there any more questions or further discussion? If not, now we can always return to candidate one for questions anytime. We think there is a common relationship between or among these candidates, but we do not yet know what. So please close no doors on your thinking."

Hearing no questions Mr. Chairman said, "Mr. Murphy, please continue with candidate number two."

Mr. Murphy began again, "Victim/candidate number two is Mr. Dag-Finn Studheimer who lived in Frankfurt, Germany. Mr. Studheimer 'became dead' on September 15, 2028, in the Barclay Intercontinental Hotel in New York City. He often traveled alone on business and had stayed at the hotel for three nights. We interviewed his New York contacts, taxi drivers, and all housekeeping staff who serviced him or his room and came up with nothing. He met with several business groups during the three days, talked with various people each day for lunch and evening meals, and was only alone during the late evening or night period. The hallway camera showed no 'outsider' entering or leaving his room. Autopsy reports for Mr. Studheimer showed no determinable cause of death. Death was officially listed as brain failure."

"Mr. Studheimer was the President and CEO of the Crystal-Steel Construction Corp. which has laboratories and factories in Frankfurt, Germany, Cleveland, Ohio, Sofia, Bulgaria, and Nanchang, China. He was the inventor of crystallized carbon diamonds. The crystal structure of a diamond is a face centered cube or an FCC lattice. This lattice can be developed into several shapes. Diamond is the most stable, hardest form of the carbon atom after graphite. Synthetic diamonds or graphite can be produced by two different methods: High Pressure-High Temperature (HPHT) and Chemical Vapor Deposition (CVD). These methods produce high quality industrial diamonds with toughness quality. Such crystallized carbon diamonds can be added to concrete during building construction and replace the steel rods. Hence high-tech building construction no longer requires steel. Mr. Studheimer not only developed the CVD methodology of producing the industrial diamonds for construction, he established the first successful factories for this replacement for construction steel. Using the crystallized carbon diamonds reduces construction costs by more than sixty percent. It has revolutionized building construction all over the world."

Mr. Bradmier asked, "So you are calling Mr. Studeimer a victim/candidate because he died on the fifteenth of a month and because of his strong high technology background?"

"And because he was a healthy robust, outdoors man who met death that was sudden and medically unexplainable," replied Mr. Murphy.

"I understand," responded Mr. Bradmier.

General Ronny spoke, "Did Mr. Studheimer have any military connections?" "Yes," answered Mr. Murphy. "He had been talking with the NATO military command about testing some of his products for tanks and artillery weapons."

"Did the Crystal-Steel Corp have a shipload of their synthetic diamonds hijacked a couple of years ago?" asked Ms. Von Eulenberg.

"No," Mr. Murphy responded. "But there were several box cars on a freight train traveling from their Chinese factory which were stolen. Some of the cars were recovered in Shanghai as they were being loaded aboard a ship. And some of the train cars were not recovered."

Mr. Bradmier spoke up again, "You have to realize that this new technology threatens iron, tin and coal mining, steel manufacturing, and construction labor jobs. It puts a lot of people out of work and closes down major exports for several developing countries."

No one around the table said anything. New technology does this. And it is a big negative against new technology. It also provides new work and more jobs; but sometimes there is a gap between the downside of the old and the upside of the new.

Mr. Murphy concluded, "The homicide investigation and a full and very complete autopsy on Mr. Studheimer was performed by the German authorities."

"What I am hearing is that there is no solid evidence that there was even a crime involved in these two deaths. Is this correct?" asked Ms. Dapper.

Then he continued, "Yes. That is my current conclusion. This is where we are. We have begun investigating the other candidates: Dr. Miroslav Nacekar, Nobel Laureate, dead in Prague; Dr. David Herman, Nobel Laureate, dead in Mexico City; Mr. Karl Trenmeister, President of Intel Biofuels, dead in Frankfurt; Dr. William Christofor, President and CEO of Voltaic USA Systems, dead in Rio de Janeiro; and Mr. Leon Odilone, Czar of High Technology of the European Union, dead in Brussels. We need and want your assistance for all of these investigations. Here is a list of the potential candidates for the MUSD, and some preliminary information." He handed a sealed packet to each commission member.

Mr. Chairman concluded the meeting. "At this point there is not enough hard information available for further discussions. We will break for now and hold our second meeting here in this room in two months. By then we project that we will have additional investigations completed and autopsy reports on other candidates. When that exact day and time is determined you will each be notified by the usual coded correspondence. Mr. President must first approve of all of these meeting. Before you leave today, I think Mr. Murphy would like to briefly request some special assistance from Dr. Von Eullenberg and Dr. Bradmier. If the three of you want to use this room, the rest of us will adjourn to our other schedules. Again, I sincerely thank you for your time and effort on this very difficult problem.

St Patrick's Day

Lá 'le Pádraig or Lá Fheile Pádraig or St. Paddy's Day is an annual feast which celebrates St. Patrick (385-461? ACE). St. Patrick is accepted as the common patron of saints of the Irish people and the day is celebrated each year on March 17. It is also a national holiday in the Republic of Ireland. This day is celebrated in many countries where there are many ethnic Irish, including the USA, but it is not an official holiday. The Catholic Church celebrates St. Patrick's Day unless it falls within Easter Holy Week.

The first St. Patrick's Festival began in Dublin on March 17, 1996. It lasted one day. In 1997 it was expanded to three days; in 2000 it became a four-day event; and in 2006 it was extended to one entire week, in Ireland. The celebration is an effort to bring together and motivate people of Irish descent and to project an international image of the Irish and Ireland as cultured, sophisticated, and honorable. The days are filled with parades containing floats and bands, contests of sports and handicrafts, dancing contests, lectures about Irish scholars and Irish history, wearing of green, drinking green beer, and promoting green three leaf shamrocks. St. Patrick had used the shamrock to teach the Irish people about the Holy Trinity.

St. Patrick, Noamh Pádraig, was a Celt from northwest Briton and a Christian missionary. Little is known or accepted concerning his life, even his birth and death dates. In general, when a child he was kidnapped from England by Irish raiders, taken to Ireland and became a slave (shepherd boy) for several years. He finally escaped and returned to England, entered the church, became a bishop, and returned to Ireland as a missionary. The places where he preached, and the people whom he interacted with are partially revealed in one of his letters. The letter states that he baptized thousands of people, ordained many priests to continue the teachings of Jesus, converted many wealthy women to become nuns, converted many 'sons of kings' into the true faith, and excommunicated several Irish warriors. One must remember that St. Patrick was not Irish but was a foreign Briton-Celt who taught against the current dominant Druid faith. And he was frequently accused of false teaching and of breaking Irish/Druid laws. It is not known with any degree of certainty when St. Patrick died nor where he was buried. But in the twentieth century he was chosen as the Patron of the Saints of Ireland and is venerated by the Catholic Church, Eastern Orthodox Church, Anglican Church, and Lutheran Church.

On March 17, 2029, the O'Reilly families would meet to celebrate St. Paddy's Day. Many of the wealthy Irish families in the Boston area met at the Irish Inn Resort near Deravies, Massachusetts, on Cape Cod Bay. This was a private club-resort complex for Irish-only members. On March 15, the FBI and the President's security detail moved into the resort, checked for bombs and other explosives, electronically swept the two cottages where the O'Reilly families would be staying, planted security cameras in key locations, and assigned security guards and metal detectors at all entrances and exits to the Inn and the near surrounding stone walls. The President and his family were coming on the 16th of March to spend two days and two nights at the Inn.

As a bright cool and sunny morning progressed, a large army UH-A Black Hawk combat assault helicopter routinely used for carrying military combat units swung over the Bay from Boston toward the resort. It carried President Jonathan O'Reilly, Attorney General Jackson O'Reilly and their 'three' families. As they flew east toward the resort area Jonathan looked down and thought,

'The three of us have been coming here since childhood, but this is the first time that only two of us are coming. We have to be extremely careful until we can rule out that Theodore's death was not personal, or Irish, or Catholic. I have increased security for Aingeal, Riona, Maire, and our children until we know more. I am sure that our extended Irish families attending the celebrations at the Inn today will not be happy with so many extra guns around, but they will understand. It is for their security also.'

As they got closer and started dropping toward the ground he looked over the newly expanded boat docks and marina, spring-like bright green 18 hole professional golf course, newly painted tennis courts, 2 navy blue swimming pools, the 250 bed - four floor rectangular shaped club house with Cape old architecture and blue-green slate roof which paralleled the waterfront, adjacent cottages near each end, and the numerous red-white-blue tiled terraces leading down from the club house and to the Bay. There were hundreds of trees and flowering shrubs and gardens on the nearly five hundred acres; all but the golf course was totally enclosed within eight-foot high stone walls. It was a very familiar and welcome site. Here, for the first time in the past year Jonathan and Jackson would be able to relax among true and faithful friends and family, not common in politics. He looked down at the Inn again and realized time had been standing still here since childhood, very little had changed. But without his 'little' brother, he feared a new type of change was in the air. Both he and Jackson felt a major war had been declared and was now beginning throughout the world. An unkind change was coming, even here, like it or not. But as of yet this new change could not be defined.

The helicopter landed on the northern helicopter pad. The club house paralleled the sea. One side faced the west overlooking Cape Cod Bay, and the other side faced inland. Sitting on the Bay side on a large open triple terrace, one could overlook the larger swimming pool and marina and watch the sun set in the west over the Atlantic Ocean. While on the land side of the Club House, there was the road entry with security gates, eight tennis courts and two large parking lots. Nine holes of the golf course were situated on each end, north and south, of the complex. One helicopter pad was located on each end of the club house on the land side. The O'Reilly families were staying in two cottages at the north end of the club house in a partial wooded area. For security purposes they used the air entrance-exit pad closest to these two extra high security cottages.

As it landed, everyone exited, ducked, and ran for the two cottages. The high security housekeeping staff emerged and started carrying suitcases and personal belongings from the helicopter to the cottages. Logistics had already been worked out. The triplet's Father had died three years ago of a heart attack; and their Mother was home in bed with a winter cold. Jonathan, Aingeal, Maira, and the youngest six of the eleven children would stay in cottage #5N. And Jackson and Riona would stay in cottage #6N with the five older children.

The younger children ranged from five to eleven years; the older children ranged from fourteen to nineteen years. Everyone was slowly adjusting to the loss of Theodore, except for Theodore's eleven-year old son, Jamie. He was small for his age, with bright turquoise blue eyes and dark curly hair. Since the death of his Father, Jamie had begun to regress toward his childhood. He still could not understand how his Father could leave him without saying goodbye; and now he had not even received one letter or telephone call. In the past, whenever Theodore had traveled, this youngest O'Reilly always heard from his Father. Why not now? Jonathan was trying to serve as surrogate Father. And Jamie and Uncle Jonathan would sleep together and spend as much time together as possible during the two-day affair.

The cottages were large and designed such that eight to twelve people could sleep in each one. Each O'Reilly selected a bed, bedmate, and roommates and settled in for a fun but difficult two days. St. Paddy's Day at the Inn had always been a blast. But this time, with Theodore's death only two months ago, the old fun would not, could not be here. But everyone would try to continue to adjust; maybe seeing other O'Reilly families and friends would help.

After lunch the three O'Reilly families met in Jonathan's cottage. They filled the couches, chairs, and floor as they faced Dad/Uncle Jonathan. He spoke loudly. "Again, we celebrate St. Paddy's Day at the Inn. Only this time it is different in two ways. The brother of Jackson and mine, your Husband, Father and Uncle will not be with us here at the Inn. But he will be watching us from above. Let us bow our heads and pray silently to God to keep him safe in Heaven."

The Catholic children knew how to pray, so there was dead silence in the room for several minutes. But even without his Father's name being spoken, little Jamie knew who they were talking about and started moaning as tears streaked from his blue eyes down his fine-featured little face. Jonathan quickly leaned over, he was just too big to pick up, hugged him and kissed him, and sat himself next to him such that they were touching. Jamie immediately sought the safety and buried his face in his uncle's arm. He probably smelled the same as his Father since they were genetically similar.

Jonathan spoke again. "The second reason that it is different this time is that we really do not know how our loved and never to be forgotten one died. It may not have been by natural causes. And if this is true, we do not know why. Therefore, with all the O'Reilly clan together, here in a public place for two days, we provide a very good target for assassins and terrorists. I ask you to enjoy yourselves but take extra precautions at all times. Play only with friends. Do not talk to or go with strangers at any time."

Jackson continued the warning talk. "We have come here often so we know most of the families, friends, and faces of guests and workers. Because many people will wear green, we have arranged for all security guards to wear dark blue jackets with a green shamrock on their chest, left side. If you see someone acting suspiciously or does not seem familiar, tell one of the security people and have that person checked out. Do not be bashful; remain alert. Remember not only is Jonathan the oldest remaining male of our three families, paternoster, but he is also President of the United States. The President is a constant terrorist target. These security people are not just from the Inn, they are from the FBI. So, do not make guesses, tell them of any possible problem, have them check things out. OK? OK!" And the two older males looked around the room, smiling and acknowledging each child one by one.

Jonathan continued, "I know that the adult's and the children's swimming pools are always heated on St. Paddy's Day. And I could tell by the steam coming off of them as we landed that they are all ready and waiting for you. The sun is shining very brightly right now. Go put your swim gear on. It is wise to never be alone these two days. Form or remain in pairs or groups. Aingeal, Maire and I will remain near the children's pool; and Jackson and Riona will remain near the large swimming pool. Look for us and anchor your activities near us. Does anyone have any questions or want to add anything to what we have said? Jack? Ladies? My beautiful little and strong big ones?"

And that last crack broke them up laughing. They all hopped up, went to their bedrooms, put on swimming suits, and headed toward the

Bay side of the Club House to the swimming pools. The adults did not down dress, but instead put on jackets to go to sit in the lovely sunshine at poolside. It was a beautiful warm cloudless spring day for children, but also a beautiful cool cloudless spring day for 'older people' And the 'older people' did bring extra towels and blankets for post swimming children.

They settled comfortably near and in the two swimming pools. The crowd was sparse as most members would drive here tomorrow and just stay for the day and evening fireworks. So tomorrow the Inn would be very crowded. Neither Father had yet figured out how to handle that situation.

Jackson and Riona settled at a table on the lower terrace near the center of the large pool; while Aingeal and Riona sat at a table near the small pool, just north of the large pool. Jonathan located close to the two women but on the large pool side so Jackson and he were in visual contact. They could directly communicate in case of an emergency. All afternoon the two men continuously stayed within shouting distance of each other. Little Jamie played in the little pool or on the nearby ground, always near Uncle Jonathan.

About 3:00 PM a well-known and popular face suddenly appeared at the small pool. Jamie was the first to see him and raced to him with his arms held high. For one second Uncle Dagda hesitated about picking up this very wet little boy; but he knew what Jamie was going through. He smothered Jamie on his large stomach, hugged and kissed him, and said, "You are still my favorite nephew."

Jamie responded, "You are my favorite grand uncle, even though you are an old baldheaded walrus."

Uncle Dagda quickly lifted Jamie over his head, placed him on his shoulder, ran toward the pool, and pretended as if he was going to throw him into the pool. Jamie loved it and was laughing and screaming his head off.

The rest of the children turned to look for the screaming, saw it was Uncle Dagda, and headed straight for him. Suddenly he had half a dozen very wet little nieces and nephews trying to pull him into the pool. After a couple of minutes of battle, he finally escaped their clutches; but not before he was as wet as they were. And then they started shouting surprise, surprise. He backed up, reached into his pocket, and pulled out five packets of balloons, ten balloons to a packet. He tossed the packets into the water and suddenly he was free of children as they all raced for the balloons. He always brought little gifts when he came to visit. They anticipated this and were ready.

Uncle Dagda and his wife had no children, so these young ones were like his own sons and daughters. His wife was an elementary school teacher, so with her profession she satisfied her motherhood instincts. But Dagda only had the O'Reilly families, here in Boston, Dublin, and London. The triplet's younger sister and family had just moved to London. Her husband had recently taken over the London Office for CELT IMPORT/EXPORT. Dagda was their only living Great Uncle, and they were his only living children. There were very strong emotional family attachments being played out. And because Uncle Dagda lived in Ireland-New York-London and the rest of the world, he only saw his Boston family once or twice a year. He was hyperventilating so much he even had difficulty helping to blow up the fifty balloons.

That evening they had dinner in the special dining room, inside the Club House, just off of the main dining area. They sat around the three round tables as individual families. Uncle Dagda sat where Theodore would have sat, and directly beside him sat Jamie. The Inn's kitchen was as large as a restaurant kitchen, so each O'Reilly ordered by menu and ate what he/she liked. The mood had again turned somber, but vigilant. And the evening went by without any unusual excitement.

On St. Paddy's Day morning, the O'Reilly's woke up one by one and simply ate cereals or light breakfasts inside the cottages. The old walrus and Jamie slept on the floor on a mattress; Jamie had most of the mattress and the old walrus had most of the floor. By mid-morning the sun was shining and it apparently was going to be another crisp lovely spring day with gorgeous multicolored flowers everywhere. The three O'Reilly families met again in Jonathan's cottage for another strategy talk.

Jonathan began, "Yesterday was good, few guests and no problems. Today will be very different. You remember other St. Paddy's Days when the Inn was swarming with people, mostly extended Irish families and friends. It will be the same today, however it will be different. It will be different because the FBI heard rumors of a possible terrorist threat. We are going to have to alter our routine St. Paddy's Day celebration. You older five can go ahead and play tennis as long as you want; but you will have to remain in a group. You can play singles, doubles, or quintuples, so long as that non-player remains with the group, keeping score or reading a book or whatever. Two FBI agents are assigned to be with you at all times, even when you go to the bathroom."

Jackson continued discussing the restrictions. "The little ones will go to the small pool and outdoor play area. The three ladies and two security personnel will accompany them. Jonathan and I will stay in the President's box which is again located on the third lower level terrace, directly in front of the center of the large swimming pool. Remember a stage had been temporarily constructed over the center part of the pool for the afternoon and evening music and dance performances. That adult pool is closed for the day. The President's box is front and center, looking directly at the stage. It has been expanded to provide room for all of us, but now has a five-foot bullet proof glass wall around it instead of the old restraining ropes. We two gentlemen will make ourselves available to our family and friends for talking business and pleasure, but they will be searched by the FBI security personnel before they enter the box to talk with us. The third gentlemen of our family will play rover. Uncle Dagda will move around the area regularly checking up on the little ones and the big ones and basically watching for possible trouble."

"At noon when you get hungry you can go as a group, with your FBI baby sitters, back to the cottage, shower, change, and join us in the Box. You can order lunch from there and it will be brought to you. Do not go to the dining room or order lunch in the dining room. Order your food and eat it with us in the Box."

Jonathan finished, "Does anyone have any comments or questions? Jack? Dagda? No? So, everyone, please rely upon our security people. They are trained to react to any kind of bodily threat. One caution, if you hear any guns going off, or explosions, immediately lay down flat on the ground, or crawl under a car or a table or lay down near a wall or fence. And stay there until the security people say that you can get up. I know this is scary; it is not our normal St. Paddy's Day fun. But we have already lost one loved one this year, we must not lose another. Be alert. Be careful. Don't take unnecessary chances. And we will see you in the President's Box around lunch time. We will then all remain within the Box for the rest of the day."

The morning went smoothly. Shortly after noon the little ones and the three ladies came to the Box and ordered lunches. At close to 2:00 PM the older ones joined the rest of the family in the box and ordered their lunches. Several music and dance groups began performing at 2:30 and would continue until 9:00 when the fireworks would begin. Again, things seemed to be going smoothly. The three youngest ones even took short naps on small mattresses which had been placed in the Box.

There were several round dining tables on each terrace and in the dining room. By mid-afternoon all had begun filling up with people. All tables had been reserved in advance. Three 12 feet long food tables were located between the kitchen and the upper terrace. They were packed with food up to three layers on some tables. All guests would help themselves when they were hungry. The open buffet would be available all evening.

At 6:30 PM the President of the Celtic Inn and Resort climbed onto the temporary stage which was located over of the center of the adult swimming pool. The musical groups had been performing from there for the past several hours. He gave a few words of welcome, especially to St. Patrick and to the President of the United States and his families. Three other 'important' people gave brief speeches involving the greatness of the Irish in America. And finally, the announcement was given that the food tables were open.

First the President, Attorney General, and their families were escorted to the serving tables. They were under the continuous scrutiny of men in dark blue jackets sporting green shamrocks. The hungry crowd understood and waited patiently. Several serving ladies assisted the little ones. Then the special invited guests, Board Members, and regular members raided the food tables. All was still going well and Jonathan began to believe that the FBI rumors were wrong. And then it happened.

Two special large round tables were located on the south end of each of the two lower terraces. The Inn had a tradition of preparing special fruit cocktail dishes for desert. These special deserts contained combinations of peaches, apricots, pineapples, oranges, cherries, grapes, and apples, and were custom prepared upon order at these tables. Two 'fruit cocktail specialists' were using fresh, intact fruit, and cutting it to fill each specific order. At one point in the evening a cook carried a platter of fresh fruit from the kitchen to the desert tables. On this platter were six pineapples. As he stepped onto the lower terrace, he quickly grabbed one of the pineapples from the platter, threw the rest of the platter at a nearby security official, ran toward the center of the terrace toward the President's box, and threw the pineapple toward the center of the Box. Dagda was sitting on that corner of the box, saw the pineapple coming, jumped up and batted it toward the pool area. The pineapple exploded as it hit the corner of the stage and water. Two FBI agents quickly pounced on the cook/waiter. The man had no other weapons. And he offered no resistance.

At the sound of the explosion people started screaming. Many dived for the ground, started running out of the area, or headed toward the parking lots. Fortunately, no one was badly hurt. Several people on the front terrace got very wet, but they were happy to be alive. The pool water and the side of the stage had absorbed much of the discharge. President O'Reilly and families were only shaken, and of course Jamie was again one very scared and unhappy little boy.

By American law, whenever the life of the President of the United States is threatened, he must be removed from the place of danger to a safe place. So, the Presidential Secret Service/Federal Bureau of Investigation guard escorted all of the O'Reilly families to their cottages and started up the helicopter. As the helicopter blades began to purr, and Jamie realized they were going to leave before he had seen the fireworks, he began to verbally protest. Uncle Dagda quickly went over to the Commander of the SS/FBI security squad. They had learned that the assassination attempt was probably a one-person effort, and that it was now probably past tense. And he talked Jonathan into letting himself, Dagda, and whichever children wanted to stay and see the fireworks, remain. Jonathan, Jackson, the ladies and those children who wanted to go could in the helicopter now. He would be responsible for the remaining children and they would come, after the fireworks, as the helicopter could easily return to get them. The flight from the Inn to Boston was only twenty minutes. The Commander would leave three of his team with Dagda, and they would all come after the fireworks had finished. The Commander had pre-school twin boys, so he did understand. Jonathan was not happy, but one look into those sad blue eyes of Jamie which had suddenly filled with tears and you just could not deprive him again, so soon.

The President and most of the family immediately flew from the area. And little Jamie cuddled up to his favorite old baldheaded walrus who was sitting on a large blanket on the ground in front of the cottages and went to sleep as the fireworks blazed over the Cape Cod Bay. Jamie needed that adult male's touch and the smell of an O'Reilly.

4

What is Nanotechnology?

A T II:00 ON A FRIDAY morning at the National Press Club Building on 14th and F St. NW, Washington, DC, Professor Chi Jiang from the California Institute of Technology, world renowned for his research in nanomedicine, was briefing the nation's members of the press about concepts of nanotechnology. He began, "Nanotechnology or nanotech innovative systems involve the use of chemistry, physics, mathematics, engineering, biochemistry, and molecular biology in attempts to control elements and matter at the atomic and molecular level. In general, nanotech systems work at the level of nanometers or one billionth of a meter or yard. In comparing one nanometer to one meter it would be the same as comparing one marble to the size of the earth. This is the comparable size of individual biological molecules found in our body cells such as genes/ DNAs, proteins, sugars, hormones, fats, and most drugs. And all such molecules are composed of a variety of atoms."

"Earlier nanotechnical products were simply atoms hooked together to make a small molecule. We have been doing this ever since man discovered atoms. Vitamins and most drugs are unique small molecules that pharmaceutical companies produce in their laboratories at levels of more than one hundred-million tons every year. These drugs are composed of 90% carbon, hydrogen, and oxygen atoms. We call them organics – all plants and animals on earth are composed of predominately organic molecules. Hence, we are organic machines."

"Small molecules (aspirin) weigh 50 to 2,000 Daltons. They can go directly through most cell membranes and may not be digested in the stomach. Larger molecules, such as proteins (insulin), weigh 10,000 to 50,000 Daltons, and are usually digested in the stomach. Plus, these larger molecules do not go through cell membranes. So, we take advantage of these differences when we design nanotech molecules of many sizes and target specific body cells or tissues."

"Historically, an early proposal that individual atoms and molecules at the Nanometer scale could be successfully constructed and manipulated was put forth by physicist Dr. Richard Feynman on December 29, 1959. It was not until 1974 that the concept of nanotechnology was defined as separation, condensation, deformation, and re-arrangement of these materials or molecules by one atom or several atoms at a time, called Nano level manipulation, by Dr. Norio Taniguchi. But nanoscience really started in the 1980s with the series of discoveries such as cluster science and the scanning tunneling microscope, development of fullerenes, carbon nanotubes, nanocrystals, and then quantum dots. Soon after the atomic microscope (AFM) was built and in the year 2000 the USA began the National Nanotechnology Initiative, somewhat like the successful National Cancer Initiative which began in 1971. In the year 2000 there were less than 1000 scientific publications concerning nanotechnology. Today there are more than 10,000 scientific publications per year. Throughout history, no other new science has grown so rapidly."

"There are two key technological developments which allowed this field to rapidly expand, in addition to the AFM. They are the Scanning Tunnel Microscope (STM) and the Scanning Acoustic Microscope (SAM). These instruments allow one to 'see' the newly constructed materials or molecules. And this initially slow visualization process was rapidly speeded up by using several types of Nano lithography such as optical, electron beam, X-ray dip pen, and nanoimprint. With this new high-tech instrumentation, all areas of nanotechnology erupted and continues such expansion today."

"Please watch the screens behind me as I will continue, from time to time, to give visualizations of some of the nanotechnology that I will discuss. The first of these are simply pictures of the STM and SAM; they will look like big boxes to most of you."

And the news people quickly agreed. For their level of science, it was enough.

"Utilization of the application of nanotechnology is readily observed by the more than 5000 nanotechnology patents now registered worldwide. There were no nanotechnology patents before 1970. Each week another eighty to one hundred new applications are considered for approval. We shall soon have many thousands more nanotech products out 'in the world'. Currently there is only a bare minimum of American or international restrictions on their production or usage. And indeed, there is little discussion concerning the ethics involved in the use of these new human life saving or life killing systems. This is a situation which is not good and needs to be brought to the attention of our lawmakers worldwide. Again, here the news media can play a constructive role.'

"When genetic engineering or recombinant DNA research began back in the 70's, there was a big outcry for control of this placement of human genes into microorganisms fearing that those organisms might become super organisms, escape the laboratory, and destroy the world. By law, every university and institute, which performed genetic engineering research, were required to have scientific and ethics committees which regulated this 'new' research. No international killer organism resulted, deliberately or accidentally. I am of the belief that the regulatory controls so developed and implemented at that time helped prevent any possible Armageddon."

"There is one big difference here. All of the initial research studies in genetic engineering were always restricted to carefully 'contained' and 'controlled' laboratories. The studies and indeed many nanotechnology products are already out of the laboratories and 'on the streets', without such restrictions in place. One can only hope this lack of significant control will be adequate. Unfortunately, nanoproducts are currently being researched, produced, and tested in 'non-contained' and 'noncontrolled' nanoproduct laboratories, factories, hospitals, offices, and homes."

"But the potential for nanoproducts, especially in the Nanomedicine-Nano-pharmacology fields is enormous. It includes: cellular and intracellular molecular surgery, intra cell/tissue molecular manufacturing, delivery of drugs to targeted cellular molecules in targeted cells, homing MoAbs which can target any cell in the body, hormone replacement in most nonfunctioning endocrine cells, replacement, re-routing or interference of selected nerve actions, replacement of specialized cell functioning such as vibrator bone cells in the inner ear for hearing or retinal cells in the eye for seeing, and on and on. Keep in mind that genetic engineering has provided a cheaper human type of insulin which now allows millions of diabetics to live more reasonably. I fully believe that nanotechnology will do much more."

"Oh! I will discuss MoAbs later."

"Now, as you know my special interest is nanomedicine. We will now look at this area first.

Evaluation of MUSD/MUSC Candidates - I

THE WEEK AFTER DANGER WAS averted on St. Paddy's Day in Cape Cod, Jonathan, Jackson, and Dagda sat in the Oval Office and discussed the Presidential assassination attempt. The SS/FBI report concerning that day had arrived and they were digesting it.

Neither Jonathan nor Dagda had yet read it, so Jackson was summarizing the report, rather than re-read the two hundred and fifty pages. "The report declares that this was indeed a lone ranger one shot attempt from a Mr. Edgar (Smiley) Bowman. Mr. Bowman had been hired the week before St. Paddy's Day, as additional food service staff are always needed for that day. He was recommended by another full-time employee, Mr. Larry Cline. Mr. Cline knew Mr. Bowman from high school days some twenty years ago. However, Mr. Cline had not seen Mr. Bowman in the past eight or ten years until Mr. Bowman approached him about helping him find a job, he was unemployed.

Why was he unemployed? Mr. Bowman and his Father had built up a very respectable farm and home store in Hector, Connecticut which provided fertilizers and pesticides for commercial crops and home gardens in the surrounding area. They had sales in the several hundred thousand-dollar range each year for nearly thirteen years. Then about five years ago a small company, Organics-For-Us, came to the area. They had received from the federal government a one hundred thousand-dollar stipend and a thirty-acre land grant to develop a small farm based on organic principles, no synthetic fertilizers and no synthetic pesticides. Within three years this Organic Company was doing so well that many of the farmers and homeowners switched to organic farming, leaving the Bowman's store in trouble. Within three years after the community's switch to organic farming, Bowman's went bankrupt. Mr. Bowman's Father killed his Mother and then himself. And Mr. Bowman had been thinking revenge ever since then. After he landed the job at the Inn on St. Paddy's Day and found out you would be coming there for the celebration, he started planning this bomb attempt. So, he has admitted to the assassination attempt; but he has not said where he purchased the bomb nor with what money. He has no police record of any kind. Basically, what the FBI are saying is that Mr. Bowman may have been psychologically unbalanced due to his recent losses; he blamed the American government, and was seeking revenge."

Jonathan spoke up, "Again, another high technology linkage. As a result of new high-tech organics this man wanted to kill someone who brought this disaster to him and his family. He could have killed all three O'Reilly families if that bomb had not been deflected away by Dagda."

"I didn't help win that national volleyball championship in my senior year at Swift-town High for nothing and win the nickname of GS – Great Spiker. And that spike on the pineapple was automatic. I did not think, just reacted. I was lucky to knock it into the water. And we were all lucky that it exploded partially under the water and the stage. That bomb had small carpet nails inside it. It was designed more to maim than to kill." Dagda explained.

And Jonathan and Jackson just looked at each other. What could they say? Every O'Reilly child was there. Indeed, they were lucky. But neither of them wanted to continue to depend upon luck in the future. Security had to be more carefully thought through. And the clustering of the three families in a large public setting was probably not a good thing to do.

Dagda added, "This new change that we are feeling may not be new, but it could be a backlash against the many new changes that our American government promoted during the past few years. I am not singling out nor blaming Theodore, but let us keep an open mind about these high technology linkages that we are seeing. Tomorrow when I describe the other five VIP candidates with medically unexplainable deaths, you will see threads of high technology everywhere."

Again, Jonathan and Jackson looked at each other and could not respond.

Two months later, at 9:00 AM, the President's Commission on Human Trafficking met in the fourth-floor conference room of the Robert F. Kennedy Department of Justice Building at 950 Pennsylvania Avenue in Washington, DC. All commission members were in attendance and Attorney General Jackson O'Reilly, as Chairman of the Commission, opened the meeting. "Welcome to our second meeting. I hope no one had any travel problems. If you did, please let me know, and we will adjust next time. We want to look more closely at the multiple worldwide deaths of VIPs who were healthy but, during the past year, became suddenly dead in a medically unexplainable and non-detectable way, MUSD candidates. I have prepared a list of these people which is included in the new packet of information on the table in front of you. You may open the packet, look at the list and follow it through our current meeting. It should be helpful."

<u>List of VIPs Who Are MUSD Candidates - 2028</u>

Dr. Miroslav Nacekar, Nobel Laureate, developed methods for stem cell conversions into other types of body cells, Czech-American, 56 years old, on January 15, 'died' of heart failure.

Dr. David Herman, Nobel Laureate, developed fertilization techniques for human cells which we now refer to as test tube babies, American, 59 years old, on March 15, 'died' of collapsed trachea (wind pipe).

Dr. Karl Trenmeister, organic chemist who invented alternative biological sourced energies, President and CEO of International Bio-Fuels Inc., German-American, 45 years old, on May 15, 'died' of respiratory failure.

Dr. William Christofor, inventor of solar conversion to electricity methodology, President and CEO of Solar-Voltaic Systems USA, American, 53 years old, on July 15, 'died' of massive bleeding in the neck.

Dr. Dag-Finn Studhiemer, developed technique of substituting carbonated diamond powder or crystals for steel, President and CEO of European Crystal-Steel Corp., German, 51 years old, on September 15, 'died' of brain failure.

Mr. Leon Odilone, High Tech Czar, The European Union, French, 52 years old, on November 15, 'died' of brain hemorrhage.

"Today Mr. Dagda Murphy will present the results of his investigations on five of these people. Dr. Studhiemer's investigation is not complete. If you have questions during Mr. Murphy's presentation, please ask. He prefers to deal with a question at the time it appears hot in your mind, not ten minutes later when it has become cold. Mr. Murphy."

Mr. Murphy began, "Dr. David Herman received the Nobel Prize in Medicine in 2004. He received the prize for the development of reproductive methods which today we call test tube babies. He was fifty-six years old when he was found dead in the Curaco Hotel in Acapulco, Mexico on March 15, 2028. He and his Forty-six years old girlfriend, Susan Panano, had been vacationing there for the past two weeks. During the evening of March 14, Ms. Panano went shopping and then met two girl friends for an evening dinner - verified. Dr. Herman was working on his next book so he apparently stayed in their cottage all evening. From the Hotel he ordered and ate a chicken sandwich and salad, and drank one cup of black coffee – verified. There was no evidence of foul play."

"Near 11:45 PM Ms. Panano returned to find Dr. Herman in bed, in his pajamas, and sound asleep. She kissed him. Undressed and climbed into the other king-sized bed and went directly to sleep. The next morning, she woke, used the bathroom, and tried to wake Dr. Herman. He was cold, and could not be roused. She panicked, called the desk who called an ambulance and the police. It was too late. He was declared dead in the early morning hours on March 15."

"Ms. Panano called Dr. Herman's sister in New York City who immediately sent a power of attorney to her such that she could request the Mexican authorities to perform a full and complete autopsy. The Mexican authorities performed the investigation and autopsy. They found no medically explainable cause of death."

"We talked with the hotel staff and found no activities or situations that would allow us to believe malicious intent on the part of Ms. Panano or any of their vacationing friends. We could not identify anyone who wished Dr. Herman harm. He was respected, if not loved by most. He was simply suddenly dead. Why would someone want to kill him?"

"One possible reason we thought of is that he broke medical ground in the late eighties for medical research with human reproduction systems. It was his work that allowed the mating of human eggs and human sperm in test tubes and then the placement of such pre-formed embryos into women; such was and still is against church edicts. This has now led to the high-tech fields of using human embryo cells as stem cells in today's attempts to create new body cells and body tissues. So, he provided the stepping stone for human control of human reproduction, not God's control."

Ms. Dapper asked, "What do you know about the relationship between Ms. Panano and Dr. Herman?"

Mr. Murphy answered. "Ms. Panano appeared to be in love with Dr. Herman. They had been living together for more than five years. All of their friends said they were very close and were highly compatible. He simply refused to marry her because he had been married twice and had five children and 11 grandchildren. He had willed most of his estate to the blood linked family. A marriage could have caused inheritance problems when he died. Ms. Panano inherited only one hundred thousand of Dr. Herman's billion-dollar estate. So, Ms. Panano had no financial reason to kill Dr. Herman. In fact, she is the big financial loser as she now does not even have a place to live."

"Was he in good health at that time?" asked Mr. Thompson.

"Yes indeed," replied Mr. Murphy. "He had been sun bathing and swimming laps in the hotel pool or in the ocean every day. His friends all agreed that he had the body of a forty-year old. So again, we are dealing with a healthy man who suddenly dies by medically unknown causes."

Dr. Batly asked, "That night when Ms. Panano returned from her outing, she kissed him while he was already in bed. Right?"

"That is correct."

Did you ask Ms. Panano if she kissed cold or warm lips?"

Mr. Murphy, "We asked and the answer was that his lips appeared normal, not cold. Why do you ask?"

Dr. Batly answered, "I am seeking a potential time frame between the time a drug might be given and the body life support systems turned off. If it is the same or a very similar drug being used in all of the cases, it might have similar lag time before action, but once action starts it 'kills' very quickly. In other words, a delayed-rapid release mechanism."

"What did he officially die from?' asked Ms. Dapper.

"His trachea was rigidly closed shut, so he could not breathe." answered Mr. Murphy.

With that statement the Commission members could only look at each other in puzzlement. This was a very unusual way to die. No one had heard of such a death. There was not much anyone could say.

"After all of these years, why kill a sixty plus year old man? He made his big discovery, didn't he?" General Ronny said out loud.

"One possibility, we might be dealing with a newly organized group, and they have just begun their agenda." replied Mr. Chairman.

And the Chairman continued, "Are there any other questions about the death of Dr. Herman? Remember we can return to any of these deaths anytime if you think you see a connection or if you want to recall something or for any reason. I feel like we are not looking for a needle in a haystack, but a needle in the newly cut wheat field."

He went on, "Mr. Femer will present his investigation of the next death. Mr. Femer is a Senior Associate of Mr. Murphy. Because this death was in Prague, it required someone competent in both German and Czech languages. Mr. Femer is so qualified, and has been working with Mr. Murphy for the past eight years. Mr. Femer, if you please?"

Mr. Femer was of average height and weight, thirty-eight years old, wore dark framed glasses, had a serious face, wore his long light brown hair in a pony tail, and was from a Danish ethnic group living in the old East Germany. He grew up in Leipzig, Germany, and was comfortable in four European languages. He is a senior investigator for Isaat and Director of the European Office.

Mr. Femer began, "Thank you Mr. Chairman. I will present another investigation of the sudden death on a Nobel Laureate which has not been explained by medically known rationale. Dr. Miroslav Nacekar was found dead in his own bed in his house in Prague, Czech Republic. Dr. Nacekar held the John Edward Jenkins Professorship at the Massachusetts Institute of Technology in Boston. He had been working there for the past nine years and simply was home on leave for a two-month period."

"His family home was in Roztoky, a small town just outside the beltway in Prague. The house was in a typical middle-class neighborhood with six to eight two story wooden houses per block and a narrow two-lane road in front. On the evening of January 15, 2028, during a heavy snow storm, his son, Michael, who lived and worked as a banker in Prague, drove through the storm to Dr Nacekar's house. He brought a couple of boxes of food. He knew that his Father, when working on a new idea, usually isolated himself for days in the house and forgot about eating. He was widowed as his wife had died of breast cancer eight years earlier. When the son arrived, he found the door was unlocked, but the house was warm and very quiet. He found his Father clothed and lying down on his bed outside the covers. When he tried to arouse him, he could not. His eyes were closed. He was dead. Rigor mortis had fully set in. He called an ambulance and the police. Emergency procedures were immediately put into motion, but he had apparently died several hours earlier."

"The local police did investigate. An autopsy was performed. No suspicious activities were observed around the house during the day of the 15th. And Dr. Nacekar officially died of heart failure. The case was closed."

"Last month I went to the house and talked with neighbors and friends. I found a slightly different story. Indeed, the son did arrive in the evening on the January 15th. But the day before, January 14th, Dr. Nacekar had several guests. According to three different neighbors there were two men and two women who visited Dr. Nacekar that afternoon. They arrived about 4:30 PM and left around 10:30 PM. Because of the continuous snow the neighbors were not able to see any faces. They were all heavily dressed and probably strangers. It was minus 10^0 C that day. They drove a white Volvo with a German tag. No one thought to write down the tag number. All of the house lights were on while the 'strangers' were inside the house, and everything was quiet. The only unusual thing that happened was a stray cat, that Dr. Nacekar always fed when he was here, had been decapitated and thrown into the back yard. The neighbor living immediately behind the Nacekar house saw and heard the decapitation. She was carrying out some garbage at the time the animal slaying occurred. According to this neighbor, one of the strangers performed this brutal act. Apparently, the police investigation was routine and had only focused on the 15th. Of course, the cat was covered by snow at that time. And what to make of this unusual event, I do not know."

"The only point I am making is that the local police found no suspicious circumstances concerning Dr. Nacekar's death, but I was suspicious about the limited police investigation of a famous Nobel Laureate who was a local hero.

Anyway, the death happened more than one year ago and I found nothing else. Do you have any questions?"

Mr. Bradmier asked, "Did you inquire about other days of December or January that Dr. Nacekar was in seclusion in his house?"

"Yes," replied Mr. Femer. "He came to the Czech Republic on December 03, 2028. During the next few days he did have several visitors. The problem is that he was not only a popular individual, but his brilliant mind surfed several cellular and molecular medical areas. His Nobel Prize was for his discovery that embryonic stem cells could be used to develop different adult or mature cell types which could be used to replace non-functional body parts in humans. Of course, this went against the teachings of the Church. I talked with many neighbors several times and tried to make a list of the visitors. My total count came to about 19 people since Christmas, but I cannot be certain how many of these were repeats. There was no written list of visitors or visitation dates found in the house. And yes, there were two Catholic priests who visited him during that time period. The visit by the priests was during the week between Christmas and New Year's. I was unable to relate any of the visits, except possibly the visit on the night of the 14th, to Dr. Nacekar's death."

Mr. Thomson commented, "So while Dr. Nacekar was in Europe, the purpose was to be isolated such that he could 'brainstorm' a new molecular or medical idea. I wonder if the new idea that he was working on could have been some high-tech system that certain 'important' people would not want developed. This could be very important."

"That is indeed an interesting thought," responded Mr. O'Reilly. When these ideas of using cells from aborted fetuses in attempts to try to develop adult human cell and tissues, which could then be transplanted into humans, the world reaction was very different. Many countries in Europe and Asia began such research and are having much success. The Conservative Right in the USA prevented this type of research and America is still behind much of the world in this high-tech medical area. Stem cell research is one of the areas that our government is strongly supporting, even though our immediate families are Catholic."

Mr. Murphy added, "Another possible high technology linkage. And you conclude that there is no supporting evidence that Dr. Nacekar was killed. Is that correct?"

"Yes. There is no such medical evidence, today," answered Mr. Femer.

Mr. Chairman announced, "Let us take a short break and have some coffee, tea, and pastries. We can continue this discussion in fifteen minutes, or go on to the next death if you are ready."

And all stood up, stretched, and helped themselves to sources of caffeine and sugar. It did not appear that they were making very much progress toward solving these MUSDs.

Evaluation of MUSD/MUSC Candidates – II

A FEW MINUTES LATER THE CHAIRMAN called them back to order as he wanted to cover all five of the potential candidates before noon. After everyone was seated, he motioned for Mr. Murphy to begin.

Mr. Murphy continued, "We must not forget the two deaths which started us in the direction of evaluating these sudden deaths of healthy VIPs, in a medically non-detectable or unexplainable manner - my brother, Mr. Theodore O'Reilly, High Technology Czar and Cabinet Member of the current government of the United States of America, and Mr. Leon Odilone, High Technology Czar of the current government of the European Union. Mr. O'Reilly suddenly 'died' of lung failure. And Mr. Odilone suddenly 'died' of a brain hemorrhage. They each died on the fifteenth of a month. It was specifically their two deaths that stimulated this Commission to be established and gave it a beginning focus."

"We have discussed the death of Mr. O'Reilly. And we will discuss the death of Mr. Odilone last."

"The next death that we wish to review is that of Mr. William Christofor, a US citizen, at the Rio Central Hotel in Rio de Janeiro, Brazil on July 15, 2028. Mr. Christofor was attending an International Conference on Solar Voltaic Energy Systems at that hotel. The Meeting began on July 11 and continued Monday through Friday, the 15th being the last day. With two thousand attendees, the meeting was very crowded during the first few days; but as is normal for such meetings only a few hundred remained on that Friday."

"During two scientific presentations, one on Thursday morning and one on Friday morning, there were verbal disagreements between Mr. Christofor and outsiders. Later it was determined that the 'several' outsiders were oil people who were working on an ocean drilling platform off the coast of Brazil. They were on holiday in Rio, heard about the solar energy meeting, understood that Mr. Christofor was the instigator of solar voltaic energy technology, so they wanted to express their 'regrets' about this new technology. On the last day, these outsiders followed Mr. Christofor and two of his colleagues to a nearby Sushi restaurant. The outsiders did not enter the restaurant but waited until the scientists came out and then started verbally expressing their feelings. They followed the scientists for several blocks and shouted, used vulgar language, and physical threats. After several minutes of abuse, Mr. Christofor and his colleagues took a taxi back to the hotel, reported these activities to the hotel authorities, who said they would notify the police. They did not. The three engineers went to bed, in separate rooms on the same floor."

"The following morning near 11:00 AM, a member of the hotel keeping staff found Mr. Christofor dead, and cold, in his night clothes in bed. She called hotel security who notified the in-house doctor and nursing staff, police, and immigration authorities as Mr. Christofor was a foreigner on a one-week visa which expired on the 16th. All concerned came immediately, notified the American Embassy, performed their respective services, wrote and filed their reports. The hallway security cameras showed only Mr. Christfor entering his room around 10:30 PM, but no one else entered during the night until the maid the following morning. His body was taken to a city coroner's office. But it took two days before his brother from Los Angeles arrived, gave permission for an autopsy, followed the autopsy to completion, and learned that Mr. Christofor had died during the night. No medically detectable cause for the bleeding was established. It was an unusual simultaneous rupture of both carotid arteries going from the heart to the brain. The mass of coagulated blood, two days after the rupture, made it very difficult to determine which blood vessel ruptured first. The cause was listed as bleeding in the neck to death."

Dr. Batley interrupted, "I have never ever heard of two ruptured carotid arteries at the same time, impossible."

"Mr. Christofor was the President and CEO of Voltaic USA Systems in Los Angeles, California. He was an electric/electronic engineer and was a key person in discovering the role of lithium in the development of the battery which is now used to store solar produced voltage energy. An early problem in the development of solar-voltaic energy was that the sun's energy was only available part of the day, but electricity was used 24 hours a day. A powerful battery was necessary to store large quantities of energy for short periods of time. The lead-acid battery was too toxic and could not be used for such purposes. Lithium based batteries now allow us to enjoy sun powered energy for cars, homes, businesses, factories, and numerous personal electric systems such as cellular phones. Of course, this is a big problem for the petrochemical industry, and even the oil well workers had learned who was after their jobs. The 'outsiders', who had hassled Mr. Christofor, were not identified nor questioned. There is no evidence that they may or may not have been involved in his death. The case was closed."

"Was the man healthy and free from previously related problem?" asked Dr. Bately.

Mr. Murphy answered. "Yes. I spoke directly with two physicians at the Voltaic USA Systems. They have a diet and exercise program which requires all senior executives and employees over sixty years of age to apply rigorously. This program is required by their health and life insurance programs. Mr. Christofor was fifty-six years old and in excellent physical condition. They even showed to me Mr. Christofor's EKG which had been taken in February of 2026. It was excellent. So, they too did not understand how a massive rupture of his neck arteries could have occurred."

Mr. Chairman commented. "Again, we see relationships with high technology and a MUSD. Are there any other questions?" He waited a couple of moments, then.......

"If no other questions now, then let us please continue. I believe that this candidate is your investigation Mr. Femer. Can you begin, please?"

Mr. Femer opened his lap top. "Mr. Karl Tranmeister, President and CEO of International Biofuels, headquarters in Frankfurt, Germany, was found dead in his house near Offenbach, a nearby suburb of Frankfurt, on May 15, 2028. He was between wives or girlfriends, or however you want to describe these relationships. He was sixty-one years old, tall, blond, handsome with an athlete's body, and was a well-known skirt chaser. He had been married three times, was currently single, and had two children from previous marriages. Mr. Tranmeister was dating a Ms. Angelique Stazey, thirty-year old lovely blue-eyed blonde who was currently modeling in various German and French cities. Ms. Stazey was staying with Mr. Tranmeister in southwestern Germany, or on weekends between modeling assignments. She stayed with him on May 12 and 13, but was on assignment in Berlin on May 14, 15, and 16. The police investigation determined that she was indeed in Berlin on those days and found no evidence linking her to his death."

"On the fifteenth of May, Mr. Tranmeister was in the company offices routinely working all day and left from work to be chauffeured home at 8:45 PM. He had eaten a quick Chinese take-out dinner in the office as he and his secretary had worked late together, and left the office at the same time. It was confirmed that the secretary went directly to her home. After dropping Mr. Tranmeister off at his home, the chauffeur also went directly home. The next morning when the chauffeur came by at 8:30 AM to pick him up, he did answer the door. The chauffeur used his pass key, entered the house, and found Mr. Tranmeister in his pajamas in bed. He could not be roused, his eyes were closed, and his body was cold. So, the chauffeur called the police, ambulance, and office. His body was taken to the chief medical examiner's building. Local police found no evidence of foul play. And the medical examiner could find no medically explainable cause of death. A full autopsy was not performed because no next of kin was available or did not wish to be involved. Officially his death was listed as respiratory failure."

"My investigation was considerably more extensive than that of the local police. In checking out the secretary, chauffeur, current girl-friend, and other close contacts, I found the following suspicious information. The secretary was a former girlfriend who was brushed aside when Mr. Tranmeister tired of her. She still resented their affair. The chauffeur was a gambler, was deeply in debt to a local casino, and was being pressed for that money. He asked Mr. Tranmeister for a short-term loan, but all he received was a look of disgust. The girlfriend had a younger boy friend with whom she regularly stayed when she was not with Mr. Tranmeister. The boyfriend had spent six years in prison for armed robbery and was in regular contact with his 'old friends'. I also learned that Mr. Tranmeister had been receiving death threat e-mails for many months. These notes were not traced."

"So, Mr. Tranmeister was a powerful, very intelligent man who was arrogant, not well liked, had very few friends, and was surrounded by people who 'did not love him'. In 2004, he was the first organic chemical engineer to develop a method to convert biomass into fuels. This is a renewable carbon energy source from various living organisms such as plants – corn, sugar cane, soybeans, rape seed, cassava and switchgrass. And today, International Bio-fuels is concentrating on using bio-wastes – municipal solid waste, agriculture residues, farm waste, biodegradable waste from streams and creeks flowing from city septic processing plants. The company went from a profit of $12 million in 2015 to more than $86 million in 2024. Because this biomass or bio-fuel technology is very new and is still developing, it is currently supported by government subsidies. This technology has started to result in decreases in sales of farm and home fertilizers. Several fertilizer manufacturers have gone bankrupt during the past few years. And the petrochemical industry is not happy with this new high-tech approach to energy production. So, Mr. Tranmeister was a man with enemies."

The room was quiet for a couple of minutes as the investigative data seemed rather straight forward – no direct evidence but plenty of unhappiness or even hatred; there certainly were possible reasons and probably opportunities to see this man and his technology gone from the current world stage.

Ms. Von Eulenberg spoke up, "I congratulate you, Mr. Femer. You didn't find a smoking gun but you found smoke so we must seriously consider that a gun must have been there. This again appears to be another situation where high technology is involved. Are you suggesting a clandestine group coordinated this possible murder?"

"I think so," responded Mr. Femer, "My gut feeling is that this death could not have been accomplished by a single individual. The deaths of some of our other candidates could probably have been carried out by one person, but not this death."

"Do you see only one person or possibly a team with one 'trigger man' involved here?" asked Mr. Thomson.

"I can only guess," Mr. Femer replied. "There may be more than one individual to whom I am referring, but it involves a group of controllers, not necessarily on sight. The 'hit' person is most likely a single hired professional, but could involve an accomplice in this particular death."

General Ronny asked, "Do you believe that we are seeing a group of decision makers/controllers who are making 'elimination' decisions, have a list of assassins whom they can hire, and are supported by several monetary sources? If so, these monetary sources would have an overall common goal or set of objectives. And, would you speculate on who or where those sources might be?"

"Your ideas are in line with my thinking," answered Mr. Femer. "I do not believe that this is a simple terrorist group. I think that their long-term goals do not involve ethnic or religious ideas, but probably business-related concepts/motives. I could even label this intellectual terrorism. Most of these targets are not common people or simple politicians, but indeed very brilliant minds. We have here several carefully designed death scenes with no remaining evidence of the cause of the death. I think that we should ask the question, what would be gained by eliminating these specific minds, one by one. Also, have such deaths stopped?

No! In fact, they have not! On 15th of March, 2021, a Dr. Bahar Edison, one of the key inventors of nanotech drugs, President and CEO of Nanodrugs USA Corp, was found dead in a hotel in Stockholm, Sweden. Upon autopsy, his death was medically unexplainable. So?"

And there was a collective intake from the group. After a few minutes of open discussion, they moved on to the last candidate. The investigation was carried out by Mr. Murphy.

Mr. Murphy began, "Mr. Leon Odilone, the fifty-two-year old Czar of High Technology, or the Commissioner for High Technology of the European Union was found dead in his bed at his home on the morning of November 15, 2028. An immediate autopsy found no medically explainable cause of death; officially he died of a massive brain hemorrhage. Mr. Odilone was near 5 ft 10 inches tall and very slim, but an acutely controlled gentleman, and an avid sportsman who regularly jogged and played tennis, summer and winter. Mr. Odilone lived with his wife at 7173 Ter Kamerenstraat just off Tervurenlaan in Brussels, Belgium; and he drove to work each day to the Berlaymont building, headquarters of the European Commission on Oudergemlaan. His wife, Dr. Jan Odilone, was a pediatrician who worked in the nearby Osfaast Family Health Clinic. They had one daughter who was married and lived in an apartment near the Old Town Square in the social-business-tourist center of Brussels. She and her banker husband had one 1 ½ year old daughter and were expecting a baby boy anytime.

On the fourteenth of November, Mr. and Dr. Odilone both went to work as usual. He had a full day of appointments and meetings. All work was routine. Late in the afternoon he received a call from his wife who had received a call from their pregnant daughter. The daughter was having some breathing problems; So, Dr. Odilone was going to the Old Town Square apartment to be with her. She would probably stay for the night. At about 8:15 PM he left his office, went down to the underground parking garage, tried to start his car, but it would not start. He notified the security and took a taxi home. When he got home, he found that the front door lock was jammed. He went to a neighbor's house, called an emergency locksmith, who came immediately and opened the door. He then entered his house, ate a salad and tuna fish sandwich the housekeeper had left for him in the refrigerator. He drank one glass of skim milk, turned on and watched the evening news, changed into night clothes and went to bed. The next morning, at 9:15 AM the housekeeper found him still in bed, cold and not breathing. She called Dr. Odilone, who had gone directly to her Clinic from the daughter's house. Dr. Odilone called for ambulance and police. Mr. Odilone was immediately taken to a hospital, and then to the city coroner's building. They brought in medical specialists during the autopsy, but found no medically explainable cause for the massive brain hemorrhage. They were not able to determine what caused the sudden and heavy intracranial bleeding. However, without any evidence of unusual or suspicious activities, only a routine investigation was undertaken by the local police"

"I saw too many suspicious things happening. So, I undertook an extensive investigation. And I found a number of suspicious activities that occurred on the fourteenth of November, 2028. First, when the daughter had lunch at a nearby restaurant she ate 'something' that caused her to have an upset stomach and breathing problems; these problems persisted all evening and much of the night. This is why Mr. Odilone's wife was not with him in their house that night. Second, it was later determined that Mr. Odilone's car had been tampered with and that is why it would not start on the evening of the fourteenth. Three, the locksmith that opened Mr. Odilone's door could not be located again. Four, the Odilone's maid was struck by an automobile and killed one week later. None of this information was recorded by the local police inspectors nor appeared in local newspapers."

Mr. Thompson spoke up, "So somewhat similar to the Trenmeister death, no smoking gun, but smoke. It would appear that these several 'happenings' indicate that there must have been one around somewhere."

Mr. Chairman commented, "Let us cluster the five deaths which we just reviewed and the two deaths of my brother, Mr. Theodore O'Reilly, and Mr. Dag-Finn Studhiemer from our first meeting two months ago. By these seven deaths can we say that the seven MUSD of healthy VIPs on the fifteenth of a month during the past year are related? And if so, are their relationships related to high technology? Also, I think whoever is doing this wants us to know they exist because these deaths all occurred on the same day of the month. It they had randomized the deaths we would not have picked up this pattern and we would still be completely in the dark. So, we are only partially in the dark. And I think that is what is intended."

Mr. Bradmier responded, "I agree. It certainly appears that way. But if it is true, where do we go from here?"

Looking at Mr. Murphy, Mr. Femer replied, "I would like to have your permission to investigate the recent death of Dr. Bahar Edison. I would think that this death also fits the pattern that we are seeing. And it occurred on the fifteenth of a month."

Mr. Murphy glanced at Mr. O'Reilly who nodded, then said, "OK, I am afraid if what we are thinking is true there will probably be more of these types of deaths. We may need to investigate these also."

Mr. Femer added, "I know Stockholm and that hotel. With our line of reasoning maybe I can find out some things that the local police missed."

Mr. Chairman said, "Are there any questions, comments, suggestions or otherwise from any commission members?"

Mr. Bradmier asked, "Dr. Batley, can you detect or do you know of any drug or drugs, nanotech or otherwise, that will kill, similar to what we have been discussing?"

"Maybe," Dr. Batley responded. "There are a few drugs, high tech, or nanotech, which have delayed action, and then 'explode' so to speak, all at once. Keep in mind that poisons such as snake or scorpion, usually initiate their effects immediately and kill within a few minutes; and they leave residual molecules in the blood which can be verified as that specific poison. Here we are seeing a delay of action, perhaps of several hours; and there are no residual molecules in the blood to tell us that there was a poisonous like substance in the body. These killing molecules/substances, whether high tech or nanotech or what, they are all very powerful, have delayed action, then seem to kill quickly."

"In trying to relate them to the current deaths that we have been talking about, there are many body targets. If I have counted correctly, we have reviewed 'officially' one death of heart failure, one death of brain failure, one death due to lung failure, one collapsed trachea, one double carotid artery rupture in the neck, and one massive brain hemorrhage."

"I do not think that all of these types of deaths could occur with a single drug. In my opinion six different types of deaths from one drug are not possible. I see at least two major problems. How did any of the drugs get into the body? And how could they act in several different body locations, unless we are seeing seven different drugs? High tech types of drugs can be specific for certain body molecules, cells, tissues, or organ systems. But it would require a super drug which had six different homing components to target six areas of the body. I have never heard of such a drug. I think we are dealing with six different types of high tech or nanotech molecules/nanotech substances/nanotech killers, whatever name you wish to use. We just do not know enough about the drug and the mechanism of killing. We should not close our minds to any type of high-tech drug-targeting system which has delayed action, the capacity to kill its target cells, and then self-destruct. Bottom line, I do not know what we are dealing with."

Mr. Bradmier asked, "So in your mind there is probably more than one drug?"

After a few seconds of thinking Dr. Batley answered, "First, probably there would have to be several highly sophisticated experimental nanotech drugs available. I say nanotech drugs because I think they are the only type of drug which might be capable of doing something like this, but even here

I do not know for sure. There are currently none that I definitely know of. But I think they are out there. I do not believe that one drug could not do all that we are seeing. And logically, why would you risk testing or trying out several new drugs if you have one that works extremely well? It would only increase your risk of failure and possible exposure. Again, I really do not know anything for certain. We need to add a nanotechnology expert to our Commission."

Mr. Chairman spoke up, "The President, Mr. Murphy and I have been talking and dancing around several theories. The one theory that seems to stand above the others is the intellectual terrorism idea. These deaths seem to be highly targeted. They seem to be related to the professional influence of the seven individuals, not to them personally. Thus, it is only logical that international conservative elements, which have the most to lose from new high technology, could be behind this. Or from the other direction; if high technology can be slowed down, stopped, or even reversed then these international conservative elements would greatly benefit."

"We did a brief news media review for the year 2028. We looked for key members of this potentially conservative group, such as church leaders, conservative politicians, presidents and CEOs of petrochemical industry, steel industry, meat industry, pharmacological industry, selected farmers and food crops companies, factory worker unions, and on and on. Another criterion that we focused on was of a cure where no known medical treatment was involved or reported; in other words, a type of a 'miracle'. One result that came from this effort was that there were six such people who had sudden life-saving miracles during the past year. And that all six of those 'miracles' occurred on the 15th of a month. To be exact:

<u>Possible Sudden Miracle Cures on the Fifteenth of a Month - 2028</u>

February 15 – Cardinal Antonio Octavus, Secretary of the Vatican Archives

April 15 – Mr. John Issac, President of the Meat Producers Lobby Intl.

June 15 – Evangelist Reverend Shepherd Exodus

August 15 – Mr. Jan van Het, CEO of Shell Oil Company

October 15 – Mr. John Tytler, President of Tytler Intl. Steel Corporation.

December 15 – Mr. Will Preston, Sec-Gen of Pharmaceutical Workers Intl

"We have no idea as to how these medically unexplainable sudden cures (MUSC) occurred, or even if they are related. But again, the fact that they all occurred on the fifteenth of a month tells us that this group wants us to know that they are out there. It almost says come find me!"

"Therefore, if you are in agreement, let us investigate these sudden miracle cures and look for linkages to each other and also to the medically unexplainable sudden deaths."

"Are there any questions or comments? If not, we will continue by exploring this which may be a tangent, may be a parallel road, may be even part of the major highway, or may be a dead end."

"And I want to leave you with an interesting, and rather macabre pun. If you list the last names of the MUSD and the names of the MUSC in chronological order, you find the following:

Nacekar – Octavus – Herman – Issac – Trenmeister –
Exodus Christofor – Het – Studhiemer – Tytler – Odilone – Preston

"And then pull out the first letters of each name and list them:

N-O-H-I-T-E-C-H-S-T-O-P

"And then you separate the letters as following, we see a warning:"

NO – HI – TECH – STOP

7

The Camp I

IT WAS SUNDAY, JULY 11 and the little Leo was struggling. It was Jamie's twelfth birthday and it was planned to be a good one. Since his Father was 'killed', and all three families had been targeted to be killed, he had become a very different little boy. Everyone could see the difficulty that he was having adjusting to the realities of the world. It seemed that some little boys, wealthy or not, were not immune to harsh world events. Before this tragedy he was happy go lucky, always into fun things and happy times, always laughing and in the middle of any happening. He now frequently became depressed, turned rather serious and withdrawn. His computer games had switched from cartoon animals to iron man and steel man transformers.

But his Mother, two older sisters, Megan and Rebecca, and the other two O'Reilly families had organized a big family picnic and cook-out at Plymouth Bay, just south of Boston. They would bar-b-q salmon, Jamie's favorite food, play croquet, Jamie's favorite game, and water ski, Jamie's favorite sport. And then Sunday night they would all watch the latest CD of Iron Man and the Nano-ray Machine, a birthday gift from Mother.

The three families, including Uncle Dagda but without Uncle Jonathan and Uncle Jackson, met at the lake after church in mid-afternoon after a brief post church sandwich lunch. It was a beautiful bright and sunny, cirrus clouds only, warm day for the Boston seashore area. The picnic started with a blast of youth energies. Being the only adult male, Uncle Dagda was in charge of driving the 290 Bowrider Sea Ray with a 240 Hp inboard which could pull three water skiers at the same time. This was necessary because the O'Reilly teenagers had logged much time boating and skiing both on lakes near Boston and in the many Atlantic bays just off shore.

With eleven children, a general rotation was set up such that the younger ones (pre-teens) got the boat first and the opportunity to ski, and the older ones (teenagers) stayed on ground with croquet and volleyball. Later in the afternoon the two groups switched. The three ladies started preparing the bar-b-q of salmon and breasts of chickens, and the dozen cold dishes that are standard for picnics such as cabbage slaw, potato salad, corn curls, Boston baked beans, green salad with tomatoes, green onions, and cucumber, hard boiled eggs, and Jamie's favorite, carrot sticks. For dessert there were apple and cherry pies, and Jamie's favorite, M&M candy covered peanuts.

Jamie was having a lot of fun. His love for the outdoors was allowing him to develop into a virtual athletic-sportsman as he had mastered both one and two skis, and the board. He could do a few turns, and even go over the jumping ramp (when it was set low at one foot). And on the croquet field he often beat some of his teenager cousins. His age and height left him at a disadvantage in the volleyball court. But he had already made plans that when his hormones kicked in, he was going to shoot up there and get big like Uncle Dagda.

Later in the afternoon, following an hour of water skiing, and two hours of playing volleyball and croquet, he curled up in the shade under a big old oak tree and took a short nap. Upon waking up, he sat down beside Mom and looked her in the eye.

He asked, "I would like to go to an international children's summer camp in August. I have one in mind. May I?"

Mother was shocked. After a few seconds she replied, "Why do you want to do that?"

He replied, "I just need to get away from it all for a while so I can think." This was one of Uncle Dagda's favorite expressions.

His Mother recognized it is as so. She said, "And where do you plan to go?" Without hesitation he answered, "Switzerland, Europe."

The shock was immediate, both for his Mother and the two aunts who were sitting nearby and overheard.

Aunt Aingeal spoke up, "Don't you think you are too young to travel so far?" Jamie's answered, "Uncle Dagda has been there and he thinks it is a really neat place. It is not like America. In Switzerland the mountains have snow in the summertime."

The three ladies looked at each other and Riona raised her eyebrows. "But Uncle Dagda is a little older than you."

"But this is a children's camp for 10 to 15-year-olds. And I am now twelve. I am already overqualified." And he laughed.

His Mother was not sure if he was bluffing or if he was for real. "How do you know about this summer camp for children?"

Jamie answered, "It was on television last night and I showed Uncle Dagda. He said Switzerland was a good place. They have children from every country in the world. You get to sleep in rooms with five or six guys. You get to hike and camp in the mountains, canoe in rivers, ride horses, do rafting and sailing, soccer, basketball, tennis, archery, learn how to tie knots, do handicraft; and you get to visit cheese factories, chocolate factories, and wine factories. That's really neat. Huh?"

The three ladies just sat back in shock. And they had thought that he was suffering from depression and wanted to escape from the world. Well this was one form of escape. The best place to hide a golf ball is in a pile of small white rocks. And it was always difficult to say no to those penetrating blue eyes. The best that his Mother could do was to simply reply, "Let us talk about it again tonight after Iron Man III."

Jamie's last comment was, "I need to figure out how to find my Dad's killer."

But his Mother was walking away and did not hear the comment.

And that night after the Iron Man movie Jamie took his Mother by the hand and took her to his room. He opened his lap top and went on line. He opened www.campsuisseland.com. And there it was, just as he had explained. He was extremely bright and was going to be an independently difficult kid as he grew older.

Three weeks later, at 3:37 on a Sunday afternoon, Swiss Airline, flight number 1537 from New York Kennedy Airport landed at Zurich Airport, in Kloten a canton of Zurich, Switzerland, Europe. This airport was only thirty minutes from the International Camp Suisseland located in the mountains near Leysine. There was a minibus with a large logo of the camp, a chauffeur and two college age assistants who were collecting children arriving for the camp. Because Jamie was only twelve years of age his Mother had notified the airlines and he had his 'personal' stewardess to 'take care of him' on the plane and to 'deliver' him to the Camp personnel. Jamie thought it was kind of neat to have such a pretty babysitter. Indeed, those snow-covered mountains in the middle of the summer were there just like Uncle Dagda said. The Camp personnel picked up his luggage and put it into the back of the minibus. Jamie and five other American children hopped in and away they went to have the experience of their young lives.

The minibus seated twelve people, so each child took a window seat. As the little bus rambled up, down, and around the winding roads toward the Camp the children were silent. Each was glued to a window staring at the fantastic summer snow caps, gigantic forests, and wild summer flowers. This group of Americans had seen nothing like this at home.

As they pulled into the campgrounds, they could see the large bright green recreation fields and several wooden buildings immediately in front of them. The camp was situated on a large mountain plateau. There were three large chateau-like buildings side by side, constructed of logs, and several adjacent small chalet-like buildings. The center three story building was the reception center with a registration desk, administrative offices, a large lounge, many couches and chairs, a snack bar, a giant fireplace on one wall and large television screen on another wall. This building also contained the dining room- cafeteria, a gymnasium for indoor sports, and several small exercise and game rooms. The two other chateau-like buildings, one on each side of the reception center, were dormitories. One was for guys and one for girls. Each dormitory had two floors with fifteen bedrooms per floor, four beds per room which totaled nearly two hundred and fifty youngsters who could be accommodated for a weekly venture. And this week it was packed.

Near the dormitories were several smaller buildings which housed the camp staff. Camp Suisseland maintained a guest to instructor ratio of five to one. More than fifty instructors, mostly young people aged twenty to thirty years, and five senior personnel were employed for a three-month summer. To the far left of the entry road was a large barn and horse corral. Scattered around the buildings were a variety of playing fields. The entire camp was more than one hundred and fifty acres; the central one hundred acres was a mostly clear pasture-like grassland, but it was surrounded by a very dense forest of deep green pine, spruce, and deciduous trees. There was a large buffer between the children and forest animals. For several miles in each direction from the Camp there was only forest. It was a summer camp isolated in a Swiss forest in the Swiss mountains with Swiss animals that serenaded the children every night. And then there were the billions and billions of Swiss stars.

The six Americans arrived at the Camp, confirmed their registration and were given room numbers and their weekly schedules. The system was set up with three groups of similar ages: group I was 10 and 11 years old; group II was 12 and 13 years old; and group III was 14 and 15 years old. With three groups of boys and three groups of girls, there were six groups of approximately forty campers per exercise group. Or at least that was the intent.

The little travelers were very tired from the nine-hour flight and the six hours-time difference between eastern USA time and central European time zones. But it was only early afternoon by local time. Each went to his assigned room with the intention of resting a little before looking around and going to dinner.

Jamie was in the boys' dormitory in room number B-125. He was planning to take a quick nap but his three roommates were already there and getting to know one another. So, his epinephrine kicked in. He got his second energy. And the four of them began a week of non-stop talking.

"My name is Jiang Li in Chinese, but Li Jiang in English. I was born in Nanking, China; but now I live in both Nanking and in Los Angeles, California. Since we will all speak in English, please call me Li. My Father is an engineer and lives and works most of the time in Los Angeles. My Father is Chinese, but my Mother was from Ireland. She died when I was little. I visited there only once, last year; and I met all of my European cousins. So, this is my second visit to Europe. I am twelve years old and do not have any brothers or sisters." said the first little boy who had dark bright brown eyes, looked very Chinese, and appeared to be usually quiet and observant. For him to speak up first in a group was unusual. However, he was rather tall and had a proud and disciplined posture, even when sitting on the floor.

Jamie was also sitting on the floor and spoke up next, "My name is James O'Reilly, call me Jamie. I am an American living in Boston, Massachusetts, but all of my family came from Ireland many years ago. I have never visited anywhere in Europe before. Maybe Li can tell me about my 'ancestor's land' sometime this week. My Father was a lawyer but he was killed last January. I have two older sisters and I am also twelve years old. I came here this week to recover from my depression due to the loss of my Father. And I know that you will help me recover." The rather small, light skinned, long curly dark-haired boy gave his roommates his gentle and seductive grin. He was rapidly maturing into a leader.

And the three boys looked at each other. They were not sure what a depression was. But if Jamie wanted to get rid of it, it must be bad. And they each expressed their desires that they would help him get better.

The slim little black boy sitting on his bed went next. "My name is Kefentse Legoase, but you can call me Kef. I live in Cape Town, South Africa. I have many brothers and sisters. But I am the youngest, twelve years old, and the smartest. I won the national spelling contest, in the English language. This European summer camp is my prize. My English is pretty good, but my spelling is really great. I would thank you if you could help me learn to speak better English. My brothers told me that you learn faster and better English if you have English or American friends. My Father is the manager of a private mining company. But my oldest brother is a nanotech technician and that is what I want to be, a nanotech scientist, when I grow up." Kef was a bean pole, all bones and skinny muscles, but quick as a cat. His long slim dark face, large lips, close cut afro and dark eyes, and a confident cocky look made you want to put him where you could sort of keep an eye on him.

And the fourth roommate who was sitting on the only desk chair contributed, "My name is Aykut Turan. I am also twelve years old and I live in Istanbul, Turkey. I have one baby sister, aged 3. My Father is a banker; and I love computers. They are my best friends. I also attend a school which teaches me in English and Turkish. My Father sent me to this summer camp to meet other boys from around the world and to learn better English. I guess Jamie will have a lot of work to do teaching the three of us English." And he laughed. Aykut's almond colored eyes and sun-tanned skin, round face and rather chunky body indicated a boy who liked his food and the summer sandy beaches. His ready grin and easy gait suggested he would be an avid follower, but could lead, where necessary.

"I will make you guys a deal." Jamie said. "I will teach you English, only if you teach me Chinese, Swahili, and Turkish."

And that broke the stranger barrier as they all began laughing at what a fun thing that would be to do.

Kef said, "If we each learn each other's languages we could set up our own secret-codes. A sentence could be spoken with 2 words of English, 3 words of Turkish, 2 words of Chinese, and 3 words of Swahili."

Jamie picked up on the idea, "Or the code could be changed to 3:2:4:5."

Li jumped into the game, "And we could change it each week; for the second week it could be changed to 1:3:2:1."

Aykut added, "Our code could be changed every day if we wanted to do so. That would be a secret code that no one would ever break. We just send the numbers in advance of the message."

And they all broke down laughing at how quickly they had jelled into a clever team. Little did they know that they would indeed develop a third language which they would use to help solve unexplainable sudden deaths.

Jamie finished, "When we can do it perfectly, we will take out a patent (he did not know what that was but he knew it was important). And then we sell it to whichever world government will pay us the most for the most secret, impossible to break code ever devised by boykind."

And four crazy little boys rolled with laughter.

Kef added, "The only problem we would have is – What would we do with all of that money?"

"We could clean up the environmental pollution all over the world." Li quickly spoke up. Nanking was one of the most polluted cities on earth.

Jamie asked, "Do we all vote in favor of the next pollution revolution?"

The vote was four to zero in favor of 'fixing' the world, and zero to four for anything else. And the crazy 'conversation' continued for several minutes until finally they got serious.

"What activities are we going to do tomorrow?" asked Jamie.

And they each reached for their weekly program which said at the top that they were all registered in group I-B-3. Jamie read Monday's activities out loud.

"In the morning, breakfast at 8:00 o'clock: 9:00 until 12:00, we can choose between field hockey, soccer, and tennis. Lunch is at 12:00 o'clock. And in the afternoon, 1:30 until 4:30, we have swimming and diving. We are then free until 6:30 for dinner. Monday night is a welcome ceremony and a Swiss mountain climbing film in the gymnasium."

The campgrounds contained one soccer, one field hockey and two general playing fields, ten tennis courts, one large swimming pool with six diving boards, one archery and golf driving range, one horseback riding corral and a circular track, plus two forest jogging or horseback riding trails, and within a thirty-minute bus ride was Lake Constantine for canoeing and rowing, and the Neu Creek for rafting and camping. So Camp Suisseland was a high-class camp with a wealth of activities for upper - middle class children and scholarship winners.

Aykut asked, "I wonder if we have to play all three sports in the morning and both sports in the afternoon?" And he chuckled and looked around sheepishly.

Li answered, "If I do that, I will have to sleep the rest of the week to get my energy back."

Kef added, "But it is a good question. Can we only do one of three in the morning, or can we do two? Someone needs to explain the rules to us. Maybe they will do that tonight."

"Also, when do we choose?" Jamie asked. "Do we choose now and tell them in advance, like tonight, or do we just walk onto the field and say 'Here we are!' They should let us manage this place then important little things like this would not become important big things later."

And again, the continuous round of grins, which was becoming contagious, happened.

Kef looked at Jamie and said, "Are you crazy, man? If I do one of these activities every day for six days, you will have to carry me back to the airplane on Saturday night." He threw his head back and laughed.

"I think I prefer the sun-bathing lessons at the pool all day each day," declared Aykut.

And the 'heterogeneous' boyhood camaraderie was being formulated and would lead to really a neat experience for four rapidly maturing young men this week, but also carry a lifetime of danger.

Hey, if twelve-year old boys cannot solve the problems of the world, who can?

As 6:30 PM dinner hour approached the four of them headed toward the cafeteria-dining room. Because of the several time zone changes for Jamie and Li, they ate quickly and returned to their bed and were sound asleep in minutes. Kef and Aykut did not have that problem so they were still awake and in motion; they ate dinner, watched the mountain climbing/hiking movie, talked with other campers, and finally turned in near midnight.

The week began with a chilly, bright sunshiny morning which found all four boys up and out, finished with breakfast and headed toward the playing fields by 9:00 AM. Jamie and Kef went to the soccer field and Li and Aykut went to the field hockey field. The fields were side by side, and each field had fifteen to twenty-five boys and girls in group I (10-11 years). Each met their coaches and assistants/teachers and began doing some loosening up exercises. Both sports required a lot of running so body stretching, bending, twisting, jumping, and short runs were needed to warm the body's muscles, especially the legs. The soccer teachers then demonstrated how to handle, control, and kick the ball using only the feet, legs, and body. While the field hockey teachers demonstrated how to hold the hockey stick and hit, push, and flick the hockey ball with only the curled end of the stick.

After the demonstrations the campers on the soccer field formed small circles of six to eight, and passed the soccer ball back and forth to each other. While the campers on the other field formed two lines of 12 to 15 each, one facing another, and passed the hockey ball back and forth to each other. The campers on both fields practiced and continued to learn the proper way to handle the respective ball on their fields. After a couple hours of practicing, the teachers described the on-field player position and strategy for each position. Each camper chose a position that he wanted to play. Teams were formed in both sports, everyone was on a team. They then played several 15-minute games, for fun. And during the part of the three-hour exercise, the teachers took their players aside and again taught or demonstrated what some were doing wrong, how to correct their catching and shooting the ball, and again about strategy of scoring. Skinny, but super quick Kef scored two soccer goals, Jamie made one assist to Kef, and Li and Aykut simply had good fun.

As the four guys walked away from the first activity session Aykut spoke up, "If all of our exercises are like this, I might lose some weight. And if I lose a couple of kilos, I will probably attract more girls. Now is that good or bad?"

All three buddies looked at him and simultaneously said, "That is bad!" And they took off running.

After a quick use of the multi-shower room in the boys' dormitory, lunch, and on to the swimming pool by 1:30 PM, they were on time. The pool was not Olympic size but it was certainly large enough to accommodate forty or fifty swimmers. Once again, the coach and his assistants/teachers had the campers perform some warm up exercises. This time the exercises included all parts of the body in bending, twisting, rotating, and lifting of limbs. For diving and for swimming you needed all muscles of the body warm, loose, and pliable.

After a few minutes of exercises the group was divided into two subgroups; one to learn about diving and one to learn swimming and how to use different swim strokes. All campers then got into the pool and swam the width (50 feet). If you could not swim the width of the pool you were not allowed to join the diving group, but stayed in the swim group the entire period. Jamie and Aykut qualified for the diving group, but Li and Kef spent their entire two hours in the swim group. The diving was only from low boards anyway. During the last half hour, it was anyone anywhere. The four of them initiated the first water fight of the afternoon, but it was not the last one. They were only children.

That evening after dinner the Four Colored Musketeers as they now called themselves, sat around the bedroom and talked away. Aykut spoke up, "My Father sent me to this camp because he heard from his friend that it was very international. He was right. Look at the four of us, four different continents, four different countries, four different cities, and four different languages."

And Kef quickly interrupted, "and four different boys." And he gave his quick laugh.

Aykut continued, "He wants me to learn everything from everyone. Would you agree to share some of our lives with each other? I mean we could each tell a little about our history, our home, and our family-life. I would be willing to go first. Maybe we could each take a different night to talk."

"I think that is a great idea," responded Jamie. "This is my first trip outside the United States and I hope to make many more; yet I know nothing about outside the United States."

Li quickly agreed, "Me too. I want to learn everything."

And Kef added, "It would be really good to have more just than four foreign names to share with my brothers when I go home. I can snow them with all of my new knowledge of Asia, Europe, and America. Let's do it."

So Aykut began, "I am ready so let me begin. The Romans first built a city on the European side of the Bosporus waterway which connects the Black Sea to the Aegean Sea to the Mediterranean Sea to the Atlantic Ocean around 500 BCE. Around 300 BCE, King Constantine the Great controlled the city and named it Constantinople, after himself, and it became the capital of Eastern Roman Empire. Later, it was called Byzantium and for the next 1000 years it was the capital of the Byzantine Empire. The Turks conquered the city and made it the capital of the Ottoman Empire in 1453. And in 1923, when the Ottoman Empire fell it remained only as a capital of past empires."

"The new Republic of Turkey made a new capital in Ankara, a small city which was three hundred miles to the east of now Istanbul. Today Istanbul is a gigantic city of nearly 20 million people and exists ½ in Europe and ½ in Asia, west side and east side, respectively, of the Bosporus Waterway. It is the cultural capital, manufacturing capital, news media capital, and banking capital of a country of 90 million people. Culturally it is both west and east, Europe and Middle East. On the streets and in the houses, you will see both types of lives – mini-skirts and head scarf covered women, clean shaven men in western suits and ties and bearded men in baggy pants and jackets. It is a fascinating contrast.'

"We live on the west side in Istanbul, geographically in Europe. My family is very modern, like Americans, and I go to a private school where we are taught in Turkish and English. My Father is a banker and a computer whiz for fun; and he regularly visits various European countries,

America, and the Arab countries on business. He speaks Turkish, English, German, and some Arabic. In Istanbul you will see people from all over the world. They come as businessmen, conference people, and tourists. Our beautiful city has many palaces, giant mosques, numerous ancient relics, renovated waterfront mansions, and many historic government buildings which were first built during the times of the empires. Istanbul has only one major disease called traffic jams or gridlock."

That was a disease that each of his roommates were also familiar with.

"Every type of restaurant and food, Eastern and Western, is available. And the city is still growing very fast. The biggest problem is that it is very crowded, with people and cars and noise. Istanbul is far behind in public transportation systems. I go everywhere by walking or by bus or taxi. The fastest way to get killed is to ride a bicycle. So, I have the bad and the good – good school and a couple of good school friends, a warm and loving Father who gives me everything, and my Mother who does volunteer work for an environmentalist organization in Istanbul. I have one cute little blond hair, blue eyed sister, unfortunately no uncles, aunts, or cousins living nearby, but a beautiful and difficult city to live in which is surrounded by water on all five sides. Before I came here to Switzerland, I did not know sparkling stars existed except over the Mediterranean Sea where we have a summer vacation house. I will probably follow in my Father's footsteps when I grow up."

A couple of the fellows wanted to inquire about that surrounded by water on five sides, but they did not want to appear dumb. They would just check the maps.

Jamie said, "Wow that was super. I learned so much so fast. I know that I want to come to visit you someday, soon."

Aykut responded, "Well I cheated a little. I always take my i-pad with me wherever I go, and I wanted to tell you about my city and life, so last night I used it to get some of the early history correct. But everything I said was true. I have a good life and I think I can become almost anything I want to be, and it will definitely be something involving the next generation of computers and electronics."

Kef added, "I wish that I had your school and your Father's money. I guess we all have to find our way in life by different roads. Can I talk about my homeland and home life tomorrow night? If I can borrow your computer, I can get my facts correct also. And then maybe you can give to me your ideas of how I can become successful like Aykut is going to be?"

"That's OK by me," Jamie responded. "And maybe we can all help each other find his road in life. I am only twelve years old and I have already had two tragedies, a killing of my Father and an attempted killing of my entire family. I don't even know which way to look, let alone go. But I still have that large warm family to help me. Can I have Wednesday night to 'open my soul to you'?" And he chuckled.

Maybe he was beginning to shed his depression! At least he was developing real friends.

Lin raised his hand, "I want to do it too. So, I get Thursday night. And then Friday night we can tell dirty stories. OK?"

And once again the 'little' boys were on the floor squealing and laughing.

A cloudy, windy, chilly Tuesday morning found the four colored musketeers wearing their jackets and sitting in the minibus at 8:45 AM waiting to be taken down to Lake Constantine for a day of canoeing and rowing lessons. For Li and Kef this was a totally new experience; though Jamie and Aykut were familiar with boats, they were not experienced with canoes.

After arriving at the lake half of the groups were sent to the canoe docks and half to the boat docks. All four went together to the boat docks for the morning session. Most of the boats were simple eight-foot long wooden boats where the single rower faced the back of the boat. The instructor led the campers through several rowing type of exercises to warm up their bodies, especially their arms and shoulders. Boating or rowing and canoeing required use of the upper body to propel the crafts. Each camper put on a vest style life jacket. They were next shown how to perform several types of rowing strokes including frontward, backward, sidewise, and turning around. Then they took turns climbing into boats that were sitting out of the water and practiced these strokes. Next, they practiced rowing in boats tied to the docks. And then they took turns rowing around in a small area, next rowing in a larger area, then rowing around a test group of barrels which were anchored in the shape of the letter eight. If they passed the figure eight test, they were then allowed to spend the rest of the time, two to a boat, and going around in the lake, each taking turns rowing. All four boys did well.

At noon everyone gathered around the nearby picnic tables and consumed a box lunch with either chicken legs or pork chops as the main protein energy source. Propelling boats was an energy consuming process.

Aykut was heard to say, 'I sure could use a couple real chicken legs. My two legs are so small they must be from a baby chicken and not an old hen."

Kef overheard him, and because he did have bigger chicken legs, he quickly traded one of his larger legs with Aykut and grinned, "I am not a big eater." He was still not near the 100 pounds or 45 kilo range.

Rather embarrassed Aykut grinned back and nodded his 'thanks'. He had passed the 100 pounds or 45 kilo level a 'couple' of years ago.

In the afternoon the four guys sat at the canoe docks and listened to the instructor talk about canoeing, paddling with different types of strokes, upsetting and right setting the canoe, while his assistants demonstrated the lesson. Each member of the group put on his vest style life jacket again. Canoeing was much more difficult because the boats turned sideways and could upset very easily; so, the Camp only allowed the campers to go in two's, never one camper, to a canoe. During the first hour one student joined one instructor, learned how to use the paddles, went through the basic strokes, and practiced canoeing in the nearby area. After each camper had practiced for a while, the instructors selected students who they considered 'competent' and let them continue as pairs in one canoe. The two water experienced fellows, Jamie and Aykut were considered 'competent' and took out a canoe named 'Deer Hunter' and played for nearly an hour around the lake. Li and Kef were not so lucky and had to watch from the docks. But later when they were all together, nothing negative was said about the canoeing afternoon. They were becoming like brothers and simply proud that two of the 'team' had been chosen. Only eighteen of the forty-six campers were found 'canoe competent' that day.

After evening dinner, they all lay down and tried to rest from two days of using muscles that were not routinely used during their home lives. They were each tired and a little sore. Kef volunteered to tell about his home and his life, so they all got comfortable on the floor or the beds, and Kef began.

"Are you ready? Cape Town, South Africa is almost as old as Constantinople. Many believe that natives settled in caves in Fish Hoek, which is now inside the city, more than 12,000 years ago. But the first foreigners, the Europeans, came in the sixteenth century. The Dutch East Indies Company set up headquarters there about one hundred years later. Because of the Indonesian Spice Islands, the spice trade through the Old Silk Road, the land route between Turkey and China decreased; and the new water route between Europe and Indonesia increased. Cape Town became the central place for all of the trading ships to dock and resupply when going or coming. Over the next several centuries the Dutch, the French, and the British controlled the city. But when diamonds and gold were discovered in South Africa, the Europeans come to stay permanently, not just for managing trade. Most of these settlers were Dutch, German, and some British."

"The European white man built and controlled Cape Town at the time it had started to become a city. After World War II the National Party, which only let the white settlers vote, won on apartheid laws, which means racial segregation. At that time the white government created new independent areas all over the country where blacks were in the majority and let them become autonomous. The government kept all of the land with diamonds, gold, or good soil for farming and raising cattle. The bad land was given to the blacks. Soon anti-apartheid action began. South Africa had a black to white ratio of more than 100 to 1, but whites controlled everything. The first true democratic election with all blacks and whites registering to vote occurred only in 1994 which resulted in a sharing of power. Many blacks became high government officials and even President and Prime Minister were black. During this fight for freedom four blacks won nobel prizes – Albert Luthuli, Desmond Tutu, F.W. de Klerk, and Nelson Mandela."

"So today all of South Africa, including Cape Town is integrated. Cape Town, known as Kaapstad in Afrikaans or Ikapa in Xhosa has more than six million people and is the largest city in South Africa. Everything is growing very fast – many buildings are being built for business and for people, lots of industry and mines of many types of metals (diamonds and gold of course), and really lots of tourists. We have tall majestic mountains and white sandy ocean beaches, national parks. My brothers say we are like California, only more beautiful. Maybe someday I can go America and see for myself."

"I have five brothers and three sisters. When I just sit quietly and listen, I learn a lot. My problem is that I cannot sit still very well. But since they are all bigger than me, they are always willing to 'teach' me things. I go to a Christian 'English' school, and I have some neat older English-speaking friends whom I play soccer with after school. Since I am faster than all of them, and I shoot a mean shot, as you saw yesterday, they always want me on their team. Then they can beat the other schools. My father is a manager in a diamond mine. My oldest brother is studying nanotechnology. But with so many children we don't have much money. I have never worn new clothes; I always got my brothers' clothes as I grew up. That is why I worked so hard to win the spelling contest. Then I could come to Europe and meet all of you really neat guys. I hope you will always be my friends."

"And then he turned around and started to sob, tears started to trickle down his cheeks. And, the little macho that he was, he was very embarrassed.

His three buddies quickly jumped up, put their arms around him and promised to always be his friends, his very best friends. Kef had never ever cried before.

8

The Camp - II

A CLOUDY AND WARM WEDNESDAY MORNING greeted the Four Colored Musketeers. They were ready for a less strenuous day. They had archery or golf in the morning and horseback riding in the afternoon. These were activities that none of them had ever done, so everything would be new. They were fast in motion from the dormitory to the cafeteria-dining room to the archery and golf fields. Both of these fields were side by side and completely fenced off such that no one could be hit by flying arrows or golf balls. Jamie chose golf because his Father and Uncles played golf sometimes. For the political O'Reilly families, golf was a social not a competitive sport and was played to meet and get to know people. He thought it must be an important game, and went to the golf field. The other three boys wanted to play Robin Hood so they went to the archery field.

Li, Aykut, and Kef listened carefully as the archery instructor talked about the first weapon of the world, thousands of years old. It was used for hunting and war. Many ancient heroes were associated with the bow and arrow: Apollo, Cupid, Heracles, William Tell, and Robin Hood. Over the centuries new and various types of bows and arrows allowed for a continuously improved weapon. It was actually studied as the first weapon science of mankind. He then demonstrated how to string the bow and shoot different types of arrows. After some questions and answers, twelve students lined up facing the twelve targets, and one by one were assisted into the proper methods of holding the bow and then loading the arrow; this was followed by directing, judging distance and air movement, aiming, and releasing the arrow at the circular target. Each boy had his turn. Li was the better bowman of the three.

Meanwhile on the golf field Jamie was learning about the oldest European (English) sport which was first played in the fifteenth century. He learned that it was usually played by hitting a golf ball with a golf club from a T-area, out and onto fairways, toward greens and then into a hole in the green. One began with low numbered clubs, and as one got closer to the green one used progressively larger number clubs. Once one placed his ball onto the green, he used a putter. And then there were special clubs for special shots such as hitting the golf ball from deep grass, from behind trees, from sand traps, or from nearby the green. To play golf well you had to learn how to use at least ten different types of golf clubs and judge distances of fifty to two hundred and fifty yards. Jamie and the other campers on the golf field learned only how to use a wooden head number two club, iron head number three, five, and seven clubs. There was also a nice sized green with several holes in it and an adjacent sand trap. Each camper was taught how to hit balls from the trap and putt on the green. Jamie leaned why it is such a difficult sport and is better played for fun and not for profit.

As noon time drew closer, Jamie slipped over to watch his buddies who were shooting arrows. As he approached, Aykut said, "How many golf balls did you lose?"

"Only two," he replied.

Aykut returned, "That leaves Kef as the winner for this morning. He lost three arrows." And he gave Kef a big smile.

After lunch the four guys headed for the horse corrals. None of them had ever been near a horse let alone on top of one. As the group gathered four 'cowboys' came riding up from a distance and raced around the circular track inside the corral. They made a lot of noise and kicked up a lot of dust. Some of the campers drew back afraid. The 'cowboys' then rode up to the group, stopped, jumped off their small horses, and each horse went down onto one knee in the form of a bow or courtesy; they then neighed and shook their heads in the form of yes. Such antics stimulated a quick change in the campers' mood. Now the horses were not so scary, maybe! And these horses were a special breed of small horses which were used at children's camps such as this. But Kef said, "This is not for me." And he started toward the dormitory.

Jamie shouted to Li and Aykut, "Come on guys we can't let him chicken out." And the three on them raced after him, grabbed him by the arms and drug him back to the corral. Jamie knew that Kef was just seeking attention because if Kef wanted to out run them, he would have had no problem doing so. He certainly was the athlete of the group.

The 'sheriff', an older guy, started talking about the history of horses as the first domestic or tamed wild animal that man used for traveling, hunting, and warring. With the invention of the wheel, horses were trained to pull chariots, wagons, carts, carriages, weapons/cannons, agricultural machines, and more. Today horses are no longer used for work but for pleasure. And riding on the back of the horse is the most common form of this pleasure. So today they were going to be shown the various types of tack, harnesses, and saddles used for riding horses.

A small horse was brought forth and placed in front of the group. The instructors proceeded to groom the horse by brushing him and pointed out the various names for the anatomy of the animal. They then showed and explained the equipment that he would wear that day, such as: a general-purpose bridle with an iron bit (goes between the teeth), a general-purpose saddle (American western cowboy style), and riding helmets. By law all horseback riders must wear helmets when riding a horse. Later, when they were not riding, there were only twenty horses for about 43 people, they could stroll through the old leather shed where on display were many types of horse-riding equipment, old carts and wagons.

The group was divided into two subgroups, two campers assigned to one horse, and one instructor to every two horses. These horses were small in stature and trained with children, always used with children, so hopefully they posed no danger to novice children. The Camp averaged less than one 'minor' accident per year with horse lessons.

Jamie took Kef by the arm and led him to 'their' horse. He said, "Cowboys are real men. You have seen the American western cowboy movies. And all cowboys ride horses. If you want to be a man you have to ride this horse."

Kef looked Jamie in the eye and responded. "If you promise that this will make me a man, I will do it."

And Jamie came back with, "Of course."

Kef again looked at Jamie and smiled. Jamie just returned the smile and reached for the bridal to start dressing 'their' horse. Li and Aykut shared a horse, no problem. They then all spent the next two hours "becoming men."

Their riding legs gave out around 4:00 PM so they went back to the dormitory a little early. None had realized that riding was as tiring on your legs as running. On the way back, Jamie spoke up and asked, "Have you guys called and talked to your families since you came here?"

And the answer was a collective no.

So, Jamie calculated, "It is now near 4:00 PM here near Zurich, then it is 10:00 AM in Boston, 4:00 PM in Cape Town, 5:00 PM in Istanbul, and 12:00 midnight in Nanking. Why don't we each call our families right now?"

The three guys looked at each other as if to say how did he calculate that so fast, and now how could they say no? Jamie, Li, and Aykut had their own cell phones. And Jamie let Kef use his phone and they each made their parents and brothers and sisters very happy to hear their voices from the middle of Europe.

That evening after dinner the four new 'men' retired to their 'favorite' bedroom and waited for more 'intimate' family stories. Tonight, it was Jamie's turn, so he began.

"In the early 1600's Puritans from England started to settle in the northeast corner of the USA and officially founded the city of Boston. Puritans were Christians who wanted to worship God in their own way and not have the Catholic Church tell them how and what to do. They brought the Protestant way of worship to America. Over the years Boston was very anti-British and played a major role in the American War of Independence by several famous events including: the Boston Massacre, Boston Tea Party, Battle of Lexington, Battle of Bunker Hill, and the Siege of Boston. And yes, this fight for independence from Britain produced famous heroes such as Paul Revere and Dr. Samuel Prescott. Boston is called the cradle of liberty in the USA."

"After independence, Boston became one of the wealthiest port cities of the world with import/exports of salt, tobacco, tea, whisky and manufactured goods. In the mid 1800's the Irish and Italian immigrants came to the Boston area in the thousands until there were more ex-Europeans than Americans in Boston. This presented major problems because the original immigrants were Protestants who came to America to escape the Catholic Church's dominance; the Irish and Italian immigrants were Catholic. The Protestants were the upper class while the Catholics were the lower class. The two ethnic and religiously distinct groups really did not solve their differences until after World War II."

"My original O'Reilly ancestors arrived in Boston around 1850. They were a family of eight, and they lived wherever they could and took whatever work they could find for whatever money they could get. With all of them living in the same house and most of them working, they did all right. Over the next years the O'Reilly family expanded into many more O'Reilly's in the Boston area. About seventy to eighty years ago several O'Reilly family members started an import-export company named CELT, Inc. Through lots of hard work this company is now one of the largest such companies in the world."

"For many years my Grandfather was President of CELT until he died a few years ago. My Father has two other brothers. They were fraternal triplets. They all grew up to be lawyers and then politicians. Four years ago, my Uncle Jonathan was elected President of the United States; he made my Uncle Jackson, Attorney General; and my Father became Head of High Technology. Then last January my Uncle Jonathan was made President again, but my Father suddenly died or was killed, we don't know which; and then some man threw a bomb on our three families at the St. Patrick's Day celebration in Boston. He didn't kill us though because my Uncle Dagda knocked the bomb into the water. He saved all fifteen of us. They caught the man and he will be punished. But my Uncle Dagda says that is why I am a little depressed. And that if I come here to this camp, and become friends with neat guys like you, I would lose my depression and be cured. So, you guys are my doctors. I hope you don't charge me too much as I only have a little cash and my Mother will not let me have a credit card." And he broke into his all toothy smile.

And then he got hit by three pillows coming from three different directions. And he shouted, "Wait. I am not finished. I have a fantastic Mother and two neat sisters aged thirteen and sixteen, named Megan and Rebecca. In fact, Aykut, Megan is really cute, for a girl."

To Jamie it seemed that Aykut was the logical one qualified for Megan. They were both a little chunky; so, they fit together the best. Then Jamie just stood up and stretched.

"Oh! I forgot. I do have a bunch of friends and a big family, so with your doctoring I guess I should be able to get back into the world without undue pain."

Kef picked up a cola straw from the desk top, winked at both Li and Aykut, and nodded toward Jamie. The three roommates got up and approached Jamie, grabbed him, and wrestled him to the floor. They then took off his shirt and Kef started using the straw as a stethoscope to check out the current health status of their little sick one.

The Thursday morning sky was filled with rain clouds. But the Four Colored Musketeers were going to be inside most of the time, so no problem. They took their jackets and a couple of umbrellas and climbed into the bus for the forty- minute ride down to Ekelburg where they were going to visit the cheese factory located in an ancient monastery. As they pulled up to the front gate, they saw the large multi building complex made of stone which had been used by the Catholic monastery and now was a large factory that made several types of Swiss cheese. This was their first visit to a monastery and a cheese factory. The bus unloaded rapidly and everyone hurried inside; it had started to rain.

The entry corridor gave the feeling of entering into an old castle: stone floors, stone walls, stone ceiling and lights shaped like torches. They then entered a large dining room, with refrigerated display cases, where later they would return and have cheese lunches. A big burly, pot-bellied, red faced older man with a bushy graying mustache and beard introduced himself as the Proprietor, welcomed them, and said that he would be their guide. He then asked if anyone liked to eat cheese. He received a unanimous positive response from the children. He then asked if anyone knew how to make cheese. Only silence came from the group. It is very simple. First, I will tell you. And then I will show you.

"First you take high quality milk from a cow; only a Swiss cow has high quality milk," and he chuckled.

"You put it into a large pot and warm it at 95°F for 20 minutes. Then you add a starter cheese culture from last week, plus calcium, and rennet. The bacteria in the culture will convert the milk sugar called lactose into lactic acid. More calcium is added. The milk will start to become thick and form clumps. This is kept quiet and warm for another hour. The milk becomes sort of like yogurt. This very soft milk-cheese is then cut with a cheese harp into small grains. The grains, which are about the size of pumpkin seeds, can be larger or smaller, depending upon which kind of cheese you want to make. Liquid called whey drains off from the curd grains; upon slow stirring the grains grow and settle to the bottom of the pot. They become thicker as the whey on top presses them downward."

"When these grain curds are just right, you can use a cheese ladle spoon and place them, one by one, into cheese forms of whatever shape you want, round, square, large, small for the shape of the final cheeses. Due to gravity the curds are pressed into one mass and the whey flows away. The forms are turned over after ten minutes, one hour, and six hours. They then sit overnight. The next day they are placed in a salt bath. The longer the forms sit in the salt bath the harder they become – minutes to hours. The forms are then placed into the ripening chamber, which must be maintained at a certain temperature and humidity for several days depending upon the kind of cheese. Some cheeses can then be eaten immediately; some cheeses must sit for several years. It is that simple,"

And one of the campers said, "That's not simple!" This caused everyone to laugh and agree.

"Let us go through the factory and see the cheese being made"

For the next 1 ½ hours, the children, in groups of ten to twelve, each group with a separate guide, walked down several corridors which separated the various 'clean' rooms of the factory. But the large corridor windows allowed excellent viewing of the various tables, ovens, and machines where the cheese making processes were taking place. The Proprietor and three of his assistants again slowly explained the cheese making steps.

Near noon all of the hungry children were more than ready for their cheese lunch. They returned to the dining room which had enough small tables to seat about fifty people. Four campers sat at each table. Of course, the Four Colored Musketeers chose a table near the open refrigerated sales desks where the cheese smells were heavenly. After each child had chosen and received a cold drink of fruit juices or water, the waitress brought to each table a large plate with ten different kinds of cheese, two by two-inch chunks, plus several hot breads, raw carrots and broccoli. The menu offered: Sbrinz, Gruyere, Appenzeller, Tetr de Moine, Vacherin, Fibourgeois, Ementaler, Shabziger, Raclette, and Munster. Many of the chunks had little flags on them which gave the name of the cheese and where it was made.

Jamie noticed that there were not four chunks of each kind of cheese, So, he asked, "If we want to try every kind, we will have to cut the cheeses into smaller pieces. I want to try each kind at least once. What do you say?"

"I have never heard of any of these cheeses," Kef responded. "Yes. It is better to make them all smaller. Then, if we find any we don't like, we can shift to another. I don't even like the smell of some of them."

And Li said, "In China we do not eat cheese very much because we do not have large udder Swiss dairy cow herds." And he chuckled.

"Our Chinese females are not as big as the Swiss females."

And they all thought that was a neat joke and laughed accordingly. Indeed, the hormones were not very far away.

But, picturing in his mind a 'full' Swiss milk cow versus an 'empty' Chinese milk cow, and then the 'full' Swiss girls versus the 'empty' Chinese girls, Li's face turned red; though he did not explain his difficult feelings of the minute.

"I will try some of these, but I will cut them into even tiny bites and let my nose, my mouth, and my stomach tell me if this cheese is good or bad for me."

While Aykut commented, 'I may have to ask for a doggy bag if we don't eat all of these beauties for lunch. By my smeller I already love all of them. It would be a crime to leave them here when we go to the chocolate factory. And tonight, we can all get drunk on cheese and chocolate; they are not going to give us any wine at the wine factory anyway."

And Jamie pointed his finger at Aykut reminding him to be a good Muslim, as they all laughed together again. "I plan to love, therefore eat them all," he added. "And I only eat what I love."

With that comment he received four strange looks of doubt.

The cheese chunks were cut into cheese pieces which were cut into cheese mini-pieces. Everyone remained faithful to his culture and had no trouble sleeping later that night.

After lunch they went to the chocolate factory near Ekelburg, only ten minutes driving time. It was now raining very hard so the group had to hurry into and out of the bus. As soon they approached the Lindtel Chocolate Factory the smell of chocolate in the air became overwhelming. Entering the front door of the factory the smell hit you. Walking into the sales salon the smell knocked you out. While inside the factory the smell was so powerful that you felt as if you were living and walking around inside a candy bar.

They saw light, medium, dark, extra-sweet, semi-sweet, and bitter chocolates of many shapes and sizes. Plus, one saw mints, pralines, truffles, classic chocolates for sale, fruit filled chocolates, and even vegetable filled chocolates.

Numerous sculptures of historical ships, trains, cars, propeller and jet airplanes, and an international space station made of chocolate were on display inside glass shelves; and every wild animal in the forest was now a brown or white chocolate. There was a calculated reason why the Camp had programmed its tour to the cheese factory first, before lunch, and the chocolate factory, second, after lunch. A complete lunch in this factory would make every child quickly satiated, and sick.

A young man, wearing a mustache, with a white yodeling shirt, green slacks and red suspenders, greeted them, "Welcome to the greatest chocolate factory in the world. Today I am going to show you how to make chocolate, so that when you go home you can make your own chocolate, in your own room with the door locked and Mom is out of town. HA! But I warn you, you can only make a small amount each day because the smell is so fantastic that every dog in the neighborhood will come barking at your door. Then the neighbors will think there is a problem and you will get caught OR you will have to share your newly made chocolate with your neighbors. And that would be Terrible!!"

The campers laughed and some, including Jamie, contemplated such risks. Chocolate WAS worth the risk.

"This is how you make chocolate. The most important ingredient is the fermented cocoa-bean. Because the bean is bitter, even bitter chocolate requires some sugar to make it palatable; therefore, sugar or artificial sweeteners are needed. And of course, Swiss milk only from Swiss cows grown on bio-organic grasses is used."

"Because all chocolate flavors are made from secret recipes, I can only tell you how to make basic chocolate. The final flavor will depend upon the quality of the beans, milk and sugar."

"First we start with fermented cocoa beans which we roast at around 300°F for around 30 minutes. Then the roasted beans are cracked and the husks are separated and recycled as plant fertilizer. The remaining nibs are next ground into a cocoa liqueur. It is combined with sugar, non-fat dry milk powder, lecithin, vanilla or a flavoring, and cocoa butter. The mixture is kept warm to keep it liquid and re-ground several times. This is continued every few hours for 2 to 3 days. Now the chocolate must be very slowly heated to 120°F and then poured into whatever molds that you plan to use for the final shape of your chocolate. After cooling it can be eaten anytime. Come let us see chocolate making in action."

And similar to the cheese factory, the campers were separated into groups of ten to twelve children. And with several assistants they walked down the corridors and looked at the 'clean' laboratories through large corridor windows. The assistants explained the procedures and the various presses, grinders, separators, ovens, and other heating and mixing machines.

At the end of a one-hour learning experience, they returned to the sales salon. Jamie saw Aykut's eyes ogling some of the chocolate animals. They were small so he could buy one of each zoo-animal. He whispered in Aykut's ear, "Don't you think that we should buy a large package of chocolate animals to munch on during Li's 'confessional' tonight?"

Aykut answered, "I don't know what a 'confessional' is, but I think it would be good to have some chocolate for tonight when Li talks about his life."

The four of them purchased a combination of white, semi-sweet, bitter, and dark, chocolates, and normal brown chocolates with truffles. Tonight, would be great, but tomorrow may be not so great.

It was still raining very hard, so the Camp tour director decided not to visit the wine factory. Many of these campers were children not yet teenagers. Besides most of the campers now had happy stomachs and looked forward to happier stomachs tonight. They went directly back to Camp Suisseland.

Jamie and Aykut happened to be sitting side by side when the announcement was made about bypassing the wine factory and Jamie said, "This is a good thing. Grape juice tastes much better than wine any day."

Aykut commented, "I agree. And good Muslims are not supposed to drink alcohol. I never touch it myself."

Jamie poked him in the ribs and they shared big grins.

The multi-ethnic, multi-racial, multi-national, multi-social group of four, now known as the Four Colored Musketeers, went 'home' to dinner. They ate lightly, as they were rather cheesed out; and they were all thinking about Li's sweet Chinese talk tonight.

After dinner they settled onto the floor in their bedroom, chocolates at hand, and Li began to tell about Nanking and his family life.

He began, "Nanking or Nanjing or Yuecheng was established before 500 BCE. Over time it has been the capital of several different dynasties including the Three Kingdoms period and the Ming Dynasty. These dynasties left behind many lovely old buildings, temples, gates, and gardens. Today it is a beautiful city, except for a very bad air pollution from hundreds of factories. But thousands of tourists come to visit every year."

"However, Nanjing is really famous for the Nanjing Massacre. Just before World War I, Mao Zedong's Communist People's Forces were in north-western China and Chiang Kai-shek's military forces were in the Shanghai area. In 1931 the Japanese army invaded and conquered Manchuria, and then invaded China. When they defeated Chiang Kai-shek's military in Shanghai, the fighting moved west toward Nanjing. Chiang fled to central China and left General Tang Shengzi in charge in Nanjing. General Tang decided to fight to the death. The result was that in 1938, in Nanjing, nearly 100,000 Chinese civilians were raped, killed and more than 300,000 casualties were inflicted by the Japanese Imperial Army. This is the worst single human tragedy ever in the world. Except for my Grandfather, all of my family was killed. And Great Grandfather was fighting with Mao in the north."

"As you probably know eventually Chiang finally left the Chinese mainland and relocated in Taiwan, the Japanese were defeated during World War II, and Mao's Communists won in China. My Great Grandfather was a general for Mao. He had two sons and a daughter. His second son, Fai, my Grandfather, had three sons with his Manchurian wife, and returned to Nanjing to live. The three sons were fraternal triplets, Chi, my Father, and Jun and Cho. I am an only child. My Mother was Irish and was killed in truck-car crash when I was three years old. My Father and his brothers are engineer-doctors and work in nanotechnology sciences, both in Los Angles and Nanjing. So, Kef, when you grow up, and if you still want to study and learn nanotechnology, let me know and maybe my family can help."

"I alternate living two years in Nanjing and two years in Los Angeles. Other than my three Chinese girl cousins, I am somewhat alone in Nanjing, but I have many friends in Los Angeles. I live with my Uncle Cho and his family when I am in China; and I live with my Father when I am in the USA. And I spend most of my time on line trying to learn about the world, and my fun hours learning Kung Fu. If we had time, I would teach you some. And I really enjoyed my trip last year to Ireland. I have fifteen Irish Uncles, Aunts, and cousins. After one month there I began to think that I was Irish on the inside and Chinese on the outside."

And he and Jamie exchanged looks of brotherly solidarity. Not only the Irish blood, but both had lost a parent at a young age. And they seemed to genuinely like each other. They would maintain a close and important communication for life.

As Li's 'confession' wound down and all of the cheese and chocolate was rapidly disappearing, the exciting day of factory adventuring began to exert itself on the four boys.

The weather had cleared by mid-morning on Friday. And the group was found wearing their jackets, windbreakers, life preserver vests, plastic boots over their shoes, canoe paddles in hand, and water hats on their heads as they cruised along the Neu Creek in a ten-person raft. The creek was very wide. The water was very cool, almost cold; but the young people felt no chill as they hollered, shouted, and screamed through their first raft ride down a pristine Swiss river valley. No civilization, no debris, no people, no noise, only many greens, browns, and blues – multi-colored flowers everywhere - nature at its best, without mankind to corrupt her. Unbelievable that such a 'pure' natural place still existed in the world; but only on top of the mountains. They also saw many small forest animals drinking along the creek bank or searching for food. When they drifted too close to an embankment an old grizzly bear roared his threat as the raft was interfering with his fishing. The raft was quickly guided back into the middle of the creek.

They cruised gently alone for about an hour, and then hit some rough water with many very large rocks and rapids, up and down swirls, and much twisting and turning. The campers of all ages loved it and shouted to each other and to the world; the wetter the better. Finally, they arrived at a lovely clear creek bank and docked the rafts. Two large campfires were blazing and the campers quickly gathered around them and warmed up and dried out. Box lunches and cold drinks were ready, so they sat around on plastic sheets since the ground was still wet from the night rain and ate lunch. After lunch the various instructors taught them how to do camping stuff such as: erect tents, tie rope knots, build a shelter with branches and leaves, construct shelving for foods and clothes, build protective fences (against night animals), make a fire, prepare meals, and identify plants which were nutritious.

Near mid-afternoon they climbed into their rafts and again continued down the large creek. They encountered rapids three more times until they finally reached the end of their journey. As they dismounted their rafts, they saw that the buses had arrived. They climbed aboard, a rather tired group of campers who had a most exciting day and a unique memory.

That night after dinner there was a classical movie entitled "Sound of Music". Only Jamie had heard of it and he explained about the musical, family, and Swiss theme. The boys agreed to watch the movie and tell dirty stories some other time. The movie was later voted as great.

After the movie they returned to their rooms for their last night together. All was quiet. No one wanted to leave his new brothers; and no one quite knew how to express their goodbyes.

Suddenly Jamie became very melancholic. Aykut noticed that tears slipped quietly down from Jamie's eyes. He reached over to try to console him.

Jamie spoke up, "I recently lost my Father, almost lost my entire family, and now I will lose all of my new brothers one week after I found them. Why is life so unfair to me?"

'You will never lose us," responded Aykut. "And none of us ever has to lose each other. Let me do this. I will arrange for the four of us to communicate anytime we want, as a group. I can set us up with a computer conferencing system, a special chat room but only for us. It will have an encrypted audio/visual exchange using a modified avatar language with a

Latinized alphabet. This will allow each of us to simultaneously see and talk to each other, at the same time – 4 to 4, and to learn a third language. By just sitting in our own bedrooms we can have a team 'silent' conference; no one else will see or hear us. Neat huh?"

And the other three Colored Musketeers jumped onto the other one Colored Musketeer and hopped up and down, cheering and laughing. They voted this the best idea of the week.

Jamie softly commented to himself, 'Maybe now I can really find out who killed my Dad.'

Saturday was the last day and both Li and Kef had to catch early afternoon planes to their homes. The four almost teenage boys spent the morning hours reliving their week and dwelling on the exciting good parts (cheese and chocolate). They exchanged e-mail numbers and pledged to e-mail each other a lot; Kef's older brother had a computer which he let Kef used since they lived next door to each other. And the Four Colored Musketeers (white, tan, yellow, and black) would meet again on-line and on conference. Just before lunch Li and Kef took the camp bus to the Zurich airport. In mid-afternoon Jamie and Aykut caught another camp bus to the Zurich airport. Each took planes directly back to their homes.

Overall it was a warm, exciting, and unique learning experience for four boys who would later play a critical role in preventing a world-wide high tech/low tech war involving nanotech killing systems.

9

Miracles

URING THE PREVIOUS MEETING OF the President's Commission on Human Trafficking a decision had been made to investigate more closely certain 'health miracles' that had occurred during the year 2028. Here at the next Commission meeting in a conference room of the Department of Justice Building in Washington, DC, this subject was taken up with fervor.

All members were present around the conference table. Commission Chairman Jackson O'Reilly opened the meeting, "Welcome to the third meeting of the Commission on Human Trafficking. In previous meetings we discussed and reviewed medically unexplainable sudden deaths (MUSD) and medically unexplainable sudden cures (MUSC). These deaths and cures occurred in several different countries.

Now let us look more closely at some specific MUSCs. However, remember comparing the two areas we were giving the following message.

NO – HI – TECH - STOP

"We do not know if this is significant or an accident, but we are taking it seriously. You will also soon see new life miracles for several well-known industrialists. Both these deaths and life miracles seem to be continuing in 2029."

"Mr. Murphy, our Assistant Chairman developed a list of all miracle cures so published in the news media on the fifteenth of a month in 2028. From that list we selected the six names from alternative months of the six deaths. The list is in the packet on the table in front of you. Please open it and read it. I know it will be useful as we review several of these possible miracles."

<u>List of VIPs Thought to Have Had Sudden Miracle Cures in the Year 2028:</u>

Cardinal Antonio Octavus, Vatican, Rome, Italy, Leader of the International Right to Life Movement, 78 years old, suddenly cured of metastatic liver cancer on February 15.

Mr. John Issac, New York, NY, President of the Meat Producers Lobby International, 69 years old, suddenly cured of advanced brain cancer on April 15.

Reverend Shepherd Exodus, Evangelist, Toronto, Canada, President of the Anti-Stem Cell/Anti-Organ Transplant Society, 73 years old, suddenly cured of multiple myeloma on June 15.

Mr. Jan van Het, Amsterdam, Netherlands, CEO of the Shell Oil Corporation, 78 years old, suddenly cured of terminal pancreatic cancer on August 15.

Mr. John Tytler, Philadelphia, PA, President of Tytler International Steel Corporation, 75 years old, suddenly cured of Parkinson's disease on October 15.

Mr. William Preston, Los Angeles, CA, Secretary General of Pharmaceutical Workers International, 68 years old, suddenly cured of terminal Hodgkin's lymphoma on December 15.

After a couple of minutes Mr. Murphy took the floor. "During our previous meetings we presented facts and information concerning the MUSDs. We knew the who, the where, the when, but not the how, and maybe the why. At least we could put together a reasonably accurate scenario as to what may have happened. This time we are also faced with the who, the where, the when, possibly the how and the why. For the MUSCs, we do not have access to all of the 'living bodies' to be able to determine the degree of the 'miracle cure'. For example, of the six VIPs, we only have access to the three Americans, Mr. Issac, Mr. Tytler, and Mr. Preston. The other three

Cardinal Octavus, Reverend Exodus, and Mr. van Het are citizens of other countries and so have their rightful legal citizenship protections."

"Here in the USA and in many other countries there are 'restrictions in the interpretations' of certain laws that presented problems in our attempts to collect data and other information on these American citizens. And I do not refer to the first amendment of the American Constitution, freedom of religion, speech, and assembly. I refer to the priest/confessor, lawyer/client, and doctor/patient protected relationships. The laws do not specifically allow direct access through any of these confidentiality relationships. And just try to obtain information on a medical patient from a hospital or a doctor and see how far your subpoena takes you – not very far. However, because we have certain superior legal powers, called upon the Attorney General of the USA on our team, we did manage to receive a certain amount of cooperation concerning the recent medical hospitalizations of the three Americans, Mr. Issac, Mr. Tytler, and Mr. Preston. So, we will give to you a summary of these three investigations today. I am sorry but it is the best that we can do at this time."

"Does anyone have any questions, before we look at the medical history of these three men?"

Hearing none, Mr. Murphy began again. "Mr. John Issac retired from farming and sold his fifth-generation inherited farm in Keokuk, Iowa in 1979 when he was only 20-years old. He had been active in the local district 16 of the Meat Producers Lobby International for several years, and had just been elected to the national office in Chicago. He sold everything and moved his wife and three boys to Chicago with the goal of trying to re-establish red meat as the national dish. During the seventies, scientific findings and numerous media reports that beef caused cancer had resulted in a major drop in meat consumption in the USA and major headaches for Midwest farmers. These farmers routinely purchased Texas yearling calves in the autumn, fattened them on home grown corn and soybeans throughout the winter, and then sold them in the spring. Corn fattened beef was the life blood of the Midwest farmer over several generations."

"Unfortunately, Mr. Issac was not successful as he watched a new agreement between Japan and the USA to grow and sell soybeans to Japan with the soy foods being prepared in the Midwest, shipped on barges down the Missouri and Mississippi Rivers, loaded onto transport ships in

New Orleans, and shipped directly to Japan. American Midwestern soy products now provide Japan with over 60% of its soy product imports. And the Midwest grown corn was increasingly used for the sucrose-sugar content by cereal manufactures and soft drinks distributers. Increases in the international sales of Coca Cola and Pepsi Cola products alone now utilize almost 30% of the corn. The American Midwest farmer still grows corn and soybeans, but they no longer routinely fed to beef cattle."

"Mr. Issac was elected President of the Meat Packers Lobby International, MPLI, in 1998. And in a state of personal depression, on January 1, 2015, he was diagnosed with a glial cell sarcoma cancer in the occipital lobe at the back of the brain. Dr. Batley will go into more detail about the medical aspects a little later. Suffice it to say, from the medical records that we obtained from the University of Chicago Hospital Center, he had surgery, radiotherapy, and chemotherapy over a ten-month period. By the end of that year he was determined to be cancer free and was released."

"He went back to work and continued to use his political contacts to try to sell American beef both within the USA and abroad, especially to Southeast Asia, including Japan. Today there are currently more than one hundred and eighty senators and congressmen on Capitol Hill in Washington who are supported by the American farm belt. And the Texas cattlemen had much lobbying power, especially when Texans were in the White House. And as the new concept that lean red meat did not cause cancer, but fat red meat 'maybe' caused cancer, and the support of chain restaurants such as McDonalds and Famous Dave's Bar-B-Q, beef sales increased, and life improved for Mr. Issac and the MPLI."

"However, in 2027 the cancer 'came back'. His re-occurring head pains were diagnosed, again at the University of Chicago Hospital Center, as metastatic cancer, probably coming from the previous brain cancer. It was determined that the cancer was not spread within the brain but was located within an area of the brain such that surgery was not possible. He was given radiotherapy and chemotherapy and expected to live no more than a few months. And then on April 15, 2028, it was suddenly announced that Mr. John Issac, President of the Meat Producers Lobby International, was completely cured of brain cancer. He left the hospital and went back to the union building on Archer Avenue in Chicago to celebrations and notoriety. The message to the public was that no medical therapy was involved in the cure. And of course, the Union had paid for everything."

"Dr. Batley, would you take over from here?"

"I will try to minimize the medical terminology," Dr. Batley began. So, if I use an expression that you are not familiar with, please let me know immediately, and I will try to explain. I want everyone to understand what may be happening here. This is not a normal 'curative' response to this cancer."

"First, the medical records that I reviewed included a total of 10 X-rays, 13 CTs, and 31 MRIs over a period of several months. This is a lot of visual information on a very deadly cancer. The cancer was there. And the second time it had spread into the back of the head-neck region into what is called the medulla oblongata. This region connects to the spinal cord below and the cerebellum above. It controls numerous critical body functions such as breathing, swallowing, the sleep/wake center, heartbeat, blood pressure, ears/balance, and assists body muscular coordination and vision."

"Because of the importance of this region of the brain, the neurosurgeons could not perform any surgery. Even radiotherapy would damage the source of controls for these many functions. And combination chemotherapy with several different drugs over several months would probably not be very helpful. Drugs injected into the blood do not easily enter the brain due to a special blood-brain barrier which naturally protects the brain from toxic substances that accidentally enter the body. So how was he cured? I really do not know how Mr. Issac was cured. But I can speculate based upon some nanotechnology research that friends of mine are performing at the NIH."

"One could prepare special antibodies specifically for Mr. Issac's cancer cells. The cells had been located and were available from a simple biopsy. From the cancer cells' membranes, monoclonal antibodies (MoABs) could be prepared; these are homing devices for targeting that specific cancer. The MoABs could then be complexed with a nanocarrier carrying four or five different drugs. If this was injected into the spinal cord, the spinal fluid is continuous from head to tail, so any drugs, or nanocarrier complexes, should reach the region of the medulla oblongata from the injection site, it would not need to go through the blood."

"If the cancer cell homing system worked perfectly, the nanocarrier complex would bind only to the cancer cells, not to normal cells, and the drugs would enter only the cancer cells. If the drugs were effective, they could kill most, if not all cancer cells. Such a high-tech mode of therapy is still somewhat experimental today. I do not know if they did this, but the medical information that I have from the University of Chicago Hospital Center indicates that Mr. Issac was injected into his spinal cord a drug named 'JXW-18T74B'. I have never heard of this drug. I do not know its composition. It is on the Department of Food and Drug's approved list. But we were prevented from learning its composition."

"In summary, from the medical reports for Mr. John Issac, I do not see a logical standard cancer treatment that was performed which could have cured his cancer 'overnight'. The only possibility is a nanoproduct procedure as I have just described. And if this cure is not a miracle, it certainly is miracle-like."

Ms. Dapper asked, "Are you thinking that this possible treatment procedure used an illegal drug product?"

"No," replied Dr. Batley. "I am certain that all drugs are cleared for legal use in the United States by the FDA. This drug was on the approval list that I saw. I am speculating that it is some type of new experimental nanoproduct. But I will follow up on this key question. Is it legally available? What is it? And where did it come from?"

"I have heard of similar 'miracle' like reactions from nanoproduct treatments in experimental animal laboratories." added Mr. Bradmier. Mr. Murphy spoke up, "Your presentation started my mind to thinking about another idea. You suggested a way to enter the brain through the spinal cord, avoiding this blood- brain barrier. We assume that this possible nanoproduct was injected. After the injection, would there be any evidence of the injection?"

Dr. Batley replied, "If an injection into the spinal cord is performed by a skilled person using a small-bore needle, especially in the lumbar area, lower back, the needle hole would disappear in a few hours."

And Mr. Murphy only grimaced and looked down at his notes on the table. He waited a few moments for more questions. Hearing none he looked at Chairman O'Reilly, who in turn nodded.

Mr. Murphy addressed the group. "If there are no more questions, let us turn to Mr. Tytler. Mr. John Tytler was born in 1953 as the fourth generation of a steel company family. His great grandfather, William Tytler, established the Tytler International Steel Corporation, TIS, in Bethlehem, Maryland, in 1888. It was one of the first steel making factories in the USA. Using abundant and cheap coal as the energy source, abundant and cheap New York City labor, the newly industrializing America gobbled any and all steel that the Tytler factories could produce. It eventually specialized in producing steel for ship manufacturing, and grew and expanded and expanded and grew for the next seventy to eighty years."

"However, in the eighties and nineties imported steel was cheaper, TIS had trouble competing and started to close down a couple of its factories. John Tytler became President and CEO in 1999. He tried to modernize, innovate, decrease labor costs but provide better working conditions for employees, and regain competitiveness. The Board of Directors was still composed predominately of family members who just did not understand the need to go for high technology. In 2014, TIS began bankruptcy proceedings for several of its factories. In 2018, John Tytler started losing his 'thinking edge', as he had been highly educated and was considered a super expert on the conventional steel making methodologies. But high technology was rushing past him and he was not willing to purchase knowledge he did not understand. In addition, his family Board did not understand the problems brought on by this high technology. Two years later he was diagnosed as having developed Parkinson's disease. His oldest son became President and CEO. And John was confined to his one-hundred-acre estate, half an hour's drive out into the Poconos."

"Would you please explain Parkinson's disease for us, Dr. Batley? And also review Mr. Tytler's medical history?"

Dr. Batley began, "Parkinson's disease usually occurs in people over the age of fifty. There are four primary symptoms which occur over a period of years including tremors in the face, arms, and legs, rigidity or stiffness in the trunk, slowness in general movement, impaired balance and motor coordination. According to Mr. John Tytler's medical records, some of these symptoms were recorded as being noticeable in Mr. Tytler as early as the year 2024. More extensive changes began after 2025, such as difficulties in chewing, swallowing, and speaking, difficulty in sleeping, constipation and urinary problems, and mental depression. Because there are no good reliable blood markers for this disease, the diagnosis of Parkinson's disease is based on medical history and neurological exams. The diagnosis is not always easy or accurate. Even a series of MRI scans on Mr. Tytler were not conclusive. However, I have summarized for you the medical history of Mr. Tytler as recorded from the famous Johnson Clinic in Allentown, Pennsylvania, up to 2028. Yes, he had Parkinson's disease."

"At present there is no cure for Parkinson's disease, but there are several drugs which are based on the biochemicals that are involved in the disease's symptoms. Nerve cells talk to nerve cells through neuro-transmitting hormones. There are three major types of these hormones: epinephrine/ norepinephrine, acetylcholine, and dopamine. Parkinson's disease is related to the cranial or 'within the brain' dopamine. It decreases as the disease progresses. Certain drugs, levodopa plus carbidopa, can provide increased levels of dopamine in certain regions in the brain. These drugs can thus relieve symptoms and may even 'simulate' cures if dopamine can be maintained at high levels for long periods of time."

"Are each of you following me?"

"Good, I very briefly want to describe the chemical/molecular level of medicine for Mr. Tytler's therapy during the last few months prior to his 'cure'."

"According to the medical records that we received from the Thomas Jefferson University Hospital and Clinics, in Philadelphia, Mr. John Tytler was admitted with a case of advanced Parkinson's disease on June 23, 2028. He was treated with the usual levodopa, carbidopa, anti-cholinergic drugs, and several experimental drugs until August 10, 2028. His symptoms were only slightly reduced. On September 5, he was given a new experimental drug which was directly injected into the cerebrum of the brain, frontal and parietal lobes. These are regions of the brain that are involved in movement and coordination of the muscles of the face, arms, legs, and body, as well as speech. This procedure was repeated on October 1, 2028, and again on October 12, 2028. On October 15, all symptoms of Parkinson's disease were gone. His family declared to the news media that he had made a miracle cure, and presented him to the world as completely Parkinson's disease symptom free. And it was reported that he had no 'Nano' therapies for Parkinson's disease. It was miracle like."

"Now you say that seeing is believing. And indeed, such surgery with the levodopa plus carbidopa would not provide such a long-term symptom-free state. The 'cure' was related to this new experimental drug. It had the name JXW-74B19F. I found this drug on the approval list of the FDA, but again special patent protection prevents us from learning about its molecular mechanism of action."

Ms. Dapper asked, "Do you think this drug is related to the drug injected into Mr. Issac?"

"I do not know," replied Dr. Batley. "But I will try to find out."

"What happened?" Mr. O'Reilly anxiously asked. He was becoming a little enthralled by all of this mystery drug/miracle cure/molecular stuff.

"If you will allow me to speculate," replied Dr. Batley. "I will guess-t-mate, as we say in the laboratory when we don't have a good solid working theory."

"The neurohormone, dopamine, is the heart of the problem for Parkinson's disease. The cells in the cerebrum region of the brain, front and center of the head, which control bodily muscle function, do not produce adequate levels of dopamine in Parkinson's disease patients. Bringing the levels of dopamine back up to normal levels relieves the symptom and 'cures' the disease. In my opinion, a properly designed nanotechnology system could possibly do this. In other words, if the JXW-74B19F drug is a Nano-dopamine factory and is placed into the critical cells of the brain, it could be possible to 'cure' this disease by continuously producing dopamine."

And that left the group rather shocked. So simple, yet obviously so difficult. And it was not yet in the marketplace! The potential of nanomedicine was becoming more obvious as they looked at these cases. But there was little anyone could say. If Mr. John Tytler was truly 'cured' of this disease by this experimental drug, the family was keeping it a secret. The public was led to believe that no medical treatment was involved; instead it was a 'miracle cure'.

General Ronny asked, "Would such a Nano-system then require a homing device?"

'That is a very good question," replied Dr. Batley. "With John Issac, an injection of a Nano-drug-carrier with a MoAb homing unit would reach the target cells inside the brain because it would be injected into a brain connected area, the spinal cord. Fluid in the spinal cord bathes many brain cells directly. However, if you injected such a Nano-system, with or without a homing unit, into the blood, it would have trouble entering the brain because of the blood brain barrier that we mentioned a few minutes ago. Can a Nano-system, even of such tiny nanometer dimensions, enter through the blood brain barrier, I do not know. I must explore that question. Thank you very much. That is a very good question."

And the big General just sat back and grinned. It was his first good question in the three meetings with this body-brain-cell-molecule-hormone stuff and he hit it right on the head. Homing was a good high-tech way to fight medical and military problems. And he knew about homing. It was his specialty, at least with rockets. Boy, will he be able to put down his buddies at the next poker game.

After a few minutes of silence, Mr. O'Reilly spoke up. "I understand your feelings, me too. The science overwhelms me. Maybe after we review the 'cure' of Mr. Preston we can open the floor to any and all questions about diseases and nanotechnology. Mr. Murphy, are you ready?'

"Yes," Mr. Murphy replied and began. "Mr. William Preston was the CEO of the Johnson Pharmaceutical Corporation in Los Angeles for fifteen years. This corporation went bankrupt in 1995 when two new drug manufacturing companies located across the bay, using high tech production systems, went on- line. He felt the pain of having to lay off 381 laboratory workers. He had known many of the workers personally and often picnicked with their families. The newly unemployed were covered by the corporation's unemployment insurance for only three months. And then they, just, suffered. He wished he could help them. So, he started working with a local public labor union to learn about unionizing. After two years working with them, he established a pharmaceutical labor firm in the Los Angeles area. His efforts were fruitful as he was perceived as honest and hard working for the 'little laboratory man', and he was an ex- CEO. The union grew and expanded eastward. Within seven years he established a second headquarters in Chicago. And five years later a third headquarters in Philadelphia was put into place. Less than twenty-five years after his labor organizational efforts, he had headquarters in London and Zurich. And he became the Secretary General of Pharmaceutical Workers International (PWI) in 2013."

"In 2023, he was diagnosed with non-Hodgkin's lymphoma. At that time, he was living and working in a new east coast headquarters in New York City. For the next five years he was in an out of cancer therapy at the Mount Sinai Hospital. On December 15, 2028, he was released for medical care and the PWI announced his complete 'cure.' The union held a press conference for him and he discussed his five years of therapy and his miracle cure. He was now back working for the pharmaceutical workers of the world. All of his therapy is documented in the medical files for Mr. William Preston which we obtained from the Mount Sinai Hospital."

"Dr. Batley, would you please review these medical files for us?" he added.

"Let me begin by describing the disease called non-Hodgkin's lymphoma," responded Dr. Batley.

"Non-Hodgkin's lymphoma is one of several cancers of the lymphocytes, white blood cells. It can occur at any age in men or women, Caucasian, African- American, or Oriental. The symptoms of this cancer are swelling of the lymph nodes, fever, weight loss, and fatigue. Mr. Preston developed these symptoms in November, 2023, and was diagnosed for this cancer on December 3, 2023, at the Mount Sinai Hospital in New York City. There are several types of this cancer because there are several types of white blood cells. In general, they are divided into children versus adult, fast growing versus slow growing, and originating from B-cells or T-cells. There are more than ten subtypes and five clinical stages"

"To assist in therapy, Non-Hodgkin's lymphoma is classified as stages I, II, III, IV, and V. The lower the Stage number the better the chance for a cure; the higher numbers are not very curable. This cancer always begins in the lymph nodes and easily spreads from the lymph nodes, called E meaning extra-nodal, and into the spleen, called S. Using this doctor's talk, Stage IE means the cancer has spread from the lymph node where it began to one other organ, maybe the liver. Stage VS+E means that the cancer has rapidly spread from the lymph node where it began to several other body organs, maybe the liver, brain, and lungs, and also into the spleen. Non-Hodgkin's lymphoma Stage IE is curable. Non- Hodgkin's lymphoma Stage VS+E is generally not curable. Mr. Preston's cancer was determined to be Stage IVS+E; it had metastasized to the spleen, lungs and liver. This is a difficult type of Non-Hodgkin's lymphoma to cure, but curable."

"The doctors gave radiotherapy and chemotherapy to Mr. Preston. They could not perform surgery because the cancer was already growing in several lymph nodes and in the lungs and liver. Over a period of sixteen months he was treated with three rounds of alternating radiotherapy and chemotherapy. The cancer was reduced by 85%, so Mr. Preston went home and back to work. On August 14, 2026, the symptoms had re-appeared so he returned to Mount Sinai Hospital. For the next eight months he was treated with two rounds of radiotherapy and two rounds of conventional chemotherapy and one round of a single drug complexed to a MoAB, for a homing chemotherapy. The cancer was reduced by 70%, and the symptoms were decreased so he again went home, but not back to work. On December 2, 2025, he became very sick and returned to the hospital. He was given injections, December 5 and December 12 of a non-Hodgkin's experimental drug JXW-35D22M. Two days later all symptoms were gone, X-rays and a CT detected no cancers anywhere. Two days later, PWI announced his 'miracle' cure. What do you think, Dr. Bradmier?"

"I think his 'miracle' cure resulted from a Nano-drug-carrier using a Homing MoAB," answered Dr. Bradmier. "But like you, I am not certain without more and better data."

General Ronny spoke up, "And this time the homing mechanism would work because from the blood it could directly enter the cancers in the liver, lungs, and other lymph nodes. Right?"

Dr. Batley answered, "Right." And gave him a thumbs up.

'Maybe this biology stuff wasn't so difficult after all,' thought the General. Not to be left out, Mr. Bradmier asked, "So   you   believe that this experimental drug JXW something was specifically designed somewhere, and provided to the doctors who just injected it by following a pre-determined protocol?"

"My gut feeling is, since each of these three cases involved experimental JXW drugs and occurred in three different hospitals with three different diseases, the level of technology is such that all three drugs were probably made in the same laboratory, somewhere in the world, and delivered to those hospitals all ready to use. Each patient had been treated for several months before the 'cure'. So, there was plenty of time to ship a biopsy sample of each potential target cells/tissue to that laboratory, prepare homing MoABs, complex them with an appropriate nanotech system containing specific drugs or chemicals, and ship the nanotech product back to the appropriate hospital. Theoretically, yes, this can be done today."

Mr. O'Reilly questioned, "So where does this leave us?"

'It seems to me that the current target should be the experimental drugs labeled with JXW," said Mr. Co-Chairperson, Mr. Murphy. "I have made a list of questions which I want to share with you and get your response:

- What is the composition of this drug or drugs?
- How does it/they work?
- Where was it/they made?
- Who made it/them?
- If it/they was/were made outside the USA how did it/they enter this country?
- How did it/they get to the correct place in the correct hospital at the correct point in time?
- What level of collaboration did the hospital and doctors provide?
- Was there a common organizer involved in these 'secret' procedures?
- Who was this organizer or group of organizers?
- Was or was not this/these drug/drugs technically approved by the FDA or another government authority?
- Can providing a drug that cures someone be considered illegal?
- Can there be any possible linkage to the suspected nanotech related sudden VIP deaths in which the death was sudden and medically non-detectable or was unexplainable?

Can anyone think of additional questions for which we need to seek answers?"

Ms. Dapper spoke, "How many laboratories in the world could make the type of nanotech drugs that we may be seeing here?"

"Very few," responded Dr. Batley. These drugs require a minimum of several types of nanocarriers, Nano factories, and even nanoelectronics because we are dealing with nerve cells, possibly gene or DNA nanotechnology, or others that we do know about. In addition, that laboratory must have the capacity to produce targeting MoABs from the carefully selected cellular membranes in the timeframe of a few months; that is very fast. And they need to complex the MoABs to the new Nano molecule(s), test it in humans, and then get the MoAB- nanotech product to the right place at the right time for proper therapy. These nanotech products are usually not stable and would probably be viable for only a few days. But yes, I feel that whoever these people are, they are indeed very high nanotech, and there is an organization behind them."

Mr. Thomson asked, "In the situations concerning the possible use of such nanotech systems involved in the 'killing' of the 'suddenly dead' VIPs, why could these nanotech systems not be found in the bodies of the VIPs?"

Dr. Batley again answered, "If I put a small round object into my pocket without showing you what it was and I simply told you that it was round. Then I took one month to travel all over the world and I simply dropped that object somewhere during my travels. I came back and said, 'go find my round object.' That is the task at hand."

Mr. Thomson simply responded with an "Oh".

Chairman O'Reilly stood up to close the session. He said, "Mr. Murphy and I will make a work list which will again include some specific tasks for each of you. It will be based upon the unanswered questions that he just read off and your capacities within the legal framework of your current working positions. If you have any additional questions please let us know. Within the capacity of this Commission, Mr. Murphy and I are always available to you at any time. If you cannot carry out the assigned tasks, or you want to tackle additional related tasks, again please let us know. I consider this my second highest priority as Attorney General of the USA. I want this problem to be solved and closed before it expands further, as I have the feeling that this is already happening. Looking at the fifteenth of each of the past several months, in 2029, we see a continuation of sudden 'VIP- deaths' and 'VIP-cures'. We will meet again as the Commission on Human Trafficking when our assigned tasks are completed, and we have some new 'enlightening' information to discuss. I hope that will be soon. Thank you for your efforts. Happy traveling."

10

What is Nanomedicine?

A s Professor Chi Jiang continued his presentation to the National Press Club in Washington, DC, he elaborated on nanomedicine. Dr. Jiang was a famous nanotechnologist, and he specialized in the biological-medical aspects of nanotechnology.

"Nanomedicine may be defined as the monitoring, construction, repairing, and controlling of human biology systems at the atomic or molecular level by using nanodevices, nanocarriers, nanostructures, nanomachines, and nanorobots."

"Nanomedicine is becoming a nanotechnology field of its own. There are more than 100 companies and 300 plus patented products in the marketplace. Nearly 3 billion dollars are now invested each year in nanomedicine research, assembly, and testing. And there is more than 20 billion dollars per year in sales. It is a very big business and growing at the rate of about 15-20% per year. It is already changing the medical industries related to pharmacology, imaging diagnostics, general, neuro-, and ortho-surgeries, immunology-bone marrow transplantation, anti-microbial genetics, gene therapy systems, and cell/tissue repair microsurgery."

"I will only discuss four nanomedicine systems that we use in my laboratories and factories: self-assembly monolayers or SAMs, nanoelectronics or NEs, DNA nanotechnology or DNA-NT, and smart multifunctional nanocarriers or SMNs. These are all related to pharmacology – drug assembly, synthesis, and delivery."

1- "**Self-Assembly Monolayers** are organized with a hydrophilic or water associated region and a hydrophobic or fat associated region. For example, a candied apple has a hydrophilic head and a hydrophobic tail or stick. This is how our blood lipoproteins, LDL and HDL, are organized. There are many types of SAMs which can be associated with certain water minerals, like sodium and calcium, and many proteins. The tails of the SAMs can associate with certain special lipids/fats such as cholesterol. This allows the SAMs to bind to cellular membranes inside or outside of cells and tissues; and it allows them to construct or build new molecules 'in place'. They can thus construct new drugs inside or outside of body cells."

2- "**Nano-Electronics** is equivalent to assembling a minute electronic/electric circuit inside of cells or tissues. It involves mini-voltages, mini-voltage initiators, and controlled switching mechanisms. A variety of synthetic polymers and metals are used to assemble a wide variety of electric circuits inside or outside of body cells."

3- "**DNA Nanotechnology** utilizes the specific and chemical molecular characteristics found in chromosomes, genes, and DNA. DNA is the chemical structure of all genes in all life on earth. Using various similar self- assembly DNA monolayers, nanomedicine can be used to construct small genes inside individual cells. These genes can then be decoded to produce proteins which the cell can use to repair itself, to enhance it own function within the cell or organ, to change cell function by blocking other intracellular actions, to repair its neighboring cells, or even select proteins which can be secreted into the blood to replace bodily proteins or hormone deficiencies. In other words, we can place a new gene into a cell and turn it off or on."

4- "**Smart Multifunction Nanocarriers** are becoming the best way to deliver a drug directly to the damaged or diseased cells within the body; it bypasses all normal cells; or it can even target only the normal cell. This can be compared with the American military smart missile-bomb which you have seen on television, go down specific chimneys of a targeted building located hundreds of miles from the launch site for that missile-bomb. Nanocarriers use this localization molecular system on the outer surface of the targeted cell to 'home-in" on. This is called biological cell targeting or homing. I will discuss this in more detail later. In this way the Nano-drug-carrier will bind only to the targeted cells and not bind to non-targeted body cells. This system has become the choice for targeting drugs to metastatic cancer cells, usually located in many different places within the body."

"I think I will break here for a few minutes, and answer questions, and then I will finish my talk. I believe you have now learned enough about nanotechnology to begin writing your current news releases and future articles on the subject of nanotechnology. One thing that you must keep in mind as you watch this science grow and expand, it is moving at such a rapid pace that what you publish today will be out of date within a couple months. It is best to make your current publications short and fast. New Nano ideas and developing Nano concepts are increasing and changing at a log rate. Both the government and private sectors worldwide are investing in this field. We now have three Nanotech Centers in the USA, and many of the developed countries also have such centers for basic research, assembly, and testing. And we are training very bright young people that have the desire to explore and conquer this new world. The only guarantee that I give to you is that within 20 years we will live in a very different world because of nanotechnology. Will it be a better world or not, I do not know, but you can help the public learn about and understand this new important science."

"Now I want to hear a couple of questions before I continue. In this way I will know if you are beginning to understand what I have said today."

Children

T HE FOUR COLORED MUSKETEERS, OR the 4-pack in shorthand, had physically separated but remained mentally intertwined. There was indeed some type of positive chemistry that seemed to create a linkage, even bondage with four very different children from four different worlds. In nature opposites attract. These guys were certainly four opposites. But they communicated every few weeks by e-Mail; similar ages, similar sexes, and similar hormones around the corner all made for many similar problems, wherever they lived.

After their exciting Swiss adventure, they had each returned to their homes and headed back to school. And of course, they all had very different schools and educational environments to live and grow in.

Jamie O'Reilly was still mourning his father, Theodore O'Reilly, Czar of High Technology in the Cabinet of his older brother, President Jonathan O'Reilly, along with his second brother, Jackson O'Reilly, Attorney General. Theodore O'Reilly had been one of the healthy VIPs who suddenly "became dead" in a medically non-detectable or unexplainable way during the inauguration process of his brother. After his father's death, Jamie first went into a depression, but later he rebounded and began to grow up very fast. With older sisters he could have easily laid back and remain spoiled as the 'baby' or 'little brother' of the family. But suddenly he became the responsible male, concerned about his females and the future. So, his attitude in school changed for the better, according to his teachers.

The family lived in Dorchester, south Boston. But Jamie attended the famous Fessenden School in West Newton which is closer to the center city. Boston has the oldest university in the USA, Harvard University, and is known as the number one education center in the world. There are more than 100 colleges and universities and nearly one million post high school students studying in the area. Boston has 11 major medical centers and of course all of the culture day and night life that can be found in most large American cities; overcrowded streets with many workers using public transportation and taxies.

The Fessenden School is a private day and boarding school for boys with kindergarten through ninth grade. It has almost 500 students and is located on a 35-acre campus with easy access to the big university campuses of Harvard, Tufts, and MIT. The school is devoted to educating the wealthy and elite for higher education. The location, established in 1903, focuses on educating the 'complete' man who will be a future leader of our nation. Over the past hundred years many famous men had attended the Fessenden School such as Howard R. Hughes (aviator and industrialist), Peter Goss (Director of the CIA), George S. Patton (five-star General), Edward M. Kennedy (United States Senator from Massachusetts), William Scranton (Governor of Pennsylvania and American Ambassador to the United Nations), and Patrick J. Kennedy (United States Senator from Rhode Island). Jamie knew he had big shoes to grow into.

During the first school years Jamie had lived at home and was driven to and from school each day. However, in third grade he elected to live on campus as he had continuous access to more of his buddies, and he only went home on some weekends. Now he was a full-time devotee to learning about life and trying to find himself. And center city Boston was a good place to learn, at least about big America city life. Both sisters were living in their boarding school for girls, so he did not see them except during vacations anyway. And even though he now considered himself the 'man' around the house, the big sisters paid him little heed. Mother was overly accommodating, so better to live on campus – more freedom.

It was early on a Friday evening. There was bitter frost, icy sidewalks, and snow flurries gently falling; only a couple of weeks before Christmas, and it was already very cold and dark. He was sprinting between the library and the Johnston House, his warm dormitory room waiting. He was hatless with only his long sleeve white shirt, slacks and school jacket; but at least the slacks and jacket were wool. He was going at top speed but trying to keep an eye open for numerous slippery spots. He cut across the lawn, up the front steps, flew through the front doors and up a set of stairs to his second-floor room. As he approached his bedroom door, he knew that his two roommates were already here. He could hear them arguing. Tim Walker and Jerald Klosky and he had gotten along very well, so far, this school year. There had only been three fights, but no blood, yet.

Before he could open the door, he heard Klosky, "It's about time you got here Curly."

And as he ran through the doorway, he replied, "If you want your tickets you had better be nice to me."

Klosky, a big tall red head with a beaming smile, answered. "Do you have them?"

Jamie responded, "Would I dare come here if I did not have them?" "How did you get them," asked Tim.

"You forget that my Uncle Jonathan is ex-Senator from Massachusetts, and now President of the USA. I asked Mr. Jake Rather, who was Uncle Jon's campaign manager when he was Senator. He always knows where and how to obtain anything. He had one of his people deliver three tickets for the Arthur Fiedler Boston Pops Review tonight at the Kennedy Theater. And it starts at 7:30, so we have less than an hour. And they are being held in my name. So be nice…."

Before he could finish Klosky reached over, picked up 'little' Jamie, threw him over his shoulder and started spinning. Then Klosky and Tim started singing 'For he is a jolly good fellow……'

Arthur Fiedler was the founder, organizer, musician, composer, director, conductor, and Mr. Everything for the famous Boston Pops Orchestra for fifty years, from 1930 to 1979. Mr. Fiedler died before Jamie was born. But the Pops music was his father's favorite music. He taught Jamie to love it. And, in turn Jamie introduced Arthur Fiedler to his roommates, who were not Bostonians. Jamie had almost every CD, converted from records, that the Pops Orchestra recorded, especially those golden oldies which were specially re- recorded from records using ultra-system-sound; Jamie really did not know what records were but that was not important. The room number seven on the second floor of

Johnston House rocked every night to Boston Pops Music. And tonight, they were going to hear a twenty-five-year live review of Jamie's, and his father's, and Tim's and Klosky's favorite music. And of course, the music reminded him of the good times when just he and Dad played together.

"Hey, you are the one who is running late," Klosky returned.

"Go wash your face, put on a clean shirt and tie, and we can catch a cab," suggested Tim.

Tim was hefty and as slow as Jamie was slim and fast. But Klosky was a six foot thirteen-year old. His father had played left tackle for the New York Giants football team. What took Jamie five minutes to accomplish would take Tim at least a half hour, and Klosky would need one minute. Tim knew that they could leave in five minutes. He took out his cell phone, dialed a cab. He knew Jamie would be ready before it got here. So, they quickly prepared to leave. The required coat and tie, routinely worn every day in class, would also be necessary to enter the Kennedy Theater for such performances.

The taxi arrived and they quickly 'mounted up'. They told the African taxi driver that they were late so he used this as excuse to play race car; and they arrived ten minutes early. They quickly looked at the gigantic marble fronted buildings which housed a large concert/opera theater. It blazed a beautiful contrasting bone white and navy blue due to the many flood lights. The three of them walked into the four-flour entry corridor, glanced up at the five multi- tiered chandeliers and headed quickly toward the main door of the hall. It was almost full so they allowed the usher to help them find their seats, center seats in row one. Boy, would they 'hear' the popular, light, and classical music created by the Boston Pops Orchestra which began in the nineteenth century, but was made famous by Mr. Fiedler. It currently was the most recorded and re-recorded orchestra on earth.

After they sat down and checked out the orchestra, especially the young blond cellist, Jamie started to read through the program he had been given. Tonight's music was a review of the music during the conductorship of Arthur Fiedler. There was the 1935 version of Jacob Gade's *Jalousie*, the 1946 version of Dimitri Tiomkin's *Duel in the Sun*, the 1949 version of Tchaikovsky's *Marche Slave*, and many others such as *I Want to Hold Your Hand, I Got Rhythm, Embraceable You, What the World Needs Now, Hearing is Believing*, a variety of medleys from *South Pacific, Capriccio*

Italien, Nutcracker, Stars and Stripes, plus many classical Christmas songs. He knew almost every piece by heart. And he felt this Boston Pops Orchestra bringing 'his music' to life. He could feel his father sitting beside him. During the rendition of *Carnival of Animals* tears streaked down Jamie's face. That had been a Christmas present from his father when he was three years old. He still had the CD and played it whenever he wanted to talk with his father, which was about weekly. His roommates saw his tears, understood, and said nothing.

Li Jiang alternated every two years with his schools in Los Angeles and in Nanking. From the Swiss adventure he had returned to Nanking for the current year. Between visiting his Mother's relatives in Ireland and getting to know the American, African, and Turk at the Swiss camp, he no longer felt very Chinese. But slowly he was adjusting again to his birthplace.

Nanjing or Nanking is one of the oldest cities of China. Throughout the 3,000 year of Chinese history, Nanjing was the capital of the Chinese people six different times under six different dynasties and in 1912 was capital of the Republic of China. It is located on the central northern region of the populous lower Yangzte River Valley, so it has always been in the center of trade and commerce. Today it is a national hub of education, research, industry, transportation, and tourism. It has a population of over seven million people and is the second largest commercial center in China after Shanghai, and ranked as fourth in the world. It recently held the Summer Youth Olympic Games. It is not surprising that the Jiang family's nanotech research and business-oriented family are headquartered here. Li's Uncle Cho, Director of the Chinese branch of JNI, lived here and had his branch office here. Therefore, Li lived with his uncle and went to school here two years, and then to Los Angles to go to school and live with his Father for the next two years. He will continue alternating his education all of his life.

Li also lived in the center of a modern, bustling, overcrowded city. But at least the traffic on many streets included bicycles as well as the usual taxi, bus and metro. And he had access to unlimited cultural activities such as Chinese opera, dance companies, art galleries, and many festivals both inside and outside the city walls. Further, with museums, libraries, theaters, and an Olympic Sports Complex it was an excellent place for a Chinese boy to grow up and learn about Chinese culture. He will need an understanding of both American and Chinese lifestyles to face his near future challenges.

Li Jiang lived only a short distance from the Jinling School on Zhong Shan Road, also near the center city. This school is one on the most competitive and prestigious schools in all of China. It was founded in 1888 as a Christian Bible School and was affiliated to the University of Nanking in 1910. The brightest of the elementary students go on to the high school and then onto the university. It is considered one of the top ten schools in China.

Like Jamie's Fessenden School, Jinling School and the University of Nanking have a long list of famous alumni: master architect Dr. Sun Yat-Sen, former Chairman of the Chinese Academy of Science and thermo-physicist Dr. Wu Zhonghua, Nobel Laureate in Literature Dr. Gao Xjingjian, and mathematician in quantum chromology and member of the Chinese Academy of Science, Dr. Gang Tian.

Because Li Jiang was at the top of his class and usually did not have very much homework, on Monday and Thursday evenings he attended his favorite pastime, Chinese martial arts, Wushu or Kung Fu, depending upon who you were talking to. Li was slim and tall for his age, a quiet, observing person so no one expected that he could take down boys bigger and older that he was, on the martial mats anyway. There are hundreds of styles and schools of Chinese martial arts throughout China. Li preferred the Five Animals and worked out every week, except for vacations when his Father or Uncle's family required his presence. One Uncle worked in Nanking, his Father in Los Angeles, and his other Uncle worked in Germany and other places.

The Five Animals, Wu Xing, represented the tiger, crane, leopard, snake, and dragon. It began in the fourth century in the Henan Shaolin Temple north of the Yangtze River, but it was now more popular in regions south of Nanking. The Shaolin martial arts evolved over time. It began with 18 techniques, in the thirteenth century these were expanded into 72 techniques, and eventually encompasses 170 techniques today. The moves and counter moves are based upon the natural offensive and defensive moves of each of the five animals. One studies and practices these many techniques for many years to become proficient in Wu Xing. But Li was well advanced for his age. Like everything else in his life, he took it seriously.

After school on one Thursday afternoon, he went to study with Chu Chi- Yong. Chu was an eighteen-year old, a little round but very fast, and was far advanced; he had qualified to become an instructor two years ago. Li arrived early at the Hop-Gar Martial Arts Center, changed clothes, and went onto the floor to warm up, exercise, and practice some of his techniques. Chu was already working with a girl of about fourteen. He noticed that the girl was very good. She was tall, but not as fast as he was. But she certainly had a grasp of more techniques. He had a feeling that the two of them had been scheduled lessons near the same time such that they would be put to challenge each other.

When Chu and the young lady took a break, Li noticed she was no longer a complete girl, but was rapidly becoming a young lady. They came over to Li. Chu introduced them.

Chu said, "Li Jiang, this is Ting-ting Chong."

Ting-ting means graceful in Chinese. And Li had to agree that when grown up she would be a very pretty and elegant lady. She was a couple inches taller than him; but he was a couple of pounds heavier. She also had a very nice long brown ponytail. He learned that she was a couple of years older and probably a little stronger. It could make for a good learning match.

Li bowed to Chu and then spoke, "Hello, I am happy to meet you. I admire your martial arts style very much. Have you been studying for a long time?"

Ting-ting responded, "About five years, and I love it very much. Chu said that if I keep working hard, I could become an instructor in a couple of more years.

Chu spoke up, "And yes I hear you thinking, Li. I did want to see the two of you work together. You are nearly the same size and about the same level. I think that you will enjoy the exercise and teach each other some new moves and counter moves. Come Li. You and I will warm up for ten minutes, Ting-ting can rest, and then the two of you can challenge each other for a while."

"During your match I will watch and correct wrong moves and suggest counter moves when you choose the wrong counter move. Li let us start."

So, for the next half hour Li, Ting-ting, and Chu enjoyed a concentrated physical effort called the Five Animals Kung Fu.

As Chu saw his two young pupils becoming very tired, he decided it was enough for today. He was correct in that the two of them were well matched so he would regularly schedule them together again. The two young ones went into their respective locker rooms, showered, and dressed.

As they met at the front door to say goodbye to Chu, Li asked Ting-ting, "Would you like to join me for tea and something sweet? You wore me out."

He was suddenly very hungry, but it was too early for dinner. Maybe a little pastry would be good.

Ting-ting smiled and thought for a few seconds, looked at her watch, and answered, "I have to be home in an hour. It is about thirty minutes by bicycle. So that gives me time. Do you know of any pastry shops nearby?

Li pointed down the street and they took off pushing their bikes. It was cold but the snow had recently melted so the sidewalks and roads were clear. They parked and locked their bikes to a light pole in front of Lo Pan's Oven, entered, found seats near the front where they could watch their bikes, and ordered. Ting- ting ordered green tea and two ping pei rolls (banana rolls). Li asked for black tea and three char siew pillow puffs filled with crème custard. As soon as the order arrived, they started to exchange life histories and found out they actually liked each other.

Aykut Turan was one of those young people who had begun to learn that he liked his own company best. He was not a nerd. He was very bright, always obtained high grades. He didn't play sports or want to learn a musical instrument. Aykut just preferred his lap top, so he took it with him everywhere. He knew all of the hotels, cafes, and tea gardens in Istanbul that had wireless connections. He communicated with many young people, but on the screen, not eyeball to eyeball.

Aykut's Father had attended Robert College, and as the only boy child, Aykut followed in Father's footsteps. Although there are currently more than thirty excellent private foreign language medium schools in Istanbul, Robert College is the oldest and still one of the best.

In 1863, Christopher Robert, an American philanthropist and Cyrus Hamlin, a Presbyterian missionary, with special permission from the Ottoman Sultan, established a private school with all instruction given in English, in Istanbul. It was located on 65 acres of forest land located high up on the mountain bluff overlooking the Bosporus Waterway running from the Black Sea, through the middle of Istanbul, and on to the Marmara Sea, Aegean Sea, and Mediterranean Sea. It was co-educational, but the girls' school was situated on the Anatolian side of the city. For the first 100+ years 'Robert or Bosporus College' was the educational institution that 'connected' wealthy children, and then became a state university offering bachelors, masters, and doctoral degrees.

Scions of Istanbul and Ankara attended this school during their formative years – elementary, middle school, high school. With such a distinguished history today's Bosporus College/University has a long list of distinguished alumni: Nobel Laureate in Literature Orhan Pamuk, Outstanding Businesswoman of Europe in 1984, Nese Erberk, President of the National Geographic Society for 35 years Gilbert Grosvenor, Turkey's first Minister of Culture Talat Halman, Bulgarian Prime Minister Todor Ivanchov, Minister of Foreign Affairs and Ambassador to the United Nations, many members of the Turkish government, and numerous business, CEOs and company and bank presidents. Istanbul is the business, banking, industrial, transportation, tourist and news media center for Turkey. Bosporus College/University is the educational and training source for much of this critical human power. So Aykut was in an excellent educational and training environment. But he probably would not follow his father into banking. Banking was too desk and client bound. The computer is limited only by the sky; and with map quest, even the sky could be opened.

One of Aykut's favorite pastimes was playing Ten-Way-Chess-On-Line. It was a continuous chess tournament played on-line with a total of ten people, located anywhere in the world, all playing at the same time. Every person played against every person. So, each person played nine simultaneous games of chess. Every time you check mate one of your opponents you score ten points. When you are check mated you lose ten points. When you lose more than fifty points you must leave the tournament for the next forty-eight hours. If your score remains above fifty points you can continue to play, but take twenty-hour rest periods any time you want, or you can drop out of the tournament for up to one week. Re-starting would be with nine new opponents in a new tournament. If you score a total of one thousand points within one month you win an honorary plaque from the Ten-Way-Chess-On-Line organization. Oh yes! It does cost you one hundred dollars a month to remain a viable playing member. Aykut had not won any plaques, and he could play for several hours at a time, before losing fifty points and having to drop out. But he was getting better.

During one of his tournaments he became acquainted with another Istanbul chess player, Ali Akman. Ali was only two years older, going to the Galatasaray School, a famous old school where all instruction was in French. Ali could not speak English, and Aykut could not speak French, but when they met at the Dove's Nest Tea Gardens, at the edge of the large Belgrade Forest in north Istanbul which overlooked the Black Sea, they were to communicate in Turkish anyway.

It was mid-afternoon on an early spring day, rhododendrons, azaleas, and camellias bursting with color, still wet from the night rain, Ali entered the gardens and spotted Aykut sitting on a stool, lap top open on the table in front of him, and staring out into the sea. Aykut arrived early and was drinking his second glass of tea.

Ali spoke up, "What are you doing starting without me?"

Aykuts's first empty tea glass was sitting on the table in front of him. He quickly hopped up, gave Ali the customary double kisses on both cheeks, sat back down and returned his eyes back toward the sea. Finally, he mumbled "Hi."

And then they both jumped as a loud boom sounded down near the water's edge. The five major rivers of Eastern Europe and Western Asia drained into the Black Sea. All that water slammed through the one mile wide by twenty-six miles long Bosporus through the center of Istanbul. The current was terrific. Large ocean like waves continuously pounded against the granite mountain entry into the waterway, which was less than two hundred feet from where they were sitting. Such giant booms happen every few minutes. One never really got used to them because they were below the level of vision from the cliff gardens and happened at random without warning.

Ali could see that Aykut was depressed and he became concerned. He asked. "What is wrong? I can see that you are down today. Can I do anything?"

"Looking at his open lap top Aykut replied, "My Father is pressuring me to think seriously about going in the direction of banking. And I do not want to. What can I do?"

"Stall, stall, stall," answered Ali. Let me tell you a recent story that will take your mind off of your Father and banking. Are you ready for this?"

Aykut murmured, "I guess so."

So, Ali began. "Do you remember last year when the Turkish Deputy Prime Minister suddenly resigned and then retired from politics? I'll bet you don't know why. I do."

"Remember the DPM was promoting a new oil pipeline from Ukraine to Turkey which would go through the Black Sea, submerged and attached to the sea bed. It was to be built by a French construction company. Well, the DPM and a couple of his associates were accumulating bribes, in the million American dollar range, in certain Swiss bank accounts, the money was coming from the French. I helped my Uncle Serdar prove it."

"What do you mean you helped prove it?" Aykut asked.

"Just call me the E-Mail Hacker," said Ali. "No, not really. It happened like this. My Uncle is an electronic engineer with a certain high-tech electronic firm here in Istanbul. I will not mention any names. He developed a Fat Thump. A Fat Thump is a small electronic switch mechanism, the size of a person's thumb. You attach it to your smart phone, Blackberry or even Green Grape which is more environmentally friendly, and it will allow you to develop a new web- wave-line on nearby computers. You must be within fifty meters. The special software within it allows you to identify the entry code for that e-mail server postal warehouse. And if you have that home e-mail number of one of the users, you can then open, search, read, and download any sent or received messages. Later, you can hook up to a printer and make hard copies if you want to. The big servers such as Yahoo and Hot Mail, most governments, and many universities have good security, so one must be careful when playing with their e-mail files. But the arrogance of private companies and many corporations with their weak or discontinuous security allows one to enter their warehouses with moderate difficulty."

'My Uncle, who did not like the ex-DPM's party a lot, invaded his postal warehouse and started reading some of his e-Mails. Not directly, but via the DPM's stupid associate. In order to prevent any correspondence from being officially recorded by the government, he used a private company's e-mail server. This company had a very weak, if any, security. For more than two years this associate negotiated ten and one half million dollars in bribes from the French company for the DPM's Swiss bank number SSD123dss876. We downloaded and made hard copies of every letter and they were sent to the DPM asking him to 'get out of politics. He did."

"But how did you find out about this?" asked Aykut.

"Simple," replied Ali. "My Uncle could not speak French. Each e-Mail was in French. He needed me to help him determine which letters were important and which were not important. I learned everything, including how to use the Fat Thumb. Of course, we only downloaded and made copies of the very important letters for possible distribution to the news media. And we threatened to send copies to *Hurriyet*, the biggest newspaper in Turkey, if the DPM did not immediately resign."

"My Uncle was so ecstatic. He made me a copy of his Fat Thumb. Sometimes I read other people's e-mail for fun. I am careful not to get caught while downloading. When you remove the Fat Thumb from your computer all traces of it disappears, I think. It is kind of fun. You can really learn neat things about your friends. So be careful. All you need is a person's e-mail number and you can, usually, read his e-mail and usually, from his postal warehouse, the e- mails of all his friends or contacts."

Aykut asked, "Can I help you play with your Fat Thumb sometime?"

"Of course, you are my best friend." Ali replied. "But if you get serious you should use a throwaway cell phone. It could become a smoking gun."

"Are you kidding? Is this a new line of transformers? I can just see it. A smart cell phone transforms into a smoking gun? Now I have heard of everything. All kids will want one."

And the best friends broke up laughing at their own sadistic pun.

Kefentse Legoase was having a difficult school year in Cape Town, South Africa. He was doing all right with his studies; it was his after-school time that had him badly shaken. His hero was Kerneels Ramla. Kerneels was the famous soccer player who led the South African national team to second place in the World Cup which took place in South Africa a few years ago. Ever since then the country, and all of the boys between ages five and twenty-five had developed soccer fever. Any boy who could out play his buddies in soccer automatically became the leader of the group. And of course, Kef was but a tall slim rabbit. He was better dribbling a ball with his feet than most people using their hands. He would never become a cricket or basketball player, but he loved soccer.

And it happened. During an intra league game Kerneel badly fractured his knee. During the next eight months he had surgery twice, once in the famous Draughtsman Hospital in Johannesburg and a second time at the Columbia University Hospital in New York City. But his knee was not healing properly. And it was becoming obvious that Kerneels's soccer playing days were over. He was twenty-four years of age. One day the entire world was kissing his feet. The next day he was looking for any kind of job just to survive.

Kef had just begun sixth grade, at the private, but government supported, Wynberg Boys Junior School, grades one through seven, on Oxford Street, Wynberg, Cape Town, Western Cape, South Africa. It was an old school, established in 1841; but it did not become big and famous like the schools that his Colored Buccaneer buddies were attending. It focused on sports and gave scholarships in school years six and seven to athletically talented boys in cross country running, tennis, water polo, diving, cricket, soccer, rugby, and basketball. Those young athletes who excelled at Wynberg were recruited by the large universities and frequently went on to play professionally. Kerneels Ramla had been one of those boys. Kefentse Legoase had thought that he wanted to be one of them.

One bright sunny afternoon at the end of scheduled soccer practice on the Wynberg soccer field, Kerneels, walking on crutches, approached the young players. He sat down on a bench and his young fans crowded around him.

The boys started asking, "How are you doing? Do you still have any pain? Are you going to have surgery again? When are you coming back to play? We love to watch you. We always talk about your two goals against Brazil in the World Cup." And on and on.

Finally, Kerneels held up his hands and asked them to quiet down. After few seconds of quiet murmurs, he began, "I have destroyed my leg and will never play soccer again."

Now there was complete silence for a couple of minutes. It appeared that not even the birds dared call out as they flew over the field.

Kerneels continued, "I love sports. And soccer was my life. The doctors have told me that my soccer life is finished. My knee is torn such that it will never heal good enough to let me play soccer again, ever. I do not regret my choice to devote my life to soccer. But I do regret devoting my life to only soccer. My grandfather warned me. He always said that a man needs to have a profession and an occupation. The profession is high gain and high risk. The occupation is for making enough money every day to put bread on the table, low gain but low risk. I did not listen to my grandfather. I put all my effort in the profession of soccer. Then I had one piece of bad luck; and now no profession, and no backup bread money via even a simple common job. I did not even finish high school. As you know, at seventeen I joined the Pretoria Warriors and played with them until the accident. Now here I am. Don't let this happen to you. Stay in school and work for both a sports profession and a normal man's occupation."

One little boy spoke up, "What about all of that money you made?"

Kerneels answered, "My contract said I would be paid several million American dollars every year. Do not believe such contracts. There were many 'management charges' and additional expenses. I took home much less money that the newspapers said."

"Can't you get a lawyer to help with a contract?" said the same little boy. "You are right," responded Kerneels. "One can never really understand these small print clauses in a contract. Besides I never was very good at reading anyway. Contracts are written by lawyers. So, you must have a lawyer you can trust. And then the lawyer becomes one of those 'additional expenses' that you have to pay."

A tall skinny thirteen-year old held his hand up, Kerneels pointed to him, and the boy asked. "What would you do if you had your life to live again?"

And Kerneels laughed, "Good question. I have been thinking about that every day for the past six months. I do not know what I would do, but I know what I want you to do."

And a group of bright eyes looked up at their god, waiting for his omnipotent advice. He looked around and made certain he had everyone's attention. He then raised his voice and tried to re-route these young lives.

"First I want you to stay in school until you finish high school. Play soccer or your sport every evening and weekends, but learn your school lessons every day. Work and get good grades. Choose lessons and courses that you like and are good in. Prepare yourself for that occupation if you should need one. If you have the brain power, go on to the university. All big universities allow you to play soccer, or your sport. Many universities even pay you scholarship money so you can go to school for free. Again, study and prepare yourself for that occupation, or possibly a second profession."

"Let me give you an example. Two good buddies of mine, no names, play for the Durban Black Tide Soccer team. They have each been playing for almost ten years. Both have million American dollar contracts. One has a university degree in business. During these years he has invested his money in three restaurant businesses. He now has a lot of money and a financially secure future; if he should suddenly have bad luck, or whenever he retires, he will be all right. His wife and children will have enough money to live comfortably. My other friend finished high school, but went directly to professional soccer and did not go to college. Today he does have a very nice house and family, but he has no investment for the future. He spends all of his money. He is getting older; and he recently told me that he will soon be like me, filled with good memories, but trying to find some bread money for his family."

And everyone started talking at once. They were trying to guess who these players might be. They did not believe such a thing could happen. Preparing for two ways to make money seemed like a lot of extra work. And it was like health insurance, it was only good if you got sick. You could not drive two cars at the same time; but maybe if you had a girlfriend, she could drive one. The message got through to some of the boys, but not to all of them.

But it did reach the ears and mind of Kefentse Legoase. Kef, when he was e- mailing with his 4-pack buddies, he thought of and talked about high school and university, because that is what they were thinking and talking about also. But when he was with his neighborhood buddies he only talked and played soccer. He was a very lucky little boy; he had an older brother who kept his interest in high-technology, especially nanotechnology, alive.

And during the next few months, Aykut kept his promise. He set the 4-pack up with a secret chat room under the screen of computer conferencing, used a modified avatar's language, and the communicators as: Jamie – Ey'tuka, Li – Tsu'teye, Kef – Na'via, and Aykut – Mo'ata. 'Computer conferencing' was a really fun thing to do.

Each of the boys already was comfortable in at least two alphabets/two languages. Jamie knew Celtic/Gaelic-Irish, Latin and English, Li knew Mandarin-Chinese and English, Aykut knew Arabic/Persian-Ottoman and Latin alphabet- based Turkish and English, and Kef knew Isizulu-Zulu and Latin alphabet-based Afrikaans and English. So Aykut sent to each of them a CD which contained the necessary instructions and codes to open their unique conference computer screens and allowed all four of them to be simultaneously viewed. It was designed such that the upper left corner was Boston-Ey'tuka, upper right was Nanking-Tsu'teye, lower left was Cape Town-Na'via, and lower right was Istanbul-Mo'ata. And the CD also contained instructions and lessons for learning a Latin alphabet-based modified version of the Avatar language. With their multi-lingual backgrounds they had no difficulties learning another language, which they consciously used when communicating in their computer conferences. It was fun and 'reasonably' secure. Just how secure they would never know until it was too late.

Adults

THE FOURTH MEETING OF THE President's Commission on Human Trafficking did not occur again until later in 2030. This time the meeting was held in conference room #4 in the Dirkson Senate Office Building on Capitol Hill. Word had gotten around that the sudden VIP deaths with unknown medical causes was being investigated by a Presidential committee, and several key Senators put pressure on President O'Reilly to allow them to attend the next meeting. The Senators, themselves, would not attend, but they could each send one Senatorial Aide who could only sit around the wall of the conference room and listen, no recording, only take notes. The second-floor conference room was reserved for this eye- opening meeting.

At 9:00 o'clock on a Friday morning in October, 2030, Chairman and Attorney General Jackson O'Reilly sat at the head of the conference table, looked around the room, counted heads of committee members, and then heads of attending aides. Satisfied, he opened the meeting.

"Welcome to our delayed Commission on Human Trafficking meeting for 2030. The reason for the delay is simply because we do not have very many substantial leads to help us solve the medically unexplainable sudden deaths, MUSD, or the medically unexplainable sudden cures, MUSC, that have been occurring around the world. To date, we count sixteen deaths and thirteen miracles in 2028, 2029, and 2030. If any of you very busy aides want to leave, you are welcome to do so. Those are the current numbers; but they are increasing"

Of the 46 Senatorial Aides present, only five stood up and left, but two would later return to hear end of meeting summary.

"Good, now, let us begin a review of our recent investigative efforts. As I said, we do not have many substantial leads, but we have a lot of very interesting data completing your assigned tasks. Mr. Murphy and I have received these reports and have organized them such that we can hopefully shed some light on this unnecessary morbid loss of human life, as well as whether we have miracles or mirages. Previously someone on the Commission used the words **intellectual terrorism**. I am beginning to agree that this phrase is becoming an apt description of our situation."

"Mr. Murphy's ISAAT has identified the sudden VIP death pattern and a sudden VIP miracle life pattern occurring on the fifteenth of every month during the previous two years, 2028 and 2029. And again, the pattern of deaths to miracles which alternate every other month seem to be continuing in 2030. Mr. Femer, would you kindly pass out a copy of our current list of deaths and miracles to Commission members only?"

"I'm sorry but we will not be sharing any printed information with you Senatorial aides. Mr. Murphy, if you could please start."

Mr. Murphy began referring to his pile of notes in front of him on the table. "Thank you, Mr. Chairman. And as Mr. O'Reilly just stated, we will not be sharing any hard copies of any data with anyone outside the committee. Members of the committee please look at your printouts."

Look at our current death list. First, allow me to go through this list.

List of VIPs Who Are MUSD Candidates - 2029

Mr. Theodore O'Reilly, Czar of High Technology, member of the Cabinet of the President of the United States, American, 48 years old, on January 15 'died' from respiratory failure.

Dr. Bahar Edison, developed techniques to grow animal meats in flasks in the laboratory, President and CEO of Safe Meat USA, Canadian-American, 51 years old, on March 15, 'died' from heart malfunction.

Dr. Bryan Tinkerson, invented biodegradable plastics, CEO of Green Plastics Ltd, Danish, 48 years old, on May 15, 'died' from a blocked swallowing reflex, a frozen trachea.

Mr. Donald Erister, founder and President of the White-Not-Red Meat Movement, Irish, 55 years old, on July 15, 'died' from a rupture of the left carotid artery.

Dr. Ellyn Rinkler, inventor of large scale solar-voltaic energy systems, CEO of Sahara Solar-Voltaic International, French, 49 years old, on September 15, 'died' from bleeding of the optic nerves in the eyes.

Dr. Eisei Ishimoto, Nobel Laureate, developed techniques to harness the movement of ocean waves which allows the production of electricity, Japanese, 59 years old, on November 15, 'died' in a sleep coma.

"Now all of these people were intellectuals who brought some new type of high technological system into the world. In some instances, they not only developed the technology but found the necessary venture capital to start up a business using their new discovery. We do not have good data and information on some of these deaths; but we were able to put together a reasonable scenario concerning the deaths of Dr. Edison, Dr. Tinkerson, and Dr. Rinkler. I will present our analysis for Dr. Tinkerson, 'killed' in Baltimore. Mr. Femer will present our analysis for Dr. Edison and Dr. Rinkler, 'killed' in Stockholm and in Tripoli, respectively. We will review these in chronological order, so Mr. Femer is first."

"Do you have any questions before we begin?"

Mr. Bradmier asked, "Are you also going to talk about the data which we provided for you, upon your request?"

"That will be included within these presentations, and then we will return to certain specifics later in the meeting," replied Chairman O'Reilly. "We thought it better to not footnote every other remark as coming from this person or that person. We are one committee with many heads and hands. I fully expect to see that we are all acknowledged as a group. It is even possible that, later, you might not want to be publicly acknowledged as a member of this committee; or you might not want to be the noted source for that specific information. Our final results may place powerful people under suspicion. And we must remember if these deaths turn out to be carefully targeted murders, we might just find ourselves in the cross hairs. For now, we are not using name references on shared hard copies."

And several members looked at each other. The Chairman was serious –cross hairs?

Mr. Femer began his review of the death of Dr. Bahar Edison. "Dr. Edison was found dead in a hotel room in the InterContinental Hotel in Stockholm, Sweden on March 15, 2021. He is a Canadian-American who developed high technology methodologies to grow animal meat in the laboratory in glass containers. He is President and CEO of Safe Meat USA. His company can grow any kind of mammalian flesh including beef, chicken, lamb, turkey, buffalo, and deer.'

"His innovative methodology begins with embryonic muscle cells from the various animals, therefore the final product is even tastier, more tender, and has no pesticides, fertilizers, or hormones in it. It is grown and sold in one or two portion sizes, so no 'slaughter' or 'butchering' is required. Cattlemen and pig, chicken, sheep, and turkey growers are not happy with this new technology. Currently, Safe Meat USA has production laboratory/factories in the USA, Canada, England, Austria, and Japan. He was discussing the establishment of an additional meat manufacturing facility in Sweden. Dr. Edison was talking with three private sector food distribution companies and the Swedish government."

"An associate, Dr. Olga Stadmieser, had accompanied him for the negotiations which had ended on the 13th of March. She had gone to Hamburg to visit her family while he was staying on for two more days to do some book hunting. Dr. Edison was an avid antique book collector, and he planned to spend a couple of days book shopping in Stockholm and then in Copenhagen, before returning to his Toronto headquarters. According to Dr. Stadmieser all of the negotiations were excellent and all was well when she left for Hamburg."

"Thanks to the assistance of INTERPOL, M15 and the Stockholm police," and he nodded to Ms. Von Eulenberg and Mr. Thomson, "we have the following data and information to evaluate. All day on the 13th of March Dr. Edison went shopping. He visited seven book shops and purchased eleven books. On the evening of the 14th of March, Dr. Edison ate at the bohemian restaurant, Prinsen, took a taxi back to the hotel, and went to bed around 11:30."

"Because of the extensive use of hallway motion-sensitive security cameras in the InterContinental, a man was observed going into Dr. Edison's room about 4:05 AM. Hotel security police were notified and went to check the room at 4:14 AM. They simply waited by Dr. Edison's hotel room door. At 4:18 AM, the door opened, a man exited, and seeing the police he drew a gun and started shooting. He tried to flee but was shot in the left leg. City police and an ambulance quickly arrived. The injured man was handcuffed, placed onto a stretcher, and carried down to the waiting ambulance. As he was being placed inside the ambulance, he suddenly rose, grabbed his head, groaned, and then a loud explosion occurred. The man's head blew off. Blood and brain scattered for 40 to 50 feet in all directions."

During this time the security personnel had opened Dr. Edison's door, entered his room and found him in pajamas in his bed. He had stopped breathing. His body was still warm but there was no pulse, no heart-beat. They called down to the ambulance and requested that one of the two emergency paramedics return upstairs. Then another explosion occurred in the street nearby. Because of the explosion both paramedics were now kept busy attending to several injured people. It was almost 5:30 AM before a more complete medical examination was made on Dr. Edison. His body was now cold. And it was confirmed that he had no pulse and no heart-beat. Later the autopsy would find no medically detectable reason for the heart to stop beating. He was determined to have died of heart malfunction or failure."

"An INTERPOL investigation of the man found that his finger prints, hand prints, and DNA profile were not on police records anywhere. He is probably a hired assassin with no previous criminal activity. Some of the unanswered questions are - Who hired him? How did he kill Dr. Edison within a few minutes without shedding one drop of blood via some medically detectable means? Did the assassin know that he had a bomb placed inside his head which could be detonated by a nearby remote?"

Mr. Thomson spoke up, "I can speculate a little about the assassin. He probably came from Eastern Europe, most likely Romanian or Bulgarian. His hands were rough so he was probably a laborer, hired and given a couple weeks of training as to how to inject someone with a syringe and a needle. A small team of controllers could have brought him to Stockholm by ship. He would have been given a picture of Dr. Edison. They would have pointed out this target while he was on the street during his book shopping, obtained a room entry pass card, given the assassin a bottle of ether and a rag, found in the pocket of the assassin, given the vial already loaded, and the empty vial was found flushed down the toilet. Near 4:00 AM, they simply said "Go inject that man. Afterward we will give you a 'few' hundred thousand Euros in cash - easy and simple, minimum risk. Probably the assassin would never have seen those Euros."

Ms. Dapper asked, "Were injection marks found anywhere on Dr. Edison?"

"Yes. And Mr. Thompson is correct. An empty bottle which had contained ether was found in the hallway trash container, and a one milliliter syringe was found in the hotel septic lines," commented Mr. Femer. "Because of our previous experiences with the possibility of an injection as a route of Nano- system delivery, extra efforts were made to try to find such marks on the victim's body. INTERPOL was aware of this; and yes, a single very tiny entry hole was found in the spinal column between lumbar #1 and #2 vertebrate. It probably would have been missed if special attention had not been made to try to find such by the forensic pathologist."

"Was this declared to be a murder case?" asked Ms. Dapper.

Mr. Femer answered, "There is a body, a 'smoking' gun, and a possible murderer found at the scene."

"So now we have hard evidence that one of our sudden VIP deaths is criminal," said Mr. O'Reilly. "But we have no witnesses. The killer is dead. And we do not know about the chemical or poison that was used to kill him. No trace of any toxic chemical was identified in Dr. Edison's blood or urine, nor was any such strange chemical found in the syringe from the hotel's septic lines."

Everyone was really beginning to appreciate the clever, well-organized group that they were up against. There were at least sixteen sudden VIP deaths, all of them medically unexplainable. Now finally a suspect is caught and he is immediately eliminated by an intra cranial bomb. And even with a 'fresh' VIP body, there was no medical evidence to substantiate the cause of death. It probably involved an injection, but an injection of what? Apparently, he was killed in just a few minutes, a bloodless death, and probably a painless death; but dead none the less.

After a few minutes of group conversation, Mr. Murphy spoke up, "Let us look at the death of Dr. Tinkerson."

And he began, "Dr. Bryan Tinkerson, another innovative scientist who invented a special type of plastic, found the necessary venture capital, and started his own company. He is President and CEO of Green Plastics, Ltd. which uses synthetic organic polymers, but not from petroleum sources, to develop and now market plastic and rubber like products which are biodegradable. They function like plastics in food and drink packaging, and like soft rubber for disposable laboratory and medical supplies. Discarded normal plastic containers require many years to biodegrade. Green Plastics products, after disposal, need less than two years to biodegrade. As you can imagine, oil exporters and plastics manufacturers are not happy about this multi-use biodegradable plastic."

"Dr. Tinkerson has his main office in the Wilkenson building on E. Lombard Street in Baltimore, Maryland. It was his routine pattern to work late most nights. On a Tuesday night, May 14, 2029, at 8:30, he dismissed his two personal secretaries. They both left the building and went home to their families. This was verified. He often drank vodka martinis later in the evening as he finished his work, and sometimes friends dropped by to talk. His office was large and lovely and equipped with all the components of a bar and kitchen, plush arm chairs and couch. On that night it was difficult to know how many martinis he drank or if he had any friends over. Only one used drinking glass was found, so he was probably alone all evening."

"Apparently around midnight, for some undetermined reason, he went into the hallway and started to go down the stairs to the lower floor. The Baltimore police report writes that he must have fallen down the stairs. He was found on the floor at the bottom of the stairs by the early morning cleaning people at 6:15 AM. His office lights and the hallway lights were on. They immediately called 911. Both the police and paramedics with ambulance arrived at 6:26 AM. Dr. Tinkerson was already dead, his eyes closed, and his body was cold. He had a large knot on his head, so everyone on the scene agreed that he fell down the stairs. However, no dents or marks on the stairwell were found where his head might have hit."

"Dr. Tinkerson was taken to the Chief Medical Examiner's Office in the Baltimore County Coroner's new building on W. Saratoga Street. From the medical records that we obtained, Dr. Tinkerson was given a routine autopsy, assuming he died of a blow to the head. However, during the autopsy an alert pathologist noticed a 'frozen' jaw. Rigor mortis had set in but the jaw area showed that the glottis and epiglottis, swallowing organs, were frozen and locked together. It was noted that he could have died of a blocked swallowing reflex. In the opinion of the Chief Pathologist the blow to the head would have caused unconsciousness, but not death."

"It was decided that they would do a micro analysis of the lower brain region, which controlled food swallowing, on the next day. Such an analysis would require several hours, and it was late in the day. So, early the next day a special micro analysis was performed. The next day the pathologists arrived at work at 7:30 AM, rolled out the gurney with Dr. Tinkerson's body, uncovered the body, and discovered the head was missing. Just how the head was cut from the body and removed from the building was never determined. A security review of the hallway cameras found no unknown workers in the corridor near the cold room during the previous two days."

"The micro analysis of the lower brain was not performed," spoke Dr. Batley. "No head, no brain, no analysis, and no identification of a possible high tech or nanoproduct. That was a very lost chance, but it does tell us that the lower brain stem area was the possible target for a possible high tech or nanoproduct. And that helps us a lot. In the future, for any sudden VIP death, we should try to have the lower brain area micro analyzed."

Mr. O'Reilly agreed, "I will immediately send such a memo to all medical coroners in the USA. Dr. Von Eulenberg, can you accomplish the same thing throughout the EU."

'Yes,' she replied. "And I will also notify the WHO and have the same set of procedures performed worldwide, at least in parts of the world where micro analysis technology for brain pathology is available."

Mr. Murphy spoke up, "Are there any more questions?"

He waited a few minutes and only heard general conversation, so he asked Mr. Femer to present the next case.

Mr. Femer stood up and began. "Dr. Ellyn Rinkler was an electrical engineer who spent her life performing research on the conversion of solar energy to electrical energy. She had focused her research specifically on large scale use of solar energy for providing electricity for large cities and even countries. This had just begun to pay off as three years ago her company, she is Founder and CEO of Sahara Solar-Voltaic International Corporation, had signed an agreement with Libya and Italy to supply electricity for all of Malta. On fifteen hundred acres of Libyan Sahara Desert, photovoltaic power pack units, 230 watts/panel, were built to generate a total 200 million kw/hour of electricity annually. The electricity was cabled under water from the African mainland to the island of Malta. The system is currently functioning perfectly and supplies 65% of the electrical needs for the entire island of Malta."

"In early November of last year, just before her death, she had arranged a second contract with Libya and Italy for an additional 10 billion kw/hr of electricity yearly for Sicily and southern Italy. And she was talking with Algeria and France about similar solar voltaic systems to be built in the Sahara, which could provide electricity for southern France. Long term calculations show that the northern half of the Sahara is large enough to provide enough electricity for all of Europe at a cost of less than 20% of petrochemical produced electricity and less than 25% of nuclear radiation produced electricity. Needless to say, the petrochemical and nuclear reactor people are not happy with these long-term calculations."

"On September 14, 2029, Dr. Rinkler and her three-person team were on the PV modular site, in the desert near Dahra. They were exploring potential new land areas for the new additional PV array modules, and they were sleeping in tents. Dr. Rinkler slept in her own tent and the three-man team slept in a separate tent nearby. According to the Algerian police, everything was normal during the evening. The weather was cool and star studded, so they had dinner outside, discussed construction strategies for a couple of hours, and then all went into their own tents and to bed around

11:00PM. No unusual sounds or disturbances occurred during the night. But when her associates went to wake Dr. Rinkler the following morning, there was much blood around her eyes and head, her body was cold, her eyes were closed, and she was dead."

"There were no doctors on site. She was taken to a small hospital in Dahra, pronounced dead, and her body was placed into a coffin box and immediately taken to Tripoli. When it arrived at the Tripoli Medical Examiners Clinic, the box was opened. Inside the box, Dr Rinkler's head was missing. Both arms and legs had been severed and lay reversed onto the body. The arms were lying where the legs should be with the fingers pointed downward. And the legs were lying across the chest with the toes located where the fingers should be. I saw a police picture of this. It was terrible. I cannot understand who would do such a thing and what the message was. So, the body was autopsied, but the head was never found."

Mr. Thomson asked, "I assume that all of this report comes from the Algerian police."

"Yes," confirmed Mr. Femer. "But I did visit the PV modular site, and I talked with two of the onsite people who were there at the time of Dr. Rinkler's death. I visited the hospital in Dahra and the doctor who examined her body. And I spent two days at the Tripoli Medical Examiners Clinic and talked with the medical staff. I simply confirmed what was on the medical report. She 'died' officially from a profuse bleeding of the optic nerves in both eyes on September 15, 2029."

"Dr. Batley asked, "How much can we trust this Algerian generated information? Certainly, the listed cause of death cannot be confirmed if the head was not available for autopsy."

"I guess they were relying upon the oral reports by workers at the site of death," replied Mr. Femer. "Just how reliable such reports are, no one will ever know."

"Were any international health care or police sources brought into the investigation, such as it was?" Dr. Von Eulenbert asked.

"Dr. Rinkler was a French citizen," Mr. Femer replied. The French Embassy was notified, but to my knowledge no special request or any request for a more extensive autopsy was made by the French government. However, her body was shipped to France and buried near Lyon."

Mr. Bradmier asked, "So neither France nor Italy requested an investigation of this suspicious death of a French citizen and a major Italian contractor? Is that right? No? Isn't that very interesting?"

"I think the whole thing stinks," commented General Ronny. "Are there any more questions," asked Mr. Murphy.

Hearing none he continued. "In my opinion we have a similar modus operandi. Each VIP is isolated, usually at night, possibly 'treated' while isolated, maybe or maybe not seen after 'treatment', and is always found dead the next morning. The time between 'treatment' and death seems to vary from a few minutes to a few hours. No medical evidence was found concerning the 'mechanism of treatment'. So, we are labeling these as sudden VIP deaths which defy a medical explanation, MUSDs. A common factor is that each death occurred on the fifteenth of a month. Another factor is that the professions of these people were at the cutting edge of several high technologies. There are certainly many people out there who would prefer to not see these new technologies bear fruit."

And he waited a couple of minutes to see if any member of the commission agreed, disagreed, or had any comments. Hearing none he continued.

"We have other information that we want to share today. As you know from our last couple of meetings, we are now also monitoring sudden VIP life miracles that occur on the fifteenth of a month. These cases are difficult because these people are alive, no bodies and no pathologists, and there is doctor to patient confidentiality on their side. In some of our investigations we used the authority of the US Attorney General's Office and obtained selected hospital records. Indeed, several of these VIPs did have the assistance of medical doctors and possibly an unknown treatment 'drug'."

"Yet in every case the recipient of the miracle claimed no medical assistance was involved in his miracle cure. Indeed, during 2028, a similar pattern of sudden VIP miracles happened in different countries around the world, and at least in the USA cases we found several JXW drugs were involved. Here again in the 2029 sudden miracles, we have identified two more drugs with a JXW number. Mr. Femer, if you will hand out a list of these VIPs to our committee members?"

<u>List of VIPs Thought to Have Suddenly Had Miracle Cures (MUSC) During 2029</u>

Mr. Philippe Pay-Lussac, Paris, France, President of Farmers Market Lobby International, 73 years old, suddenly cured of brain cancer on February 15.

Dr. Pauline Nuvier, Geneva, Switzerland, CEO of World Kidney Transplant Center, 64 years old, suddenly cured of debilitating atherosclerosis on April 15.

Mr. Jeffery Harrver, Atlanta, Georgia, USA, lawyer, conservative Senator from Georgia, 73 years old, suddenly cured of metastatic urinary bladder cancer on June 15.

Mrs. Marie Van Beterson, Switzerland-Netherlands, CEO of Iron Salvage International, 61 years old, suddenly cured of metastatic ovarian cancer on August 15.

Dr. Samuel Anders, Chicago, Illinois, USA, President of the US Chambers of Commerce, 68 years old, suddenly cured of Alzheimer's disease on October 15.

Mr. Topper Norton, Pittsburg, Pennsylvania, USA, President of the Clean Coal Lobby, 72 years old, suddenly cured of metastatic terminal prostate cancer on December 15.

"If you will carefully read through this list you will notice several things. There are a wide variety of 'cures' from a terminal illness that one can observe in the list. Each of these people had their sudden cure on the fifteenth of a month, just like in 2028. And if you look back, the sudden VIP deaths occurred on the fifteenth of the odd numbered months in both 2028 and 2029. The sudden VIP miracles occurred on the fifteenth of the even numbered months in 2028 and 2029. Our investigations of the 2029 miracles showed that at least three, Mr. Jeffery Harrver, Mr. Samuel Anders, and Topper Norton, did have medical treatment in a hospital that involved an experimental drug with a JXW number attached. We do have JXW numbered drugs associated with five cures, but no numbers for any drugs/chemicals associated with any deaths. In addition, all of these 'miracle cured' people are conservative in their professional and political orientations – lobbyists, lawyer-congressman, iron and coal salvage, and live organ transplantation."

"The final thing that I want to leave with you is this. If you will remember at our last Commission meeting, when we listed by chronological sequence the sudden VIP deaths and sudden VIP miracles in 2028, took the first letter from their last names, and wrote them we found the following macabre pun.

NO – HITECH - STOP

"Now if we repeat this process for 2029, we get:

O'Rielly-PayLussac-Edison-Nuvier-Tinkerson-Harrver-Erister-Beterson-Rinkler-Anders-Ishimoto-Norman

And then pull out the first letters of each name and list them:

O-P-E-N-T-H-E-B-R-A-I-N

And then you separate the letter as following, we see another macabre pun or warning:

OPEN – THE – BRAIN

Does anyone have any questions or thoughts?"

Chairman O'Reilly offered, "We are either dealing with some crazy people, or maybe just desperate people, or very clever people with a long-term macabre plan. These killing/cures certainly have been planned and almost perfectly carried out over several years There have been several this year, 2030. The ones that we have evaluated are very similar. But we will discuss them at another time. It certainly is a unique type of surgical terrorism on carefully selected key intellectuals. There are no massive armies, no hundreds of airplanes, tanks, and missiles, no big guns, no big noises, no massive killings to hit the single individual target, no suicide bombers, no collateral damage, no news coverage and therefore no fear factor spreading among the common folk. And yet somehow I have the feeling that they are winning."

General Ronny cringed, because he agreed. A talking buzz began among the Senatorial Aides.

Again, Chairman and Attorney General Jackson O'Reilly spoke, "Listen you young know-it-all-children sitting along the walls. You tell your bosses that this is why we are keeping the findings of this Commission quiet. And we are going to keep everything we say and do here quiet. If there is one smell of what this Committee is doing or finding that is placed into any news system, on paper, audio, video, or on-line, I personally will track down the person that released that smell and see that he, and his boss, suffer. And I am not talking about some little slap on the wrist. Let this be a warning to all of you. Keep your mouth shut during happy hour."

Dr. Von Eulenberg suggested, "Why don't we take a long break, have some coffee, chat a while, and then perhaps the Committee could meet later today in our previous Department of Justice Committee Room and decide where we should go from here. I have several ideas which I do not want to share with non- Committee members."

"That is a great idea," agreed Chairman O'Reilly. "For the next few minutes we will continue informally over coffee and try to answer any questions the Senatorial Aides might have. Let us break and the official Committee on Human Trafficking will reconvene at the Department of Justice building on Pennsylvania, at 2:30PM.

How Do Nanotechnical Systems Work?

"I T IS NEAR LUNCH TIME so let me finish my first National Press Club presentation by discussing targeting or homing for Nano-systems, and mechanisms of action." responded Dr. Chi Jiang. A key part of the efficiency and success of using nanotech systems in medical therapy is targeting. I mentioned earlier MoABs and Aptomers, and how we make them. MoABs are the most common method that we use to identify specific molecule(s) on the outside of cell membranes which we are targeting. How do we do this?"

"The surface of every cell in our body has thousands of membrane-bound molecules sticking out into the blood. We pick out one or two groups of these molecules that are unique only to the cell we are targeting. Example:"

"If you fly slowly over the surface of the earth in a small airplane or a helicopter, you can look down and see billions of 'things' sticking up at you; mountains with many combinations and shapes of large and small boulders; multi-shaped rocks, scrubby trees, deep ravines and high cliffs; forests with many combinations of large and small trees and shrubs, and streams; grasslands with numerous varieties of grasses, small trees, ponds, streams, rivers, flowers; deserts with many combinations of different cacti, thorny shrubs, waves and waves of sand dunes; and some areas will have combinations of several of these earthly projection systems. And all of these change every season."

"You would see a similar type of picture if you could 'fly' in a Nano-submarine through the blood and look out the windows and see the body cells as you went by them. All body cells have many combinations of 'projected things', molecules, sticking up/down/out toward you. And like a biologist or a geologist looking at the earth's surface, using special medical training, you would be able to recognize a cell or a group of cells by recognizing the cell surface. This is what medical pathologists do. The most common way to distinguish a normal breast cell from a breast cancer cell is by recognizing changes in the structure of the cell which includes the surface. By law, the medical pathologist analyzes and determines the difference of whether a body cell or tissue is normal, diseased, or damaged by comparing its surface features on a slide under the microscope."

"Obviously nanotechnology is not necessary for this legal form of diagnosis of a disease. The medical pathologist has been using surface structures to recognize cells and tissues in our bodies for more than two hundred years. Nanomedicine is only 20 to 30 years old. So how does the targeting in a nanotech system play a role in medicine?"

"When flying in a helicopter over a forest and trying to determine what forest you are in or where you are in that forest, you need very specific targets or groups of targets. -special trees, flowering shrubs, certain rocks, unique bodies of water, and on. The same rationale is critical to identify a specific 'surface' of any body cell membrane."

"In a similar way, our targeting must focus upon one cell or a small group of cells. We must find and identify a unique or specific molecule or combination of molecules that are found only on that surface of that cell; and then we prepare antibodies which will 'recognize' only that area, therefore that cell. These are called monoclonal antibodies, MoABs, which are prepared via a HYBRIDOMA. These MoABs are prepared and attached to the Nano-system which we want to use. Hence that Nano-system can now 'find' the cell via recognition of that one unique molecule or group of molecules on the surface of that biological cell among the millions homing element of cells in our bodies. MoABs provide very powerful **guides** or **homing devices** for any or all Nano-systems, used for both diagnosis and therapy."

"So, I repeat, a **Nano-technical system** is usually composed of a **MoAB plus a Nano-system**. 1) one MoAB molecule as a homing component – it finds and attaches to the target cell; 2) one or more active Nano-tech molecule - these Nano-tech molecules directly initiate a variety of actions at the specific cell membrane attachment site."

"Now, the last thing I want to leave with you is how the Nano-system works after it finds the target."

"First the MoAB binds to the target, and then the Nano-system directly affects the target. The Nano-system can now rupture cell walls or membranes, digest small holes in the walls, stop the cell from working, freeze the cell, increase the cell's activity, decrease the cell's activity, repair the cell, improve the cell's function, carry something such as metals into the cell, place new small genes into the cell, turn on new genes brought to the cell, initiate synthesis of new proteins in the cell, and on and on."

"Where do we obtain our ideas about how to make a Nano-system do any of these things? From nature! We use the ideas for designing Nano-molecules which are similar with active molecules in venoms. For example, various venoms contain the following molecules which can cure or kill:

- Neurotoxins – block nerve to muscle function (block muscle function)
- Phosphodiesterase – cuts phosphates (rapidly decreases blood pressure)
- Phospholipase – cuts lipids in cell membranes (ruptures cells)
- Cholinesterase – block nerve action (freezes muscle cells)
- Oxidases – digests many cell membranes (ruptures cells)
- ATPases – short circuits the energy system inside of body cells
- Hemolases – stop heart beat and close down blood circulation
- Neurolases – short circuits the body's nerve cells
- Lipolases – short circuits brain nerve cells
- Osteoclastases – digest bone cells and ruptures bones
- DNAases – digests DNA (destroys all types of cells)

"Most types of venoms, from reptiles, scorpions, insects, jellyfish, certain ocean fish, and marine microscopic animals, have molecules or substances that are deadly; this is how their venoms can block cell/tissue activity or kill cells, therefore people. And we do use the molecular shape or structure of these venom molecules to help us design Nano-molecules, Nano-substances, Nano- carriers, and Nano-products to kill bad cells such as cancer cells."

"Also take note that many of these toxic venom molecules have their own built-in homing component! They only associate or bind to specific cells/tissues and thus exert their effect only on those cells/tissues!"

"So, today I have tried to briefly review for you the state of nanotechnology as related to medicine. In my opinion nanotechnology will benefit mankind just like the discovery of human body cells more than 200 years ago. Using targeting MoABs attached to any Nano-technological system we can specifically attach to any single cell or group of cells in our bodies and change that cell's action."

"With a properly designed nanomachine – carrier, activator, constructor, builder, digester, enhancer, expander, opener, renovator, manufacturer, duplicator, OR inactivator, reducer, destroyer, smasher, destructor, demolisher, pulverizer, dismantler, ruiner, killer, assassin, one can effect one or a small group of cells in the body without effecting the other 99 % of body cells. This means very little or no side effects from diagnostic or therapeutic treatments."

"However, if that 1% of body cells are necessary for life, such as brain cells, lung cells, or heart cells, then the MoAB plus nanomachine can kill those cells, thus the body."

"It also means that we can use new creative ways to control the bad cells without killing them. In the past we only used surgery, radiation, and drugs for therapy. Now the door is open to use new or yet undiscovered methods to prevent and cure diseases in our bodies."

"I sincerely thank you for your time and attention. I will stay here for a few minutes to answer any more questions. Those of you who have more important obligations may leave. You are dismissed."

And he laughed as the audience laughed with him; they gave him a standing ovation for several moments and then slowly trickled downstairs to the Club's dining room.

One big burly, bald headed fellow, who was not a member of the National Press Club, but had been attentively listening, came forward. The new gentleman introduced himself as Mr. Dagda Murphy. Mr. Murphy invited Dr. Jiang to lunch just down the street at the White House in the near future, where they would be joined by President of the USA, Mr. Jonathan O'Reilly, and the US Attorney General, Mr. Jackson O'Reilly; an invitation Dr. Chi Jiang could possibly not refuse.

The Quest Unfolds

THE FOLLOWING YEAR, THE FOUR Colored Musketeers were in the middle of a lengthy discussion via their computer conferencing system when Ey'tuka asked, "Have any of you guys read about the nanotechnology that may have killed my father?'

Mo'ata responded, "Yes, it was in the Turkish newspapers last week that many very important people may have been killed or cured with Nano- molecules during the past few years. Your father's name was on the list."

"It was also in the South African newspapers," added Na'via.

Then Tsu'teye spoke up, "Yes I read about it. And did your papers give a JXW labeled nanodrug that could be involved?"

"Yes, those letters were in my paper," answered Mo'ata.

"That is what I was afraid of," replied Tsu'teye. "My father's company is called Jiang Nano Control International, JNI. Their nanoproducts are labeled with JXW. J is for Jiang. X and W for the Chinese warrior god named Xan Wu – so JXW."

And all four boys were suddenly silent. Was it possible that one of Li's father's nanoproducts or nanodrugs killed Jamie's dad?

Ey'tuka tried to rescue the situation. "Just because those nanoproducts or drugs or whatever might have been labeled with JXW does not mean that they came from your father's company."

Tsu'teye returned, "But I have to find out! Will you help me?"

After a few moments of brief questions and answers and ideas, Ey'tuka, Na'via, Mo'ata, and Tsu'teye agreed to pursue a double quest, or maybe the same quest doubled. They would try to find these JXW nanoproducts and Jamie's father's killer at the same time. So, the children's quest began.

Li Jiang was currently going to school at the Jinling School on Zhong Shan Road near the center of the very modern city of Nanjing. He was living with his Uncle Cho Jiang who was an industrial-electronic engineer and who was responsible for the Chinese branches of Jiang Nanotechnology International. Their headquarters was on Zon Da Road, also in central Nanjing; but their JNI factory was down the Yangtze River at Yangzhou. Li's uncle worked in both places.

JNI was an international corporation which had been founded by the three Jiang triplet brothers. They were fraternal triplets, not identical triplets. But they looked very similar in body size and facial characteristics. However, their personalities were very different. Dr. Chi Jiang was Jamie's father, President and CEO. He taught at the California Institute of Technology and worked at the JNI factory at Silicon Ledge in Temucula, just outside of Los Angeles. He was well loved by his students and was a super researcher. He was also the real brains behind the Nano-systems research programs and concentrated on the establishment and development of all types of new ideas in nanotechnology. He was also the Director of Nanomedicine, so he spent much of his concentrated effort in research using chemical models on the computer and animal models in the laboratory.

Dr. Jun Jiang, the second brother, was a chemical engineer and Director of Nano-chemistries. He was sort of a ghost as he was on the road most of the time. He was the courier who transferred all initial test Nano-systems from the USA to China, and the final tested products were distributed around the world, usually bypassing customs controls where possible. He maintained houses in Berlin, New York, and Nanjing. He also worked with the third brother, Dr. Cho Jiang in the startup efforts of these initial human test Nano-systems in the Chinese factories.

Dr. Cho Jiang was a Professor at Nanjing University and Director of Nano- multi-systems in the JNI. He was responsible for all new products which were assembled in the Seven Dragon's Gang's Parlors nearby Yangzhou, just east of Nanjing. Initial human testing was carried out at the Ming Ancient Castle Cluster in Jincheng City, located north of Nanjing. And more extensive human testing was carried out in Syria under the control of a Syrian agent. Chi, Jun, and Cho Jiang were very difficult people, but they all played a role in the success of the JNI.

Li knew about the two Chinese JNI locations, but he did not know about a secret Syrian location. So now he had to figure out how to get into the two Chinese factories. He also knew that he must obtain a list of all JNI nanoproducts which had been assembled in the Yangzhou assembly plant during the past three years. It might also be necessary to confirm that these same products were indeed later tested at Jincheng City.

The assembly plant was in the middle of Seven Dragon's Gang's Parlors. That is where the difficulty lay. That area of Yangzhou was the private fiefdom of the Seven Dragon's Gangs. He needed some help from the family, after all it was a family 'factory', and he was family who would inherit the JNI, some day.

One evening, about a month after the 4-packs's decision to investigate the nanoproducts of JNI, Li was eating dinner in his uncle's large 8 room mansion. He sat on the floor across the short table from his Uncle Cho. Uncle Cho's wife, Li Mei, and his two daughters, Lian and Xiu, always ate separately from the males. That evening the two males were eating xiaolongboa, special Chinese noodles, one of Li's favorite foods. Because the two usually ate alone, Li had recently worked his way into the good graces of Uncle Cho. So, they were not friends, but they were closer than most Chinese uncles and nephews.

During the meal Uncle Cho asked Li, "Do you still like your chemistry lessons at school the best?"

'Of course," Li responded. "I seem to have developed a special love for atoms and molecules." This was not exactly true, but he knew that was the answer his uncle wanted to hear.

"Your father said that he hoped that he hoped that you would like this area of knowledge because by using chemistry in nanotechnology an entire new world of science has begun," replied his uncle. "He also told me he hoped that you would find this knowledge area as a true challenge and join him in helping to solve the world's diseases. And of course, there are only two Jiang sons, you and your Uncle Jun's son, Lin Fu. The two of you will inherit all of the JNI someday."

Li did not know how to answer. He finally said, "I always try to do what my father wants me to do."

"And now how old are you?"

"I will soon be fourteen years old."

"Have you ever seen our Nano-factories in Yangzhou or Jinching City?" asked Li's uncle.

Li thought for a minute. He thought that here might be a chance to learn about those JXW numbers. So, he answered, "My father took me to Yangzhou several years ago when I was a child, but I did not understand anything. At the time, I did not even know what an atom or a molecule was. Now I even have an idea about Nano-tech molecules. But I know that I have much to learn. I would be very pleased if you would teach me."

Uncle Cho said, "I will discuss this with your father by e-mail this weekend and then maybe next week you can go with me to the Yangzhou JNI factory.

The following week Li began his new schedule. He went to school during the week, took his Wu Xing martial arts lessons on Monday and Thursday afternoons after school, and then on Saturday he went to the Seven Dragon's Gang's Parlors region of Yangzhou to the JNI factory with Uncle Cho. During the one-hour trip by the chauffeured JNI limousine, Uncle Cho briefly told Li the history of the Seven Dragon's Gangs and their Parlors.

"As you know Yangzhou sits on the southern bank of the Yangtze River, just down river from Nanjing. It was first settled in 485 BCE, and was a capital and major leading economic and culture center from 581 to 617 BCE under the Sui Dynasty, from 618 to 907 under the Tang Dynasty, and over the next 1000 years under the Wu Kingdom, Five Dynasties, Ten

Kingdoms, Ming Dynasty, and the Qing Dynasty. So, it has played an important role in Chinese history."

"With the Yangzhou riot in 1868, in which the British and Christian missionary offices and residences were destroyed, began the downfall of this history. From the Taiping Revolution until the end of the Communist Revolution in 1949 Yangzhou was almost destroyed by many battles and wars."

"It only began a major revival in 2018, but then it had been taken over by several mafia gangs who called themselves the Seven Dragon's Gangs. They controlled most commerce, trade, prostitution, gambling, and even legitimate businesses within various districts which they had divided into the Seven Dragon's Gang's Parlors. Anyone doing business in Yangzhou today must deal with them. We do. We pay several million US dollars each year for complete and permanent security for our factory. But then we don't need factory guards."

And as he laughed out loud, Li became nervous about coming here to work, or spy as was the real reason for coming to the factory.

"Now, do not forget! We are within two of these Parlors. One is called the Golden Dragon Gang which is run by Liang Wu. The other is called the Destroyer Dragon Gang which is run by Xiong Wu. The two leaders are not related. I know both of them. In fact, I think that none of the seven gang leaders are blood family. And they are not nice people. But they certainly give to me the feeling of total security. We are not producing something that they understand such as jewelry or guns. I don't even think they can pronounce Nano- technological-systems."

And he broke down laughing. This time Li joined him in his mockery of the illiterate criminals and hoped he would somehow be able to circumvent their 'security'.

At about 8:30 AM they arrived at the factory which occupied a major portion of a city block. There was a twelve feet high steel-razor wire fence completely around the complex of buildings. This was necessary as much of the area was filled with empty and deserted factories and warehouses. It was a harsh, desolate area. On could see why the factory security was in the hands of gangs. The JNI factory included three 3 floor buildings called Buildings B, C, and D, and one larger 5 floor building, at the front of the block, called Building A. Most of the nanoparticle construction laboratories were on the top 4 floors in Building A.

The outside of the buildings was built of old brick and some had most of their windows blocked. Inside Building A, one found the modern germ-free technology. Floors 2, 3, and 4 were for stage P2 germ free laminar flow rooms, hoods, and sterilized instrumentation for first stage nanoparticle construction. Floor 5 was for stage P3 germ free lamina flow rooms, hoods, and sterilized instrumentation for last stage nano-molecule construction and initial testing. He never learned what buildings C, D, or E were used for. In fact, he was only allowed in Building A during the times while studying in his family's Yangzhou JNI factory.

Uncle Cho and Li were driven through the front gate, exited the limousine, and then entered the front steel door of Building A. They went directly to Uncle Cho's office near the back of the building on Floor 1. This floor contained all company offices, a small library, and the computer-oriented Nano-systems design labs. Uncle Cho was going to have a busy day so he had arranged for one of his junior technicians to spend the day showing him around and answering his questions. They would meet back in his office for lunch.

The technician arrived and introduced himself, "My name is Wan San. I am twenty-six years old and have been working for JNI for the past three years. I work six months here in the labs and then study at Nanjing University for six months. I hope to receive my doctorate in physical-electronic chemistry in two more years. Cho Chiang is a great boss. And JNI is a great place to work."

'As you have been briefed, I am sure, my name is Li Chiang," responded Li. "My father is the President and CEO of JNI. Cho Chiang is my favorite uncle. Therefore, I am currently trying to decide whether I want to follow in my family's footprints. Maybe you can help me."

And this was the beginning of a close friendship which would be positive for both young men for several years. But it would inevitably end in disaster.

For that entire morning Wan showed Li around the factory. They put on surgical scrub suits to enter Floors 2, 3 and 4. However, Floor 5 was off limits to all but a select, very highly experienced group of technicians. He would never be allowed to go up to Floor 5.

Li walked from one lab group to another and asked questions, limited to his level of knowledge of course. But he did make a couple of more friends, and enjoyed learning how atoms and molecules could be assembled to produce new disease fighting instruments. He concluded that his family's company was doing good things.

At lunch time Uncle Cho took Li to the Emperors Club which was located on the fifteenth and top floor in a building on the Yangtze River. As he sat down and looked out of the floor to ceiling window, he saw the numerous ships in the river.

He was amazed and said, "Wow, I see oil tankers, trailer transports, LPG transports, automobile/truck transports, steel transports, grain transports, wood/lumber transports, military destroyers and transit ships, border patrol and customs ships, and numerous fishing boats. I did not know that there were so many types of boats. Are they all going up river to Nanjing?"

Uncle Cho laughed, "No. Some are going up river, some down river, some stop here, and most of the fishing boats are local. Historically, movement of people and life's needs took place by river in China. We have numerous rivers and these rivers have always been our mode of transportation and natural way of life. Even today, more goods are moved within China and to/from China by water, both river and ocean."

"Not our goods," smiled Li. We can put one billion of our nanoparticles in a water glass, seal it, and carry it anywhere."

"And with those one billion nanoparticles you can treat millions of sick people," said Uncle Cho. "That is one of the big plus factors in nanotechnology."

Li replied, "But only if the nanoparticles remain in good hands."

Uncle Cho suddenly spotted two business friends walking into the restaurant and waved to them. They came to his table as they were going to join him and Li for lunch.

Uncle Cho introduced them. "Li, Dr. Chou Lo is a physician who works with us on certain special cases where we are testing difficult nanoparticles. And Mr. Lou Jou is the President of the Yangzhou Charter Yachting Club. He has a lovely thirteen-year old daughter who I want you to meet someday. Mr. Jou has invited us to sail with him out into the East China Sea one weekend."

And he continued, "Li Jiang is my favorite nephew and is the only son of the President and CEO of our Jiang Nanotechnology International, also my big brother." And he smiled.

"Thank you," Li returned. "I would be happy to sail into the Sea. I have never even been on a sail boat. But you must teach me."

Looking Dr. Jiang in the eye, Mr. Jou said, "He is just as anxious to learn as you said. Let us go out to the sea on the last week end of this month. But we would leave from the docks here in Yangzhou. Can you find a way to get here from Nanjing?"

Li replied, "I will find a way."

The three men laughed and the group settled down into enjoying a pleasant lunch.

After lunch Uncle Cho and Li returned to the factory. Another young man was assigned to show Li around the Nano-systems design offices in Building A on Floor 1.

"My name is Wak Han, and I have been working for six years in nanocarriers design systems. I will show you how we use ideas sent from the USA, modify or alter those ideas, mock up the designs on computer, and computer test it with various human test tissues and organs. We can test any nanocarriers design on any human molecule, cell, tissue, or organ. Dr. Jiang said that you might work with us someday in the design offices. That would be very nice and I think that you would find it very exciting. I do. And I could help you at every step in your learning. First it will seem difficult, keeping in mind all of the bonding rules of different atom-atom interrelationships. But I know that you will learn quickly, and I am sure that you will soon be constructing more sophisticated nano- molecule designs than I can do. I will give you some books to read and we can work and study together."

And indeed, Li was being drawn into the challenge of putting atoms together to make molecules to make life saving drugs and substances. He asked and received permission from Uncle Cho to come with him to the laboratories on all Saturdays. Uncle Cho allowed him to come to work, but only in Building A on Floor 1 with the Nano-systems design people.

Li also knew that these same computers held the data that he needed concerning the JXW labeled drugs. He would thus work with those computers every weekend. If he could just find the proper file and download it for Jamie and the brothers, they would have successfully completed the first step in their quest. He could bypass the 'security' of the Seven Dragon's Gangs and their Parlors. He would simply bypass the gangs and ride into the factory with the boss.

147

Group Nano Systems

AN EMERGENCY MEETING IN 2031 was to be called. At shortly after 10:00 that morning members of the Commission had arrived. The uncle and nephew had closed certain of their files and opened other files in front of them.

All members were present, including Dr. Chi Jiang who was now a temporary member. Chairman O'Reilly began, "Thank you for coming on such short notice to this emergency meeting. We have several new happenings and we need to make some decisions as to where to go from here. We have finally had reasonable progress! And, indeed our killers have changed their program. This current year the MUSDs have continued on the fifteenth of every other odd month just as during the past three years, 2028, 2029, and 2030. However, we will show you the change in several patterns. Mr. Murphy, can you present the cases, please?"

Mr. Murphy spoke up, "First let me hand out copies of the MUSDs for 2031."

<u>List of VIPs Who Are MUSD Candidates – 2031</u>

Dr. Alvin J. Knowler, founder and President of Knowler Bio-Sciences International that markets a gene for alanine aminotransferase which when placed into wheat seeds allows the wheat to grow with sixty percent less nitrogen fertilizer, American, 58 years old, on January 15, Dr. Knowler, his wife, and five children simultaneously 'died' from ruptured kidneys.

Dr. Rodolfo Paletti, inventor of Ocean Acoustic Waveguide Remote Sensing (OAWRS) which involves a new sonar device that detects pockets of non-life with summer North Arctic Pole melts. This can be used commercially for one season for the growing of any fish or sea life so seeded there, Italian, 63 years old, on March 15, he, along with his wife, two sons, and three daughters simultaneously 'died' from ruptured livers.

Dr. Mary Smith-Johnson, CEO of Commercial Space Systems, Inc. As various governments moved from government support to private sector contracts for the exploration of outer space, she developed a fleet of shuttle ships to move supplies and materials to and from the outer space orbiting units, American, 54 years old, on May 15, she, her husband, three daughters, one son and his girlfriend simultaneously 'died' from frozen-ruptured small intestines.

Dr. Jansen Wilson, won the Nobel Prize for developing suspended animation system methodology using hydrogen sulfide which replaces oxygen in the cooled down body for indefinite periods of time, American, 66 years old, on July 15, Dr. Wilson, his wife, and three sons, simultaneously 'died' from pyloric sphincter rupture (exit valve/door of the stomach).

Mr. Alexi Stoleneskwi, founder and CEO of Water-Life Systems International which is a company that developed a plastic spray that prevents 100% heat convection, uses it to enclose gigantic blocks of ice, then tows the so wrapped ice through the seas to countries to be used for agricultural purposes, Polish, 49 years old, on September 15, he, his wife, one daughter, and two sons simultaneously 'died' from ruptured spleens.

[The deaths of a family of eighteen illegal Syrian immigrants in Kadıköy, Istanbul, Turkey; all deaths occurred near the same time and each died because of ruptured colons.]

Mr. Femer went to the front of the room and began: "Dr. Paletti was a tall, slim gentleman with a permanent sun tan and uncombable white hair and beard. His father was a fisherman in Napoli/Naples; Dr. Paletti's life was the sea, as when a child, he and the sea became one."

"In his books he states that he never missed a day in his life when he was not in or on the water. He was also a professional scuba diver and certified sea rescue coordinator. He owned three boats; one was for family pleasure; one was for river and sea coastal explorations; one was for deep water research. He taught at the University of Naples. And he was so popular that he had an abundance of students who kept all of his boats clean, in good repair, and in motion. With more than two hundred scientific publications and twenty-four books, he made a great effort to understand and teach about the waters in which our continents are situated, but islands under them continuously drift."

"He developed a solar device which he named the Ocean Acoustic Waveguide Remote Sensing system. This sensor device was capable of identifying Arctic ocean melt pockets which contained no life; these pockets could be used for one season of growth of any sea animal, predator free. He identified and sold the longitude-latitude locations to fish farmers who, rent-free, produced large quantities of fish and sea foods in a few months before the melt pocket closed. And he spent much of his time lobbying against commercial over-fishing in all oceans around the world."

"On March 2, he took his family of six across the Mediterranean Sea on their family yacht down the Suez Canal, and into the Red Sea. They had never been in this area and were going to spend a warm winter week, scuba diving on the coast of Sudan. All family members were certified scuba divers. They arrived on March 12 at the coastal city of Sawakin, loaded aboard food, drinking water, other supplies, and two 100-pound oxygen tanks with which to fill their diving tanks. They planned to be totally self-sufficient for several days so they could go to various coves and bays where the coastal shelf and reef areas would make for warm water March diving. The youngest daughter, Eve, had a large photographic collection of underwater plants and animals and wanted to include pictures from the Red Sea."

"On March 17, because their yacht had been anchored in Bayi Bay for three days and no one had been seen on board for the past two days, a local fisherman and his son stopped and tried to arouse anyone on board. The son climbed into the yacht, entered the terrible smelling central cabin and found many people dead and cold. Each member of the Paletti family was lying on a bed, on his back, bloated bodies, with eyes closed.

Upon seeing the morbid scene, the native boy panicked, ran and jumped into his father's boat, explained what he saw, started paddling away; and they immediately used their cellular phone to call the police. The police and other governmental authorities arrived in one hour. After a two-hour investigation and finding no obvious causes for the deaths, the bodies of Dr. Paletti, his wife, two sons, and three daughters were taken to a nearby morgue."

"The Italian embassy was notified. Autopsies could not be performed until they received permission from Dr. Paletti's father back in Italy. No permission was given. The bodies were flown back to Naples and finally autopsied four days after the determined time of the killing of March 15. The official cause of death for each was a ruptured liver; the abdominal cavity was completely full of blood."

Ms. Dapper interrupted, "What were the results of the police investigation? What about those air tanks?"

"Yes, there was a problem here," replied Mr. Femer. "Two large supply tanks were indeed found on board after the yacht had been re-docked at Sawakin. They were empty. All of the individual diving tanks were missing. The large empty supply tanks had been returned to storage for two days, and then refilled. The problem was that by the time we arrived there to perform a follow up investigation on March 21, many things were missing or unaccounted for. At that time, in carefully checking the books we learned that the two large refilled tanks were not the same tanks that the Paletti family had taken aboard their yacht. They had been switched. The tanks used on the Paletti diving cruise were missing. Obviously, there was a switch made on the yacht, probably after their deaths."

"Was there anything else missing from the yacht?" asked Mr. Thomson.

"Yes, their expensive underwater cameras, electronic components for computer picture analysis, and most of their diving gear were missing. Other people either boarded the yacht or the killers deliberately tried to make it appear as a robbery. However, no fingerprints were taken and the entire investigation was performed with less than western standards."

Mr. Ronny commented, "And I suppose no one saw them for the entire week as they sailed from cove to cove, anchoring here and there."

"I am sure that the locals must have seen them. But this area is very fundamentalist Muslim; I am guessing anyone who saw the non-Muslim foreigners said nothing so that they would not get into trouble with their neighbors later," responded Mr. Femer. "We tried to interview several locals in or near three of the coves where we think the Paletti family anchored. However, the yacht's log book was missing, so we cannot even be certain about these anchorages. The fisherman and his son who discovered the yacht had disappeared, so we could not talk to them. Final result, no locals saw or heard anything, not even a foreign Italian boat."

Dr. Bradmier spoke up, "May I ask Dr. Jiang a question? Can you give us an idea about how long a Nano system would remain intact in the human body such that it could still be detected? I assume that the several days interval from death to autopsy would be much too long. If tests had been run within two days, do you think that a Nano system could have been detected?"

"This is possible," Dr. Jiang replied. "Certainly, the shorter time the better. But what you have in these deaths is that there was a massive amount of bleeding which would cause major metabolic problems in the bodies during their death throes. The killers knew what they were doing. By creating this mass of coagulating blood, they allowed many new non-normal molecules to be produced which would have created many false Nano system tests."

There were several sighs around the room, but no more questions.

After waiting a few moments for more questions Mr. Murphy said, "Let us look at the Wilson murders. We can always return to the Dr. Paletti family again for additional questions or comparisons as they arise. Then he continued:

"Dr. Jansen Wilson was a stout, dark skinned, green eyed chemical pathologist at New York University Center in New York City. Fourteen years ago, he won the Nobel Prize in Chemistry for discovering that hydrogen sulfide could replace oxygen in mammals if the animal was cooled down to near freezing temperatures. It also protected against freeze damage of all types of frozen tissues. With this new technology many surgical procedures, such as transplantation surgery, were revolutionized; and human or near extinct animals were placed into frozen storage for indefinite periods of time. Several people with terminal diseases have now been so frozen in an attempt to wait until a cure for their specific disease has been discovered. This has created a major problem among conservative Christians as many believe that this is an infringement on God's rights."

"Dr. Wilson was the outdoors type. He loved camping, hunting, and fishing. And what Dad likes the entire family likes. So yes, the entire family of father, mother, three sons, one daughter, and two dogs, both German shepherds, were camping out in Canada. They had entered into the wilderness in the upper part of Parc des Grandes Jardins in the Reserve Faunique des Laurentides in Quebec on July 8. Later, during our follow up investigation, when talking with his colleagues we learned that the Dr. Wilson was the type who moved around a lot. The family would have not stayed in one location for more than a day or two."

"Nevertheless, on July 18, following a strong putrid smell, two naturalists walked into an area where there were no animals, probably because of the smell. They guessed it was human death. They placed cloths over their mouths and noses and entered the putrid area, found several tents, and checked the tents. One or more Wilson was laying in each a tent, on his back, eyes closed, cold and dead. They dialed 911, and twenty minutes later two helicopters delivered a medical team and a police team into a nearby clearing and an investigation of the Wilson deaths began."

"The investigation showed that the Wilsons had probably been at this location for five or six days. And from subsequent autopsy results the time of death was placed on July 15, so they had been dead for three days before they were found. It was a warm July and decay had fully set in. The deaths were caused by a ruptured pyloric sphincter, which is the valve or door that controls the release of stomach digested food entering the small intestine. Acid gastric secretions had been released into the abdominal cavity and digested areas of the small and large intestines."

"The Royal Mounties and their investigation team went through the campsite and surrounding area with a fine-tooth comb. No human footprints other than those of the family and the two naturalists were found. The area was full of bears but no bear tracks were found in the camp. There had been a heavy rain on July 14 and 15, so there should have been fresh tracks of many types after the July 15 killings. But the investigation report stated that the only foot prints that were found were from the two naturalists, two wolves, and many birds."

"Were the dogs also killed?" General Ronny asked. "Yes, they were shot with an old hunting rifle."

Dr. Bradmier followed up, "Did the Wilsons have guns with them?"

"That is a good question. No guns were found at the campsite. But, as part of our follow up investigation we talked with several of Dr. Wilson's camping buddies. They informed us that Dr. Wilson would never go deep into a virgin forest area, especially if bears were known to be present, without at least one 'bear' gun. They guessed that each of the boys would also have a gun, even if the hiking and camping trip did not have hunting on the agenda."

"Should we assume that Dr. Wilson had certain enemies who wanted him dead?" inquired Ms. Dapper.

Mr. Murphy responded, "I asked the New York City Police and the Quebec Royal Mounties if there were known criminal types in the forest areas of north and eastern USA and Canada. I received a negative response from both. As to personal enemies who wanted him dead. He did occasionally receive death threats. But the letters were not taken seriously, and there was never any follow up."

Mr. Murphy waited a couple of minutes as the group discussed these two different but similar family killings. Finally, he spoke up. "If there are no other questions, let us look at the next case."

He began: "Mr. Alexi Stoleneskwi, a Polish oceanographer was a tall, large boned, light skinned, blond haired son from a mixed Russian-Polish marriage. As a young man he purchased the patent for a new plastic with super non-heat convection; it prevented passage of heat and air. Blocking 100% of the air for house insulation could cause dangerous problems. But for packaging large blocks of Arctic or Antarctic ice, up to one million square feet at one time, and towing them to countries all over the world that needed fresh water, no problem. Twenty years ago, he established his company, Water Life Systems International. He then retired from his oceanographic studies and devoted full time to providing water to North

Africa and the Middle East. Mr. Stoleneskwi has made a fortune from his company such that he now provides much venture capital for start-up of high technology companies located in Poland."

"During last spring his seven-year old daughter entered a name in a Belkin Foods Company food contest. She entered the name of 'tomatoriffik" to describe catsup. She received the grand first prize. The prize was a one-week vacation trip to Palms View Resort on Waikiki Beach in Honolulu, Hawaii. The trip would begin on September 12, all expenses paid except travel, for the entire family. The daughter was the baby of the family; her two brothers were in high school and college. With pressure from the three hard studying children and a loving wife, father agreed to purchase the round-trip air tickets."

"They arrived, were picked up at the Hawaiian International Airport by a Palms View service bus and taken directly to their water front villa. This was the special six-star villa in the five-star resort. It was somewhat isolated from the normal villas. And it was surrounded by numerous flowering shrubs and many trees. It was a private, quiet area in the middle of a four million populated city. There were five bedrooms, one very large salon, three bathrooms, a TV and games room, and a large kitchen. They could cook, order from the resort restaurant, or go out to other restaurants. Taxis were readily available."

"From police reports that we read, the neighbors said that the family ate their meals everywhere. For the first few days they swam and water skied in the ocean, things not routinely done in Warsaw. The weather was 85 to 90°F with brilliant sunshine every day. The younger ones concentrated on the outdoor world. They were on the beach mornings and afternoons with special attention to obtaining nice suntans to take home to show their friends. Mom and Dad were more conservative and lived under the umbrella, but on the beach."

"According to police reports the week was going beautifully for the Stoleneskwi family, until Thursday, September 15. Resort neighbors all confirmed that the Stoleneskwi children did not appear on the beaches that day; in fact, no noise was heard from inside the villa. Perhaps they had gone sightseeing for the day, so no police checks were made."

"The next morning around noon two maids came to change the sheets; every two days this was done. As they entered the villa a terrible smell emanated from the bedrooms. It was so strong that one maid vomited and the other quickly ran to the security desk and reported the putrid smell. The security police entered, found all five members of the Stoleneskwi family lying on their backs in their beds, cold and dead, with their eyes closed. They notified Honolulu police and then immigration authorities. The bodies were taken to the city morgue, and American immigration authorities and the Polish consulate became involved. No autopsies were allowed without permission of next of kin; so, the bodies were flown back to Poland. In Warsaw routine autopsies revealed that each family member died about the same time. Cause of death for each was a ruptured spleen. Therefore, the abdominal cavity was filled with blood, which created the terrible smell."

'Were the other villas close enough such that physical disturbances could have been heard or detected? asked Mr. Thomson.

'In my opinion," replied Mr. Murphy, "Yes. Nearby villas were somewhat out of view, because of the vegetation. But the area is very quiet; usually there are only gentle ocean waves in the evening hours after sunset. So, sounds do echo. Because none of the neighbors reported hearing anything during the day or nights of July 15 or sixteen, we have to assume that the family members had to have been quietly subdued with drugs. Certainly, there was no loud physical resistance."

Dr. Von Eulenberg asked, "Did the resort security not see or hear anything during those two quiet nights?"

"During the nights of July 14, 15, and 16, there was a rock concert in an amphitheater which is located about three blocks away. We were told that the noise from the concert would carry into the villa area of the resort complex, but should cause minimal noise at the Stoleneskwi's villa directly on the water. The Palms View Resort security relied upon the concert noise as an excuse for missing the murder of five foreigners within their jurisdiction."

Mr. Tomson added, "I assume that there was no connection established with the Belkin Foods Company and the resort or the murders."

"None was established."

Dr. Bradmier said, "Dr. Jiang, I need to ask you something. Concerning the molecular mechanism of action, how could these Nano systems cause these types of deaths? Previously you explained that hitting the target was dependent upon the homing MoAB for the various regions of the brain. Would this also be true for the abdominal organs?"

"Of course,' responded Dr. Jiang. "Every military missile now requires a homing device."

And he deferred to General Ronny, who in turn nodded.

"All of these deaths probably resulted from holes cut into or digested from tissue/cell walls or membranes. I will make an educated guess, which we frequently do in the medical laboratory research world. The Nano system probably contained a Nano scissors, what we call a protein protease which degrades or digests structural proteins which are present in the cellular membranes. And this Nano scissors would be guided by a specific MoAB for each body organ: kidneys, liver, small intestine, colon, stomach, and spleen. Thus, these deaths are somewhat similar to the brain regions-initiated deaths that occurred in 2028, 2029, and 2030. It is very possible that the deaths we are discussing today could have occurred via one Nano destructor or Nano-scissors, six different MoABs, and six sets of multiple deaths. I am assuming that each family member received a similar Nano system. And the Nano system would have to be introduced into the body by way of an intravenous injection, not into the spinal cord."

"This is a very scary thing," replied Ms. Dapper. "These Nano systems can strike anywhere in the body and leave no trace; and you can be completely healthy when it happens. They are like deadly ghosts."

"No, they leave a trace," Dr. Jiang said. "We just do not know what to look for. For example, after a ferocious wind storm on a desert road you find a body. The body was obviously hit very hard by something, possibly run over. But there are no footprints or vehicle tracks. What do you do to try to find the killing mechanism? – a group of people, motorcycle, automobile, truck, train, helicopter, airplane. If an automobile, then what kind of an automobile? – Ford, Chevrolet, Toyota, BMW, Mercedes. If a Ford, then what kind of a Ford, what was the license number, who was driving. You might need all of this information to try to track down the killer from his killing mechanism."

"If you have some good information about the murder weapon, you have a better chance about finding the murderer. If you have no information about the murder weapon, you will probably never find the murderer."

Elizabeth Dapper, famous international lawyer though she was, shuddered. She was only afraid of snakes, but this new knowledge did not give her any comfort.

Dr. Von Eulenberg, "I am curious. Are the sudden VIP miracles still occurring on a bi-monthly basis, at random, or have they almost stopped?"

'Yes, they continue, but they are very difficult to recognize," answered Mr. Murphy. "Only when there is national or international publicity of the miracle can we investigate it. When we do investigate, we find the same thing; on the 15th of a month, a covered up medical assistance, sometimes a JXW numbered experimental Nano drug is involved, and indeed, full cure at least for the short period is recorded. We have never found a JXW numbered Nano drug associated with a death. In fact, we have yet to identify a Nano drug in a death that could be traced to the cause of death. We still do not know if they are one of the smoking guns."

Mr. O'Reilly commented, "We have been carefully evaluating these deaths and miracles for the past four years. With these last deaths I officially declare these to be murders. Mr. Murphy and I have some more thoughts that we want to share."

"All right," said Mr. Murphy. "The three cases that we have just looked at and the other two on our 2031 MUSDs show a change in the modus operandi of our killers. For example:

- Each complete family was on a vacation,
- Each family was in a foreign country,
- The deaths were not found for a couple of days,
- These deaths probably did not involve the brain as previously,
- An intra-body catastrophe was created which would produce many false molecules,
- These deaths all involved organs in the abdomen and large-scale interior bleeding,

"And comparing the deaths over the past four years, the killing pattern has changed from secret assassinations or single MUSDs to obvious murders of entire families. The time until the discovery of the deaths and autopsies has been deliberately lengthened; the internal body systems have been self-contaminated; and the scene of the death has been carefully sanitized. Why? Does anyone have any ideas?"

"The only macabre thought that hits me is that selling four or five Nano systems would be much more expensive that selling one Nano system; therefore, whoever is manufacturing these guys is getting rich faster, Mr. O'Reilly commented.

But there were no smiles this time or even comments.

The Quest Quickly Reaches Maximum Velocity

AFTER A COUPLE MONTHS LI had mastered the JNI computer filing system at Yangzhou, stole certain entry codes from his uncle's office, and successfully downloaded a copy of all the JXW numbered nanoparticles onto a flash drive. At mid-night Chinese time and mid-day USA-Europe-Africa time he set up a computer conference with his Colored Musketeer buddies.

He began, "Tsu'teye is present. Who else is present?"

In response he heard: Ey'tuka is present. Mo'ata is present. Na'via is present. He continued, "Excellent. I have very good news for you. I have a copy of the JXW numbered nanoparticles from JNI. There are more than fifty from the past three years. Now what should we do with the list?"

And there was complete silence, no answer. No one had thought Li would find the numbers, let alone what to do if he was able to obtain them. After all, it was just a bunch of numbers. As far as they knew there were no linkages with those numbers and the sudden VIP deaths. The newspaper articles simply mentioned the numbers and the deaths and the miracles in the same paragraph. It did not say the numbers caused the deaths or the miracles. They needed more.

"Let us consider approaching the authorities," said Ey'tuka. "Not reported, but I know that there is a Presidential Commission which has been investigating all of this for more than two years. Two of my uncles are Co-Chairman of this Commission. I have overheard them talking about the difficulties in finding hard evidence. What about if I talk to my Uncle Dagda? He is also a famous detective; I could ask him what we might do next."

Tsu'tey was the first to respond, "That is a good idea. I will fax the JXW list to Ey'tuka tomorrow. I cannot do anymore here without risking getting caught. Besides I do not know what else to look for. I am inside the factory which makes many of these nanotech systems. So, if I know what question to ask, I can try to find some more 'hard evidence'."

Na'via and Mo'ata did not have additional suggestions so they kept the computer conference short, closed off, and decided to wait until Ey'tuka talked to his uncles.

One month later Uncle Dagda was in Boston on business. Jamie had called and asked him to stop by their house when he was in town. So, Dagda and Jamie were now in Jamie's father's den/office. With his mother's permission, Jamie had moved into the den and began studying there a few months ago.

Jamie began, "Thank you for coming to see me."

"I would walk miles to see my favorite nephew," replied Uncle Dagda. And he gave Jamie an old bald-headed walrus squeeze. Jamie was becoming too old to still receive such shows of affection; but Uncle Dagda was not too old to still give them.

"Several summers ago, I went to Switzerland to a summer camp," continued Jamie, "At the camp I met three boys, one each from China, Turkey, and South Africa. We developed close personal relationships, call ourselves the Four Colored Musketeers, and talk as a group via a cryptic signaled computer conference system. The Turkish buddy is a computer whiz and special designed this system for us. We even use Avatar names, not our own; and we use a modified avatar language when in conference. Now we have learned that you and Uncle Jack are Chairmen of a Presidential Commission on Human Trafficking, but which is really investigating the sudden VIP killings and miracles which occurred, but there was no medically determined way of death was found. I believe that my Father was one of those killed. Is that right?"

And all Uncle Dagda could do was loudly respond, "Stop. Where are you getting all of this information?"

"Uncle Dagda, I can read the newspapers too. The Commission and what it is all about is not a big secret."

"All right, you are right. You have told me nothing that the public does not know. And yes, we think that your father might have been one of the victims. So?"

And that made Jamie mad. He responded, "If I told you that I know where the JXW labeled drugs were being made, would that be something new?"

"What? You must be teasing me. Our Commission has not uncovered that information, replied Uncle Dagda.

"Here!" Jamie shouted. And he gave Uncle Dagda the hard copy of the list of 55 JXW numbered drugs.

Uncle Dagda spent several minutes reading through the list. Finally, he asked, "Where did you get this list?"

And Jamie replied, "If you will be nice to me, and treat me like an adult, I will tell you everything. Agreed?"

What could Uncle Dagda say but, "All right."

Jamie sat back, took a pose of I am important, and began again. "This is a list of JXW nanodrugs which are made in Yangzhou, China. They are made in a factory owned by Jiang Nanotechnology International. I know because my Chinese buddy works there and downloaded this list from their secret files. I also know that you have several complete numbers from some of the victims with which you can compare. I think that you will find your numbers on this list." The latter statement was a bluff; but he was correct.

"I can tell that you want something," said Uncle Dagda. "What is it?"

"Yes. We want to help you find my father's killer," he answered. "This is our deal. We will work with only you, the rest of the Commission must not know, not even Uncle Jackson. You provide us with the types of deaths, and maybe some additional information as we need it; we will learn how the Nano systems are made, how they work, and the people involved. We think that there may be several factories in several different countries involved." Another of Jamie's bluffs, which also turned out to be correct.

Uncle Dagda thought for a few moments and finally responded. "You have a deal, on one condition; that you only do the spying. When we need to physically confront or arrest some people, we do it. I will not live with my favorite nephew in physical danger, nor any of his musketeer buddies."

Jamie quickly said, "I know how walruses take care of their children."

And they shook hands, broke down laughing, and did the mature walrus hug.

After Jamie received the list of VIP names and types of deaths, and also miracles, he initiated the next computer conference.

He began: "Et'tuka is present. Who else is present?"

In response he heard: Tsu'tye is present. Mo'ata is present. Na'via is present. "Good. I have talked with one of the Commission Chairman who agrees to our conditions. He has provided us with the list of names of death and miracle types. I will send it to Na'via by fax tomorrow. He can code it. Let me know if you do not receive it immediately. Now, in brief, how do you plan to use it?"

Na'via replied, "My brother is a senior technician in a nanotech company. I have already talked to him about a theoretical friend of mine who died of brain disease when he was treated with a nanocarrier therapy. He will inquire among his colleagues and let me know. He wants me to also go into nanotechnology. We can have additional technical questions that I am sure he can help find answers for us. He would never guess that I am working with a big shot Commission in America to solve world problems. I will not tell him."

"Hey, be careful about such talk," blurted Mo'ata. "Ey'tuka and Tsu'teye could get into real trouble if anyone found out about our efforts. Remember we are looking for killers. Do you think they would stop with just eliminating international VIPs? And they would not kill us? We would just disappear, forever. Stay cool."

"Yes, you are right, I am sorry," Na'via apologized.

Ey'tuka closed out, "That is all I have. The ball is in your court, Na'via. We want only goals." And the computer program was closed down.

The list of deaths arrived. Kef looked over the list which contained several deaths which were probably related to brain function. That is what some of those newspapers had previously reported.

On the following weekend Kef and his brother, Baryti, went to the seaside. They lived only a few houses apart and several blocks from the sea so they often went to their favorite café, the Blue Way, and had a nice lunch while overlooking the Atlantic Ocean. They talked for a while about football, would the Black Arrow soccer team win the national championship again this year? And then they discussed pluses and minuses of the science of nanotechnology. Kef was still playing football after school, but he knew that he could not make a career in sports, and his brother's descriptions of nanotechnology were always interesting. He understood that this new science was a young science. That meant it would grow a lot in the future, just like he was growing a lot right now. He was now fourteen years old and already approaching six foot.

Finally, Kef asked Baryti, "Have you found any answers to my question about curing brain diseases with nanotechnology?

And Baryti began a small lecture: "Nanomedicine usually requires two components – a Nano-activity-unit and a MoAB.

"First, a nanodrug is usually a molecule designed and synthesized to carry atoms; therefore, it is technically a nanocarrier. My colleagues told me that to affect any type of nerve or brain usually iron or other heavy metals are carried. When the iron atom enters the nerve cell it short circuits the nerve and causes a block of the electrical impulse, like the shortening out of a house's electricity when lightening is nearby."

"A MoAB is a monoclonal antibody which is a homing device that is attached to the nanocarrier. Only certain blood cells, B-lymphocytes can make these MoABs. We cannot synthesize them in a chemistry tube. I have never worked with MoABs, but we have an entire group of technicians who do no nothing else but make very special MoABs. If I understand correctly, you remove or extract a protein from the outer membrane of a cell or tissue or organ that you want to target. You inject this protein into a mouse. The mouse's B- lymphocytes make the MoAB. You take those special mouse T-lymphocytes, make them immortal, then they will grow forever, and now you have a small factory that continuously synthesizes and secretes your specific MoAB. You then fuse that homing MoAB antibody molecule onto your nanocarrier."

"So, to affect nerve cell function your complete drug is the nanocarrier plus iron which are fused to the homing MoAB. This complete drug will home in on only the target cells you want to kill, or stimulate, or affect in some way. It should not affect any other cell in the body."

Kef responded, "So it is like a guided missile that America uses all the time."

Hearing no response from his brother, Kef continued, "If I understand, no single technician makes the complete nanodrug. Is this right?"

"Correct. Let me think for a minute. There are several different types of technicians who: 1) remove pieces of the potential target tissue or organ, biopsies or sometimes complete human organs are required; 2) prepare the membrane proteins from these organs; 3) inject the mice and make B- lymphocyte factories in the mice; 4) prepare homing MoABs and test them; 5) design an appropriate nanodrug; 6) construct a nanodrug molecule; 7) test the nanodrug in free growing cells, for example brain cells in culture dishes; 8) fuse the nanodrug to the homing MoAB; 9) test this complete Nano-system in animals; 10) test this complete Nano-system in humans; 11) put it into the marketplace to sell as special Nano-drug-systems for certain nerve or brain diseases, or even other diseases; 12) repeat the process with changes in the atom carried."

"So, there are several technicians and usually several different laboratories that are required to manufacture one good Nano-drug system."

Kef was impressed. This was not simple. It was difficult and complex.

Baryti continued, "I am only involved in constructing nanocarriers. And I do this in a laboratory that is separate from the other laboratories. I would like to learn more about making the MoAb because it fascinates me. But I need a university degree and then I would probably have to get special permission."

Now it was Kef's responsibility to report to the 4-pair. A few days after talking to his brother he called up a computer conference.

He began, "Na'via is present. Who else is present?"

In response he heard. Tsu'teye is present. Ey'tuka is present. Mo'ata is present.

Na'via began again. "Our luck is running good. I have learned that one can indeed make nanodrugs which directly affect any cell in the body, including nerve cells and brain tissue. But the production or manufacturing requires many steps, many different technicians, many laboratories, and many tests in animals and humans. These various manufacturing steps can be done in different places in the same building or different places in the world. Yes, I said world. In other words, if ten steps are needed, they could be done in ten different countries."

There was no response and only silence after that last comment. How could they possibly find out about all of this? Or did they need to learn about each and every manufacturing step?

"One secret of nanodrug actions is a monoclonal antibody, called MoAB. A MoAB is a specially made homing protein molecule which is fused onto the nanodrug to allow the nanodrug to target one specific type of body cell or tissue. It is similar to the homing device attached onto missiles which make them guided missiles. So nanodrug plus MoAb make for a complete Nano-drug- system. That is what is used in medical diagnosis and therapies."

Ey'tuka asked, 'Could you write these many manufacturing steps down, as best as you can remember, and code-fax to me a copy? I think I understand, but I want to correctly explain it to Uncle Dagda. Then we can ask his advice as to what we should try to do next."

"Please send a copy to me too," said Tsu'teye. "Certainly, Nano-molecules are made in the factory in Yangzhou. And I think JNI has another factory in Jincheng City. I think there may be a third factory, which is kept secret, in Syria."

"But I am not sure. I also do not know what is made on Floor 5 of Building A where I work. Only certain technicians are allowed up there. There are the 3 other buildings within the factory complex that I have not been into. And the workers in each building are always kept separate. So, I need to do a lot more snooping around."

"Please be careful," Mo'ata added. "And if you can find the location in Syria, let me know. I will try to get information about it. Syria is not far from me."

"Is there anything else that I need to tell or ask my Uncle Dagda?" Ey'tuka asked.

"No? Well if anyone thinks of anything please code- E-Mail to me immediately because I will try to talk to him as soon as he is in Boston again; or I could telephone to him on his private line if you think it is necessary."

And the conference program was closed down.

A couple of nights later Li was lying awake in his bed. He could not sleep as he was trying to figure out some way to learn what work was being done on the top floor of Building A and in Buildings B, C, and D. He visualized in his mind a map layout of the JNI factory:

'The city itself is still trying to rise from the dead and modernize. With the Seven Dragon's Gangs in control this will not happen soon. And this area of the city is filled with many empty factories. The JNI factory has four buildings which occupy one complete square block and is encircled by that tall steel fence. It is very prison like in character. And because there are only a few windows in each building, it is very prison like inside as well as outside. I do feel like a prisoner confined just working there.'

'The workers in each building are always kept separate. Each building has several midi-buses, which pick the workers for that building from service locations all over the city, bring them directly to the door of their building, and then after work again pick them up at the same door and return them to those same service locations. Each midi-bus is electric and is re-charged from the many solar energy panels on the roofs of the buildings. Each building has its own small cafeteria where the workers are required to have their lunch. It does appear that there may be several different labs, or distinct work facilities within the factory.'

'Now how to find out what is happening in those buildings, and on the top floor of my building? The small library is in Building A on Floor 1 near Uncle Cho's office. It has a window which looks out into the back central courtyard between the four buildings where the midi-buses load and unload, and where delivery trucks arrive and unload. Maybe if I read and study near that window, I can monitor who and what and how people come and go. And I think I can pump Wan for some help at identifying the work going on in each building.'

The factory was currently on a six-day work schedule. So, for the next several Saturdays Li spent the morning in the design labs and the afternoons at 'book study time' near the library window. He noticed that the people in Building B usually wore nice clothes, jackets and neckties; deliveries to the building were mostly laboratory glass/plastic ware and chemicals – laboratory technicians. People working in Building D wore uniforms and the deliveries included mice, rats, animal cages, animal food and other supplies for animal care – animal caretakers. While the people working in Building C wore coveralls and frequently appeared outdoors carrying hand tools – probably maintenance of buildings and transportation systems.

The workers on Floors 2, 3, and 4 of Building A were technicians who made most of the nanomachines, especially nanocarriers. Floor 5 of Building A contained predominately doctor scientists and senior technicians. All workers in Building A ate in the same cafeteria, so he saw both the junior and senior technicians. These observations told him that Floor 5 was probably a laboratory for fusing the nanocarrier and the MoAB and for testing them in tissue culture flasks. Building A was therefore the heart of designing and constructing the nanomedicine projects.

One day Li drew Wan over to the corner of the cafeteria for lunch. He opened the conversation, "I want to thank you for all of your assistance in helping me to learn about nanotechnology and how to design nanocarriers. I will go to the USA in a couple of months and will attend school there for the next two years. Then I will return. I hope you are here so we can work together again."

Wan was at a loss to reply. Finally, he said, "I thank you for the opportunity to teach you a little. You learn so fast. I only show you and then you do it, usually better than I do it. You are a super student. Yes, I hope that I can work with you again. It would be my great honor."

'There is something that I have not learned though. I understand how to make nanodrugs such as nanocarriers. But how do these drugs find the target cells inside the body. I read that MoABs are needed. Is this true?"

"Yes, we also make them here in Building B. But that is not part of my job and we are discouraged from discussing science that does not directly relate to our current work effort."

"So that is why Building D has so many rats and mice, "commented Li. "We cannot discuss these things here."

Li looked Wan directly in the eye and asked, "Our factory in Jincheng City, where is it located?"

Wan swallowed, looked around, and finally answered, "Yu Tower."

So, Li understood that the Yangzhou factory had many of the necessary laboratories to manufacture or produce Nano-medical-systems. However, there was no building designed for human testing of these systems. He would have to make a quick trip to Jincheng City before he left for the States.

School was out for the summer, and he would soon leave for Los Angeles to live with his father and go to school at the JJ Mortin School in San Clemente. Hence, he needed to hurry and make a quick trip up to Jincheng City. He made reservations for 8:15AM on the express train from Nanjing to Jincheng City. It would take three hours to reach Jincheng City. He would then return the same night on the return express which departed Jincheng City at 1:30 AM. That would give him a long afternoon and an evening to explore the area where the JNI 'factory' might be located.

After settling into a first-class coach car, he ate some rice crackers and drank his morning green tea. He then opened his small folder on the history of Jincheng City, which he had downloaded the previous night. He wanted to learn more about the city before he arrived. He had a map so he could move around without getting lost. And he also had a six-inch long concealed knife, just in case he might run into problems.

Jincheng did not have a reputation of being a gentle city. It was born in agriculture, but was now filled with ex-farmers and ex-mountain dwellers as during the past few years the weather had been extremely dry, almost to the drought level. Families that had relied upon regular rains for survival were now in deep trouble, even to the point of coming to the city to find food.

The history of the Shanxi Province dated back several thousand years. The land is hilly, mountainous, and fertile. It is famous because the Shen Nong Diving Farmer helped the ancestors of the Chinese make the transition from the nomad way of life to pastoral living. It is only in the recent years that drought like conditions has persistently caused a partial return to the nomad life style. It is also famous as the major Taoist Center in the world with statues of the 28 tutelary gods of the 28 constellations of Taoism.

The Old Jincheng City has had a long turbulent political existence especially during the Ming Dynasty (1368-1644), the early Qing Dynasty (1644-1911). The First Ancient Castle Cluster in China was built here during these times.

There have been more than fifty castles in the area including several large structures: the Heshan Tower, the Double City Ancient Castle, the Yu Tower, the Guoyu Castle, and the Diyi City Castle. Wan had said the Yu Tower was the location of a JNI factory. And it was located in a very decadent part of the city, a long walk from the train station.

Yu Tower is a seven storied castle in Guoyu Town and is next to the Heshan Tower. Yu Tower is very large and is today filled with numerous levels of moderate to squalor living areas, apartments, shops, businesses, corridors and secret tunnels. It contains several separate cities on various levels. And it is a poorly lit complex of rooms and passageways that is not safe to walk through during daylight or night. 'This might be more dangerous than I thought,' Li said to himself.

As the train pulled into the station in Jincheng City, Li looked out the train window and saw his bodyguard waiting for him. Chu Chi-Yong, his martial arts teacher had contacted his older brother who was a black belt in Wushu. His name was No Chi-Yong. He lived nearby, and Chu thought it might be nice to have a friend in that Tower.

Li debarked, walked over to No and expressed his thanks for some assistance. "My name is Li Jiang. I am pleased to meet you. Your brother Chu Chi-Yong has been my Wushu teacher for many, many years. After reading about Jincheng City and the Yu Tower I am very thankful that you are willing to escort me today. He told me you were a black belt and that you defeat him nine times out of ten matches. Chu beats me nine out of ten matches. So, I guess I would have to fight you twenty times to even win once" And he laughed.

No Chi-Yong was 6 foot 4 inches tall and a solid 210 pounds. He gazed at Li who was 5 foot 9 inches, 165 pounds and responded, "I am honored to meet you. Chu has told me about you and your problem of finding the JNI factory in the Yu Tower. I have lived in Jincheng for the past ten years. And I know where it is located. But it will be most difficult to enter. It is best to learn about it from the factory's neighbors first. Then we can discuss if entering is necessary. And do not worry. If we fought twenty times, you would have to be lucky to win one time." And he laughed. The two of them were going to get along just fine.

No led Li through the new modern city into the old city, a long one hour walk through heavy people and vehicular traffic. And Li played tour guide as Li was interested the militant history of the city, and also the Taoist connections. As they approached the Wu and the Heshan Towers in the Old City suddenly living conditions became more dismal as the streets and most of the old stone buildings needed extensive repair, pot holes and falling roofs were common. Cars disappeared and transportation seemed to be only by bicycle, cart, and on foot. The street trash level increased remarkably. And suddenly ill-dressed people of all ages with old and dirty clothes appeared on many street corners and from the many narrow side streets. Street peddlers and beggars were also suddenly popping up as the two 'wealthy strangers' came walking down the street. They had indeed entered the slums of Jincheng City. Li was happy to have No beside him. Li began to understand No's previous suggestion that they begin by talking with some of the neighbors of the possible JNI factory which was on part of the fourth and the fifth floors of the twelve-floor structure. They entered the old stone castle-tower through one of the five gates, walked up to the fourth floor, found a small restaurant, and sat down to gather food for the stomach and food for the mind.

Over the next several hours the two of them explored the JNI factory neighboring restaurants, shops, and businesses on the fourth and sixth floors. They sought out employees, gave small amounts of money in exchange for information concerning about what kind of a factory was in this place, did many people work here, did street people often enter and maybe never come out, what kind of supplies did they receive, did strange noises come from there, any unusual events happen.

And then after interviewing more than a dozen neighbors, they asked the critical question. Did the JNI factory have any secret tunnels connecting it to the outside of the Wu Tower? The answer was yes. Everyone had 'private' corridors, stairs, elevators, and underground tunnels.

So, their many questions and answers were meaningless as certainly all clandestine activities would occur behind the guarded and locked entry doors and entry and exit would be via secret tunnels. They would have to go inside the factory rooms, or discover and check out the tunnels. Either effort would require a high degree of risk and take several days to plan. Li did not have the time, and No simply declared it to be too dangerous unless they had a group of armed commandos to assist them.

Li asked, "Do you think they have secret and possible illegal things going on inside the factory?"

"Very definitely yes," No replied. "And I think by now we have attracted the attention of some 'security members' of the factory."

"So today we can do no more, do you agree?

"We would be not just foolish but stupid to try to learn more without a military expert to help plan something. Besides, we have already compromised ourselves by asking so many questions to so many neighbors. It is almost midnight. I will walk you back to the train station. You do have a train to catch in a couple of hours."

Li did not respond, but when No got up to leave Li followed him. Inside this castle-tower was not a place to be without a friend like No, especially late at night. As they left the area No said, "Don't turn around but we have a tail. Do not walk faster but let us try to select streets with more lighting. We will be in the better part of town in a few more minutes."

No sooner had he said that when suddenly five young men appeared on the sidewalk in front of them, while three young men came up behind. These men did not appear to be armed, but they were indeed street toughs.

No said, "In one minute, turn around. Those three are yours. These five are mine. Begin with tiger and then switch to snake. I will use tiger and leopard. Remember we are not playing. Strike to disable. Now when I say go, attack."

Both of them crouched in the tiger position. Then No and Li both roared like tigers and they simultaneously attacked. The eight men were planning to attack, not to be attacked, and certainly not by skilled martial arts strangers. Within two minutes, there were eight hoodlums from the Old City lying on their backs. Some were unconscious, some were conscious, and one had even managed to get up and start running back toward the Old Town. Li and No were now jogging toward the newer part of the city and in the direction of the major business district.

As they entered a well-lit central shopping area, which was open all night, No put his arm around Li and said, "We are not even sweating, but I do need a cup of tea. Just across the street is one of my favorite noodle shops. Will you have enough money left after you pay me to buy a cup of tea?"

Li responded, "I thought only pet tigers eat noodles. Real tigers eat red meat. Since we just ate yellow meat, I guess we are certainly no one's pets tonight."

The two of them clicked an American high five and broke down laughing. They had indeed become lifelong friends. And No promised that he would 'watch' the JNI factory in the Wu Tower to try to find out just what type of 'research' that was happening there. The two new brothers exchanged e-mails and would talk when No learned something important. He had only lived near Jincheng City for a few years. But because he was the best martial arts teacher in the area, and the #1 in Wushu, he had many students and friends.

17

When is a Killer Not a Killer?

W HEN LI RETURNED HOME TO Nanjing, he immediately opened a computer conference with his buddies in the 4-pack.

He began, "Tsu'teye is present. Who else is present?"

In response he heard: Mo'ata is present. Ey'tuka is present. Na'via is present. He continued, "I have checked out each of the possible buildings of the JNI here in China to determine if they have different types of Nano-factories in them. Three of the buildings in Yangzhou probably manufacture nanomedical systems including MoABs. And certain heavily restricted rooms on the fourth and sixth floors in the Yu Castle in Jincheng City probably perform human testing. I did not learn anything about a possible factory in Syria. That is the best spying that I can do for now. I will go to Los Angeles this fall, live with my father, and go to school there for the next two years. Maybe I can learn something in the JNI factory in Silicone Ledge."

"I have some interesting news for you guys," Ey'tuka spoke up. My uncle recently told me that those JXW numbered drugs were not related to the sudden VIP deaths. They were related to several sudden VIP miracles. During the investigation of five of the sudden VIP miracles a JXW numbered drug was involved in each. The list from JNI that Tsu'tye obtained had all five of those JXW numbers. No drug of any kind has ever been found with any of the sudden VIP deaths. So Tsu'tye may have tracked down the drug factories which are saving people's lives, not which are killing people."

"Where does that leave us?" asked Mo'ata. Na'via commented, "With no place to go."

"Wait just a minute," Ey'tuka said. "I understand that these Nano-systems can cure or kill. Tsu'tye has done a super job of learning about a Chinese factory that makes these Nano-guys. He checked it out even though it was his own father's factory. As of now we do not know for certain how the JXW drugs are used, except that some maybe have helped to cure people. I will pass on Tsu'tye's latest information to my uncle. During the past few months I have learned that more sudden VIP deaths have occurred. And I still believe that Nanodrugs or Nano-systems are involved. Let me talk to both of my uncles. And as our original agreement, I am using none of our names when I talk to them. I only say my Chinese, Turkish, and African buddies. So that will at least partially protect all of us if things should become difficult."—They hope!

A few weeks later Uncle Daga dropped by to see his nephew. Because of Jamie's insistence, they always met in his father's den. It was quiet, comfortable, and secure. They sat and began an exchange of information.

Jamie went immediately into a summary of the several months of efforts by the Four Colored Musketeers. "So, we have identified drug numbers which match those numbers found in several of the sudden miracles for which it is claimed that no medical assistance was used during therapy. And we know, in some detail how these drugs are made and where they are made. What we need is one of the drugs used in one of the sudden deaths for which no medically identifiable cause was found. When you find a death drug, I feel certain it will also have a JXW number associated with it."

"However, you cut the cake. My team has been more successful than your Commission. Don't you agree?"

Uncle Dagda did not respond for a few moments. These children had indeed uncovered a lot of interesting hard data. And no one had yet been hurt. To date, it appeared that all JXW drug numbers were for drugs that had cured, not killed. He knew that Ms. Dapper would never recommend going to court on this hard data. But he would run this past her at the next Commission meeting in a couple of months.

He responded, "You fellows have indeed beaten us, 5 to 0 if we kept score. Did you find an American connection to this Chinese company which uses the JXW numbering system?"

"Of course," Jamie quickly answered. "It is the Jiang Nanotechnical International Corporation, JNI. The President and CEO is Dr. Chi Jiang who is also a Professor at California Institute of Technology. Their factory is in Silicone Ledge in Temecula, California. They are one of the leading nanotech companies in the world." Again, he was bluffing; but so far, his bluffs had all been correct.

Uncle Dagda had to catch his breath on this one. "I think you are so far in front of us I don't even see your tails," said Uncle Dagda and smiled, "All right. I will brief the Commission on all your findings. No names or source will be given. I will tell them this is a lawyer-client relationship that we have. I will try to convince key Commission members to place a legal monitoring ring around this JNI, follow their drugs and any courier personnel, and see what happens. We cannot go to the Chinese government yet. I will keep you informed of our progress. In the meantime, it would be good if we had a spy inside the JNI factory."

Jamie smiled, "We will see what we can do."

Attorney General and Commission Chairman Jackson O'Reilly and Co-Chairman Dagda Murphy were sitting at a small dining table next to the East Room in the White House. They were discussing the 4-pack team of spies that their nephew had put together.

Mr. Murphy spoke up, "Of course I am amazed that the 'kids' have found so much in such a short time. I first agreed to continue to help them in their quest because it really began as their quest. But if it should get rough, we need plans to place each of them 'out of danger'."

Mr. O'Reilly said, "You design such a plan and I will help you implement it. And we should probably do it the sooner the better."

Mr. Murphy knew who the other three Musketeers were. With his own security and investigation web reaching into most countries, and the blanket interception of wire and wireless communications thanks to the US Department of Justice and the National Security Agency, how could he not know? America would provide shadow security as was necessary.

Just before 1:00 PM Dr. Chi Jiang was escorted into the room. Introductions were made. Five minutes later President Jonathan O'Reilly entered the room and again introductions were necessary. They sat, Dr. Jiang across the table from President O'Reilly.

Mr. President had been briefed by his brother, so he understood why Dr. Jiang had been invited to this luncheon. "Dr. Jiang, we want to thank you for coming to have lunch with us on such short notice. But some interesting and troubling events have occurred, and we need your expertise and advice."

Dr. Jiang responded, "I sincerely thank you for your gracious invitation. I have only been in Washington twice in my life, and this is the first time in the White House. When Mr. Murphy invited me, one-hour ago, I thought he was playing games. But I am beginning to understand that this is not a personal lunch, but a professional one."

'Yes, we may have a major international problem on our hands, and we need your help," said Mr. President. "I will let Mr. Murphy explain the details of the problem to you, as we eat if you don't mind. I have a meeting with the Chinese President in 45 minutes."

Turning to the butler, the President asked that lunch be served.

As it was being served Mr. Murphy asked, "Dr. Jiang, would you please very briefly review your education and training for the three of us. Thank you."

Dr. Jiang spoke, "Of course. I was born in China but educated in the United States, married an American-Irish lady, she gave to me a boy child, but a few years later I lost her in an automobile accident. I was educated in universities in New York, London, Boston, and Los Angeles. The field of nanotechnology has always been my love. So, after being thoroughly educated in this new field by the best professors, and with the monetary support of your government, my research has blossomed. I fully believe that we will soon be solving many of today's unsolvable diseases such as .... "

The other three gentlemen at the table had previously received a file on Dr. Jiang and therefore knew his life history, but they wanted to hear it from the source. They wanted to hear the adjectives and adverbs that he would use in his spontaneous talk. They also knew about both of his American and Chinese companies. Today, they were really interested in his outlook on life, his projected role in science and medicine in the world, and his directional thinking in national and international politics. They were especially looking for direct or indirect connections or possible hidden reasons why he might be involved in any type of international conspiracy, conservative or otherwise. They could find none.

After a few minutes, Mr. Murphy spoke up, "It seems that you have been studying all of your life." And he smiled.

Smiling in return, Dr. Jiang commented, "I have and will probably never stop. When one is teaching bright young people in the classroom and laboratory you must run fast just to stay even with them, let alone get and stay ahead of them."

And he chuckled while the other three gentlemen smiled.

From recent experience with his nephew Uncle Murphy knew what the good doctor was talking about.

"The field of nanotechnology is so new, and there is so much to learn that I fully believe that I will indeed study it for the rest of my life. I consider my advanced students as my legacy. I will die someday, my discoveries will disappear into the waste bin of history, but my students and their trained minds, filled with my ideas, will continue long after I am gone; and then there will be their students, where many of my ideas will still be viable; and on into the next several generations of discovery, I hope. So, my ideas will exist long after me. And that is the way all research professors think. We may be mortal. But our ideas can become immortal, if they are truly nature's truths. Studying 12 to 16 hours a day 6 to 7 days a week is the price one must pay to find these truths. If the truths were already known, we would all be immortal. Not in my lifetime!" And he chuckled again.

The President looked Dr. Jiang in the eye for a few moments, and then he said, "We have a problem that involves nanotechnological systems, involving some secretly known truths. During the past several years several healthy, very important people have suddenly 'become dead', in just a few hours, and no medically detectable cause has been found for any of them. These deaths have occurred in several different countries. There is a Presidential Commission investigating this problem. So far, they have failed to produce any good leads. The Commission believes that nanotech machines are involved. Is such a thing possible?"

Dr. Jiang asked, "Can you please tell me what was listed as the cause of death for each?"

Mr. Murphy opened his briefcase and took out some notes; he read. "The sudden deaths were officially listed as heart failure, heart malfunction, frozen trachea, frozen esophagus, respiratory failure, massive bleeding from the carotid arteries in the neck, bleeding through the optic nerves in the eyes, brain failure, and brain coma. And apparently the deaths occurred after a few minutes to hours. Oh, and the victims always had their eyes closed. My understanding is that when we die our eyes usually remain open. How does one explain these things?"

"Let me think. I do have some ideas, but the dinner table may not a good place to discuss these possibilities," replied Dr. Jiang. "Each of these deaths have common control points in the brain. I would investigate these brain regions very carefully."

"In brief: At the top of the spinal column and connected by the spinal fluid are several areas of the brain which control all of the areas of the body that you just mentioned – these include the medulla oblongata region controls swallowing, breathing, heartbeat, blood pressure, and the wake-sleep center; the cerebellum region controls muscle and body coordination; the occipital region controls the eyes. As you can see, a neuronal short circuit of any part of these three regions could interfere with a variety of major life threatening processes."

"If you wish I would be pleased to write my ideas down on paper and send them to you. After you have had a chance to evaluate them, I could return, and we could discuss these ideas in detail."

"That is a very good idea, "said Mr. Murphy. "For several reasons we have been suspicious of brain involvement in these deaths, but we did not know how or where to begin."

"I have just one question right now, commented Mr. Murphy. "Could one nanotech drug control or interfere with the function of one or all of these brain areas? And if so, how?'

"Yes, "Dr. Jiang responded. "What we call a nanocarriers containing iron atoms would interfere with nerve function; and what we call a specific homing MoAB could allow targeting to each brain region or even selected sub-regions."

Mr. President looked at his brother and uncle, smiled and asked, "Would you consider joining our Commission which is working on this problem? It might be good for the Commission members to hear your thoughts. And I think that you could make a positive contribution toward solving this problem in the future. You see, these deaths are still occurring."

"I would indeed be honored to assist in any way that you think I may," Dr. Jiang replied.

"Excellent, we will discuss the possibility and let you know immediately," said Mr. President. "For now, let us enjoy the rest of this delicious Chinese- California chicken salad."

And catching the pun, they all chuckled.

An hour later in the Attorney General's office Mr. Jackson O'Reilly and Mr. Murphy were talking about Dr. Jiang. Mr. O'Reilly was analyzing, "Yes, he appeared upright and honest. We obviously need someone of his expertise to help us on the Committee. I sort of liked him."

Mr. Murphy came back, "I have several problems. He appeared or acted like he had not heard about the Commission; it has occasionally been in the news media and there have been implications of possible linkages to nanotechnology. He did not inquire about the sudden miracles, which are in the same news media. Also, he only talked about his university research; he did not mention his factories in Los Angeles or China. But yes, I do like him also. Maybe we will be able to see him better if he works on our Commission. But I still think we should place a legal circle around his factory and any couriers, especially to and from China."

"Before the next meeting, let us talk to Ms. Dapper about what type of legal 'observations' that we can employ," concluded Mr. O'Reilly.

A few months later the Presidential Commission on Human Trafficking adjourned in the conference room in the Department of Justice building.

Mr. Murphy had communicated with each member separately, explained the situation concerning Dr. Jiang, and received their approval to invite him to become a 'temporary' member of the Commission. Dr. Jiang was so invited and accepted. He was to bring his ideas concerning the possible involvement of nanotechnology in the MUSDs.

At 9:00, Chairman Jackson O'Reilly looked around the room, counted heads, checked faces, and opened the meeting. "Thank you all for coming to the fourth meeting of this special Presidential Commission. I think that each of you have met our new member Dr. Jiang." And Dr. Jiang raised his arm in a hello gesture.

"The goal of this Commission is unchanged. We are trying to understand and possibly solve the series of now more than twenty sudden VIP deaths all of which occurred in a medically undetectable way. We have also been attempting to keep track of and investigate a series of sudden VIP miracles, where it was claimed no medical treatment was involved. We think the deaths and miracles are linked."

"Over the past year we have had difficulty identifying the sudden VIP miracles because, unless the person was truly a known VIP, the news media do not pick it up, and we may have missed it. The best we can do is to say that these miracles are continuing."

"Certainly, the sudden VIP deaths are continuing, even into this year. In the packet in front of you is a list of the latest victims for the year 2030. Please look over the list:

List of VIPs Who are MUSD Candidates - 2030

Mr. Meridith Wilson, developer of the concept of Climate Cloud Engineering, creation of artificial and modification of natural clouds to control both the length of light per day and intensity of sunshine in desert areas of the earth, President of Climate Lobby, American, 39 years old, January 15, found dead of large brain embolism.

Dr. Haaston Van Klyberon, inventor of President of Tidal-Mills Corporation, harnessed tidal movements by using under water kites to produce electricity, Austrian, 54 years old, 'died' on May 15 of massive bleeding in the ear/neck area.

Dr. Jose Gonzales, CEO of SLFI (Synthetic Life Forms International), created synthetic life forms, especially algae which can very rapidly convert carbon dioxide to oxygen and hydrocarbon energy for fuels, Spanish, 60 years old, 'died' on July 15 due to respiratory paralysis.

Mrs. Patti Gerbero, Organizer and President of the NGO entitled Green, Water, and Life (GWL) which promoted growing large green leaf vines down the sides of tall buildings to provide both long term heat and cooling systems for that building, American, 42 years old, on September 15, bled to death through the optic nerves in the eyes.

Dr. Peter Jerkins, CEO of SVEA (invented solar-voltaic plastics which can be placed on airplane exteriors that will provide all necessary energy during flight, Australian, 63 years old, on November 15 died of a ruptured coronary artery.

"We have the most complete data on Mr. Wilson, Dr. Gonzales, and Mrs. Gerbero; so, we will review these MUSDs today. I will give you a minute to look those three deaths over more carefully."

After a couple of minutes, he asked, "Anyone need a little more time?" Not hearing any such requests, Mr. Murphy began:

"Mr. Wilson had lived and worked in the White Sands area near Alamagordo, New Mexico most of his life. He was currently living in a small one-bedroom rancher on a flat one-acre plot with only a couple of trees. The nearest neighbors were some 500 feet away."

"Over the years it had become obvious to him that cloudy days were much more comfortable that beautiful sun shiny days. In the very dry summer, the Navajo Indians always attempted to 'convince' clouds to 'make' rain. He thought that if these natives had been doing this for centuries, why should our professional weather people not be able to 'make' clouds 3, 4, or 5 days each week. He calculated that this would save more than 80% of the water that was now evaporating each summer. This would be a gigantic boost for the people and the numerous commercial farms in the state. So, he simply organized the voters of New Mexico, and voted in like-minded Congressmen in Albuquerque and Washington. This idea soon spread to other southern states which have hot and dry summers; and then countries with large deserts began promoting the idea. Today climate cloud engineering is a common way to control summer heat and evaporations all over the world."

"Mr. Wilson was a confirmed bachelor. On the night he became dead he was alone. The following day a male friend who frequently came over to Mr. Wilson's house to play cribbage, found him in his bed. He never locked his door because he had a large German shepherd dog. However, the dog was found behind the house. He was also dead. He had eaten some poisoned meat. A routine autopsy by local authorities found no medically explainable cause of death. There was indeed a large blood clot on the back of his head, but how it happened was not determined. It was not due to an external physical blow. It was caused by some unexplainable internal parameters."

"So, we have a simple case of a man 'dying' and no causes, no witnesses, no motives, no way of knowing how or why. His eyes were closed. He was either awake when he died during daylight hours, or he died in his sleep, but his eyes somehow were not open – unexplainable."

Dr. Jiang asked, "What tests were run during the routine autopsy?'

Dr. Batley answered, "I can answer that for you. Each state has slightly different protocols for autopsy analysis. The state of New Mexico performed visual anatomical dissections and simple blood and urine tests looking for alcohol or other incapacitation drugs, and possible analysis for normal chemicals such as sugars, blood proteins, lipids, creatine/urea, acid/base, and so forth. They would not perform more sophisticated tests such as HPLC, high precision liquid chromatography or GLC, glass liquid chromatography."

"That is what I suspected," responded Dr. Jiang. 'No routine tests would ever pick up any type of nanodrug or nanoparticle. Nor would directly using those listed tests be of any help. That is like trying to find a marble in the ocean. You need to strain the ocean first."

Mr. Murphy added, "I would guess that most of these sudden VIP deaths were autopsied without any special pathological testing."

"What would you recommend if you suspected a Nano-system?" asked Dr. Bradmier.

"You would have to first separate, concentrate, and then analyze," answered Dr. Jiang. "For example, you might begin with some type of vacuum ionic filtration system, VIFS. Then perform a freeze dry of several fractions from the VIFS. Now individually concentrate the many freeze-dried fractions with micro liquid suspensions. Only then they can be analyzed via HPLC or GLC or even with a Nano-analyzer."

Several members of the Commission were rapidly writing down this information. Already they were learning from Dr. Jiang.

Mr. O'Reilly said, "Thank you. During the entire time of our investigations we have been ignorant of these special autopsy procedures. We will be certain that they are included in the 'routine' pathology of any future MUSDs." And he nodded to Mr. Murphy and Dr. Batley.

"I assume that the local sheriff's office made a careful check of the area around the house seeking any evidence outside or inside, such as footprints and fingerprints," inquired Mr. Thomson.

"They did the usual, the minimal. The police found nothing." Mr. Murphy responded. "After all Mr. Wilson was a simple man. He was not a local hero. He was an international hero who had been forgotten. He made his contribution to the idea of climate engineering over ten years ago. Why kill him now? Was this a belated punishment of some kind? I really do not understand."

"Were there any relatives or locals who might have had a reason to kill him in this way?" again Mr. Thomson was inquiring

Mr. Murphy responded, "The police investigation did not look into this. And because Mr. Wilson was not a high-level VIP we did not get onto the case until about 3 weeks later. There were no other MUSDs on January 15, 2030. Indeed, he was a very high-level VIP a few years ago, but not today."

Dr. Jiang spoke, "If a Nano-system was used in this killing it would have been a very expensive murder weapon. The Nano-systems that we sell begin at $250,000."

That brought the Commission members to a round of murmuring. There were certainly cheaper ways to kill someone, whatever your reasons. This was especially true for a bachelor living by himself in a desert.

Mr. Murphy asked, "Are there any other questions? We can return to Mr. Wilson later if anyone wants to do so."

Hearing nothing, Mr. Murphy asked Mr. Femer to present the results of the next investigation of Dr. Jose Gonzales.

Mr. Femer began:

"Dr. Gonzales was a Professor at the Complutense University of Madrid, Spain and a member of the Royal Society of Physics and Mathematics. He was a good friend of Dr. Fedrico Mayor Zaragazo, past Secretary-General of UNESCO. The two of them were together the night that Dr. Gonzales was 'killed'. But first:"

"Dr. Gonzales had been experimenting with creating new biological cells which would reproduce themselves, in other words create new forms of life. For many years he had been using atoms and simple molecules to synthesize DNA/genes in a test tube. He then placed his newly made DNA/genes into cell- less flasks with growing solution at 35^{0}C. He placed these flasks under various plant grow lights. Eventually plant like cells formed and began to multiply. He had known the short DNA/genes sequences for algae, so that was the DNA/genes that he had placed into the flasks. And yes, he was successful in creating new algae cells from naked DNA/genes, not from other algae. He created new life forms. Not being satisfied with this, he continued to create more algae in other experiments until he had created super algae that could convert carbon dioxide into oxygen and hydrocarbon precursors one thousand times more rapidly than normal algae."

"In summary, Dr. Gonzales created not just new life, but he created a new life form that helped clean the air of carbon dioxide, placed into the air oxygen, and produced energy which could replace hydrocarbon fuel. All of this was accomplished using only the energy from sun. It is expected that he would have received a Nobel Prize for this discovery in the next year or two."

"This is the best that I can do with this complicated science; so please do not ask me any questions about DNA and genes as I will simply say I do not know and pass the question to Dr. Jiang."

And the group, as one, turned and looked at Dr. Jiang. Suddenly he was beginning to grow in demand; only he knew this biology and chemistry stuff. Dr. Jiang just smiled and nodded.

'To continue, let me turn to the night of July 15, 2030. Dr. Gonzales was staying for a week with Dr. Zaragazo in Dr. Zaragazo's seaside house just south of Valencia. He had done this several times in the past as the two had been friends for many years. It was a family estate located on a high mountain side, on Cape de la Nau, with a gorgeous view of the Western Mediterranean Sea, Spain's Levant, and a direct drop of more than 200 feet to the sea from the edge of the estate. The sea side road into the area was like a snake which reached elevations up to 500 feet and down to sea level. It was difficult to drive this twisting and turning road in the daytime. At night it was quite dangerous."

"July 15 was a Saturday and they were hosting a weekend party with nine guests. The house was large enough that everyone could stay over. Late in the evening they began to run out of white wine. Dr. Gonzales volunteered to drive down to Alacant, about ten miles away, and pick up some more good Spanish wine. Dr. Zaragazo would stay and continue to entertain. According to the guests Dr. Gonzales left the house around 10:30 PM. He drove his red Fiat 250A. Before midnight, they noticed that Dr. Gonzales had not returned. Dr. Zaragazo and several of the guests became worried."

"First they called Dr. Gonzales' cell phone. No answer. Next, they telephoned to Mario's General Store in Alacant. Dr. Gonzales had been there, purchased ten bottles of various wines and left, perhaps an hour previous. Dr. Zaragazo became very concerned. The road was difficult, and he suggested that several of them drive down toward Alacant and look for Dr. Gonzales, he might have had car trouble. In two cars, Dr. Zaragazo and three of the male guests started driving very slowly toward Alacant. After about fifteen minutes they saw skid marks on a sharp outer curve on the sea side lane. They stopped and looked down toward the rocky shoreline. There was enough moonlight to see a red car at the bottom, smashed on the rocks, half in and half out of the water. They immediately called the police and an ambulance. It took about more than an hour for an ambulance helicopter to retrieve Dr. Gonzales body and take it to a hospital in Valencia."

"This entire on-site scenario was carefully documented and verified by the Spanish National and Valencia police authorities. The following day, our SAATO people from Madrid, via President O'Reilly's assistance arrived and were allowed to follow the investigation at the death site and the autopsy in the State Emergency Hospital in Valencia."

"In the beginning it was assumed that Dr. Gonzales' death was a driving accident. However, a very careful and extensive autopsy was performed. Dr. Gonzales was a very famous Spanish VIP, and the President of the United States had a special interest in the case. All normal and special laboratory tests were performed. Dr. Gonzales had many bruises, but because he was still locked inside his seat belt there were no physical blows considered to be life threatening. However, the car's crash balloons did not inflate. The car ended right side up and Dr. Gonzales' head was up and out of the water in the open air as the windows were down. But cause of death was determined to be respiratory paralysis. His lungs were literally cardboard stiff. A form of rigor mortis had settled in the lungs but not in the rest of the body. And his eyes were closed. How could such a thing happen? I don't think that this type of death could happen because of an automobile accident. We had orders not to mention the possibility that some Nano technology might be involved. And we followed these orders."

Dr. Bradmier asked, "Did they perform any type of special test such that they might have found some type of Nano-technical-system in Dr. Gonzales' body?"

Dr. Jiang spoke out, "At this point in time there is no single test or group of tests that can be performed in clinical diagnostic laboratories which indicate the presence of a nanotech component. I will discuss this in more detail later in our meeting."

"Good," replied Dr. Bradmier. "I am supposed to be Director of Science and Technology for the USA and I know very little about these Nano-guys, certainly not enough."

"Did they completely eliminate the possibility of a second party involvement in the automobile accident?" Dr. Von Eulenberg asked. "Such as, could Dr. Gonzales' car have been stopped on the road after he left this store, could he have been accosted, could he have been injected with a nanodrug, and then could the car have been run off the cliff imitating an accident? From our previous cases we have begun to understand that spinal injections can heal in a few hours. If the killer knew this, he probably assumed that the car and body would not be found until the next day, and by then the injection site would have completely healed."

"I personally talked with several of the Spanish police detectives," Mr. Femer answered. "And I know that they thought about the possibility of second party involvement. I watched them search the road bed around the accident site all the way back to Mario's General Store, about three miles. No off - the road car tracks were found. And, of course the road was asphalt."

"Is it possible that any of the guests were involved?" Mr. Thomson asked.

Mr. Femer responded, "We had permission to listen to each of the video- audio recordings, of the investigative interviews of the guests and three estate servants by the police detectives. And we obtained a list of all the guests, and their current work and home addresses, who were at the overnight party at Dr. Zaragazo's house. During the past few months we have been running background checks on each of them. To date we have found no information which would allow us to suspect any of the guests, servants, or the host."

"Are there any other questions?" asked Mr. Murphy.

He waited a few moments. Hearing none, he began.

"Let us review our last case for this meeting, Mrs. Patti Gerbero. She was a hobby ancient historian, and even wrote several books on Persia. One of her favorite subjects was the Hanging Gardens of Babylon. She was enthralled by the idea of a desert city growing vegetable and flower plants down the side of its building walls, or in major cities using such ideas to provide a natural form of heating and cooling for tall or mountain side buildings. When Babylon was destroyed by wars and earthquakes, this idea of wall-hanging gardens became a lost form of agriculture-architecture."

"In the 2,300 years following the destruction of one of the seven wonders of the ancient world, no single building or city in the world had ever tried to duplicate this phenomenon. And Mrs. Gerbero decided it was time to re-awaken the world to these beautiful and very practical green efforts. So, she organized an NGO entitled Green, Water, and Comfort. She received a lot of publicity on the subject because she had received a $450 million government grant to promote her ideas. The money was used to build two new buildings, in New York City and Los Angeles, with exterior vinyl tubing frameworks that served as support systems to grow large green leaf vines; a water drop supply, electronically controlled, hence would guarantee correct amount of water supply. Within 5 years of completion, both 'green' buildings, were providing 'free' energy for heating and cooling all year round. Plus, the cost of construction of the building's exteriors was reduced by 75%."

"Mrs. Gerbero lived in Montebello, New York, about a 45-minute drive to New York City, with her two children and husband. Her husband, William, worked at HSBC Bank in Manhattan. And during the day both children, Mary and George, were in Montebello Middle School. The family lived only two miles from the large New York State Park where they frequently went for hiking and picnicking."

"Golden mushrooms were a favorite of hers. And in September she knew that they were plentiful in the Park just north of Lake Sabago in the southern part of the seven lakes region. On September 15, she had wanted to add mushrooms to her beef casserole for dinner. So, she decided to run out to the park and gather very fresh mushrooms. It would only take a couple of hours. She left a note for the children as to where she had gone and when she would return. She placed the note on the table under the pencil. However, after she had gone out the door, the pencil rolled off the table and the note fell into the waste basket. Let me say at this point that this latter event was only a guess because the next day the pencil was found on the floor and the note was found in the waste basket. It is possible they could have been put there."

"Nevertheless, Mrs. Gerbero was not home when the children returned from school around 4:30 PM, and yet not home when the husband returned from work near 6:30 PM. William started calling around to friends. The two children, Mary and George, went house to house in the neighborhood asking if anyone had seen their mom. Her car was missing. At approximately 7:05 PM, they called the police and reported Mrs. Patti Gerbero and her green 2003 Ford Sunset, New York plate FZ2952 were missing. Notification bulletins went out to all state offices. As is their pattern, the State Park police drive through the park at closing time, 9:00 PM, to be certain everyone is gone. They spotted Mrs. Gerbero's car, radioed it in, and a massive 'woman' hunt began."

"The search lasted for two hours, no luck. So, they brought police search dogs into the very densely forested area. The dogs found her in half an hour. She was not breathing, was lying on her side, her eyes were closed, her face was full of blood, ants and other insects were already crawling in and out of her mouth and nose. The police managed to cover her, place her on a stretcher, carry her almost two miles, put her into the ambulance, and took her directly to the Spring Valley County Hospital. The husband and children were taken home."

"Mrs. Patti Gerbero was on our list of VIPs to monitor as a potential MUSD. Our computers picked up her death the following afternoon. Our Attorney General Chairman immediately notified the New York police that they would now directly cooperate with SAATO during the investigation and a complete autopsy of this death would be performed."

"I took my five-best people with me and we went into the woods just north of Lake Sabago. The forest was all natural, very few paths. We found numerous tracks made by many animals, but only a few people. We took pictures and made cast prints of the human tracks; they are on file if we should ever find a suspect. To date we have no suspect. There was no evidence of a fight at the death site. But the mushroom site was a least a half mile further. We were informed that a basket filled with fresh mushrooms was found at the site. Later when the mushrooms were tested, several were found to be poisonous. However, before we arrived, the case was being written off as death due to mushroom poisoning."

"Our investigative results yielded a few additional pieces of information. 1) The mushrooms in the basket did have mushrooms from the north lake location, but the several poisonous mushrooms were from somewhere else; they were a day old and probably later added to the basket by someone. 2) At the death site the tracks of Mrs. Gerbero came from the direction of her car, not from the mushroom area. 3) The only other human prints around the death site were made by three children, probably near ten years of age. No adult human tracks were found. 4) The mushrooms were still covered with dirt and mud, not a tasty mouthful; no dirt was found in the mouth of the dead Mrs. Gerbero. 5) The analysis of her blood and urine did not reveal any type of toxic substances including known mushroom poisons. 6) No known mushroom poison causes bleeding of the optic nerves in the eyes. 7) When the police found her, about 6 hours after she was reported missing, her body was already cold."

"It was not death due to mushroom poisoning. If you will remember the death of VIP Dr. Ellyn Rinkler in the Sahara Desert in September 2029, this death has many similarities. – the month of September – nature setting – bleeding to death through the eyes – the difference is desert versus forest."

"I assume no one saw Mrs. Gerbero, going, coming, inside the forest, or even late in the afternoon," said Mr. Tomson.

Mr. Murphy confirmed. "Mrs. Gerbero was seen only by one friend as she was driving to the park in mid-afternoon. No other reported sightings."

'And I assume that you checked this friend out and found her not to be a potential suspect," declared Mr. Tomson.

"The friend was a social friend of Mrs. Gerbero for many years." "It would still be a good idea to check this friend out."

"We did and found nothing to raise our suspicions of her."

"Ms. Dapper asked, "Did you check to see if the husband was at work all day that day?"

"He was."

"How many entrances and exits are there into the park?" asked Mr. O'Reilly. "Many. At least a dozen."

"And we had an extensive analysis of her blood performed. But from what I think we are going to hear in the next hour, I believe that any extensive analysis will not detect any type of Nano-technical-system in the body. We need special tests that are not yet routinely available in forensic pathology labs." Mr. Murphy replied. And then he continued.

"If there are further questions let us discuss them after a coffee break. I'm sorry but my elderly throat is becoming hoarse from talking too much."

No one disagreed so the meeting adjourned thirty minutes.

18

It Begins to Get Rough

THE JAGUAR CONVERTIBLE WENT FLYING down Morrissy Boulevard toward South Duxbury, Massachusetts Bay off to the left as they passed every car they could. For every green car they passed Jamie got one point, for red cars Tim Walker received one point, and for white cars Jerald Klosky was credited with one point. The loser had to pay for dinner tonight at the Bay Side Retreat Restaurant at Wallaston Beach. Just beyond was Merrymount Park where tonight was the big Friday night Sound Off. They had reservations for the Sound Off, and then the three of them would spend Friday and Saturday nights at the nearby beachfront Stars Light Motel on Sea Avenue. It was predicted as the last 90°F weekend before autumn weather hit the Boston area.

The car belonged to Klosky's big brother. It was borrowed for the weekend. And big brother would find this out when he returned from his New York City weekend. Klosky was sixteen and was driving. Oh, how he was driving.

He shouted, "I love the Romp and Stomp Band and Reida. She is my black bombshell. I am glad they are the last act tonight so we can just stay up and swim in the ocean for the rest of the night."

Jamie, riding shotgun shouted, "Cara and Mara are the blonds of the night. After them I will not even be interested in Reida."

And Tim, from the back seat shouted, "You guys and your dream girls. They would not notice you if they were sitting on your laps." Ha!

Jamie came back, "Just because Klosky and I have real girlfriends back at school; you shouldn't be jealous if we want something bigger and better." And then they all laughed.

It was only 5:30 PM, and the Sound Off started at 9:00 so they went to the hotel, checked in and headed out the door onto the beach. There was nothing like a good cold swim to relieve the tension of the past week. They each had just finished major exams; and even when you think you did well, exams have a way of letting you know that you could do better.

The physical one, Klosky, was the first into the water. The waves were high, and the tide was coming in, so he was out to the two-hundred-foot marker before his schoolmates even got their feet wet. But they soon caught up with him. They were all excellent swimmers, so they swam the incoming waves for a couple of hours and forgot about books and school.

Each was a growing boy and they had just worked up an appetite. The next anti-school venture was the Bay Side Retreat Restaurant which served only sea food. They had the unfortunate task of choosing between New England clam chowder, raw oysters, clams, scallops, mussels, lobster, crabs, octopus, squid, and then there was the fish such as salmon, haddock, tuna, cod, sea bass, swordfish, sole, and halibut. There would not be time for vegetables. But they could eat there again tomorrow. They agreed to each select different foods; in this way they could share and try everything, almost. Only boy sized stomachs saved the restaurant from running out of food.

They played at becoming whales, when Jamie asked Klosky, "Klo, are you going to follow your father into law?"

Klo replied, "I want to be a trial lawyer. I want to get the bad guys, or the good guys who have gone bad. I think there are more of them anyway. I have a cousin who is a trial lawyer. I have gone to court to watch him several times. The most exciting case is when they are trying a banking CEO for fraud and embezzlement. The guy is officially making five hundred thousand dollars per year, and he owns ten houses in ten countries." And he eyed each of his buddies.

"If the guy had only three houses in three countries, he would not have been caught in the first place. That is what I love about the good guys turned bad guys. They have a disease called GREED."

"And that is why I love my music," Tim spoke up. "Musicians don't care about money as long as they can do their thing. I am making my parents happy by finishing high school. What they will soon learn is that I am not going to college to business administration. My father built his electronics import company, I-International, from scratch. That is what he wanted, so he did it. And now he is fifty-five years old and looks eighty years old. I am not even sure he would be around to see me graduate from six years of college. I really do not want to follow my father into his business world. He knows but does not accept my decision."

"Fortunately, I have an older sister who likes that stuff. She is thinking in that direction. But there is one problem. Dad thinks women belong in the home, not in the executive office. What am I to do? Tim continued."

"Maybe your father will have his heart attack before you graduate from high school and then you can just help your sister take you father's place." And he smiled.

"I do not know what I want to do," said Jamie. "At least you, Klo, know what you want to do. And Tim knows what he does not want to do. I do not know either. I lost my favorite consultant a couple of years ago, my father. Since then I have much trouble even thinking about my future. It is sort of like; whatever happens I will accept it and do it. That is not so good is it?"

And the conservation, concerning the advantages or disadvantages of knowing or not knowing about where you want to go and how to get there, or where your parents want you to be in life, began. And there was always the unanswerable question as to why parents think they need to be involved in helping make your life's decisions. Until suddenly they realized it was 9:30 and the grand music was going on without them. So, they quickly paid the bill, ran out to the car to the park to the blood moving sounds.

As they sat on the second row from the concert stage, the noise level was such that talking was not possible. Jamie and Klosky were in musical mania. But their timid roommate, Tim, was thinking, 'A Boston Pops or a Mozart concert would have been better. I play the cello. The cello has been common in Europe for hundreds of years, the American electric guitar is a relative baby in historical time, yet the cello has not found a place in American music. And I do not think it will. American children need noise to help them lose themselves. But I had to come tonight to supervise these intellectual brothers of mine.' And he chuckled to himself.

About 2:30 AM the concert began to wind down. Tim was asleep. Jamie was one step away from sleep. Klosky was still in full motion. Klosky punched Jamie on the shoulder. They each took one arm of Tim and moved slowly toward the car. Fifteen minutes later they were asleep in their ocean side beds. And even the waves had gone to sleep as the tide was now going out.

At 5:30 PM the next afternoon the three boys were declared missing persons by the Massachusetts State Police. During the morning hours Jamie's Mother had tried calling Jamie on his cell phone several times, no answer. She called Tim's Mother and Klosky's Mother. They each called their sons on their cell phones, no answer. After pushing the panic button at the Stars Light Hotel and learning the boys were not in their rooms but the car was there, Mrs. O'Reilly called her two brothers-in-law and told them Jamie had disappeared. Within one hour, the entire area, land and sea, was filled with state police, national guard, and US border patrol. When the President speaks, people jump. Several hours of searching did not find the boys nor reveal how they were kidnapped. The theory was that they were taken during the night and placed onto a boat.

And the theory was correct. Later Saturday afternoon, Jamie began waking up. He had a terrible headache, which could not have been from alcohol as the boys were underage and had drunk only colas. He was tied up, hands and feet, and there was a pillow case covering his head and face. He could tell that he was in a large boat as the engine sound was a big purring noise. And the gentle swell of waves told him they were moving slowly in some bay or near a land mass, not out in the ocean proper. He hoped that Klosky and Tim were in the boat and tied up just like him. And then he began to wonder what these guys wanted from the three of them. But he was not afraid. He knew what death was; he had faced it before, recently.

There was a marine guard booth at the entrance to the official parking lot between the White House and the west Executive Office Building. On the following day, Sunday afternoon, a little boy approached the two guards standing on duty. The little boy said, "I want to share my candy with the people that make me feel safe in my country."

He reached up and gave each marine a wrapped candy sucker, smiled, and walked away. Suddenly the boy dropped a small package and took off running. The two marines did not know what to think, but they were trained to do, not think. They immediately backed away. One marine ran out to stop all traffic; the other marine called the bomb squad. One pandemonium hour later, it was determined not to be a bomb, but a person's finger and a letter to the President of the United States. It was so delivered to the Oval Office.

Two hours after the package was again carefully screened for any explosive or poisonous materials, it was given to Mr. Jonathan O'Reilly, Jamie's uncle. The President opened the package. A note inside the package said:

DISBAND THE COMMISSION OR YOU WILL BECOME A FINGER COLLECTOR

And the package also contained a small finger of the left hand. On the finger was a small ring with the image of Cu Chulainn, the Irish folk hero who, after being badly injured in a battle to save his homeland, tied himself upright to a boulder and continued fighting to the death. It was Jamie's. He immediately recognized the ring because he had given it to his nephew Jamie after his brother, Theodore O'Reilly, Jamie's father was killed. At that time, he promised Jamie that his uncle would be there when needed. He now understood the kidnapping of the three boys. He immediately called his other brother, Jackson to come to the Oval Office. They had a first priority problem.

A half hour later the President and the Attorney General of the United States sat together to try to decide who was more important, their little nephew, or the people of the world. After a serious discussion of pluses and minuses the President said, "I am empowered to establish commissions, to de-establish commissions, and to re-establish commissions. Call Uncle

Dagda, de-establish the Commission on Human Trafficking and explain why. But tell him to continue on his own with the NSA. Now I really want those guys."

His brother stood, saluted, and walked to the door to begin to carry out his new orders. Going out the door his comments were, "It is just not fair for you to get both the brains and the logic in this family." And he looked back and their eyes and smiles met.

Sunday evening Jamie was still in a lot of pain. Last night they had removed the little finger on his left hand. But they also took his ring. He would have readily given them his finger if they had just let him keep his ring. But they took both. He was doubly sad. He told the kidnappers of the pain, he had not yet seen their faces, and they gave him some more pain killer. They obviously planned to release him, or they would not be so 'nice' to him. Or else they were just afraid of his two uncles. He knew he would soon find out.

The following Tuesday, two bodies were found washed up on the shore in Ipswich Bay, just north of Gloucester, Massachusetts. They were the bodies of Jamie's roommates, Klosky and Tim. The bodies were only partially eaten by fish, so they had only been in the sea for a few hours. Uncle Dagda Murphy had flown in from Europe and was overseeing the search for Jamie and his friends. After finding the bodies of the two boys, he immediately had complete autopsies performed; and he took body fluid samples from the boys and sent them to the JNI Laboratories in Los Angeles. Dr. Jiang would test the samples for any possible Nano systems. And as expected, Jamie's two buddies did not die from drowning. They died two days earlier due to heart failure, and were simply thrown into the Bay such that they would be found by the authorities; a reminder to the President that they were serious. And a final postal note to the White House—

DISBAND THE COMMISSION OR PAY THE PRICE.

One week after the Boston kidnapping, at mid-afternoon, Jamie was found walking through Merrymount Park, again. He was very dizzy, probably because of those drugs. He thought at first it was all a dream, and he was back to the concert, but there was no music. But when he felt his little fingerless left hand, he knew it was a nightmare. He found a policeman, told him who he was, and the American security system went into motion.

Several hours later, sitting in his father's office chair in his father's office, now his, den, in the privacy of his house, secure and talking to Uncle Dagda, Jamie tried to remember what happened.

Uncle Dagda spoke up, "Now I am recording everything you say for legal police purposes, then maybe you will not have to go to the police station. Remember both Tim and Klosky were killed, so I want you to tell me about them also."

Jamie agreed, "I do not remember a lot. Everything was a dream and I kept going in circles. After the concert, it was very late; we came back to the motel, the Stars Light Motel on Sea Avenue. It was directly on the beach. Before the concert we had gone swimming there. We all went directly to bed and to sleep. And the next thing that I remember was that I was lying in a different bed, my hands and my legs were tied and there was a pillow case like sack over my head. The sack material was thin enough so I could tell it was daylight. And I knew that we were in a big boat because the motor noise was strong and purring. We were moving very slowly as the ocean swells were gentle, sleepy like. My mind seemed to come and go in rhythm to the swells."

Uncle Dagda asked, "Did you hear any noises?"

"No. Everything was quiet and peaceful. And then they did it." "They did what?

"They cut off my finger. Why did they do that?"

Uncle Dagda hesitated, and then decided Jamie was old enough to digest the undeclared that was in motion. He responded, "Your father was killed more than two years ago because some people did not like what he was doing, helping high technology advance in the United States. Several more people who were super experts in different high technology fields have also been killed. Your Uncle Jonathan set up a Commission to try to find the killers of these very important people. And, as you know we are making progress, your musketeers are helping us a lot."

"Now those 'some' people want your Uncle Jonathan to close down that Commission so they won't get caught. To encourage him to do this they kidnapped you and your roommates. They cut off your finger which had the ring your uncle gave to you after your father was killed, sent your finger and the ring to your uncle, and told him to close down the Commission or they would cut off more of your fingers. And to enforce their demands they killed both Tim and Klosky, threw them into the ocean such that they would be found. And they were killed using a Nanotech system; they did not drown; they died quickly without pain. Again, this was done to try to convince your uncle to stop searching for them. The Commission has been closed down."

And Jamie's eyes filled with tears and trickled down his face. He could not say anything for several moments. "Uncle Jonathan chose me and let the killers go free?"

Uncle Dagda replied, "We haven't stopped our investigation, we have just stopped the Commission. Now please finish your story."

After a few minutes of hiding his wet face in his hands, he finally spoke up, "All right. After they cut off my little finger, they injected me with some pain killer and gave me some pills and the pain went away. Later, they then put on masks and took the pillow case off my head. They untied my hands and brought to me some good food. And they put some chains on my legs, loose enough that I could go to the bathroom, but not go very far if I got out of the room. The windows were covered from the outside, but I could tell if it was day or night. For the next days, I do not know how many, they gave me injections every few hours, I went into circles and had many crazy dreams. They also gave me pain killer medicine when I told them that I was in pain. When they did that, I knew they were going to release me someday."

"Did you hear these people talk? Did they have any accents? Could you tell how many of them there were? Several or just a couple?"

"I did hear them talking several times. Sometimes I heard them speaking in English but I did not understand it very well. Sometimes they spoke in another language. I think there were several, all men on the boat."

"Did you see or hear Tim or Klosky at any time?"

"No. I do not know if they were on boat or somewhere else. I never saw them after going to bed in the motel."

"Were the ocean waves always gentle, or sometimes were they more ferocious?"

"Yes, most of the time they were gentle, but sometimes they were big and I had trouble staying on my bed."

"Let us start and talk about it all one more time. Maybe you forget something important the first time you told me."

19

One Nanotech System - Multiple Deaths?

TTORNEY GENERAL AND CO-CHAIRMAN OF the Commission Mr. O'Reilly called everyone back to the table and continued with the meeting. After all were seated, he announced, "It appears that we have been dealing with something for almost three years of which we know very little. So, I have asked Dr. Chi Jiang, Professor of Nanomedicine of the California Institute of Technology, to brief us about nanotechnological systems. Dr. Jiang, if you please."

Dr. Jiang began, "Thank you for your kind invitation to talk to you about my professional children, Nano-somethings." And he gave a big smile.

"I assume by now you agree with me that they are just that, Nano-somethings, because they do come in every color, flavor, feel, sound, and smell. This is one of the reasons that makes it extremely difficult to detect one in the body's fluids. It is best if you know what you are looking for. If you go into the woods to hunt a deer, you take a rifle. If you go to the river to catch some fish you take a fishing rod and reel. If you go shopping you take your billfold, or credit cards. And on and on. You know what you are looking for before you leave home; so, take with you what is necessary to find it. When you go looking for a Nano-tech system, you may not know what you are looking for, because there are many types. How can you find something if you do not know what it looks like, or smells like, or feels like, or sounds like? Most difficult."

"Second, the quantity of nanotechnical systems is incredibly small. Again, imagine if there was only one deer in the entire United States and you went out to hunt it, most difficult. Imagine if there was only one fish in the Chesapeake Bay and you went out to catch it, most difficult. Or imagine if all the shopping malls were closed on Sunday except one and you did not know where it was located, and you needed to buy a pair of shoes or something, again most difficult."

"Third, many nanotechnical systems have a very short life span when placed into the body. It may naturally disintegrate, or it may be designed such that it will disintegrate or be digested in a specific period of time. And each nanotechnical system will be different."

"Fourth, in order for the nanotech-something to find a specific target in the body, one must prepare and attach to this nanotech-something a monoclonal antibody, MoAB. This is a homing component which will recognize any specific cell, tissue, or organ in the body for which it is programmed. A nanodrug plus a homing MoAB programmed to find cell Q will find only cell Q, associate with cell Q, and/or affect the activity of cell Q. The affect may be to stimulate cell Q, kill cell Q, make cell Q go to sleep, make cell Q wake up, or many other things."

'To identify a nanotechnical system in body fluids we need to; Isolate, Separate or Partially Purify, Characterize, and Analyze."

"Let me give you another analogy. If you are looking for a small round white unbreakable diamondized marble in the Atlantic Ocean, first you drain away most of the water; vacuum up most small white rocks; strain the small rocks through two different wire screens such that the very tiny rocks and sand go through screen #1 and the remaining rocks which are the approximate size of the marble will go through screen #2; place the rocks from the screen #2 onto a black surface and tilt the surface such that only the round rocks will roll; collect all of the white rolling rocks; run the small strained white rolling rocks under a rock crusher. Within the remaining uncrushed rock should be your marble. These procedures allow you to have a high percentage chance of finding your white unbreakable round diamondized marble from the Atlantic Ocean."

"We must use similar types of procedures to 'find' a nanotechnical system in body fluids. Of course, if your marble is radioactive, you can probably use a sophisticated radiation counter to help you find it faster and easier. If your marble is filled with iron, you can probably use a sophisticated magnet to help you find it faster and easier. Such labeling can help one find a specific Nano- system. If you know the specific characteristics of your marble you can design a fast-easy way to detect it – a specific nanotechnical system diagnosis. If you do not know about the physical characteristics of the nanotechnical system that you are hunting for, it is extremely difficult or near impossible to find. Today such general diagnostic tests are not available."

"In brief, that is why you did not find any nanotechnical systems from all of your recent investigations; you did not have a proper diagnostic system. There is no such test for diagnosing all nanotechnical systems. But with time the various systems will fall into categories, based upon their molecular structures. Then we will be able to design tests for the various sub-nanotechnical systems."

Mr. Murphy spoke up, "I hear you saying that we would not recognize a nanotechnical system if we were looking directly at it. Is this true?"

"Yes, answered Dr. Jiang. "There is some truth in that. If you had never seen the Loch Ness Monster, how would you know what it was if it walked across the road in front of you? If you had never seen or heard of a mammoth, how would you know what it was if you met one in a forest? The point being is that our forensic laboratories have not 'seen' these nanotechnical systems. How can we expect them to recognize something that they have not 'seen'?"

"I think I understand," said Mr. O'Reilly. "The experimental laboratory science is far ahead of our clinical diagnostic science with regard to nanotechnology. We have to live with this gap until it is closed. How many years do you think?"

Dr. Jiang responded, "I really do not know. But it will not be long. Capitalism is a powerful motivating factor. Soon there will be companies which will be developing and marketing diagnostic kits for certain nanotech factors or for sub-nanotech factors. There will be much money to be made by harnessing this new diagnostic technology."

Mr. Murphy said, "I want to sincerely thank Dr. Jiang for his presentation. I am now relieved. It was not obvious to me that I could not find the thing because I had never seen the thing; and that I would probably not recognize the thing as a thing even if it bit me on the tail."

And he not only got a nice laugh but also applause from his Commission colleagues. They all felt the same way. Hurry up and bring on the diagnostic kits so these potential killing things could be identified, and the killers could be caught.

Dr. Jiang got the final word. "Recently, when I was having lunch at the White House, President O'Reilly asked me a question and I promised that I would answer him. The question was: Is there a possible relationship between the various deaths and the brain?"

"My answer is as follows. Mr. Murphy informed me that the MUSDs officially involved the heart, lungs, neck/throat, eyes, and brain. All of these organs are controlled by five adjacent regions at the back of the brain. The spinal cord has a liquid-fluid in the center called the spinal fluid. It runs the entire length of the spinal cord and at the top it bathes the nerves in the brain regions that control the death targeted organs which I just mentioned. Therefore, theoretically, one nanodrug, if injected into the spinal cord, could go to the brain and could 'control' any of these five nerve regions in the body. That is assuming there was a different homing MoAB, for each brain region or sub-region, attached to that drug. One drug, five MoAbs, and you could account for most of those recent eighteen deaths which were medically undetectable. The drug could be a simple nanocarrier with iron which could short circuit the specific nerve cells in the specific region of the brain that it entered. This could shut down the area of the body that those brain cells controlled."

"I hope this helps you better understand nanotechnology and the problem we are facing. Mr. Murphy, if you would kindly pass this answer on to Mr. President."

General Ronny spoke up, "What I am hearing is that your theory is based on the idea that our Tomahawk missiles can hit and destroy different targets hundreds of miles apart and far from the launch site, if they have a homing device on each missile for each target. You are saying that this military concept is similar to a nanocarrier attached to a MoAB injected into the spinal column which travels via this fluid to its specific brain target. One can use the same or a similar nanocarrier as long as it is attached to a specific MoAB for each specific target. Is this a reasonable comparison?"

"Very good!"

There were no further comments or questions from Commission members. That was enough science for these non-scientists.

Group Actions

ONE SUMMER SATURDAY MORNING IN Kadikoy-Istanbul, Turkey, in an apartment on the fourth and top floor of a dilapidated old wooden house, sixteen bodies were found, each lying on their back, eyes closed, facing the ceiling. Later it was determined that each man, woman, and child, for there were several of each, had died about the same time during the night. There was no blood or body marks anywhere, just 18 bloated bodies.

The Bosporus courses from the Black Sea through the center of Istanbul into the Marmara Sea; and then It continues into the Aegean Sea, the Mediterranean Sea, and the Atlantic Ocean. Speculation has it that it was created at the time of the historical/religious Noah's Flood. Today nine million people live on the west side, in Europe, and seven million people on the east side, in Asia Minor. The last major suburb on the east side of the Bosporus as it enters the Marmara Sea is Kadikoy (ancient Chalcedon). Three thousand years ago the first settlers in the Istanbul area built their homes here. Soon the gods told them to move to the European side as the view toward the Asian coastline was more beautiful. Thus, the two-thousand-year old walled city of the Eastern Roman-Byzantine Empire and later the Ottoman Empire was built as the last suburb on the west side of the Bosporus looking at Kadikoy.

The current view of the Kadikoy coastline includes two unique historical structures, the Haydarpasha Train Station and former Selimiye Military Academy. It now houses the Marmara University Medical and

Law Schools. Old shops and houses separate the two. The Haydarpasha Train Station is a large U-shaped building with tall circular columns on each corner. It was the end, or beginning, of the Silk Road to China, as well as the steel railroad associated with trade and the transportation of armies from Europe into the Middle East region. The old Haydarpasha Military School is a large square building also with tall circular columns on each corner. It was the royal school for the training of all senior officers of the Ottoman armies.

The apartment house where these unusual deaths occurred was in a slum area between these two historical structures, perhaps 300 meters from the train station. All houses in the neighborhood need extensive repair; although many are historical, so by law they can only be renovated as they were in the past. The façade cannot be changed. They cannot be torn down. And the cost of renovation is such that most owners lived elsewhere and just willed the properties to their children or grandchildren. Let them worry about the future of the neighborhood. Hence there was no known owner of the building containing the eighteen bodies on that Saturday morning.

For the past thirty-five years the Marmara University occupied the Haydarpasha Military Academy building. On Saturday mornings they held Computer-On-Line-Search-Contests for various age groups. During the past several weeks Aykut had been crossing the Bosporus by the Vapur, the ferry boat, from Beshiktash on the European shore, to the Haydarpasha Train Station on the Asian shore. Crossing back and forth between Asia and Europe by a Vapur took only fifteen minutes, bus travel via bridges required an hour. So, it was always quick and easy. He crossed often.

But this Saturday morning everything was chaotic at the Hadarpasha Train Station. The Gendarme-military police, and Istanbul police were everywhere, checking people, identifications, examining packages, and asking where one was coming from and where one was going to. He finally made the routine ten- minute walk to the university in one hour where he found everyone who had come for the contest in a state of shock and panic. The contest had been called off. And of course, he learned about the horrible deaths in the neighborhood he had just walked through.

After he learned, by community grapevine, just how horrible the deaths really were, he called Jamie in Boston and told him of the unusual and simultaneous deaths, not of one person, but three families of eighteen people, all illegal immigrants, men, women, and children. Jamie called Uncle Dagda and told him about the Istanbul deaths. And Uncle Dagda arranged, through his nephew the American President, for permission to allow him to go to Istanbul and for his ISAAT to observe the investigation of these 'murders'.

Uncle Dagda had been in Vienna, so he flew directly to Istanbul in two hours. His plane touched down at 5:30 PM and two of his people met him at Atatürk International Airport. As they drove toward the Istanbul Governor's Office, Murat and Selcuk told him what they knew.

Murat said, "Early this morning a family member, who lived in this fatal apartment but had gone to dinner and stayed all night with a friend of his in Uskudar, about three miles up the Bosporus on the Asian side, returned home and found his now dead family. Can you imagine walking into your house and finding every family member lying on his back, abdomen bloated, eyes closed, a terrible smell emanating from each body, and all are cold and dead?"

Selcuk responded, "Let Allah protect us all from such hell." "Please go on Murat."

"Soon after the young man arrived, and with the apartment door open, several people in the building smelled a terrible odor. One of these neighbors called the police. They came, saw the situation, called the ambulances, and all bodies were taken to one of the five nearby hospitals. It was certainly several hours too late. Every person in the apartment was dead and apparently died at nearly the same time. There was no evidence of any fights or disagreements. Each was on the floor or in a bed in a normal position of sleep" Murat finished.

They arrived in Istanbul Governor's Building and were immediately taken to the Assistant Governor's office. The Governor was currently meeting with people from the Office of the Turkish Prime Minister. They were discussing this tragedy, as all the dead were illegal immigrants from Syria, and none had passports. Mr. Murphy was introduced to Mr. Dogan Kavlakoglu. Mr. Kavlakoglu was tall, slim with graying mustache. He did not give his title but he was probably a member of the Turkish MIT, equivalent of the American CIA or British MI6. They were all seated around a small conference table in this office. Mr. Kavlakoglu had two police detectives with him. They would brief Mr. Murphy about the tragedy.

Mr. Murphy spoke, "I am Mr. Dagda Murphy, CEO of the International Security Assistance and Anti-Terrorism Corporation. Today I represent the President of the United States of America. I bring his utmost condolences about this terrible set of deaths. And I thank you in advance for sharing your investigation with us. Mr. President has a strong interest in this case and asked me to tell you that if he can help in any way, please let us know."

Mr. Kavlakoglu responded, "Thank you, and we are impressed that your President is interested in this tragic happening. Police Detective Mohammad Bozkurt has been directly involved in the investigation; and the Governor has requested the he present our findings to you, as they become available. The other Police Detective is Ali Sapanoglu who is in contact with the Department of Immigration in Ankara. As you know none of the victims were Turkish citizens. We three speak English so we should be able to cover more ground more quickly. Mr. Bozkurt, why don't you begin?"

Mr. Bozkurt, short, dark haired with a small scar on his chin started, "Thank you. The Kadikoy police precinct received a call from 3517 Elma Street at 9:15 this morning. A nearby policeman from that neighborhood checked it out. Fifteen minutes later, all hell broke loose. Forgive my French. With the discovery of eighteen bodies, eight men, six women, and four children, the area became a whirlpool of police, Gendarme or Military Police, ambulances and other official cars. Two hours later the area, house, and apartment where the bodies had been found were cordoned off and the initial in-depth investigation had begun. The forensic people and our homicide detectives were collecting what hard information they could; which has turned out to be relatively little. The situation, as of now is as follows."

"Three families from the Kahalife clan in Aleppo, Syria were all killed sometime during the late hours last night. They had entered Turkey illegally over the past couple of years. The males were working in building construction and two of the women were working as house maids. None of the children were going to school. All eighteen were living in this three-bedroom apartment near the Haydarpasha Train Station in Kadikoy over on the Asian side of Istanbul. No one knows when they gradually began moving into this particular building, probably over a several month period so they would not attract attention. The building is nearly one hundred years old and is dilapidated, but it has not yet been condemned. This is a common method by which illegal immigrants settle quietly into a slum area."

"There were actually nineteen people living here, but a fifteen-year old boy, named Sargon Kahalife, was with one of his friends during the evening and all night. He discovered the bodies when he returned home around 9:00 this morning. The Turkish friend, Serdar Aktas, has been interviewed and supports his whereabouts during the night. Neither are suspects. In fact, currently no one has been arrested and there are no suspects."

"What was the cause of death?" asked Mr. Murphy.

Mr. Sapanoglu, brown haired with blue eyes and a serious face answered, "Each victim died of a ruptured colon and associated blood vessels, blood and excrement filled the abdominal cavity, basically they bled to death internally. It also appears that each died at about the same time, just after around midnight, and after they had all gone to sleep for the night. We do not yet know what caused the colon to rupture. We are testing all food, water and other plants in the apartment, looking for any kind of poison. We can go and see the place if you would like."

Mr. Murphy agreed, so the group of six left the Governor's Building, climbed into a bullet proof SUV and took the Fatih Sultan Mehmet Bridge across the Bosporus to Kadikoy. On route they continued to discuss details of the tragic event of last night.

Upon arrival in the slum area Mr. Murphy immediately thought of blood feud revenge assassinations. He knew that the Kurdish regions in eastern Turkey, Syria, and Iran had never been forced to undergo land reform. There were many villages 'owned' by one family. Disobedience by villagers of other families or between village heads was often punished by entire family killings. So, he asked, "Could this be a blood feud mass murder?

Mr. Kavlakoglu responded, "Yes, that is a very good possibility. The newspapers are calling it terrorist killings. Some of us are looking in the direction of blood feud revenge killings. All of the deaths were in one family; men, women, and children. All were killed in a very brutal way.

The method used did get, is getting, extensive publicity. I think that right now some village chieftain is feeling like a god and pointing to his enemies to lookout, they may be next. We will know more in a couple of days as we have sent agents into Syria to inquire about these possibilities."

As they climbed the rickety stairs and looked through the building and the various apartments, the Khalife's apartment floors were filled with recent body areas drawn in chalk. It was bad enough to imagine it from the chalk marks. But to see it in person as the one young man had, this was a sudden hell from which he would never escape.

All food and water had been removed by the police to be tested for poisons. But under the back corner of one bed Mr. Murphy noticed a one-quart plastic bottle of water which was still sealed. It had the word Pinar written on the side. He asked about this water. He was told that in Istanbul the tap water is for washing and flushing, one purchases water for drinking; even slum dwellers do this.

Mr. Sapanoglu quickly dialed his cell phone. In one minute, he said, "Our detectives found a carton with two remaining bottles of water from Pinar Mountain Spring Water Company. Usually these cartons hold ten bottles. So, they took those last two bottles and are analyzing them for poisons. That unopened bottle that you have must have been from the carton."

And immediately Mr. Murphy thought about Dr. Jiang's words, 'to find a nanotech-thing one must isolate, separate, partially purify, characterize, and analyze.' He was certain that this would not be done by the Turkish authorities, so he asked if they could see the site of the terrorist murders, as the news media was now labeling the event.

Mr. Murphy asked, "May we take this bottle with us and analyze the water with some new high technology research procedures that we have only just begun to use?"

"I will have to check," replied Mr. Kavlakoglu, and he took out his cell phone and dialed.

Mr. Murphy stepped outside and took out his cell phone and dialed.

Mr. Kavlakoglu's first phone call received a positive response. He then dialed again.

Mr. Murphy"s first phone call received a positive response. He then dialed again.

And the bureaucratic tape began to wind. Within the United Sates a sequence of encrypted phone calls occurred such as to the Department of Justice and the White House in Washington, DC, the Central Intelligence Agency in Langley, VA, the Pentagon in Arlington, VA, and the National Security Center in Landover, MD; within Turkey a sequence of encrypted phone calls occurred to the Cumhurbaskanlık (President's Office), Basbakanlık (Prime Minister's Office), Milli Istihbarat Teshkilati or MIT (CIA equivalent), Genelkurmay (Military Headquarters), and the American Embassy, all in Ankara; Istanbul Valilik (Governor's Office), and Jandarma (Military Police), and the American Consulate, all in Istanbul.

Within two hours a positive response from all the above centers of power came (a miracle unto itself). Mr. Murphy's plastic water bottle was immediately police shuttled to the Chorlu Military Airbase outside Istanbul, loaded aboard a Turkish F15, flown directly to Norco Air Force Base just outside of Los Angeles, CA, and the police shuttled it to the JNI Company in Silicone Ledge, CA. The plastic bottle of mountain spring water, priced $1.35, arrived approximately thirty-five hours after its owners had been killed. That special transportation cost more than fifty thousand American dollars.

Several weeks after the terrible murders, Aykut was sitting at his favorite café on the Bosporus in Bebek. He had his laptop open and was reading a CNN report concerning the 'Istanbul massacre' that he had previously downloaded. The report had several terrible pictures. He read about Sargon Khalife, the only family member who escaped death that night because he had been staying at a friend's house. One of Aykut's school mates was a Syrian fellow named Asu Kalan, the number one student in school. At a recent party at Asu's house, he met a Turk Ali Aktaş, Sargon Khalife's friend. Sargon was not at that party so he had not met him. Recently he had received word from Jamie, which came from Uncle Dagda, which came from Dr. Jiang, that there was indeed some type of Nano-system in the water in the plastic bottle. So, if they could learn any more about the mass deaths, maybe they could learn more about the source of the Nano-system.

In the proper Turkish way, Aykut reciprocated by inviting Asu who invited Serdar who invited Sargon to lunch. In this way Aykut could meet and talk with Sargon about his family's tragedy without raising suspicion. Each had accepted and should arrive anytime.

All three arrived at the same time. Greetings and introductions went around the group of fourteen to sixteen-year-olds. Aykut opened the conversation, "I am very sorry for your family. I hope you are adjusting."

Sargon, who was small for his age and had the permanent tan of outdoor laborers responded, "Thank you. It was a monstrous nightmare which is beginning to recede."

Asu jumped in, "That is because his favorite soccer team, Fenerbahçe Canaries is on top of the Super League, and my team, Galatasaray, are now down in third place."

And for the next fifteen minutes they discussed the players and the teams of the major Turkish football scene and whether the Turkish Nationals would make it to the world cup next year. Eventually, as Aykut felt Sargon begin to relax a little he gently asked what he was now doing.

"Many people have helped me." Sargon explained. "The state has given to me a Turkish Identification Card, not a passport, and a five-year visa and work permit. The CEO of the DAKO Construction Company is a Syrian-Turk. I am tentatively living with his family and going to a state vocational school near his house. He will employ me in the summers. I hope to find my own apartment in a year or two. I guess things are not terribly bad; except every night I still see a floor filled with my dead, bloated loved ones. The doctors said I may see this image forever."

And the boys were silent for several minutes, each looking out into the water of the Bosporus, each avoiding Sargon's eyes, each wanting to help him quickly heal. What else could they do but offer their sincere friendship, which they did.

Aykut asked, "Do you want to go back to Syria someday?" "Oh no! I would be killed too.

Why would you be killed?

"My family was not killed by a bunch of terrorists. I know who killed them." He answered. "But I have already been told that I can live as long as I say nothing."

All was quiet again for a few moments. "I do want revenge, very badly; but how?"

"Do you know some kind of new poison might have killed your family?" said Aykut.

Sargon answered, "Yes, I know that and I know where it comes from." "Where?"

"From the past, Masyaf." And he would say no more.

Serdar changed the subject and asked Sargon if he wanted to join them next weekend to watch the speedboat races in the Marmara Sea, about one hour from here by car. The boys were going to make extra effort to help Sargon return to the world of the living.

Two hours later they had finished their lunch and started to head toward their homes. Aykut asked Asu to walk with him for a minute.

As they walked along the walkway beside of the Bosporus Aykut asked, "What did Sargon mean when he said that the poison that may have killed his family came from the past, Masyaf?"

Asu grimaced, "The Citadel of Masyaf was the center of the Hashshashin. Do you know what that is?

Aykut thought for a second and answered. "The word hashhash is the Turkish word and hashish or opium is the English word for it."

"Correct," said Asu. "Masyaf is located in northern Syria about one hundred kilometers from Aleppo, where Sargon's family is from."

And Aykut thought to himself. 'I wonder if this is the Syrian location for the Chinese company that is making Nano systems. I need to call up a computer conference right away. He asked Asu one last question, "Are there very many Syrian-Turks, who are from this region of Syria, currently living in Istanbul?"

Asu responded. "Oh yes. My family is from that region."

After a few more minutes of discussion, Asu caught a taxi to go to his house. Aykut kept walking and thinking.

'What I need to do is to obtain home e-mail numbers which are in a possible nanotech factory in the Masyaf, learn about northern Syria and Masyaf, and develop a plan to go there. Using the Big Thumb, I could download from those e-mail server postal warehouses. And of course, I must get out without getting caught. So first I need to talk to my buddies and get their help.'

A Presidential Mistake?

IT WAS MID-MARCH AND THE two Chairmen of the disbanded Presidential Commission on Human Trafficking were meeting in the Office of the Attorney General on Pennsylvania Avenue in Washington, DC.

Jackson O'Reilly spoke, "It seems that we have a lot of interesting data coming from the Turkish boy's downloads of the Masyaf e-mail directories. NSA had identified several names and places and dates that are worth following up. Where do you want to go first?"

Dagda Murphy replied, "There appears to be a leader in this effort to slow down the many advances in high technology. He apparently calls himself the Korrectorizer. But he has a group of 'friends' who are definitely helping him. He calls irregular meetings at different castles in Romania. My intuition is still unchanged. I think that these 'friends' are from various outmoded or soon to be obsolete industrial or commercial systems who meet with him, help with decisions such as targeting, and provide any necessary support such as communications, transportation, and money. For example, most names that we have identified include people from many different industries and commercial establishments such as steel, petrochemicals, metals, silicon chips, and transportation systems."

"To me it is obvious that a group of Korrectorizer's friends are seriously concerned about their industries and commercial endeavors having survival troubles if high technology is allowed to expand at its current pace. As you well know, such has happened in history again and again: horses to automobiles, candles to light bulbs, bow and arrow to guided missiles, writing ink to computers, animal skins to synthetic textiles, telegraph to smart phones, clay bricks to steel/cement structures, sundials to electronic watches, petroleum- based energy to solar based energy, and on and on. And looking at some of the names that NSA has provided to us, the concern is probably correct."

"It is waning industries versus waxing technology!

"The bottom line is that many industrial and commercial groups prefer that the status quo be maintained; they simply resist change if it means that they might lose. I appreciate the enormity of the problems that high technology creates. But a war will not solve these issues.

"KILLING IS ILLEGAL ON EARTH AS IT IS IN HEAVEN!"

He paused for a few moments to catch his breath. He obviously had been thinking about all of this for a long time. He understood the problem, did not know the solution, but was determined to stop the abominable solution that was now in motion.

"Do you have enough information about the eight people that you mentioned to me previously?" asked Mr. O'Reilly.

"Yes and No. We think there are at least eight decision making committee members, if I may temporarily call them a committee, and a group of Nanotech system providers. Within the group or committee, no one uses his real name, address, or profession. They use the names of ancient gods and prophets. We think that we have determined some of the connections, and possibly several of the suppliers. But we certainly do have enough data to put them under 'legal' surveillance. Are they a group that just gives advice in general? Or do they help select targets? Do they determine and or supply various Nanotech 'weapons'? These are critically important questions for which we do not have answers."

"However, if we put them under obvious surveillance it would be declaring war on them," replied Mr. O'Reilly. "And from the last warning with my nephew, we should expect some swift and very negative repercussions. Maybe we can put them under very individual non-obvious surveillance. I think that we can figure out a way to do that. Certainly, we can use the terrorism laws to tap their cellular phones as well as their on-line systems."

"I agree. We cannot look the other way."

"With regard to this Korrectorizer, who seems to have organized this method for slowing the development of high technology in the world, we have identified several possible candidates. I am guessing that it is someone who profits, at least monetarily, from providing or is a direct supplier of the Nano systems," commented Mr. O'Reilly.

"Yes, we have several excellent supplier candidates who I think we should put under legal or not-so-legal surveillance. Tapping their cellular phones and on-line systems are a good place to begin."

"One possible candidate, Mr. Boris Kukrynisky is founder and CEO of two nanotechnology factories, St. Petersburg and Celjabinsk, Russia. Mr. Kukrynisky is an oligarch who survived the government cleansing when the government re-nationalized the country's industrial systems. He bought his way clear by returning his microchip manufacturing companies and continued with his high-tech science companies. One of these companies is doing nanotechnology research and manufacturing. They really do not do research, but they are very successful at purchasing, stealing, and acquiring international patents. They copy and manufacture several Nano-systems which are marketed for medical diagnosis."

"Another candidate, Dr. Frans Heinz is a chemical engineer, trained in medical nerve biology, and President of Nano-solar LTD, which has one large industrial plant in Rosenheim just outside Munich, Germany. It is a large company, reported profits of almost one hundred million dollars in 2030, and is involved in both research and manufacturing of several Nano systems for energy conversions in medicine and transportation systems. Dr. Heinz teaches at the University of Munich; and his brain power comes predominately from his German graduate and postdoctoral students."

"A possible candidate is Dr. Mario Kemps, who is a sixty-year old Professor of Nano chemistry in Buenos Aires, Argentina. He is the Director of the University Technological Institute. His research is human disease oriented. And like many established professors his research is carried out in the university laboratories while the profitable manufacturing occurs in a nearby nanotech factory, Medical-Nano-Systems Corporation, MNS. Some of the profit from the factory does go to support students. Dr. Kemps is founder, but Dr, Gustavo Cortazar is CEO. We know that they produced two of the Nano drugs that produced sudden miracle cures during the past two years."

"A very good candidate is Dr. James Wiley Walters, Professor at the University of Ontario in Ottawa, Canada, where he founded the Canadian Center for Nanotechnology. It is one of the largest such research centers in the world. They employ more than one hundred teachers and educate nearly six hundred students at all levels. All areas or research and application in nanotechnology are studied. In the past few years, several companies have sprung from this research center and are located in surrounding suburbs. Most of these rogue companies are founded by professors from the Center. And these rogue companies/factories provide support money for university research projects and salaries for faculty and students."

"Now, with the example of the Canadian Center for Nanotechnology there are probably many such university rogue companies so affiliated and producing Nano-tech-systems which escape legal inspections and controls. These companies may or may not be controlled by the university or government regulators. Turning a substantial profit and paying taxes on their profit is all that is necessary to function. One good patent on a Nano-tech-system could bring in millions of dollars in a few years."

"You certainly are right," said Mr. O'Reilly. "I recently read an excerpt on super patents and super profits. For example: The Wright brothers designed and flew the first 'airplane' in 1903 from a small research building, with a four- person team. Within 3 years there were five laboratory/factory units in three countries, building and flying 'air-planes'. Soon every modern country in the world was producing and flying thousands of 'air-planes'. Today, many millions of 'airplanes' are flying. The author of the article said that if the Wright brothers had a patent on their first 'airplane', today the Wright descendants would be by far the richest people in the world."

"So, you can't blame these young people for reaching for the golden ring on the carousel, as long as they do it within the framework of legal restrictions and controls. In the United States the Food and Drug Agency reviews and approves all drugs and their patent rights. Europe has its own regulatory controls for all drugs; most countries have approval control of their drugs and patent controls. I only hope that these many different controls are adequate for the quantity of Nanotech systems that are coming into the marketplace."

"And of course, we have to consider the Jiang triplets. We are aware of the Nano drugs with the JXW labels that are produced by the JNI, drugs that apparently initiated sudden miracle cures. This company was founded by Dr. Chi Jiang, who is the President and CEO. He and his two brothers, Dr. Jun Jiang and Dr. Cho Jiang, are all major shareholders. We think that they have at least four factories researching, manufacturing, and marketing nanotechnology systems – Los Angeles, USA; Yangzhou and Jincheng, China; and Masyaf, Syria. However, we can only confirm the Los Angeles and the Yangzhou factories. We are receiving no cooperation from the Chinese or Syrian governments concerning this problem."

"Dr. Chi Jiang lives only in Los Angeles, teaches at the California Institute of Technology where he has his student-based research division. He rarely visits China. Several of his students are supported by JNI scholarships. Dr. Cho Jiang, wife, and two daughters live in Nanjing. We think that he is the Director of the Yangzhou and Jincheng factories. While Dr. Jun Jiang is a citizen of China, Germany, and the USA. He lives with his wife, two daughters and one son in Berlin, but has houses in China (location not established) and New York City. He markets the JNI Nano-tech-products all over the world. He also has two pharmaceutical import-export companies of which he is owner and CEO; so, he has his own jet and travels much."

Unless you can think of a better way, I suggest that we establish a new Presidential Commission with a new name, same objectives, and add an international banker, accountant, cybertechnology expert, customs and passport control experts, and any others who might be needed to set up tight investigative rings around all of the people that we have just discussed. Let us find out where they are going, what they are doing, and how they are living, today. The so called 'committee' of the Korrectorizer will be difficult because I know the individuals change periodically. But this group of possible Nano-tech-system suppliers should be easier targets."

"I support this decision. And I think it would be wise to drop Dr. Jiang and add another nanotechnology specialist, Mr. O'Reilly commented."

On May 17, 2031, a newly established Presidential Commission on International Drug Smuggling was meeting in the fourth-floor conference room in the Department of Justice Building. Again Mr. Jackson O'Reilly and Mr. Dagda Murphy were Co-Chairmen. Many of the old Commission members were there, and several new people were added:

- Mr. Dartworth Jefferson, international specialist and senior partner with Jefferson, Taylor, and Cottons Law Firm in New York City, tall, slim, long dark hair, mustache, fits a three-piece gray suit perfectly.
- Mr. Leopold Mueller, retired Director of the Central Bank of the European Union, Brussels, big man with large stomach, balding with grey hair and small hazel colored very alert eyes.
- Ms. Leonette Beauchamps, CEO of Goldheim International Accounting Firm in Geneva, short, long brown hair, heavy make-up, dangling earrings, bright colored suits and very high heeled shoes.
- Dr. Donald Mackelroy, recently retired Director of the Department of National Intelligence of the USA, average height, red-gray hair, bulbous nose, blue-gray staring eyes.
- Dr. William Stronger, Chairman and professor of the Department of Nanotechnology at the Massachusetts Institute of Technology in Boston, middle aged African American with light skin and dark green eyes, tall and walks with a limp, extremely intelligent.

Mr. O'Reilly had just finished introducing the previous returning members and the new members to the Commission. He then gave a summary of the problem.

"In conclusion, we have some good information, but not hard evidence of several people who may be involved in this effort to stifle the momentum of world-wide high technology. This stifling has involved several medically unexplainable sudden deaths, what we call MUSD. Most of these deaths are of high technology specialists."

"Now these people, killers, are very capable of eliminating their pursuers or family members of their pursuers. We are now their pursuers. What I am trying to say is that your lives and the lives of your loved ones may be in jeopardy by participating on this Commission. At this point in time we do not plan any personal security for Commission members or their families. So, **this is a warning**! If any of you wish to resign and leave, now is the time to do so. You need not give any excuses. I will simply thank you for your time and hope that you would be available to us in the future."

All was quiet for several minutes while Commission members, new and old, quietly discussed the security implications for themselves and their families. They seemed to agree that the 'killings' needed to be stopped and the 'killers' needed to brought to justice. No one left. It appeared that no one could resist this Nano-tech-system challenge.

After waiting for a while and answering several relevant security related questions, Mr. O'Reilly continued. "Now allow me to turn the meeting over to Mr. Dagda Murphy, whose International Security Assistance and Anti-Terror Company, ISAAT, has led our quest for the past three years. Mr. Murphy, please."

"We have identified several people who we think are directly or indirectly involved with this organization. We plan to closely monitor these individuals. We will also monitor all nanotechnology research and manufacturing in the medical fields, throughout the world if necessary. So, we begin with a gigantic agenda, which we hope can be reduced to a limited agenda in the near future. Our guess is that there may be ten to twenty people directly involved in these anti-high technology efforts. Or goal is to find them and bring them to justice."

"One last thing, please notice there is a microphone on the table in front of you. This microphone will indeed amplify your voice so everyone can hear your comments better, and it will also record what you say. There is no need to say your name as we are using a high-tech voice wave identification system to establish who said what. Feel free to say what you think, ask what you want, and make any suggestions you have. We may want to again go over this brain storming discussion later. What may not be so relevant today could become very important tomorrow as things develop. You have a general picture of our problem; please help us find approaches to solve this problem. We promise that what is recorded here today will be codified and placed deep in Mr. O'Reilly's special deep freeze."

And finally, there were a few smiles and the atmosphere around the room relaxed a little.

After a few moments, and hearing no comments, Mr. Murphy continued. "Dr. Bradmier, Director of the US Office of Science and Technology, will you please begin?"

"Thank you. It has become obvious to us that Nano-tech-drug curing systems and Nano-tech-weapon killing systems have been developed which can strike almost any cell, tissue, or organ in the human body. The Nano-tech-drug curing systems are helping cure diseases which previously were not even treatable. It is obvious that the Nano-tech-weapon killing systems can kill a single person or groups of people. Both systems apparently leave no or non-detectable traces of their presence. We are afraid that these Nano-tech-weapon killing systems may be used by terrorists and/or military groups on a large scale in the short term. With such weapons, terrorists would not need one suicide bomber to kill a dozen people. What do you think General Ronny?"

"At the Pentagon we have an entire Department of War Intelligence that spends all of its time looking as just such potential problems," responded General Ronny. This group of army, navy, marines, and air force personnel do not just perform computer simulated battles at various latitudes and longitudes all over the globe, air, land, and oceans. They also focus on exotic weapons. And yes, if you do not know the weapon, how can you fight it or even protect against it? I totally agree with you, Mr. Bradmier. We need to stop this type of potential weapons' development immediately. If not, at least understand what it is, what are its weaknesses and strengths, and is there prevention or cure?"

Mr. Mueller spoke up, "It seems to me that we cannot and should not even try to stop the development of high technology. That is apparently what these people want us to do. And that would put us in a position of recommending a new science committee of some type that would continuously sit in judgment of what is good and what is bad high technology. Was nuclear fusion good or bad technology? Was the internal combustion engine good or bad technology? Was miniaturization good or bad technology? Were silicon chips good or bad technology? I would hope that the objectives of this Commission do not involve singling out and stopping one certain type of technological development."

"That is a good point. That would certainly play into the hands of these people."

"Concerning the nanotech systems that enter the body, how many ways can they do this?" asked Dr. Von Eulenberg."

"To date we have some evidence that they have been injected into the spinal fluid and the veins, and perhaps through the stomach in the drinking water."

"Do you think that they are planning additional routes of bodily administration?"

Dr. Batley answered, "Certainly if they can introduce it through the air or skin, then they have the full range of methods for invading the body – spinal fluid, blood vessels, gastrointestinal tract, and lungs."

"Do you think they will try the air or skin?"

"Yes, I think that they are experimenting with all types of Nano-tech-systems and routes of administration into one body or a mass of bodies."

"Certainly, for a major war level effort they must have a capacity for bodily mass attack," the General spoke up.

"Can you please tell me, do these Nano-substances kill like snake venom?" "Yes and no," Dr. Stronger answered. "One component of a Nano system is a MoAB homing component which can be targeted to any cell or tissue in the body, like General Ronny's Tomahawk guided missiles. They have this one homing device plus one synthetic destructive molecule, a Nano-molecule, which directly affects the target cell. And they may have a delay of action built into the system."

"Snake venoms are composed of twenty or thirty different substances that are toxic and attack several different cell types. Some snake venoms have only one or two substances and only attack one or two cell types, such as nerve cells or red blood cells. The same is true for other animal venoms from scorpions, and certain other fish and reptiles. The beginning action of animal venoms are usually immediate, there is no delay."

Mr. Murphy said, "I think we can agree that we have a problem that involves some type of new weapon system, never before used singularly or in mass killings. Now as I mentioned earlier, we do have several candidates, not yet suspects, who may be involved in manufacturing or using these, probably, Nano systems in an illegal, clandestine, and lethal way. We currently have little evidence that would hold up in a court of law. Or first efforts will be to try to find evidence that will allow us to decide, who is a suspect or innocent bystander. Please give us your ideas about how specifically we could proceed."

Ms. Dapper, specialist in American criminal justice responded, 'You must always keep in mind the concept of probable cause if you want to properly investigate these candidates, not suspects. When a highway patrolman is driving down the road following a car, and he thinks that the driver is an illegal immigrant or has illegal drugs in his trunk, he cannot just signal for that car to pull over, confront the driver, and search the car. He has to have probable cause. Now probable cause may be something simple. It can be that a tail light is out, the turning light doesn't work or he forgot to use it at the latest turn, speeding, ran a yellow light, not driving properly in his traffic lane, passed to another lane without signaling in advance, and more. So, if the patrolman follows the car long enough, he can usually find an excuse to stop him and check his driver's license and car trunk. But he does require probable cause. If he does not have 'legal' probable cause, everything discovered about the driver of that car, including any drugs in the trunk, cannot be used in a court of law in America. This is true in most western countries."

"What I am trying to say is, even though time is critical, do not take too many shortcuts to 'find' evidence to make your target a suspect and don't move too quickly on to an indictment. As long as you have cooperation within the proper venue or jurisdiction, given time and careful observation of the candidate, physically and electronically, one can usually find solid evidence if the person is guilty. It could be something as simple as an accusing affidavit from an unhappy business partner, or movement of suspicious packages across a national boundary or a suspicious vacation trip out of season. With such efforts, one can usually justify for judge approved search warrants and writs. But again, your investigative teams must be careful not to cause harassment of your potential suspect or the suspect's lawyer will legally block you."

The new international lawyer, Mr. Jefferson added, "Ms. Dapper was referring to the USA and other modern westernized countries. I noticed several 'developing' countries from the list of this Korrectorizer's group of friends and the list of potential Nano system supplier suspects. Many 'developing' countries do not have such conforming laws. In these situations, money often speaks louder than proper legal procedures. It might be expedient to purchase subpoenas or writs to obtain permission to perform an investigation on one of their citizens or to work outside the framework of normal international protocols. Political pressures may also be useful to expedite the investigation. It is also probable that your candidate or suspect may have local political connections to block your investigative efforts. Challenge him slowly and carefully. You did remind us that these people can be or are killers. Even if he has local political muscle, he probably will not have an international contact who would be in any position to help him. So, hit him from international directions."

"How and what specific types of questions should we be asking?" asked Mr. Murphy.

The experienced and retired Director of National Intelligence of the USA, Dr. Mackelroy immediately spoke out. "You must follow three major areas; his personal and professional living standards; his electronic personal and professional bookkeeping and records; all of his bank accounts."

"Allow me to be more specific with a few examples for in-depth investigations: personal – family, close relatives, friends, daily habits, relaxation times, vacations: professional – business confidants, senior colleagues, select junior colleagues, select bookkeeping personnel, personal secretary, daily work habits, degree of control in the office, laboratory, or factory, international business travels, all electronic phone and office affairs; annual reports such as IRS statements (personal and company), tax records of company and all foreign affiliates, lists of local and foreign sales focusing on any suspicious international transactions, bank records from local and foreign banks (personal and company). All of this can be done legally, on the record and therefore can be used by for prosecution in a court trial; or it can be accomplished not so legally in which it can only be useful to provide pre-prosecution information."

Ms. Beauchamp chuckled and said, "This focus of data collecting on a potential killer's lifestyle and pocketbook, instead of data collecting on his killing parlors reminds me of the good old days of chasing the mafia. Any ownership or lifestyle which is above the reported income allows for suspicion of extra unreported income. Like the mafia of old, we can still catch many bad guys when the IRS notices that their tax payments do not correctly reflect their level of living."

And a general series of murmurs began going around the room. Everyone knew that in the middle of the twentieth century key leaders, Dons of the American/Italian mafia were put into prison, not because of their numerous crimes, including murder, but because of income tax evasion. The five New York families of Gambino, Luccese, Bonnano, Genovese, and Colombo, controlled organized crime in New York, Chicago, Boston, Pittsburg, Cleveland, and Philadelphia for many years from 1924 to 1959. They were rarely caught, found guilty in court, or served any prison time for their criminal activities. It was their selfish attitude or greed to not report or pay their taxes, or to hide massive amounts of monies in illegal places that finally brought them down. Many mafia Dons spent time in prison only after being found guilty in court of simply not paying their taxes. Today, throughout most societies, such greed still exists. So, this approach to trying to find candidates or suspects involved in the Nano system killings was a logical area to spend much investigative time.

The meeting continued until late in the evening. Two rounds of meals were catered into the Commission meeting as everyone had an idea or suggestion which they hoped would help identify the 'world-killers'. The word terrorist was not spoken during the meeting. Apparently, there was agreement that these targeted killings separated them from the world of random killings which are usually associated with terrorism.

And it was becoming recognized that the investigations and collection of information and data from the western world could be accomplished easily and quickly. However, trying to investigate possible candidates/suspects in many of the 'developing' countries could be difficult. All committee members agreed that if necessary, the President of the United States should use his political leverage where necessary.

They would meet later in the year. At that time a list and current information on possible suspects would be given to all Commission members.

Two weeks after the May meeting of the Presidential Commission of International Drug Smuggling, a little boy ran past the black fence and threw a package onto the front lawn of the White House. He ran down the street, jumped on his bicycle, which was waiting for him just around the corner, and disappeared. The guards immediately halted all traffic entering and leaving the parking lot, moved people away from the package, called the bomb squad who came immediately and checked the package – no bomb. The package was addressed to the President of the United States. Presidential Aides picked up the package, ran it through security control at the west entry door of the White House where it was opened and checked for toxic chemicals. No danger. They took it up to the Oval Office where the two O'Reilly brothers were talking and gave the opened box to the President. Inside was a small envelope which contained leaves of the following spices – biltong, bobotie, sosaties, frikkadel, bredie, and potjiekos. These plants are not common in America. They are common to South Africa. The small note read:

-YOUR CAREER HAS BEEN ADVANCED-
-WE NOW CROWN YOU COLLECTOR OF THE BODIES!-
-YOU HAVE ONE MONTH-

Masyaf of the Assassins

T HAT NIGHT AYKUT ASKED FOR a computer conference.

He began, "Mo'ata is present. Who else is present?

In response he heard: Ey'tuka is present. Tsu'teye is present. Na'via is present.

He continued. "Very good. I have some exciting news. Remember the Turkish terrorist massacre a few weeks ago, that did not involve terrorism? It was a blood feud massacre. As you would know it might have involved a nanotech system as the killing agent. I have learned where that killer may have come from. The families that were killed were from northern Syria, near Aleppo. Just south of Aleppo is a city called Masyaf. It is one of the historic homes of the Hashshashin Sect, which is Arabic for opium and it also means assassin. There is a very large castle/fortress/citadel there where assassins were trained for hire all over the world. I have learned that this castle has recently been renovated. Some of it is open for tourism and some is private. The private area has been under renovation for the past several years. I think that the private area might be a high-tech factory. It might even be the one that Tsu'teye thinks is Chinese. I want to find out. And I need your help."

Suddenly several voices spoke up at once.

Mo'ata broke in, "Let me finish. I need Tsu'teye to obtain the e-mail directory of his Uncle Cho or Uncle Jun. They both work in China and are possibly in contact with any Syrian associates, maybe from Masyaf. I need a home-based e-mail number inside the factory if there is a factory.

With such a number I can hack in and download all letters in that e-mail server postal warehouse and obtain the e-mail directory. I can do this with my Big Thumb hacker. If I can do this, then I will need Ey'tuka to ask his Uncle Dagda to have the letters translated from Arabic or Chinese or whatever language they are using. If we can do this, the information might help us learn something about these worldwide killings."

Na'via spoke up, "But what can I do? I want to help. If any of the languages used are African, let me have them for translation. OK?" Kef was still thinking this was a great game and was having difficulty taking everything seriously. Since all of the players on the field were above the Equator, he felt left out. You cannot score if you are not passed the ball. He did not know that the entire ball game would move to his front yard very soon.

Ey'tuka said, "Let us not cross too many bridges too soon."

Mo'ata agreed, "Yes, I have to get into and out of the assassin's nest with my head still on my shoulders."

And that allowed all of them to chuckle and relax a little. This entire affair needed to be discussed thoroughly before implementation. So, they began. It took about half an hour to design a plan that they all agreed would work. But it took another half an hour to discuss what a Big Thumb was all about. What could it do; what could it not do; could we all have one, and when? Hey, they were all very computer literate; and listening in on your friends could be a lot of fun.

And they were still children at heart!

On August 27, 2031, Li Jiang was flying over the state of Alaska in a Cathay Pacific Airlines 747-400 jumbo jet. He flew from Shanghai International Airport and they were now flying the North Pole route to the USA. This flight only took twelve hours. His two years of living and studying in Nanjing, China were over. And he was flying to Los Angeles to live with his father and study in an American school for the next two years.

Living with the computers in the Yangzhou Factory every Saturday for the past months had allowed Li to have easy access to his Uncle Cho's e-mail sites. There were six and Li downloaded the e-mail directories from each. He placed all six directories on a flash drive and sent it to Jamie who shared it with his Uncle Dagda. Uncle Dagda shared it with the NSA who identified four e-mail addresses and their three postal addresses in Syria, but in the cities of Tortus, Latakia, and Hama. These were cities on various sides of Masyaf. There was no website related postal address in Masyaf, itself. Was this camouflage? If so, clever! Jamie sent to Aykut those three e-mail addresses and their home addresses, but names were probably false, and maybe the home addresses were also false. But they believed that the possible factory was inside the Citadel and hoped that at least one of e-mail addresses would work such that Aykut could retrieve information about any nanotech factory in the region.

As the plane was approaching the Los Angeles International Airport Li saw a Chinese man walk past his seat who looked just like Uncle Chi Jiang. It was not, but it brought Uncle Chi to his mind. He thought:

'I have not seen Uncle Chi for more than a year. When he does come to China, he stays in the JNI guest house in Yangzhou and comes to the factory during the week. He never visits the Nanjing headquarters or his brother in Nanjing. They transact all of their 'secret' talks in Uncle Cho's office in Yangzhou. On Saturdays he must go to Jincheng City, or somewhere else in China. I know he has houses in New York City and Berlin. And I know he is involved in bringing information with him from Los Angeles sometimes. I also know he is involved in marketing JNI nanoproducts to the entire world. So, I never see him. I wonder if his son does.'

The plane landed. He debarked, and because he was a double citizen, Chinese and American, he went directly through passport control. He picked up his single suitcase, cleared customs, and exited the international area. His father was there waiting for him. They hugged, kissed, looked each other directly in the eye, re-expressed their very solid bonds, and even walked toward the car holding hands. He loved his father very much and really missed him. They had a lot to talk about, but deaths due to Nano-systems would not be mentioned. That was not the Chinese way.

As they walked to the car Li looked up to his dad, but not very long and thought, 'Dr. Chi Jiang was a father to be proud of. Dr. Cho Jiang was an uncle he struggled to even like. While Dr. Jun Jiang was an uncle he did not know. And he was not sure that he wanted to get to know.'

—∘∘⊰❁⊱∘∘—

Aykut was on-line searching and downloading everything that he could find about Aleppo and Masyaf. It was fascinating, but scary stuff.

Aleppo was one of the oldest cities in the world dating back nearly 6,000 years. It was the capital of Greater Northern Syria and was successively controlled by the Amorites, Assyrians, Persians, Alexander the Great (Macedonians), Romans, Byzantines, Arabs, Seljuks, Mongols, Mamluks, Ottomans, and again the Arabs. Between 700 and 1700 AD was the general timeframe when the Citadel of -Masyaf, south of Aleppo some 200 kilometers, became a key control point for the international *Federation of the Assassins.*

The Citadel was built on a high rocky promontory above the lush Orontes Valley. For hundreds of years it served to protect the many trade routes in the area including the Silk Road. The village of Masyaf slowly developed around it and provided support services. At that time the area was under Muslim control. And during the Crusades, numerous Muslim Principalities were formed throughout northern Syria in order to afford protection from the various European Christian armies that kept coming through the area. It was directly on the land route from Europe to the Holy Land. At this time Hassan Sabbah used the Citadel of Masyaf as a major fortress for his army, including the assassins, in attempts to fight the Christian armies.

Hassan Sabbah officially established the *Federation of Assassins* in 1090 in a mountain fortress near Alamut in Persia just south of the Caspian Sea, north and east of Aleppo. It was called the Eagle's Nest and remained as the mountain capital and home to the Ismaili Sect. This Sect elected not to build a great and powerful city, but to establish 'islands of power'. They controlled more than one hundred fortified settlements in northern and western Syria at one point in time. Because of its strategic location Masyaf was one of the key settlements.

Just as power from many fortified settlements was a unique choice of the Ismailis, so also was their choice of individual or personal assassination of key officials and leaders. The assassins did not use bow and arrow or sword, neither did they use lance, armor or horse. Political assassinations with scimitar styled daggers and poisons were their tactics, and they used sleeper commandos to carry out 'assignments'. These commandos were trained in languages, science, trade, politics, and so on. The most common tactic was covert infiltration of an enemy position, in a house or office or business establishment or the battle field, remain undercover and strike the targeted individual within a pre-arranged timeframe. Known as the Fedayeen, and with their skills so well known, many of their political goals were accomplished with just the threat of killing, such as leaving a Hashshashin dagger on the pillow. Several Christian leaders of Crusade Forces were killed by the daggers of the Fedayeen.

Hashshashin, Hashishin, Hashashiyyin, or Hashasheen mean both hashish user and assassin. Hashish is opium. It is thought that when the Fadayeen killed, they were high on hashish. Hashish was the common hypnotic drug that was used by these assassins, so they were basically fearless during an assignment. Fortunately, these killers disappeared over one hundred years ago. So Aykut only had to deal with their ghosts, he hoped.

Aykut was not a brave person. He still was a little overweight and was not sport inclined, so he would have to anticipate potential problems when walking the streets. He did not want to encounter any major problem. But he had the feeling that these sudden international deaths were not going to stop with this last massacre. If any information about the killing mechanism might be found in Masyaf, he must try. So, he developed the following plan.

For his school history course, he would write an article on Masyaf. He would convince his father that he must travel to Syria to see the real thing. The Kurdish unrest along the Turkish border was in Iraq, not Syria. And the Syrian government in Damascus, 400 kilometers south was always focused on Israel. The Aleppo/Halab region had been quiet for many decades. A Turkish tourism company, Dunya Gor, See the World, organized weekly tours to the region. All air and ground travel, hotels, food, and site seeing was on a schedule – Istanbul to Aleppo was two hours by Turkish Airlines, three days in Aleppo, surface travel to Hamma and Homs, and then three days in Masyaf. Back to Aleppo on day six and return by Turkish Airlines to Istanbul. All surface travel was by bus. He would be with twenty to thirty other Turks all of the time. He did not need to involve his friends. And of course, his father would not know the real purpose of the trip. He was able to borrow the Fat Thumb for one week. And he had his smart phone, an IBM-OB1-20a, in peak condition for probably only an hour or two of hacking, if he was lucky. He thought the risk was minimal.

The Aleppo/Halab region hit the upper 30ºC during the summer, hot. But in early October it would be in the 20ºC range, comfortable. And during the second week of October there would be a four-day Bayram, a religious holiday, with all schools closed. So, he talked his father into letting him go, his father arranged his ticket for the tour, and on Sunday afternoon, October 12, he flew from Istanbul to Aleppo with 26 other Turks, adults and children.

As the plane was descending, Aykut looked out the window and remembered what he had read about Aleppo. Today, Aleppo is the second largest city in Syria, population of more than two million, and is the capital of the north. He could see the old city in the center with a large stone wall surrounding it. The city was both old and modern, a typical Arab city filled with thousands of houses and apartment buildings which were the same: four to eight floors in height, flat tops, and many twisting tree lined streets. It sat on the Quweq River, about fifty kilometers from the Mediterranean Sea, surrounded by cultivated and irrigated fields, and only fifty kilometers from the Turkish border. It should be an exciting adventure. His curiosity was beginning to overcome his fears.

The next morning their guide, Sabeen, a very pretty, twenty-year old girl with a lovely olive complexion, dark eyes, and long dark hair in a pony tail, was waiting for them in the hotel lobby. Aykut was sorry that she was too tall for him. But since he was the only 'unattached' tourist, all of the others were couples or families, she did 'seem' to give him the 'eye', he thought. And she even spoke good Turkish.

She would take them on a walking tour of the old walled city. Sabeen began, "We will begin in the Citadel which, as you see, is a large fortress sitting on top of a high rise which dates back to the thirteenth century. It was the heart of Aleppo for the next seven hundred years. Let us enter and see what life was like five hundred years ago." And off they went.

As they left the Citadel and walked for a few minutes toward the south wall, Sabeen continued: "Over there is the Madrasa Halawiye, built in 1124 on top of the site on the Cathedral of St. Helen which had been built in the tenth century by the Mother of Constantine the Great. In those years, as the Christian Crusaders pillaged the surrounding countryside, the Chief Judge of Aleppo converted the church to a mosque, and soon the religious school was added. There are approximately one thousand madrasas and mosques in Aleppo. There are several very famous mosques such as the Great Mosque of Aleppo, built in 715 and rebuilt in 1158, which is the only mosque in the world that has four different façades on the four different sides. The Kushruwiya Mosque was built in 1547 by the famous Ottoman architect Mimar Sinan. We will visit the Al- Nuqtah Mosque or drop of blood mosque, supposedly the blood of the Prophet Husayn. I have a list of most of the other famous mosques. If anyone wants to visit or go to pray, please let me know and I will make arrangements. But as of now we will only visit the mosques in and near the old city."

"In addition, today and tomorrow we will visit several famous or prominent non-religious buildings such as the Beit Achiqbash Museum, the National Library of Aleppo, the Clock Tower of Bab Al Farj, the Grand Saray d'Aleppo which was the former seat of the Governor. And tomorrow we will take a bus out to the Khanqah Al-Farafa, a thirteenth century Sufi monastery."

The days would be filled with walking and seeing history. And he will try to catch Sabeen's eye a couple of times, but it would do his ego no good when that is all he catches.

On Wednesday morning the group left by bus for Hamma on the Orontes River. It is in a major agricultural area and is famous for its innovative norias built during the tenth century. A noria is an aqueduct for purposes of irrigation. They had developed three types; 1) a vertical wheel which is slung with buckets, - animals turn an attached second wheel which when turning causes the first bucket wheel to turn, 2) a vertical wheel which is slung with pots connected to a second wheel which is connected to a wind mill, 3) a vertical wheel slung with buckets which is connected to a water wheel which is located in an artificial waterfall. Hamma boasts the largest noria in the world, twenty meters tall. It was to see this gigantic noria that they stopped for lunch in Hamma on the way to Homs. There were three such side by side wheels, twenty, eighteen, and sixteen meters tall. They were indeed monstrous.

After lunch they rode to Homs, also called Hims, which is now the third largest city in Syria, and which is located in a very fertile mountain valley on the Orontes River. It has always served as a key link between the interior cities and the Mediterranean coastal cities. Historically, it went through a similar series of conquests and reconstructions as did Aleppo. Then, as well as now, it is a major center for trade, industry, especially cotton and textiles, and many agriculture crops. They saw the famous folklore museum of Azze Hrawe Palace, a Mamluk era museum, which depicted life during the twelfth and thirteenth centuries during the reign of Saladin, the Muslim leader who drove the Christians out of Jerusalem.

Then they traveled on to Masyaf and arrived late in the evening, checked in at the Gazzan Hotel, ate a quick meal, and went directly to bed.

The next morning, they had the standard breakfast of cheeses, tomatoes, cucumbers, olives, hot pita bread, honey, and brown tea. A couple again sat with Aykut. Each meal, and often when strolling along, one or another couple would sort of 'get to know him' and 'keep their eye on him'. This was the Turkish way. A child, at any age, never left the family nest. And at this moment of his fourteen years he was once again in the 'Turkish family nest'.

Across the table sat Bulent and Verda Gurer, and to his left side sat Attila and Yildiz Ulusoy. They had been his two most insistent/consistent family babysitters. Mr. Ulusoy asked, "So what do you think of northern Syria so far, Aykut?"

Aykut responded, "I liked the Azze Hrawe Palace in Homs. The exhibits really let you imagine what life was like for the Mamluk tribes. And I thought the noria in Hama was neat. But living in Istanbul with water on five sides, I don't think they will sell there." And he laughed.

Mr. Ulusoy commented, "If you lived in Ankara where we do, not even one river, you could sell one hundred of those things."

And Aykut laughed as in Istanbul it rained at least once a week; in Ankara, the Turkish capital, it rained less than once a month. He had spent one month in dry Ankara in April and swore never to return.

Mr. and Mrs. Ulusoy were the only two non-Istanbulites on the trip. The Ulusoys had been on vacation in Istanbul for the week with Mrs. Ulusoy's brother, Mr Gurer. And they had all decided to take a tour to see Aleppo and Masyaf. Their five children were nearly the same age and were being babysat by an aunt. So, the two couples had sort of adopted Aykut back in Aleppo. It was all right. He knew when and how he would ditch them and do his hacking. He already had a copy of the floor plans of the Citadel of Masyaf, and he was currently memorizing it.

Mr. Ulusoy asked Aykut, "What profession do you plan to enter someday?"

"I do not know yet," replied Aykut. "My father wants me to go into banking with him. I want something more exciting than just moving money from here to there or there to here. I love my computer. Maybe I will study robotics. Robotics is seventy five percent computer and twenty five percent mechanics. And someday we will be building electronic people who can do all types of dangerous work that humans should not be doing or cannot do."

Mr. Gurer spoke out, "I will introduce you to my twelve-year old son who wants to go into Nano sciences. Maybe that area would interest you."

Aykut quickly looked at his plate and quietly said, "Maybe."

They talked for a few more minutes and then Aykut excused himself. He went to his room to get his smart phone. This was the latest and best. He would use a single ear plug, tune it in to a local radio station, keep his downloaded music ready, open and close his phone with and without the Big Thumb attached at different times to try to pick up cell phone noise from the Citadel. Occasionally he would flip into the camera mode, take a few pictures, and then turn it off and turn the phone or radio back on. At locations where he had good phone noise he would return later and try to hack in and download it using one of the numbers that Jamie had given him.

The tour group met in front of the hotel. Their tour guide, Yusuf Shazon was a dark-skinned older man with narrow eyes, a balding head, thick graying mustache, and a rather difficult disposition. He began, "Welcome to Masyaf. Today we will walk, as a group, and please stay as a group, for a couple of hours through the village area. As you can see the village is south of the Citadel. The population is nearly twenty thousand and throughout history has only provided support service for the famous Citadel. So, history of the city of Masyaf is really the history of the Citadel of Masyaf."

The group began walking towards the center of the village and continued to learn Middle East history. The tour group had no choice but to follow and listen to the Syrian tour guide, as there were several armed police studying them.

"Human settlement began here in the eighth century and a small village existed until the tenth century when the Hamdanid dynasty came to power in northern Iraq and Syria. Based in Aleppo, they started building fortified outposts to guard the mountain trade routes. The Citadel of Masyaf was one of the first. Between 1098 and 1200 AD, during the era of the Christian Crusades, the region became chaotic. Different Christian armies were coming and going, raiding and burning and killing and then moving on. From the twelfth century onwards, Masyaf and the Citadel became the Capital of the Nizari Ismaili state. The Ismaili conquered many of the other outposts, strengthened them, and became a power in northeastern Syria for several centuries. It was during this time that the methods and techniques of individual assassination developed and personal assassins were trained using the Hashshashin dagger."

"Later the Mamluks conquered several of the fortified outposts and citadels in the region; eventually the Ismaili and the Mamluks shared the area until the sixteenth century when the Ottomans arrived. The Ottoman Turks captured the Citadel, allowed the Ismaili emirs to remain, and improved, expanded, and enhanced its military capacity. At the end of the Ottoman era in the twentieth century, the military capacity began to diminish. And after the First World War, during the French mandate, the Ismailis evacuated the Citadel."

"Now we have reached the shopping sector of Masyaf. I will allow you to have one hour to shop. Do not buy too much as we will not have time to return to the hotel before we go into the Citadel. We will meet back here at 11:15 sharp. Then we will go up to and enter the Citadel."

And he walked off toward a heavily shaded tea house to have some tea and sweets, and to chat with his friends. The Turks looked at each other, shrugged their shoulders and started looking at trinkets and souvenirs. They had already paid for their guide, too late to request another now. But if his rather arrogant behavior continued, they would inform the travel agency when they returned to Istanbul.

At exactly 11:15, the guide started walking up toward the Citadel, and the Turks hurried to catch up. After five minutes he stopped and said, "From this spot one can see most of the Citadel. Look and I will explain."

"The Citadel of Masyaf is located on a mountain spine that runs north to south. The Citadel is one hundred and fifty meters long and sixty meters wide. There are natural terraces along the east, south, and west sides, but not the north. These terraces were expanded; many walls were built on the terrace edges; and hundreds of rooms were built next to and in the mountain side. There are five levels; each level is divided into outer and inner rooms, streets and corridors. And each level is compartmentalized like a bee's honeycomb. Plus, there are numerous secret corridors, tunnels, caves, and stairways inside and even below the mountain itself. Conquest of this fortress was accomplished only by hand to hand battles. Even long-range cannons were not very helpful in trying to conquer this stone-mountain city. It is the only city/fortress inside a mountain anywhere in the world. Or as some people say, it is a mountain that swallowed a whole city, or a mountain that swallowed a city whole. Ha! Ha! Ha!"

And still the Turks were having a hard time trying to find him funny.

"Here on the south end you will see that there are more extensive defense walls and cannon placements because the approach toward the Citadel is shallow. On the northern end the mountain drops off very sharply so the defenses are less. There are more than one thousand rooms inside these walls and fifty-seven stairways, plus eleven ramps, no elevators. We will enter through one of the dozen entries at ground level. I will take you to a nice restaurant, Hamdi's Restaurant, which has a spectacular view of the surrounding mountains. You can have your lunch and then I will show to you some of those one thousand rooms, but not all of them. You don't pay me enough to show all of them to you. I will give you two hours for lunch."

He laughed. And again, the Turks just looked at each other and wondered where this guy really came from, a local of course. But his Turkish was reasonable; so, one understood most of what he said most of the time. It required about a half hour to walk to the Citadel and to climb to the fourth level. Fortunately, there was a nice breeze and the view was as promised. They sat down to a nice lunch and looked out at the lovely brown-gray-cream-orange mountains At 1:30 PM, when Yusuf announced that lunch time was over and that everyone would now meet outside the restaurant on the fourth level street everyone agreed.

Outdoors he started, "I expect you to stay with me as a group, but if you do get lost ask anyone and they will help you. In the summer the narrow streets and corridors are very crowded and getting lost is common. But now the heavy tourism season is over, the big crowds are gone, so we should not have that problem. But there are a couple of rules I must tell you. Several years ago, a foreign company purchased the northern 25% of the Citadel. They are still renovating that part and it is off limits. You will occasionally see doors that have signs that say do not enter. This company is currently renovating space on all levels, but construction supplies enter and leave from the ground level on the north corner. So there has been no interference with tourism, and we will simply avoid those construction areas. The other 75% of the Citadel has been fully renovated much like it was a few hundred years ago. You will find it fascinating, I am certain. Are there any questions?"

One lady spoke up, "Are there police inside the Citadel to help us if we have a problem?"

"Of course, there is a police station on each level."

An older gentleman asked, "Are there toilets on all levels?"

"Yes, there are several on each level. All right let us go to the Palace first." For the next several hours they walked and looked at sites on each level such as: the inner Palace on levels four and five in the center of the Citadel, bedrooms and living facilities of the ruler and family on the inner fourth level, tombs on the inner fourth level, special defense towers on level five and the outer fifth level, housing accommodations for the ruling class on the inner third level, the Ottoman House on the outer fourth level facing west, a large defense complex on the second level facing south, large shopping area on the outer second level facing east, barracks for military on the first and second levels outside, a very large open courtyard on the first level near the main entry stairway. Stairways were for people; ramps were for animals and wagons or carts. And there were several underground cisterns for storage of rain water, caves that were used as general storage areas for everything from food to military supplies, and of course a large prison with extensive torture facilities.

As they walked from area to area Aykut continued to test for phone signals, sounds, or voices. At the end of the day he decided that he received the strongest signals from the area of the tombs. So tomorrow he would return to this area to continue sightseeing. He would pretend to look for the names of famous families that were buried there. And he would determine the names of those families while he was playing on-line tonight.

The tourist group was on their own for the day. The following morning the bus would leave the hotel at 2:30 PM to return to Aleppo and then by plane directly to Istanbul. Therefore, the entire trip rested on having a lucky last day in Syria.

The next morning Mr. and Mrs. Gurer and Mr. and Mrs. Ulusoy joined him at the breakfast table. Mr. Ulusoy spoke, "Where are you going this morning, Aykut?"

Aykut swallowed twice and finally said, "I think I will just wander around inside the Citadel for a while and finish the film in my smart phone. If you would please just slide closer together I can take your pictures."

They slid closer together and he quickly snapped a couple of photos. Then he looked down at his phone and commented, "Oh! Oh! I see a problem with my wireless computer mode. Excuse me I need to run upstairs and adjust it before I go out this morning. Excuse me please."

He quickly ran up the stairs to his room. Now he would have to wait until his friends/babysitters left the hotel.

One half hour later they were gone so he quietly left for the Citadel. He slowly walked up to the fourth floor, stopping along the way on the second level to purchase a couple of presents for family and friends. He picked up two more tourist copies of the floor plans of the Citadel. These plans showed all five levels and some of the underground caves of the public sector area; but they did not show the private sector area which was under renovation. The area around the tombs was on the far north end, east side near the closed off area where he speculated was a possible nanotech factory. It also seemed logical that if the factory occupied several floors, the upper floors in the private areas would house the offices and possibly computers and phone systems.

He slowly approached the tomb area, took out his list of famous Ismaili families that should be buried there. No one was around so he plugged in the Big Thumb and opened his smart phone. He tried each of the numbers. He heard nothing on Number one. But numbers two and three were hits. He downloaded for six minutes on number two and eight minutes on number three. He then closed it as he did not want to run out of luck. While waiting for the downloading to finish, he had found more than nine of the Ismaili graves dated seventeenth and eighteenth centuries. No one had approached him. So, he packed away his smart phone and started to leave.

As he went along the fourth floor toward the Palace area two policemen approached him and commanded, "Stop, what are you doing here by yourself?"

Aykut was prepared, "I am writing a research paper for my class in Istanbul. I am studying the Citadel of Masyaf and the Ismaili royalty. See my study information." And he gave to them his notes.

Both of the officers were Syrian, could speak only a little Turkish, but could read no Turkish. They did not want to embarrass themselves; so, they carefully looked over Aykut's notes, and nodded, "This is very nice. More Turks should study the Ismaili. You can go."

As he quickly left the Citadel and started walking back toward the hotel a man started to follow him. The man was poorly dressed and sort of rough looking; he made Aykut nervous. Aykut knew the way to the hotel by now, so he decided to take a short cut down an alley. About half way down the alley another man entered from the far end. He was even more ruffian looking. Aykut turned and tried to return up the alley but the first man blocked his way. At the same time the second man closed in from behind. Both men revealed knives from under their shirts. They were even uglier looking up-close. Aykut tried to stare them down; and then he saw that they had Hashshashin daggers, not just knives. He assumed that they wanted his smart phone and started to take it off when both of them approached with the daggers raised, Aykut shut his eyes and prayed.

Suddenly he heard two shots. He fell to the ground. He thought he was dead, but suddenly realized that those two men had daggers, not guns. He opened his eyes and saw the two daggers lying on the ground and the men running toward the Citadel. From the hotel direction Mr. Gurer and Mr. Ulusoy came running. Mr. Ulusoy had a gun in his hand. And Aykut knew his prayers had been answered.

Mr. Ulusoy helped him up and asked, "Are you hurt? It looks like we got here just in time."

Aykut looked his body over, felt around, saw no blood and answered. "I guess not. Why? How?"

Mr. Ulusoy, seeing that they were indeed on time, smiled and responded, "I am a government agent. Your father arranged that my wife and I enjoy this tour with you. He also suggested that we may be prepared to help you if you should need any help. After the Haydarpasha murders we sent several agents to Aleppo. They are still here. I arranged for one of them to provide me with a gun and to help keep an eye on you. A couple of minutes ago he called and told us that you had just left the Citadel and was cornered in this alleyway. He did not think that he could get to you on time to help. We were at the hotel, which as you know is just around the corner, and fortunately we were on time."

Aykut was still shaking a little. "Thank you. I was in deep trouble. You did save my life. Will you tell my father? He will ground me forever."

And he gave Mr. Ulusoy that please smile. Mr. Ulusoy had a ten-year old son. Mr. Gurer had a twelve-year old son. They looked at each other. Mr. Ulusoy reached down and picked up the two daggers, gave one to Mr. Gurer and said, "These tourism shops really know how to make very realistic knives."

They both turned around and walked back to the hotel. Aykut, who was sweating, but smiling, followed behind them. For the rest of the day they were no longer strangers. And that evening all members of the tourist group returned safely to Istanbul.

23

Breathing Can Be Dangerous

O N July 4, 2032, the American President and his three families were outdoors in the White House Rose Garden celebrating Independence Day by watching, along with a few thousand other Washingtonians, the fireworks display over the top of the Washington Monument. One of his Aides interrupts and gives to him a quick briefing on a recent CNN report. The Aide then opens his smart phone and he and the President tune in to CNN, then BBC, and then EURO News. A second Aide had already dialed the State Department which had received the same information via encrypted e-mail from the American Ambassador in South Africa several hours ago; but because of the holiday they considered that it was not high enough priority, so they delayed in sending the information to the White House.

The report said that in Bloemfountain, South Africa, 212 Africans had been killed in a diamond mine. They had been killed by some kind of unknown toxic substance in the air. The lungs of each miner had been digested or dissolved. Everyone died by immediate asphyxiation.

The President of the United States was now a Collector of Bodies. Was this the first 212?

Three days before July 4, Kef and his older brother, Baryti, had gone to Johannesburg, the capital of South Africa, to look at a new Nano-technique method for cancer diagnosis at the Department of Nanotechnology in

242

the University of Johannesburg, and to pick up some special laboratory supplies. Baryti was a level three laboratory technician in a small Nano-research company, CTNano Corp., in Cape Town. Kef was following, more and more, in his brother's footsteps, and big brother was encouraging him to do so. When Baryti asked Kef if he wanted to join him for a trip to the capital to visit the UJ Department of Nano-technology, he answered with a yes, yes, yes. They arrived late in the evening of July 1, after a three hour South African Airlines flight, took a room at the Ekala Hotel, and went directly to sleep.

Johannesburg is the largest and richest city in South Africa with over five million people. It is the center for the large quantities of gold and diamonds that are mined nearby and in the vast hinterlands, and sold in Europe, Asia, and North America. It is about 800 miles from Cape Town and within 200-300 miles of Botswana, Zimbabwe, and Mozambique.

Removal of gold from the earth is accomplished by several processes and techniques. Most of the gold discovered in California 200 years ago was by way of panning, sluicing, dredging, and using metal detectors. However, over the past 100 years more modern methods include hard rock mining from underground tunnels or from open pits, extraction of gold away from the ground rocks using cyanide, a very toxic and poisonous chemical, and storing the used cyanide in nearby manmade ponds.

Diamond mining also now utilizes several extraction methods. Whereby gold forms near the earth's surface, diamonds form deep in the earth, usually more than 100 miles deep. They are then carried toward the earth's surface by volcanic activity. Most diamonds are found in the Kimberlite Pipes, which are champagne like flute glass shape areas, large at the top and small at the bottom. They may be several thousand feet deep, and form as volcanoes erupt. Later, the center of the extinct volcano droops and fills with water allowing shallow lakes to form on top of the old volcanic opening or at the top of the flute glass. It is directly under these lakes in the old lava chamber that the Kimberlite Pipes form. They contain complex matrixes of rock mixtures. Most such mixtures include some diamonds of gem quality on down to alluvial deposits of tiny machine grade diamonds. The lake water is pumped off and these deposits can then become open pit mines. Tunneling is used for diamond extraction only when horizontal Kimberlite types of pipes form from the large vertical pipe. And surface mining is used in locations where alluvial deposits are very near the surface of the earth.

Johannesburg is ranked 47th out of the top 50 cities in the world as a center of commerce, has the country's largest stock exchange, and has recently been expanding from a mining center to heavier industries such as steel and cement. The city encompasses almost 800 square miles, including the township of Soweto which played a critical role in the anti-apartheid movement. Today many consider Johannesburg to be the most advanced metropolitan city in all of Africa. With over ten million planted trees, a man-made urban forest, it certainly is one of the greenest cities in the world. It is filled with numerous excellent highways, shopping malls and native crafts centers, so it has successfully converted hundreds of thousands of slum dwellers into home-owners and has begun attracting tens of thousands of tourists each year.

On July 2, they woke up and Baryti asked Kef, "Well, are you ready to see a real nanotech research laboratory? This is the best in Africa, you know."

Kef responded, "Yes. I want to see how they do research and meet some of the doctors. I must decide whether I want to study nanotechnology for my entire life. And that will be a long time."

And the brothers' eyes met. They both smiled. They had grown close over the past couple of years. The new science called nanotechnology was the common magnet.

So Baryti and Kef spent the entire day at the Nanotech Laboratories in the University of Johannesburg and watched a demonstration of this new diagnostic technique. Baryti liked it very much, called his laboratory director, recommended buying it, received permission to buy two test kits, and bring them back with him. They would try the test on blood samples of their patients from the local small cancer hospital in Cape Town. They stayed at the University all day, watched several research projects in motion, talked with doctors and students, and even ate dinner with several of the nanotech laboratory workers that evening. There were only six nanotech laboratories in all of South Africa, so it was good to get to know each other.

The next morning Baryti asked Kef, "I have completed my work for this trip. We saw what nanotech research was, and now know several nanotech researchers such that as they develop new products, we can learn from them. We probably will not return to Johannesburg for a while, would you like to see some of the city?"

Kef had already thought about this and replied. "Yes, if we have time, I want to see the Mandela Family Museum, the Apartheid Museum, and the Hillbrow Tower, which was the tallest structure in Africa at 300 meters."

Baryti agreed, so off they went to play tourist.

The Mandela Family Home, in Orlando West in Soweto, had been turned into a museum and was living history. Nelson Rolihlahla Mandela was one of the world's greatest leaders. He spent his entire life fighting racial oppression in South Africa, including twenty-five years in prison. Eventually, as President of the African National Congress and Head of the Anti-Apartheid Movement, he was a key person who led the nation toward multiracial government and majority rule. Mr. Mandela was awarded the Nobel Prize for Peace and became President of South Africa. He is revered by most black South Africans. The house where he lived was converted into a spectacular museum; and Kef went through every room and read everything.

They then left the museum and took a taxi north and east to Gold Reef City to have lunch. Baryti heard Kef say, "He sure was a superman. In prison one year and the Nobel prize winner the next year."

Baryti chuckled to himself, but agreed.

After lunch near the Apartheid Museum, they entered the museum. Kef found all of the massive killings very depressing; "How can human beings do that to human beings?" Yet it resulted in a clear final victory for his people.

The museum tells the story of the human spirit triumphing over human repression. It is the first and only museum in the world to tell the story of the rise and fall of apartheid. The museum illustrates in detail the events and human stories of fifty years of struggle by twenty million black Africans, natives, against total control under a few thousand white Europeans, foreigners. The numerous exhibits include film footages, photographs, text panels, and many artifacts of the now past era. Kef spent the entire afternoon going through the twenty-five exhibit centers which tell the very emotional story of a state sanctioned totally on racial discrimination, and how this was finally overcome.

As they left the museum and started walking the several blocks to the Restaurant of the Wilds, Kef had only one comment, "This is something that must never happen again."

They entered the restaurant which was decorated like a dozen village domed houses, the walls filled with spears, long knives, and animal heads. And each area had a central fire pit with a small fire burning, for ambience only, and several round tables with four chairs. They chose the alligator house which had the skin of a 35 feet long alligator on one wall.

As they sat down and looked over the menu, Bartyi asked Kef, "Would you like to go to school and work here someday, maybe at the Nanotech Laboratories at the University?"

Kef studied the menu and replied, "Only in my furthest dreams."

Bartyi replied, "I have some friends who might be able to help, if you had super grades in high school, that is."

Kef returned, "It is a deal. I will get the grades. You get the money."

And they both seriously did high fives. It was a good incentive for a young man with the energy and the motivation to go and do, but he also needed a solid road to follow. Certainly, Nanotechnology in sports medicine was not yet even an academic program.

"This is our last night in Johannesburg so I will have duiker antelope," said Bartyi. And what are you going to have?"

"I want a double portion of the black rhinoceros," responded Kef. "Who needs vegetables?"

Bartyi looked him in the eye to see if he was serious, and yes, he was serious. So, he got his double meat protein. He could eat his vegetables when he got home.

After dinner Kef liked it so much that he thought he might have to grow a couple of rhinos in the back yard. In that way he would have this powerful protein more often.

But they ate with little conversation. Having decided in what direction his studies would go, especially after the heavy messages that emanated from the day's two museums, they just ate slowly, and went back to the hotel to bed. Kef was happy but a bit depressed. He was ready to return home. He was the last in the nest and that had certain security.

Their return flight to Cape Town was scheduled for 11:00 AM on the fourth. So that next morning, they woke, had a light breakfast, took a taxi, and arrived at the Tambo or Johannesburg International Airport near 9:45 AM. As they were walking through the terminal there was a mass of confusion. All television sets and every channel were announcing the massive killing of 212 workers in the Saatfordam Diamond Mine near Bloemfontain. Their father was the manager of a working crew at this mine; and they knew he was working a night shift this month. It appeared that it was the miners on the night shift that had been killed.

Bartyi simply said, "We must go."

As they changed their tickets to Bloemfontain they heard from the televisions that the miners' lungs had dissolved and they died of asphyxiation.

Kef's first response was, "Could that be a Nano-tech system?" Bartyi immediately agreed, "What else could it be?"

Three hours later they landed, rented a car, and took off for a one hour drive out to the Saatfordam mine. Bartyi had been here several times, so he knew that the mining headquarters was on the west side of the half mile diameter open pit. As they arrived, he headed directly to the headquarter buildings which were surrounded by a twelve high barbed wire fence.

The military seemed to have everything under control and stopped them at the entry gate. Once they explained that they were family members of a miner on last night's work crew, they were allowed to go directly through. It was obvious that the mine's security forces were not enough as many families of the workers were enquiring about their loved ones. They were bringing up and out the bodies as fast as they could. The brothers learned that these bodies were being laid out in a back- parking lot. It was hot and there were not enough refrigeration units to place the more than two hundred men. So, they were laid on the asphalt and simply covered with plastic sheeting. This allowed the families to more easily search for their men, but also allowed the pall of death to fill the air.

The brothers identified their father, notified a soldier who then checked it off his list of dead miners. They asked to be left alone with him for a few minutes before they moved him to another area of 'identified dead'. Because the soldier was in heavy demand, he told them he would return in fifteen minutes. The soldier walked away.

Bartyi said, "Stand between me and the soldiers."

Kef moved over and blocked the view of most of the soldiers as he bowed his head in prayer over his father. Bartyi bent over the body, pretended to pray, removed a needle attached to a vacuum blood collection tube from his pocket, taken from the supplies and nanotechnology test kits that he was taking to Cape Town, withdrew several milliliters of blood, capped it, and placed in his pocket. Because the syringe had an interior coating of a potent anti-coagulant, the partially coagulated blood re-dissolved as it entered the tube. He would take his father's blood back to his laboratory and have it tested for presence of any kind of Nano-tech system.

Bartyi and Kef then went down onto their knees and for the next fifteen minutes they prayed over their father; neither could resist the flow of tears as he was a very good father, and a very good man. He had raised a big family; and every child had become a successful adult, Kef was on his way.

Soon the soldiers came and took the body to a room in an adjacent building and the brothers filled out identification death forms and made arrangement to have their father's body sent to Cape Town. While Bartyi was dealing with the official process, Kef went outside and using his brother's cellular phone he called their mother, and then each brother and sister. At that time, he could only tell them that all of the miners died at the same time during the night, and their lungs were dissolved so they died quickly of asphyxiation, probably without any pain. Their father's funeral would be on Sunday and he would be buried in their communal family plots.

Two weeks later, Kef initiated a computer conference of the Four Colored Musketeers.

He began, "Na'via is present. Who else is present?"

In response he heard: Mo'ata is present. Ey'tuka is present. Tsu'teye is present.

But before Na'via could respond the air was filled with "I am very sorry about your father. Are you all right? How are your mother and family doing? Is there anything we can do……?

Na'via's father was the second father of the 4-pack to be killed by a Nano- tech-system in the past three years; he reminded them of this. And a question that was still up in the air, were they each killed by a nanoproduct from the factory on a certain one of their fathers?

He continued, "Thank you. We are good. We are surviving. And I want to tell you about the mass killing of my father and his entire work crew of more than 200 men in the Saatfordam Diamond Mines. My brother, Bartyi, and I were in Johannesburg, nearby, when this happened. So, we arrived only a few hours later. They were still bringing the bodies up and out from the tunnel when we arrived. They were laying the bodies on the ground in a large parking lot just behind the main building. We found him right away. And when no one was looking Bartyi took a blood sample and we brought it back to Cape Town."

"As you know Bartyi is a senior technician in a nanotech company here. Because I am seriously thinking about studying in the nanotech sciences, he has been teaching me about how different Nano-tech systems work. Allow me to remind you. Usually they require two major components; the nanoproduct which is a molecule made up of many carbon atoms and is called an organic molecule, and a homing MoAB which guides the nanoproduct and which is a protein molecule. They are only lightly bound to each other so they can be easily separated in the laboratory."

Bartyi found a Nano-tech-system in our father's blood. His laboratory has what is called a new model high precision liquid chromatography column, HPLC, with a NYT-3943-d column, and a TO-183 Mass Spectrophotometer Analytical. Using these instruments, he found a nanoproduct, but no MoAB. Ey'tuka, tell your uncle that we may have a Nano-killer, and that this is how Bartyi found it. Ask him to let us know if he wants us to send to him a sample extract to compare with one of the JXW labeled nanoproducts. Bartyi says that he can do no more because he has no standards to compare it with. He cannot determine how it caused the lungs to digest or dissolve."

Ey'tuka responded, "I understand."

"All of the miners died at the same time. Their lung cavities were partially filled with blood and fluids and membranes, otherwise they were empty. All of the cells in the lungs, which are similar to millions of grapes filled with air, had burst. Apparently only some membrane cell walls remained. Now that is scary!"

Eu'tuka asked, "I thought that most diamonds came from open pit mines, not from tunnels in the ground. Your father must have been in a partially enclosed area if this Nano-system came through the air and into the lungs."

"You are correct, "answered Na'via. "Tunnels are only used if there is an offshoot cone of very rich diamonds that are too deep to reach from an open pit. I know from talking with my father that this cone where they were digging was loaded with alluvial deposits of tiny diamonds. Such diamonds are now becoming more valuable than large jewelry style diamonds because of their new use in chips in electronic products. So yes, they were deep in a long narrow tunnel or cave."

Ey'tuka asked, "Do you know if that tunnel has had air circulation problems in the past?"

"I am not certain. And I think that it is the only tunnel or cave mine at the Saatfordam Diamond Mines."

Mo'ata commented, "If I am correct these killers have gone from individuals to families to group killing. What next?"

"Does your brother think that this Nano-system did not have a MoAB because it obviously targeted the lungs and was somehow placed into the air, so the miners just breathed it?"

"I did not ask, and I do not know." Na'via replied. Probably the bigger ups must be investigating all of that."

And indeed, the bigger ups were investigating the mass murder of 212 South African miners. After a President to President clearance, Mr. Dagda Murphy and his ISAAT team of five investigators traveled to South Africa on the 10th of July. They first stopped at the South African Ministry of Police in Johannesburg, and then were escorted to the mine at Bloemfountain by the Ministry's investigators who had carried out the investigation on the mass murder. At the mine they talked with the mine's security people, and even spoke with some of the dead miners' families.

They were informed that the deaths of the miners were probably due to a toxic microorganism which originated from the tunnel's walls during the drilling process. Although they tried to identify and isolate this microorganism, they were not successful. But they did believe that it originated within the tunnel's air and that the miners did breathe it; the inhalation is what caused the deaths. They also were not able to identify or isolate this toxic microorganism from the bodies of the miners. The South African investigators were not even thinking about nanotechnology; Mr. Murphy did not bring the subject up. All of the miners had already been buried. No blood samples were available to take back to the States for evaluation.

Mr. Murphy did learn that all the killed were at the far end of a 280 feet long tunnel and in an adjacent large cave. They had begun work at 7:30 PM. At 11:00 PM they exited the tunnel and ate their dinner by sitting on the ground in the open pit. They always carried their food with them. At 12:00 midnight they all returned into the tunnel to work. Near 3:00 AM the air seemed to become stagnant, so the crew's manager, Kef's Father, ordered an air purifier/circulator machine brought into the tunnel and turned on. This was done. The night shift was routinely finished at 4:30 AM; but the current working crew had not yet left the tunnel when the next shift began arriving at 5:30 AM. The mine security entered the tunnel and found all of the miners lying on the ground, at their work stations. They were on their backs, eyes closed, with a peaceful look on their faces. All were dead and almost cold. Later the purifier/circulator machine was carefully checked for toxic biological organisms; none were found. The person who had delivered the machine to the tunnel upon request, had disappeared. It was determined that he was not an employee of the mine, but apparently a stranger.

The deaths were officially attributed to natural causes, a toxic microorganism from the tunnel's walls. Therefore, this worker was not of importance. Case closed.

24

The Evidence Is Rolling In

Autumn had begun and the leaves in Washington were falling. Mr. Dagda Murphy and his ISAAT investigative teams had been following the advice and recommendations of the members of the Presidential Commission of International Drug Smuggling. They had been working overtime and taking advantage of the expertise and contacts of the other eleven members of the Commission. So, this was the last meeting of this year and there was a lot to discuss.

On October 26, 2032, all Commission members were sitting around the conference table on the fourth floor of the Department of Justice building in Washington, DC. Each was anxiously waiting to hear the results of these difficult and extensive efforts in information and data gathering, not all of it legal and legitimate. But the dangers involved were such that legality was for the future and the courts could decide that issue when or if it should manifest itself.

Mr. Jackson O'Reilly opened the meeting, "Welcome. We have much to cover so let us begin immediately. At our last meeting we informed you that there were many possible candidates for a leader who could be orchestrating these MUSDs. We narrowed it down to four plus a family group of three. We feel that each of these seven men has the facilities and are capable of working with nanotechnical systems at the international level. This reduction in candidates was necessary in order to reduce our work load such that we could perform in depth investigations in a short period of time. It does not eliminate other possible candidates on our list, nor prevent us from adding to the list. Recently, Mr. Murphy and our investigative teams in Russia, Germany, Argentina, Canada, China, and the USA, have been working 24/7 collecting information and data concerning these seven people. So, I will turn the meeting over to Mr. Murphy."

"Hello again," he began. "I will present most of the information today; and I wish to present to you the summaries of our investigations such that when you have a question, please ask it, do not wait until later. We are looking for a person who calls himself the Korrectorizer. I will begin in Russia, circle the earth and end up in China."

"Mr. Boris Kukrynisky was born and raised in Moscow. His father was a general in the Soviet army; he saw to it that his only son was educated in London and New York, as well as the International School in Moscow. At a young age, Boris developed international friends in the two largest banking cities in the world. When the Berlin Wall fell, USSR and Communism fell, and national industrial systems were sold to people who became known as oligarchs. Boris Kukryknisky was an A+ oligarch."

"But when Russia became a smaller republic, the government was reorganized. Part of that reorganization was re-nationalization of many of the previously now un-nationalized industrial systems. Many such entrepreneurs, like Mr. Kukrynisky made hard and fast deals just to survive. But a wheeler- dealer he was."

"In 1998, Mr. Kukrynisky was the President and CEO of five companies involved in transportation, mining, textiles, and microchip manufacturing. By 2012, three of those companies had been returned to the Russian government. He maintained control of Russian Chip International, RCI, and Moscow Nanotechnology Incorporated, MNI. He had used his friends in New York and London to become a major player in high technology manufacturing. His companies did little in the way of research; but they followed the Chinese model - steal the patent, copy it and add one comma, manufacture the product, and sell it to the company holding the patent. He could produce it 50-75% cheaper. Over the years he had begun to focus on nanotechnological systems in medicine."

"Mr. Kukrynisky now is fifty-seven years old, has three sons who are currently in schools in Copenhagen, Tokyo, and Los Angeles, and one daughter who is a student in the Faculty of Sciences at the University of Moscow. He has houses in Los Angeles and New York City, a large Moscow flat, and a lovely dacha outside of Moscow. His wife lives in the Moscow flat. A plethora of girl- friends rotate through the other three homes. He spends his work days at both of his company's headquarters on the 32nd and 41st floors in the Moscow International Business Center, commonly known as Moscow City, on the Presnenskaya embankment; both offices have a spectacular view of the Moscow River. In addition, he regularly rents apartments and offices in nearby buildings within Moscow City, to be used officially, of course. The RCI factory is in Voykovski and the MNI factory is in Ryazanskiy. Both are between the second and third Moscow Ring Roads, within easy access to Moscow City or his dacha."

"With regard to Mr. Kukrynisky's financial status, he is currently a billionaire. He has bank accounts in Switzerland, Cyprus, and the Canary Islands, that we know about. He regularly travels to and does business in France, USA, and China; part of his travel involves stopovers in Monte Carlo, Las Vegas, and Singapore where he often spends several days gambling. He has close business contacts in Paris with Jean-Pierre DeRond, who is known to be associated with the Royal Cross Mafia, and in Hong Kong with Lin Won Do, who is the Titular Head of the Yellow Tiger Mafia. Mr. Kukrynisky has the capacity to produce Nano-tech-products and to move these products through illicit groups on at least two continents."

"Therefore, Mr. Boris Kukrynisky has many fires to fuel, much money coming and going, friends of dubious character, a track record which is less than pure, and he has a factory that produces a variety of Nano-tech products."

The international lawyer, Mr. Jefferson asked, "Has Mr. Kukrynisly been indicted for any crimes in the recent past?"

"Prior to 2010 yes, several times. In the last dozen years, he has led a 'clean' life."

Dr. Thomas, CIA, asked, "Does Mr. Kukrynisky have any connections to western, perhaps the USA, nanotech companies where he might finance specific research projects and then manufacture the product from his factories and sell it?'

"If you will remember; the famous Soviet expression which was taught to every grade school kid was: If you want to hang a capitalist and you do not have a rope, do not worry, you can always find another capitalist around the corner to sell you a rope!"

"As you know, the world's capitalistic system allows anyone to contract research or production of commercial products. Just look at the massive outsourcing of today. The exception is for products that have been proven dangerous and highly toxic; but even those can be produced and sold under strict local and international regulations. To my knowledge, no Nano-technological product has been declared dangerous or toxic. So, what you are suggesting, buying a nanoproduct from a Nano-factory, is easy to do."

Mr. O'Reilly spoke up, "Today, the Nano-tech market cannot be compared to the gun market supported by the National Rifle Association. But, if we can prove that these killings are caused by Nano-tech systems, we hope to change the laws to control their manufacture and sales. Are nuclear fueled systems controlled today? Yes! Why? Because they have been proven to be dangerous."

After several moments of silence, Mr. Murphy continued, "If there are no more questions for now, let us look at Dr. Frans Heinz, President of Nano Solar LTD, whose factory is in Rosenheim, near Munich, Germany. Mr. Femer was in charge of investigating Dr. Heinz. Mr. Femer, if you please?'

Mr. Bryan Femer, Director of the European Division of ISAAT, began his presentation. "Thank you, I will try to be as succinct and yet as informative as my boss." And he smiled at Mr. Murphy.

"Dr. Frans Heinz has been a Professor for the past nineteen years in the Division of Science and Engineering at the Technical University of Munich, in Garching bei Munchen, or Garching, Germany. He lives in a modest house near the A9 Autobahn toward Munich, and close to his nanotech factory. He only became President and CEO of Nano Solar, LTD seven years ago. Currently, each week he spends three days teaching and four days in the factory. The company is moderate and had sales of two hundred million Euros in 2030. Its major research and production efforts are in the field of using nanotechnology for solar-voltage energy associated with new transportation systems; one example is a solar-voltage skin for airplanes. But he has been producing medically related Nano systems during the past 3-4 years, because they are further developed, in higher demand and have a bigger profit margin. His brain power comes from his students at the university. He was a typical University Professor of Chemical Engineering and over the years had seen several of his research ideas go into mass production. But his luck turned bad just a few years ago."

"In 2026 his mother was in a terrible automobile accident, broke her neck, and has been bedfast on total life support systems ever since. She is housed in a nursing center near the family house; she has all of her mental facility, but is officially as 90% disabled with no hope of recovery."

"Dr. Heinz is divorced and does not see his ex-wife; he has two adult, married children. One lives and works in Berlin. The other lives and works in Bonn. They both are married, have children, and do not visit with him regularly."

"In 2027 his father developed a very progressive form of Parkinson's disease. Currently he is physically stable but has lost most of his mental facility. The father is housed at the same nursing center as mother, but on a floor separate."

'The mother and father no longer see each other, nor do they know that the other is still alive, let alone live in the same building. To maintain both of his parents in the same full-time nursing time facility costs Dr. Heinz nearly ten thousand Euros per month. He has recently sold his summer house, several real estate possessions and much of his stocks and bonds. And there is no way to determine how much longer this parental burden will be on his shoulders. Dr. Frans Heinz has a major financial problem."

"In 2027 he was personally approached by a Chinese, Dr. Sam Wu, CEO of Chinese Natural Drugs Incorporation CND. We do not know exactly what arrangements took place, but we do know that a secret contract was signed in which Dr. Heinz would develop and supply nanotech products to them. CND would then market these products. Our understanding is that he would prepare Nano-tech systems for solar-voltage products that would involve electron transfer systems at the atomic level. Can you confirm this for me Dr. Stronger?"

The MIT Professor of Nanotechnology answered, "That is correct. If you will remember, most of the MUSDs during 2027 to 2029, probably involved nanocarriers transporting iron atoms which could short circuit targeted regions in the brain by interfering with nerve function. Hence one of the first death mechanisms for MUSDs apparently was interference of nerve activity. Dr. Heinz's research involves nanocarriers, albeit linked to solar systems. It should not be difficult for him to design nanocarriers linked to other systems such as nerve cells or muscle cells."

"Dr. Frans Heinz has a major personal financial problem which is open ended," added Mr. Femer. "He has the capacity to provide Nano-tech systems, and a linkage to a company which markets via legitimate and non-legitimate markets. It is for these reasons that we have Dr. Heinz on our list."

"Are there any questions?"

Mr. Mueller, EU Central Bank Director asked, "Have you checked all foreign bank accounts for Dr. Heinz, and have you checked to see who is paying the bills for his parents at the nursing center?"

"We have looked for bank accounts in Europe, Asia, and North America in the name of Dr. Frans Heinz," replied Mr. Femer. Do you think that we should look for accounts in the names of his children? And no, we have not looked at the nursing center's accounting. Thank you. We also need the German government's permission to do this, as German banks are involved."

"Yes, I think that you should also look for foreign bank accounts in his parent's name. Also, remember the son is now legally responsible, via power of attorney, for both of his parents. Hiding money in bank accounts or in securities in their names would still allow him to have direct access to 'clandestine' monies."

"Again, I thank you. We have not looked at that possibility either, "Mr. Femer embarrassingly replied.

Dr. Von Eulenberg, INTERPOL, spoke up, "Remember in Europe any transfer of foreign currency of 10,000 Euros or greater must be registered with the EU Central Bank and INTERPOL, and in the USA transfers greater than 10,000 US dollars must be registered in the USA."

"We cannot reach the banks in certain countries such as China, so this is a problem."

Mr. Mueller commented, "Come talk to me later and I will show you a couple of less than legal financial tricks that might be helpful."

"Thank you again," broke in Mr. Murphy. "Are there any other questions about Dr. Heinz?"

After a few moments, he continued. "Then let us continue on and finish our review of all seven of our candidates. We have set aside the entire afternoon to re-discuss everything and continue on to some possible action programs, based upon your ideas and recommendations."

"I will next review the information and data that we have concerning our investigation of Dr. Mario Kemps, who is a sixty-two-year old Professor and Chairman in the Department of Nano-biochemistry at the University of Buenos Aires, Buenos Aires, Argentina. He is famous in Argentina as the first doctor to bring nanomedicine to his people and is known to have developed two nanodrugs that cure two rare types of cattle parasites which grow on pampas grass."

"Several years ago, Dr. Kemps became Director of the University Technological Institute, and soon thereafter, with both government and private sector money he established the first nanotech factory in Argentina, Medical- Nano-Systems Corporation, MNS. He is the founder and President. But Dr. Gustavo Cortazar, a forty-six-year old Nano-chemist, is the CEO. Of the eight sudden cures of VIPs that we investigated, one of those cures was via a nanodrug produced by MNS. Dr. Cortazar remains with the university and factory, while Dr. Kemps travels much as they are trying to develop an international patient base for their current nine marketable nanodrugs and to seek new disease targets for commercial farm animals, especially in Africa and Asia."

Dr. Kemps has a self-destructive personal life. He has just married his fifth wife. He had two children by wife 1, one child by wife 2, three children by wife 3, and two children by wife 4. So, he is currently paying alimony to four women and supporting eight children in schools, primary through university levels. And it appears that there is from one to three bank accounts for each ex-wife. So, with his personal expenses and company expenses we totaled that he uses thirteen different bank accounts in five different Argentinean banks, plus at least one bank account in Jamaica, one in the Canary Islands, and two in Switzerland. He receives income from the university, the factory, and 'several' consultantships concerning nanomedicine projects."

Dr. Kemps travels much, routinely sleeps with different women, and lives very well in one large seven-bedroom city estate, one small five-bedroom sea side villa in Bahia Blanca, and one large nine-bedroom hacienda on two hundred acres in Cordoba where he raises several hundred head of cattle. His father was a politician, a close friend of the Peron's, and known as the kingmaker. The son knows many of Dad's political cronies. It is said that Dr. Mario Kemps could walk across water if he wanted to do so."

Because he has the capacity to produce a variety of Nanotech systems, and because he is of dubious character with several unsavory friends, we consider Dr. Kemps as a candidate for the Korrectorizer and/or a supplier of several types of Nano-weapons."

Mr. Murphy looked around and saw many members of the group comparing notes of the three men that they had just heard about. He just let the conversations continue for a few minutes.

Finally, Mr. O'Reilly spoke up, "Why don't we take a short break. I can smell fresh coffee coming through the door. It must be sitting in the corridor waiting for us. Let us not let it wait any longer and let it get cold. I will have it brought in and we can walk, stretch, and recharge our bodies with caffeine and sugared donuts. We begin again in twenty minutes."

Twenty minutes later Chairman O'Reilly asked, "Please let everyone be seated and we will continue the presentations. Unless there are questions about Dr. Kemps, I suggest we turn to Dr. James Walters. Mr. Femer are you ready?"

Mr. Femer began his review of their Canadian investigation. "Dr. James Walters is a Professor at the University of Ottawa in Ottawa, Canada. Several years ago, adjacent to the university campus, he established the

Canadian Center for Nanotechnology Research, where he is now Associate Director. This has become one of the largest and most respected nanotech centers in the world. The Center employs twenty professors and teachers and has more than fifty students. Most areas of basic and applied research in nanotechnology are pursued.'

"Over the past few years many small nanotech companies have sprung up in the Ottawa area. Most of these are combinations of university faculty and students focusing on specific nanotech products which are only a few steps away from the marketplace. These rogue companies provide research projects for graduate students and their profits are frequently used to financially support the students.'

'Professor James Walters is a typical academic with a small family, stay at home wife, three children, two dogs, three cats, moderate salary, and moderate living in a four-bedroom house within walking distance of campus. His bank accounts were within normal professor salary scale until about five years ago. At that time his oldest son began the eight to ten-year medical school program at the University of Montreal. Three years later his daughter was accepted into the Columbia University Medical School in New York City. She began that six-year internship/residency program two years ago. And the last son enrolled in engineering at the Massachusetts Institute of Technology in Boston, a six to eight- year program. Dr. Walters is currently supporting his three children's university educations at nearly fifteen thousand dollars per month. His professor's salary is five thousand dollars per month. And this deficit will continue for the next several years. So, Dr. Walters has been borrowing from everywhere."

"Several years ago, he began to help select young professors and certain students establish neighboring 'rogue' Nano-tech companies. For this assistance and continued consultation, he approves the specific Nano-project, and he becomes a silent partner of that company at 15% of the profit. During the past couple of years, he has been approached by foreigners to perform research and/or manufacture specific Nano-systems which meet their needs. We have identified at least three such companies in other countries which currently have five projects in motion. As far as we can determine the projects are being financed by two east African governments, Zimbabwe and Mozambique."

"Professor Walters, after a solid career of teaching and research, may be turning to clandestine efforts to support his children's education. Do these clandestine efforts involve producing Nano weapons? We do not know. But he has need for extra salary, and he controls several small rogue Nanotech companies with are currently supported by two less than stable democratic governments. We are seeking international bank accounts in his or his wife's names."

"Has he mortgaged his house?"

'Yes and no; in 2028 he took out a three-hundred-thousand-dollar mortgage. However, two years later he paid off this loan. We cannot determine where the money came from. And it was not reported on his 2030 IRS filings."

"Are you thinking that this is another honest man who is turning to underhanded efforts because he suddenly now has expenses far above his salary level?"

"For now, we are saying that in the near past he has used a slight of hand in the neighborhood of three hundred thousand dollars. His annual salary is 20% of this. And he has placed himself in a working position to possibly obtain more 'unaccountable' income. We agree, Dr. James Walters is a proud man. He has had a very successful career and has raised three wonderful children. But sometimes proud men will do 'incorrect' things just to maintain that 'honorable' state; this is especially true when their children are involved."

"I hope you are wrong; but I agree with your logic. He needs to be put under the microscope as bankers always say,' responded General Ronny. And he looked over at Mr. Mueller, Director of World Bank, and smiled.

And that brought a round of light applause. Things had gotten very serious. A little so-called humor, especially from the military was unexpected, but welcome.

After a couple of moments, Chairman O'Reilly asked, "Are there any more questions? We can return to any of these reports in the afternoon. No? Mr. Murphy will you present the difficult information and data on the three Jiangs?"

Mr. Murphy began: "We have been focusing on this next group of three men for the past three years. The Jiang brothers are fraternal triplets, born in China, educated and now live in several different countries, including China, USA, and Germany. Their father was a high ranking general with Mao Tse-Tung; so, their schooling was supported by the Communist Chinese government. Allow me to briefly review each man, one by one."

"Dr. Chi Jiang was the first born, was the brightest, and had the highest energy levels. He sought a maximum education and life challenges from the beginning. He was educated at universities in New York City, London, Boston, and Los Angeles. He holds two doctorates in Chemical and Molecular-Cellular Biology, and is currently a Professor of Nanotechnology at the California Institute of Technology. He is founder, President and CEO of Jiang Nano- Control International, JNI, which is in Silicon Ledge near Los Angeles. His brothers are equal co-shareholders. We have non-official data that they also have factories in Changzhou and Jincheng, China, and possibly in Masyaf, Syria. But these two countries have not cooperated in our investigation, so our information comes from other, but very reliable sources."

"Dr. Chi Jiang is a very popular teacher and a creative researcher. The company has seventeen patents in the area of nanomedicine; this includes diagnostic Nano-tests and Nano-drugs. We have identified several of their drugs with JXW labeling that were involved in three of the VIP sudden miracle cures. Apparently most of the ideas for nanoproducts originate with Dr. Jiang and his students at Cal. Tech.; and he employs several of his students at the JNI factory at Silicon Ledge. Nano-research takes place both in the university and the factory."

"He works at both places ten to twelve hours a day, six to seven days per week. All his free time is spent with his only son, fifteen-year old Li, who was born to his Irish wife. She died when Li was still a child and he did not re-marry. Li alternates living with his father in Los Angeles and father's brother, Dr. Cho Jiang in Nanjing, every two years."

"Dr. Jiang is very likable and personable, and was on our Commission for a short period of time. We have no direct evidence that he might be this Korrectorizer or is providing any nanoproducts to this group of killers. But his company does have several clandestine Nano-tech components, as you will soon see. Also, his brothers are not so clean."

"The second born was Jun Jiang. He was educated in China, USA, and Germany. He lives in Berlin and New York City, and possibly a couple of places in China. So, he travels much, and apparently is the company executive who is most active in promotion and sales. He owns and is president of three companies in Germany and the USA. These companies are involved in transportation and pharmaceuticals. He is not directly involved in Nano-research or Nano- manufacturing, but he attends international high-tech meetings and seeks new markets for the family's nanoproducts. He has a PhD in chemical engineering. And he regularly visits the California, Changzhou, and Jincheng factories. He has been seen in northern Syria near Masyaf."

"Dr. Jun Jiang's family, wife, one son and two daughters, reside in a large house in Potsdam, the vicinity of old imperial capital of the German Empire, ten miles west of Berlin. The headquarters and offices for JNI and his own companies are in Berlin, just off Unter den Linden Strasse, only a couple of blocks from the Reichstag, the German Parliament. So, he has good access to prime contacts in Germany. The JNI and Dr. Jun Jiang's company's regional headquarters are in the same building in New York on 8th Avenue and 42nd Street, just off Times Square; his condominium flat is located on Columbus Avenue and West 56th Street, near the Lincoln Center. Again, he lives and works in prime business locations and promotes JNI and his own companies' products. We think he has his own offices and living accommodations in China, possibly also Syria. We have no proof that he is producing or moving illegal drugs. He does have bank accounts is several countries."

"We believe Dr. Jun Jiang is a good candidate for this Korrectorizer and/or a prime supplier of Nano-killer type of products. We are now carefully monitoring his private and business movements and activities."

"The youngest of the Jiang triplets, Dr. Cho Jiang, grew up in China, went abroad for education and then returned to live and work in his home country. He received his PhD in Industrial-Electronic Engineering from the University of Chicago. He then worked for several years with Yakin Electronics Incorporated in Seattle, Washington, and then three years with Jacksoner Medical Diagnostics in Los Angeles. After these work experiences, he returned to Nanjing. By then the Jiang triplets were establishing their nanotechnology laboratories and factories. Dr. Cho Jiang set up the JNI factory in Changzhou. His wife and two daughters live in Nanjing and he commutes about an hour to the factory. Basically, he lives and works in China and travels occasionally to New York or Los Angles to meet with his brothers."

"Because of the lack of cooperation from the government of the People's Republic of China, his movements, work, life style, and bank accounts are almost impossible to follow. Suffice it to say, this Dr. Jiang is also involved with the manufacture of nanotechnology products, is in a position to perform human testing on new products, and has regular contact with both brothers who are in the nanotechnology business."

"The three Jiang brothers are not close friends. They are arms-length brothers. When they do meet, it is usually for business. In fact, Chi is interested in basic research in nanomedicine. Jun is the business capitalist type. And Cho seems to flow with the tides, using Chi's ideas and sort of following Chi in the production and marketing world. There is a general coolness between Chi and his brothers, Jun and Cho. Their families do not know each other. And there is more family disharmony than harmony."

The CIA Office of Science and Technology Director Bradmier spoke up, "I understand that we have numbers for several Nano-drugs that JNI has manufactured. And that each of these nanodrugs was used in the sudden VIP cures. Do we have any numbers for any Nano-products that may have been used in the MUSDs? Are any of these people who you have presented to us under direct investigation for any specific nanoproduct for any specific sudden VIP cure or specific MUSD?"

"Some of the numbers that we have obtained matched the JNI and MNS companies." replied Mr. Murphy. "But each of these matches was for nanodrugs used in sudden VIP cures. We still have not identified any Nano-killing type of drugs or products, so we do not have any such numbers. Identification problems result from obtaining the nanodrug several hours after it was activated and in inadequate quantities. We have been able to determine that Nano-substances have been present in a couple of the MUSDs. But without standards, we could not determine what type of nanosubstance it was."

"If we can link nanotech products to any of these killings, we can argue in Congress to place them under the anti-terrorism laws," responded Chairman O'Reilly.

British MI6 Director Thomson asked, "When nanotech products are internationally shipped, are they labeled as nanotech products?"

"No, they are not," replied Dr. Stronger, Nanotech Professor from MIT. "This is an area that has been of concern for many of us. Nanotech products and other types of drugs or medical chemicals are labeled and shipped in a similar fashion. And because we have not been able to establish that certain nanotech products may really be poisons, not curing drugs, there is no such warning on the shipping labels. They are simply labeled as toxic, like many medical chemicals."

"So, there is no simple way to follow production, shipping, or even utilization of nanotech products because they are not separately identified," replied Mr. O'Reilly. "Is this correct?"

Dr. Stronger just smiled and nodded his head in the affirmative. Maybe the establishment was going to wake up after all.

"As I understand that most Nano systems are composed of two major components, an organic nanoproduct and a homing protein MoAB, at least for medical use," said General Ronny. "Can one make these two components separately, ship them separately, and then put them together just before use?"

"This is possible," replied Dr. Stronger. "However, it would be unlikely for two reasons. One - the manufacturer would not want to give away his 'secret' methodology. Two - even if one had a written recipe, to accomplish this you would need considerable knowledge of Nano-chemistry. If a molecular product was produced with one atom out of place it would not function properly. And yes, the possibility of manufacturing and shipping the Nano-product and MoAB separately, and then binding them together just before administering them, is very possible. But a person from the manufacturer's laboratory would have to be trained in advance to make this delicate chemical reaction just before use."

Mr. Murphy spoke up, "We have reviewed for you several candidates that we think may be involved in this, now at least a six-year killing spree. Each person can or has access to developing and manufacturing Nano-weapons that can kill a person, several people, and even groups if clustered.

I want you to think through the information and data that we have just reviewed for each of these candidates and give us your opinions. Who do you think are good candidates and why? Who do you not think are not candidates and why? And where should we go from here with each one?"

"It is nearly noon," announced Chairman O'Reilly. "We will go downstairs to our private dining room. The food will be delivered to us in that room. After we are all comfortably seated and the food has arrived, please allow the waiters to leave the room. Two of my Aides will confirm that the room is free on non- Commission members, only then can we feel free to discuss what we heard this morning. After lunch we will return to this conference room, the chairs are more comfortable, and we will re-review each of these seven people. We want to make decisions. Do we forget, simply follow, or initiate legal circles around any or all of them? What type of legal circles should we use? Which, if any of these 'gentlemen', are potential international killers - suppliers of Nano-weapons or the administrators of those weapons? What and where should we go next?"

25A

The Conservative Manifesto - I

FOR THE PAST SEVEN YEARS, a group of conservative industrialists had been meeting annually in secret in a different one of the more than seventy old castles in Romania. And every three years the composition of the attendees was altered, three exchanges always took place, but names remained the same. Just as the names of the ancient gods and prophets never change. So!? This meeting was being held on November 20, 2024, in the Bran Castle, otherwise known as the Castle of Vlad Tepes, otherwise known as the Prince of Wallachia, otherwise known as the Castle of Dracula. The Bran Castle was originally built in 1212 by the Knights of the Teutonic Order. In the late thirteenth century it was conquered by the Saxons. It was in the fifteenth century that Vlad Tepes, a powerful and merciless conqueror and ruler, whose conquests and special types of execution including rectal impalement on ten-foot shafts and slow bodily dismemberment become known. He had numerous very bloody conquests. This is how the name of Dracula became associated with Prince Tepes and the Bran Castle.

Surrounded by gigantic mountains and forests, perched upon a sharp 200 feet peak, the fortress/castle has numerous imposing towers and turrets, plus the myth of Dracula created by the British writer, Bram Stoker. It is a frightening location to visit, especially at night. During the past century it has been renovated and is now a very popular tourist attraction. Visiting hours are from 10:00 AM to 4:00 PM. When eight male and female tourists split off from the tour group of forty- five at

3:55 PM and went down a side corridor, the others paid no attention but continued to follow the tour guide, finished the tour, and left the castle.

The splinter group went down a circular staircase to the second floor below ground. This level was marked 'area closed'. The leader of the group withdrew a key from his pocket, placed it into an ancient metal lock on a 4 X 10 feet old oak door, turned it twice, the lock screeched, but with a gentle shove the door opened. As they entered the cave like room, movement sensory lights came on and lit up a modern styled conference room with beautiful mahogany wood paneled walls and ceilings, a reticular birch wood conference table with twelve large comfortable arm chairs down the two long sides and at one end. They entered, the door was shut, and with fresh coffee brewing, tea, canapé sandwiches and pastry smells in the air, it felt like one was in the Hyatt Regency's elite conference room in Paris.

Each of the tourists in this splinter group helped themselves to refreshments and then took their assigned seats denoted by a name plate at each chair. Each attendee looked around with the intent to communicate with their neighbors for the next couple of hours, but after the meeting they would go their separate ways, and forget all names, faces, and discussions. They would take home to their sponsors only the final decisions made during the meeting.

The Leader, as he was called, or Korrectorizer as he was otherwise known, sat at the head of the table. Each of the attendees was seated in front of their names which were taken from mythical gods and prophets. The Leader nodded and each person opened the small packet located in front of them on the table. After a few minutes of silent reading, they replaced the material back inside the envelope which would be returned to the Leader after the meeting. Nothing could be taken from the room, except the verbal decisions.

And the 2024 meeting of the Committee of World Conservatives, CWC, began. The Korrectorizer had organized this Committee six years ago, and he, as always, was the Chairman.

Leader/Korrectorizer began, "Welcome again to Romania and to the most famous castle in the world. Or if not the most famous, certainly the most feared. After that two-hour tour and learning the fifty bloodiest ways to kill someone, I am rather proud of our death methodology which is almost bloodless." He smiled.

"Our procedures are designed to be painless and bloodless. But we are still learning and sometimes we are not always completely successful. But we are getting better. The delay, which we have built into some of the recent Nano- systems, allows the person at least to die during the night, frequentlly when asleep, so it certainly makes the death painless compared to the Dracula methodology. Mr. Dracula, or Prince of Wallachia, seemed to get his jollies from the pain induced before death."

And this statement allowed for mixed emotions from the committee members. Some laughed, some just smiled, and some inwardly groaned. They obviously were not in total agreement concerning the method of eliminating their world competition.

One of the participants spoke out, "Dracula should take lessons from us!"

And a second round of facial expression appeared. The Leader carefully watched and noted: 'The degree of acceptance of our Nano-killers is not unanimous. Is there a better way? But it will still be a good meeting. I am sure they will all agree to an increase in my fees for my next, and certainly my best idea.'

And he stood up and shouted out! **"And what is change?"**

"To a two-year old little boy change is when Mommy brings home from the hospital a new crying little monster who now takes all of his Mommy's time. To a five-year old child change is when he breaks his favorite electronic toy and loveable Dad will not buy a replacement because the child had been careless. To a nine-year old girl change is when her dog is run over and killed by a car and she learns that it will not come back to life. To a sixteen-year old girl change is when her boyfriend, who promised to marry her, is seen kissing her best girlfriend. To an eighteen-year old boy change is when he is not accepted into Harvard University in Boston but is accepted at John Watts Jones University in Ashish, North Dakota. At any point in time for any child change comes when Dad moves out of the house and the child gets to see Mom during the week and Dad on weekends. And one of the most difficult changes occurs for an entire family when a middle-aged Father and or a single parent Mother loses her job and can no longer pay living expenses for the family of four. All of these changes regularly occur everywhere. No one is immune to them."

"Change begins very early in life and continues throughout life. Older people may remember the changes in entertainment during the past eighty years from radio to television via mechanical, cathode ray tube, stereoscopic, multicolor, broadcast, electronic, digital, high definition, and 3-D television. And with each change one is required to buy the newer higher technological system which is always a more expensive model. Older people may also remember the changes in the technology of communication systems such as speaking tubes, modulate electric circuit, electric telegraph, switch hook, cross talk, dial switch, touch tone, mobile, cable, cellular, and multifunctional (smart) personal cellular phones. One can only speculate on the new modes of visual/acoustical entertainment and communications that will become available during the next 80 years. A new stock market, NASDAX, was created just to speed up the current change."

"If there is one thing that schools should be teaching, it is how to adjust to change. Unfortunately, this subject is not on any school curricula in any school in the world; in fact, it is not even in the minds of our school administrators and teachers. Parents are a little better, but they are still guilty of not consciously teaching their children how to adjust to change. It is very common that many parents somehow have the idea that they must protect their children from change. A child must be over eighteen, leave the house, and be financially independent before he can make 'all' of his own decisions concerning the changes that he needs to make in his own life. Is the close protection of our children by our teachers and parents a service or disservice?"

"When children graduate from high school, get a job, go to college, they leave the protective nest behind. They now appear to live 'independent' of 'some' parents. Thus, they immediately face changes which could be career or even life threatening; and they face these changes with minimum learning and minimum experience. Most decisions during one's twenties and thirties determine success or lack of success during the rest of his/her life, personally and professionally. When one hits the forties, it is difficult to go back and make those decisions for previous changes a second time.'

"We all face personal changes every day of our lives. Hopefully professional changes happen less often but represent even more difficult responses or adjustments. Losing a child or your spouse is traumatic.

Losing your job is traumatic. Losing your business is traumatic. Losing your house and financial support for your family is the ultimate, because you have been making decisions not just for yourself, but your entire family. If your family had some knowledge or skills at adjusting to change, all adjustments would be much less traumatic."

"The biggest problem concerning most change is that it allows some people to win and some people to lose. Change creates winners and losers. If the change for you is to win, all is great. If the change for you is to lose, it is not so great and possibly traumatic. The winner is happy. But the loser is not happy. Then the question arises, what should the loser do about this change: try to anticipate and prevent it, ignore it, confront it, reverse it, destroy it, or eliminate it entirely? If the loss is traumatic, the last choice may be a viable option. It is only a matter of selecting a modus operandi to eliminate this change. And today in the world, not only is change rampant, but modus operandi is plentiful and some are highly sophisticated."

"Every day new technology is giving birth to new systems. Acceptance and growth of these new systems frequently crowd out or even destroy existing systems. In the past, inertia of motion was a problem and a stumbling block to the development of new systems. The concept of high technology began in the seventies, but in the nineties, it began its momentum with both cellular phones and computers. Why, because today government incentives, venture capital, and high-risk decision making have allowed many new systems in numerous areas which are now called high technology, even though some of those systems are simply re-writes of old systems with higher profit margins."

"Some old systems can also become new systems and thus a threat to the other old systems which cannot adjust to successfully compete, so they must simply die; a good example is coal energy to solar energy. The sun made the coal; but soon the sun's child will no longer be needed in our high-tech world. So, the definition of old or new is not important, adjustments to change must occur in such a way that there is survival: – winners survive – losers usually do not survive."

"Are we going to allow the Darwinism of God's nature also control survival of Industrialism and Commercialism of Mankind?"

"The losers, or non-winners, in this fast forward world of change, can better prevent or slow down this rapid new technology of change if they organize. And if they organize, how far should/could/would they go to stop or slow down the forward momentum of the high technology train in the twenty first century? Some potential losers see the disaster far enough in advance and can change themselves into a more competitive system in time to prevent a disaster, if their administrators can and want to do so. Other losers may just disappear, like the dinosaurs. Of course, it is these latter losers that are more tempted to initiate a counter movement or simply seek **preventive revenge**; or as the military call it **pre-emptive action**. If a preventive revenge is the decision of choice, then it is only necessary to select the appropriate target and the appropriate revenge methodology. Mass bombing disappeared almost one hundred years ago. Today laser guided missiles, drones, or unmanned attack vehicles (UAV) are high-tech weapons of choice on a small or large scale. While now the MoAB guided nanotech weapons are the choice on the microscopic, small, or large scale."

"In our recent past we have been using only the microscopic scale. But we may soon switch to a larger scale to continue our preventive revenge efforts."

"Yes, you will see very soon that our MoAB guided Nano-tech killers can be used on a larger scale. I promise you that before this year is finished, such weapons will destroy half of the world's most rapid high-tech change makers. It will also prove to you that your money is very well spent."

The Korrectorizer sat down and a general discussion began among the various committee members. As the comments moved back and forth, he sat back and looked carefully around the room. After a few minutes he spoke up, "Let us go around the table. I want to hear from each of you and the industrial or commercial system that you represent."

The Leader had created this Committee of World Conservatives for two reasons: 1) to provide a market place for testing his Nano-systems, 2) to slow or even roll back the rate of growth of selected high technology. In his opinion only one form of high technology should be allowed to continue to develop because it could help everyone – Nano-technology. Or at least that was his altruistic rationale.

The CWC was composed of eight of the largest industrial and commercial groups in the world who were suffering because of the train of high technology. One representative from each group was selected and served on the committee for three years, and then he was replaced by another selected representative from that group. In this way the representation did not derive from a single country, but from regions of several countries all of which were involved with that specific product. No names were used, only a single e-mail address which changed with every meeting, disposable cellular phones, and the name of an ancient god or prophet. Currently the members were:

- Vulcan – Petrochemicals – currently from Saudi Arabia
- Mars – Steel – currently from India
- Saturn – Hoofed Meat Industries – currently from Argentina
- Minerva – Metals Chemistries – currently from Germany
- Mercury – Transportation – currently from Japan
- Jupiter – Silicon Based Chips Products – currently from the USA
- St. Abraham – International Gold Consortium– currently from Israel
- St. Peter – Agriculture Crops – currently from the USA

The Leader started on his right, "Vulcan, let us hear the thinking of your people."

Vulcan began, "The petrochemical industry has more than 650 million employees, including gas station attendants, throughout the world. If it was 'put out of business' during a five to ten-year period of time the entire world would go bankrupt. It must be protected, and we recommend several ways to accomplish this. Other forms of energy such as wind, movement of water, sun, and bio-fuels should not be allowed to come into existence. Recycling energy systems can only create insurmountable changes. The costs of developing, building, and supporting these new possible systems, plus the cost of purchasing their related consumer products, of course which would appear in an ever more competitive market place, is an unforgivable loss to the world's economy. You don't change from a horse to a pony in the middle of the river even if the pony eats less food and runs faster."

"My commercial group wishes to continue to eliminate all forms of competition in the re-cycle-able energy research in the world; this may include elimination of individuals or facilities. All mechanisms may be used, from negative publicity to lab-factory destruction to conversion of key leaders into a non-breathing state."

"Thank you very much," responded the Leader. "That was straight and to the point. Everyone should understand that point of view. Mars would you like to express your thoughts?"

Mars began, "We have many problems in steel production and new construction concepts. I will be brief, but also direct. As all of you know, steel is produced by fusion of iron and carbon atoms; hence it is an iron carbon alloy. Iron is first smelted in a blast furnace with limestone and coke carbon; it is then converted into a molten pig iron. Next, certain impurities such as sulfur, phosphorus, and copper are removed and combinations of magnesium, nickel, chromium, vanadium, and other selected atoms are added in order to produce the type of steel wanted. More than one billion tons of steel is produced every year in the world."

Several carbon allotropes such as graphite and diamonds are used as carbon raising components, increasing carbon levels in molten steel. Graphite is not expensive, but natural diamonds are very expensive. However synthetic diamonds are now becoming more available; they are not so expensive. Using synthetic diamonds, carbonated diamond power, and natural alluvial diamond deposits allows the finished steel to be stronger, harder, and more durable. I am talking about a several fold increase in these characteristics. So, twenty-five tons of high carbonized steel can now accomplish what one hundred tons of iron- graphite-coke steel used to do. Adding the cost of these diamondized components allows production of higher quality steel at 50 percent less cost. Sales of our 'normal' steel have dropped more than thirty percent in the past five years. With the switch to high carbonized steel we anticipate that our 'normal' steel sales may drop at least thirty percent in the next five years. Iron and coal mines will go out of existence because much less iron and coke will be needed in this new type of steel. It is a tragedy that is happening now!'

"If you will remember, fifty years ago most tall building were built with 100% steel I-beams. Then the new construction technology began to use cement and less expensive re-rods. And now we have aluminum/plastic tube construction technology for gigantic domes of athletic stadiums and certain major large buildings. These new technologies have decreased the use of steel by more than 30%."

'Therefore, synthetic highly carbonized components, synthetic diamond factories and diamond mines, and new high technology construction designs have now become the steel manufactures' enemy number one."

"Thank you very much, Mars," said the Leader. "Next can we have Saturn? Saturn began the report which had been composed by his colleagues: "Most of you grew up eating meat; you and your family and your friends eat red meat cut from animals that have hooves or feet. And that includes cattle, pigs, lamb/sheep, goat, buffalo, turkey, chicken, plus many types of wild game such as deer and duck. This type of meat is the most nutritious food of any food in the world in that it has every vitamin, every mineral, and all of the necessary carbohydrates, fats, and proteins with all of the essential amino acids. It has 99% of everything that we need to live healthy lives. Ten thousand years ago our ancestors ate only meat and survived very well, otherwise we would not be here today."

And he received a nice round of smiles and a couple of short applauses.

"No single plant source can provide such a complete nutritious diet. And while fish and seafood have most of the necessary nutrients, there currently are not enough of these water creatures for all of mankind. So, our survival problem is not related to a sudden decrease in the consumption of meat, it is decreased consumption of meat from animals with hooves or feet."

"Today there are more than three hundred meat production **laboratory-factories** in the world. Most industrialized countries are experimenting with them. Unfortunately, they are having much success. I am talking about both red and white meat production in test tubes – **test tube meat**."

"These laboratory-factories are growing and marketing meat from cattle, pig, lamb, turkey, and modified chicken. They begin with embryonic or tissues from fetal animals. They remove the embryo or baby from the mother, cut off the skeletal muscles, digest these muscle tissues with a bunch of chemicals, and place the digested muscle cells into flat plastic flasks. They then add some of the mother's blood plus the necessary nutrients that the mother would have provided to the baby if it had been born. The muscle cells grow, fill the flask, become muscle tissue, and then are frozen."

"For marketing they remove the tissue-meat and sell it frozen or thawed. These procedures allow for marketable tissue-meat 'cut' into various sizes. It is marketed by comparing the nutritional parameters of our 'normal' meat with their tissue-meat, they are similar. They claim that their tissue-meat is more tender and tastier, maybe. They can sell it at 70% less than 'normal' meat; we can compete with this. They claim a fat content of 90% less than 'normal' meat - it is. And finally, they claim that their tissue-meat is free of plant pesticides and fertilizers and that the animals are free of growth hormones – it is."

"So how do we fight this kind of high technology without burning down every meat production-laboratory in the world? Or maybe we should do this!"

The room immediately filled with discussions about test tube meat. After a few minutes, all again became quiet, the Leader asked for the group to move on by asking if Minerva was ready.

Minerva answered, "Six thousand years ago the Egyptians used many metals for both life and death. This included a wide variety of toxic metals such as gold, silver, lead, copper, zinc, and arsenic. When the ancient Egyptian society disappeared, metal chemistry disappeared. Not until the twentieth century did the Germanic peoples resurrect this noble science and they remained number one in the world in the chemistry and physics of metals. Much of this became associated with tall buildings, bridges, trains, trucks, automobiles, airplanes, ships, and numerous weapons such as tanks and artillery."

"The Germans almost won World War II because of their superiority in the metal sciences. If it had not been for their defeat at that time, they would today be the frontrunners in inner and outer space vehicles. In fact, the utilization of metal chemistry for military weapon systems from non-radar detection aircraft to multiyear submersible water craft has stimulated enormous research in metals and other inorganic atoms. Chemical engineering and electrical engineering have combined to produce electronic engineering which has evolved into Nano- technology."

"There are four types of atoms which are classified as metals: alkali metals, alkaline earth metals, transition metals, and rare earth metals. All of you are familiar with many of the common metals such as gold, silver, copper, aluminum, zinc, mercury, calcium, mercury and on. You are not familiar with other now very important metals such as lithium, lanthanum, promethium, cerium, europium, nobelium, dysprosium, and on."

"You do recognize uranium, the uranium metal 235 which America used to produce the first atomic bomb. Uranium ore as mined from the earth usually has a ratio of 500 parts uranium metal 238 to 1part uranium metal 235. Uranium metal 238 is stable, uranium metal 235 is unstable. So, the two atoms are separated by gas centrifuges to produce enriched uranium which is 95%+ uranium metal 235. When the enriched uranium metal 235 is placed into a closed container, one neutron is added and it becomes uranium metal 236 which is extremely unstable and explodes immediately - hence an atomic bomb. The explosion gives off massive amounts of energy, depending upon the purity and quantity of the uranium metal 235. And when it explodes it produces many small atoms such as barium, krypton, thorium, cesium, iodine, and on. Several of these new atoms remain radioactive for thousands of years."

"Thus, the concept of changing the characteristics of atoms by adding neutrons, electrons, and protons to an atom, as well as fusing two or more atoms using nanotechnology is now commonly used in many laboratories and factories. Expensive metals/atoms can be converted to cheaper metals/atoms. Common metals/atoms can be converted to rare metals/atoms. I can give to you many examples of Nano-conversion research in progress: production of titanium, beryllium, palladium, rhodium and iridium which are critical for the external skins of missiles, supersonic aircraft, space vehicles, and deep-sea vehicles."

"And of course, nanotech atomic fusion is being used to produce gold, silver, copper, aluminum, and other expensive or in-demand metals. The current research trend will lead to the closing of thousands of metals mines in the world within ten years because the commonly available metal will be converted to 'rare' or more expensive metals. There are more than 120,000 mines in the world employing 100 million uneducated people. If cheaper, easier to obtain metals/atoms are so converted, chemists, chemical engineers, as well as miners will need to be re-educated. Already the entire field of metal chemistry is entering a mass confusion because of the speed of movement of high technology, especially these Nano-conversion mechanisms."

"This high technology thing must be slowed down such that the people of the world can also adjust to warp speeds."

The Leader asked, "Do you recommend on how this slow down should be pursued?"

"Every way possible," Minerva replied.

"All right, let's move forward to Mercury. Are you ready?"

Mercury began, "Thank you for allowing us to participate and be heard. Please allow me to present some of the problems of the transportation industry. Transporting ourselves, our families, and our necessary living goods has been a problem since there was humankind. It currently involves different modes of travel on rails, roads, cables, air, tunnels, waterways, canals, pipelines, and space. To allow these various modes of transportation to function properly we have developed railway stations, refueling stations, bus stations, truck terminals, airports, and sea terminals. To accomplish this travel we have built and re-built and re-built again bicycles, automobiles, trains, buses, trucks, ships, aircraft, and spacecraft. And to power or move these many types of vehicles we have designed and re-designed and again re-designed steam engines, internal combustion engines, electric motors and engines, and jet engines or rockets. I have not even begun to calculate how many people have been employed in designing and building the millions of vehicles that we use for travel. And of course, every man, woman, and child over the age of sixteen who has money personally utilizes at least one of these vehicles every day of his/her life."

"What would you say if I told you that I could snap my fingers and all of these transportation systems would disappear, and yet everybody and everything would still go to where it was planned to go. I would give this new transportation system a single name, **teleportation**."

'Teleportation is a new high technological system which will have the ability to transport any person or object from one place to another. Teleportation is no longer science fiction, but is in a sustainable research mode that we will see it begin to function within our children's lifetime. Several forms of teleportation are being studied: de-atomization, de-molecularization, de-materialization, quantum teleportation, superluminal teleportation, fourth dimension teleportation, and time travel. It is probable that mankind will develop more than one type of teleportation system depending upon the need for movement of one entity versus several entities, distances involved, time during teleportation, humans versus things."

"Teleportation is not a new idea. In the New Testament of the Bible Acts 8:39, Phillip is teleported from Gaza to Azotus by the Lord."

"When such transport becomes truly functional, just imagine the changes imposed upon the people of this earth. We will teleport ourselves to work, to home, to the shopping mall, far away vacation spots anywhere in the world, hopefully in just a few seconds of time. We will teleport all products from the farm to the supermarket to the home or restaurant. And generals will be able to move complete armies behind and attack his enemies from the rear, assuming such frontal wars still exist in a few years. I can also see how terrorists might penetrate previously secure structures like banks. It will indeed be a very different world."

'Other modes of travel cannot compete. We will no longer need any physical type of transportation vehicle, vehicular motors, vehicular stations, vehicular parking lots, and on and on. If you can just step on your teleportation pad in your house, enter a code for your name and a code for your destination, push a button and a couple of seconds later you step off the pad in your office, or shopping mall, or golf course first tee."

This caused a variety of sounds in the room, some liked the idea, and some thought it crazy. Mercury waited a couple of moments until silence returned, and then continued.

"Maybe this will be a good thing for my grandchildren, but it is too much for me today. This is another high-tech change that needs to be slowed down; I do not think it can be stopped. It would not bother us if it was stopped today and allowed to begin again for use by our children and grandchildren. I am too old to be de-atomized and re-atomized every day."

And indeed, this statement resulted in even more conversation among committee members.

After several moments, the Leader spoke up, "Did you try to calculate how many people would become unemployed if no physical transportation vehicles were designed and produced, and paths for their travel was not built or maintained?"

Mercury answered, "I thought that I would leave that number up to you to solve. I am too old to be de-atomized and re-atomized every day."

The committee members from very different walks of life again began conversation with their neighbors. Will the attendees, perhaps, warm up to each other? Probably not, they are simply second lieutenant level not starred general level representatives who were sent from their international industrial or commercial groups to seek help in slowing, stopping, or even reversing the too rapid progress in high technology. But the talks certainly were making it obvious that they each had the same common enemy.

The Leader had signaled for another round of coffee, tea, and pastries. It had arrived, so he called a fifteen-minute break. This would also allow for a few more minutes of general conversation. Things were going very well. The world wide call for 'anti-technical help' was spreading.

Conservative Manifesto - II

SOON THEY RETURNED TO THEIR chairs and the Leader asked Jupiter to speak. Jupiter began, "For the first several thousand years of life on this planet there was only one type of electrical system, lightening, and perhaps the electric eel.

In the mid nineteenth century, Ben Franklin, playing with kites during an electrical storm began to develop the basic understanding that electricity was the movement of electrons. In 1897, Thomas Edison invented the first electric light bulb, and the Serbian-American Nikola Tesla, enabled transmission of electric power. And in less than twenty years the world went from dark to light, slow to fast, down to up; this was because of electrons moving within copper wires."

"During the twentieth century, with the invention of vacuum tubes, diodes and triodes, and all varieties of switching controls, radios, telephones, television, and numerous electric instruments and machines became available to the common person. As the circuitry became larger and more sophisticated, one major problem occurred, HEAT. Copper has poor thermal conductivity, so overheating was commonplace. This heat was a severe limitation in the development of such instruments as calculators and computers. Soon the invention of special vacuum tubes, transistors, and integrated circuits with combinations of resisters, capacitors, and transistors laid the foundation to high speed electronics for such things as computers. But it still had the same problem, HEAT. So, silicon metal was chosen to replace copper metal because silicon had one hundred times greater thermal conductivity than copper."

"Today several thousand transistors and integrated circuits can be placed on a silicon chip the size of a dime. But with the increased demand for electronic chips that have even greater capacity and are faster, the heat conductivity of silicon is not sufficient. Just as copper had its heat limits which we surpassed, now silicon has its heat limits which we have surpassed. So, what is next, alluvial or synthetic diamonds have heat conductivity one hundred times greater than silicon, and also negligible electrical conductivity."

"Current research has proven that diamond-based chips have greater speed and a larger information storage capacity than silicon-based chips. Already, silicon chip manufacturers and all instrument, machine, vehicle, and even space system manufactures are fearful of losing their 'soon to be worthless' patent rights and their current share of the marketplace. And this is not just changing a chip or a circuit board. The switch to diamond-based chips for industry has initiated a new science which will cost billions of dollars in re-structuring and re-education in the entire electronics field."

"For several thousand years man had only to look at and fear lightening, During the past 150 years he has harnessed the basis of lightening, electron flowing, first with copper, then with silicon, and now with diamonds. With each change came major 'modernization' and an increase in the volume and living speed of humans."

Jupiter finished, "We agree with our colleagues sitting at this table, the changes are too fast and too expensive, monetarily and psychologically, for peoples of the world to absorb in too short a period of time. We also agree that this new technology will eventually be good and will allow for more advanced systems, hopefully for the betterment not the determent of mankind. Only time will provide that answer. So, our feelings are that we need a slowdown, not a stoppage, in the development of diamond-based chip technology. The method that is used for a slowdown is not of concern to us. You are being well paid to make and complete those decisions."

Mr. Leader said, "Thank you my Roman gods." And he tried to bring out a few smiles from the group. He was not successful. Seriousness was their business and pleasure for today.

"We want to hear from two more gentlemen, first St. Abraham."

St. Abraham began, "Forever in the history of humans, gold has been the most sought after and most valuable metal. As you just heard from our metal chemistry colleague, gold was even used to help guarantee that the dying pharaohs of ancient Egypt would never die. Although I have not seen any of them walking around recently."

And that comment finally brought a few smiles.

"Because of its perceived value, continuous attempts to convert lesser metals into gold have been in motion for thousands of years. However, the dream of converting lead to gold may be just around the corner. Many metals have been added together, and numerous metal and non-metal mixtures have been tried, in attempts to create synthetic gold. Some methods have been more successful than others. But today gold metallurgists have a variety of laboratory chemical tests which are used to determine the percent of true gold in a piece of jewelry. Synthetic gold is now easy to detect, except for one metal, a recent advance in high technology, using the mercury metal."

"Mercury, iridium, platinum, thallium, and gold are almost identical. Why?" "All atoms have a nucleus containing protons (plus charge with mass) and neutrons (no charge with mass); in addition, electrons (negative charge without mass) circulate around the nucleus. An atom's **atomic number** is the number of protons in the nucleus. The **atomic weight** is based on the calculated nuclear weight of the protons and neutrons which are located together within the nucleus of the atom. Circulating electrons have no weight. In normal nature, protons and neutrons do not routinely leave the atom. Circulating electrons come and go.

This leads to following possibilities:

	atomic number	atomic weight
- Iridium	77	192
- Platinum	78	195
- Gold	79	197
- Mercury	80	200
- Thallium	81	204
- Lead	82	207
- Bismuth	83	209

"However, atoms can be changed, using human technology, from one atom to another atom, by adding or removing protons or neutrons from the nucleus; but not by adding or removing orbit circulating electrons. In nature, we just heard about the movement of orbiting electrons in electric wires and electronic systems. Copper exists in two forms, with 2 electrons or 3 electrons. But whether 2 or 3, it is still a copper atom. Uranium atom 235 can be converted to uranium 236 by adding one neutron. It is now a new form of the uranium atom.

"In all biological forms of life, movement of orbiting electrons is the simplest form of energy flow – sugar conversion to water and carbon dioxide involves the flow of 20 electrons through 22 different atoms/molecules in every body cell."

"However, movement of the nuclear located protons and neutrons is not common in nature. One atom does not naturally or commonly change into another atom. Such must be forced as when a neutron is added to uranium 235, it explodes, and is converted to several smaller atoms, each with atomic numbers that are smaller than 235, during the atomic bomb blast."

"The most common way to convert one atom to another atom is by adding or removing a proton or neutron. As I said, this does not routinely happen in nature. But man can do this in the laboratory with a particle accelerator, nuclear reactor, neutron generator, or neutron absorber. The latest and most successful research efforts involve high tech proton absorbers or neutron absorbers. If you compare the atoms of mercury, atomic number 80, with gold, atomic number 79, you can see that one must remove one neutron from mercury to convert it to a 'synthetic' gold which has almost all characteristic of true gold. Many new Nano-methods are used to do just that, convert mercury to gold, and platinum and iridium to gold by removing or adding neutrons or protons."

"Because platinum and iridium are rare and expensive, and mercury is common and not expensive, most research efforts are focused upon the mercury to gold conversion. Once the methodology is perfected, it will take only a few years to eliminate gold as a precious metal in the world and it will disappear from the market place. There is currently more than 100 trillion tons of gold stored with individuals and countries. Today gold is valued at 25,000 dollars per ton. If you calculate these numbers you can determine that more than 2 billion- trillion American dollars of gold metal will become worthless in a very short period of time."

"Does one call that positive change? It cannot be allowed to continue. Such synthetic gold will replace the major monetary commodity and destroy the world!"

Mr. Leader looked around the table; the potential 'synthetic' gold scenario could indeed be a problem for everyone on earth. He waited for a couple of minutes but the room remained rather quiet. Was this high technology at its best or its worst?

Finally, he asked, "St. Peter, can you please finish our round of talks?" St. Peter began the last presentation.

"The only physical thing in the world that is more precious than gold is food. And this could be in for major changes in the near future."

"Mankind has been incredibly irresponsible, even downright stupid in the food crop world. All major food crops have been highly inbred, re-bred, cross pollinated, re-pollinated, and hybridized thousands of times, such that today we do not even know what the true or real chromosomes or genes were thousands of years ago of most of our food crops. Today every major commercial crop has hundreds of extra genes and many extra chromosomes. Let me give you four quick examples, as the overall problem is the same for each."

"Soybeans have 20 pairs for a total of 40 chromosomes. However, there are 2 or 3 copies of each chromosome. There are 46,000 genes which are 40 to 65% repetitious. The soybean has from 3 to 10 copies of each specific gene, except the DNA sequence in each specific copy of that gene may vary 10 to 30%. The genes in the soybean plant are multiple, heterogeneous, scrambled, and very difficult to determine their function."

"The corn plant has been less bastardized. It has 10 pairs for a total of 20 chromosomes. There has been extensive cross breeding or hybridization of the corn, such that there are thousands of 'types', or 'strains', but each strain has approximately 20 similar sized but different chromosomes. The genome of the corn seed is being determined such that soon we will know which genes code for which proteins and which serve which functions for the plant."

"Wheat has been grown for more than 5,000 years. So, it not surprising that it has very abnormal genetics. It is considered that the wheat plant has 21 pairs for a total of 42 chromosomes. There are at least three related copies of every chromosome. There are probably 3 to 6 copies of every gene, well over 100,000 genes. It is not known if every copy of every gene on every chromosome even functions."

"Sugar cane is a younger plant and has only been grown commercially for the past 4,000+ years. In the beginning, like the other commercial crops that I have described, there were probably 8 to 10 chromosomes. But today, the sugar cane plant has 80 to 120 chromosomes. This is called acute polyploidy or multi- copying. There are probably 5 to 15 copies of each chromosome and 10 to 20 copies of each gene, possibly more than 250,000 genes. What do all of these extra genes do for the plant, we have no idea."

"Keep in mind that we humans have 23 pairs for a total of 46 chromosomes which contain nearly 100,000 genes. We only use 20,000 genes for functional purposes, 80,000 genes are apparently not necessary to make a human. So, we only have four times more genes than we need."

"In summary, most commercial food crops have a super abundance of extra chromosomes and genes in the nuclei of their cells. Many of these plants which are carrying five to one hundred times extra genetic units are at an extreme handicap as they must continuously manufacture these genes and chromosomes every time one cell makes two cells. For a sugar cane plant, one seed produces more than 10 billion cells which mature into a plant and produce sugar cane. If the excess of genetic units were removed, the energy required to grow the plant would decrease proportionally, at least by 90+ percent. This would translate into much less fertilizer, hence greatly decreased growing expenses. And I have not even tried to calculate the massive decrease in artificial fertilizer production and sales that would be required to grow a 'leaner' commercial food crop"

"The new science of chromosomal cytology has started focusing upon this problem. Using high technology, one can expose the chromosomes of a cell under a micro-dissection microscope and systematically laser and destroy selected genes and chromosomes. The remaining chromosomes can then be placed within an enucleated cell and allowed to grow. Using this new technology one can eliminate most of the duplicate or extra chromosomes and create a cell more representative of the original cell. It certainly can remove the excess of genetic units in the cell allowing for a crop that will require less energy to grow, hence more commercially competitive."

"Such high-tech research will drastically change the food crop industry. The old methods of cross breeding or hybridizing, will disappear, hence so will billions of dollars of 'excellent' patents. The new methods of 'trimming out' unnecessary chromosomes are beginning. Likewise, there will be a new era of billion-dollar patents beginning. And these new 'trimmed' crops/food will have difficulty getting accepted, just like genetically engineered crops and genetically modified foods of the past. But because of the commercial advantage, it will be accepted. And thousands of companies will be buried along with the soon to be dead patents."

The Leader interrupted and spoke out, "Let me try to understand. Each of you is telling me that there is a big need for a slowdown or even elimination in the development of high technology associated in your industrial and commercial areas which are currently causing undue competition. In my opinion, complete stoppage or elimination of some of this high technology is not possible. Slowing it down is possible and we can and will do that. Before the end of this year, I will give to you a vivid demonstration that will prove this to you."

"Please let your colleagues know that I understand their past frustrations of supporting conservative political parties and NGO groups in trying to slow down the development of high technology. Political conservatism focuses on status quo, tradition, stability, unchanging communities, opposition to modernization, and promotes a return to past mentality. These values are of some help to you. But then there is the social conservatism which includes selected religious values, the right to have physical protection in the home; only two sex marriages; against all abortions; rigid law enforcement; restricted immigration; anti-environmentalism; military power and military interventionism. These latter values are of no help at all in slowing progress in high technology. So, all in all, where do you turn to obtain direct help with your problem?"

If our elected politicians cannot help us with our problems, we have to help ourselves. And that is just what we are doing. I am proud to be of some small assistance in our efforts to solve these problems. Suffice it to say, in my recent past I have been in a position of die or live, and I am proud to say that I survived. Your industrial systems will not only survive, but continue to lead far into the future."

"Today, one must take control of one's own fate!"

"One cannot wait for chance to do it for you. Chance can be good or bad, it can change in the blink of an eye, and it allows the bad as well as the good to prevail. Waiting for chance is simply wrong."

"All right," continued Mr. Leader, "if you have questions or further comments that you do not wish to share as a group, please e-mail to me. The new packet that I am now giving to you contains your specific new codified system and a new text for one time three-digit reverse coding. Each of you have new and different codes so, as usual, I will know who you are by the codification. Before you leave please write your new e-mail number, place it in the envelope. After every meeting we always start with new communication systems. So, please burn all previous communications and codification programs."

NOW MY SPECIAL-SECRET ANNOUNCEMENT

"You can inform your colleagues to watch for a massive strike on high technology in a repeat location but water born. It will be an early Christmas present for our common enemies at a location where they do not even celebrate Christmas."

"See if you can guess who, what, where, and when. And you will all be very pleased, I am certain."

The Korrectorizer finished, "I thank you for coming. In addition to your new e-mail number, please leave your annual fee, cash only, and your list of suggested new targets in the same envelope. Kindly place your envelope into the large Roman amphora which is sitting to the right side of the lovely 1000-year old door. I will see you next year."

As his clients slowly left the basement room and the castle, one by one, his thoughts were 'organizing this world-wide conservative cartel was the smartest thing that I have ever done. My fee is certainly more than adequate for this group of clients. But I probably should take on a partner at some point in time just in case difficult problems occur on down the road. We are causing many exotic deaths of very important people which is making some very powerful people very unhappy.'

26A

World Entrepreneurs - I

I T WAS LATE OCTOBER, AYKUT was lying on a beach chair with his dog, dreaming about his days as a tour coordinator in Istanbul and trying to recall the facts such that he could brag to the scientists about famous-historic Istanbul, when they soon arrived for a week-long conference, if he should be called upon to do it. He typed on his iPad the following -

'The land mass located between the Black Sea, Marmara
Sea, Golden Horn, and the Bosporus was first settled in
7th BCE. Here the Thracians developed a small fenced city,
Lygos. In 330 ADE the Eastern Roman Empire established the
Byzantium Empire and the Roman Emperor
Constantine I dedicated
the new Rome or Constantinople. In 1054,
the West-East Schism between the
Latin Roman Empire in Rome and Constantinople resulted in the
split in the Christian Church, thus was born
the Eastern Orthodox Church.
In 1453 ADE the Ottoman Sultan Mehmed II conquered it and
re-established it as the new capital of the Ottoman Empire.
Now it is Istanbul, with ten million people, the major tourist-
business center in the Republic of Turkey. There are fifteen palaces,
winter and summer palaces of the Ottoman Sultans,
and numerous original scenic areas because the city was

*never bombed during any war. The Bosporus partitions
Tukey into Europe and Asia. It is the only city
in the world where you can go from continent
to continent without a passport.'*

Suddenly his little brother, a 212 pounds red-golden black faced, super lovable, Anatolian Shepherd Kangal dog, Amber, started licking his feet. He was being told that it was time to play. A frisbee had been placed on his legs. When he tried to pick it up, a loud woof rang forth, the favorite toy was snatched away and his chair was knocked over. Aykut was only 130 pounds, so he was at a distinct disadvantage. But he and Amber had been growing up together for the past six years. They were like brothers with simply different capacities for loving and playing. They had the beach to themselves so they took off running and jumped into the water. Amber was faster on the run, on the swim, on the physical, and on the thinking, at least many times he caught the social movement of the immediate surrounding first. In a city the size of Istanbul it was good to have a 'body guard' that was twice your size. Plus, he was both the Turkish National and Turkish Military dog. Aykut took Amber everywhere that the social system of human beings allowed. And Amber will repay Aykut with all of his heart and soul, soon to be totally understood.

He stopped playing for a minute and sat down under the umbrella to cool down. He gave the last of his drinking water to Amber, who downed it in a few seconds. And sitting under the vivid yellow sun, he looked south across the turquoise blue of the Mediterranean Sea toward Egypt. Aykut was trying to lock in his summer olive sun tan before winter arrived. His father and little sister, Gül, had gone up into the nearby mountains to go snow skiing. This was the Turkish Riviera near Antalya which had numerous multi-story five-star hotels with indoor and outdoor swimming pools, exercise rooms, tennis courts, golf courses, beautiful white sandy beaches, and a warm sea as late as November.

The Sultan Osman Hotel even had several serving tables which were continuously filled with the most delicious food – five hours for breakfast, five hours for lunch, and six hours for dinner. Aykut was really having a good time. Mother was upstairs packing as they were returning to Istanbul by Turkish Airlines that night.

The three-day vacation was nice. But he was worried as he kept reading in the newspapers about the World Entrepreneurs Congress which would start tomorrow at the Ciragan Palace - Kempinski Hotel in Beshiktash on the Bosporus in European Istanbul. He had bad feelings about such a conference of super high technology brains and their financial support systems at the same place at the same time. At the last 4-pack computer conference, Jamie said that his Uncle Dagda was also worried about it; so that worried all of the Colored Musketeers. After he returned to Istanbul, tomorrow he would contact a couple of his Syrian friends. Maybe they smelled something, and he thought now they might be willing to tell him if they knew or even suspected anything coming from Masyaf.

Early Monday morning, Aykut's father, Bulent Turan, who was Vice President and Director of Applied Projects of İşbank, the largest bank in Turkey, was in motion by 7:00 AM. His chauffer driven Mercedes had picked him up an hour earlier than normal as they needed to get ahead of the rush hour traffic. Aykut had begun to look more and more like his father, average height, a little overweight, round face, brown hair and eyes, and very intelligent. Mr. Turan had quickly grabbed a slice of toast with some goat cheese for breakfast, so he would have to find a way to grab a pastry before the congress got under way; he didn't want to be embarrassed if his stomach started growling during the presentation of the Turkish President.

They were speeding down to the mountainside toward Beshiktash and to Ciragan Palace and the associated Kempinski Hotel on the European side of the Bosporus. The Ciragan Palace was one of more than a dozen palaces of varying sizes, along the Bosporus. In the old days each small palace was the temporary home of one of the Sultan's family members, special associates, or favored Ottoman Generals. When the Republic of Turkey was established in 1923, all the palaces were nationalized, so now they were open for tourism and frequently used for national and international meetings and conferences.

The Ciragan Palace, built in 1864, plus the newly added Kempinski Hotel, had become the prima donna meeting site in Turkey. It routinely held the big important conferences of NATO, UNICEF, UNESCO, the G-Twelve, the G- Twenty-Five, OPEC, OECD, WHO, OSEC, OIC, WTO, and on and on. Like all palaces on the Bosporus it faces the water as the Bosporus has been the water highway number one for several thousand years. The river like channel is one mile wide, twenty- six miles long, begins in the Black Sea and ends in the Marmara Sea, splitting Istanbul into Asian and European halves.

The spectacular renovated palace had three floors, an all-white marble exterior with six marble columns facing the water, a mixture of randomly distributed red and crimson brick and stone interior walls, no two walls were the same. The ground floor contained one large auditorium and several small meeting rooms. The second level had four medium sized meeting rooms, one on each corner of the rectangular building, each with 210 seats and named after famous Sultans. And the third floor was arranged into several small, casual conversation rooms with arm chairs and couches, where coffee, tea, cakes, and pastries were continuously present. This upper floor was where personal negotiations and private small meetings were held.

Immediately adjacent to the old palace was added an architecturally matching five-star Kempinski Hotel which can sleep 800 guests. Thus, the congress attendees could sleep and eat in a first-class environment and walk one minute through a covered connecting walkway or stroll around the outside of the palace to the front door of the palace which faced the Bosporus. They could breathe and talk in the environment of past Sultans, Emperors, Kings, Queens, Princes, Princesses, Dukes, Countesses, and other royalty from Europe and Asia, plus elected world leaders such as Presidents and Prime Ministers. No negative 'incident' had ever happened here.

The palace - hotel complex was surrounded by a 25-feet high 5-feet wide stone wall with only two large entry gates. The hotel faced the palace but the palace faced the water because there was only one land side road in the area. The Bosporus and the single road remained as the major mode of travel in the Ciragan Palace area of Istanbul. So, many people still come and go, over, or across this body of water and pass by the palace on this one road, every day, a road which would be closed during this coming week during the conference.

As Mr. Turan's car entered the Bosporus Road in Beshiktash, with less than one mile to go, he opened the congress program book and the supplemental list of attendees with their addresses. He started reading through it. He knew that the attendees of the World Entrepreneurs Congress were carefully selected each year by the WE Congress Organizational Committee. Two hundred and fifty of the world's top high technology scientists were invited to spend three days with four hundred representatives of the world's financial groups. These groups provide venture capital and continuous investment support for beginning and all stages of high technology research and developmental projects.

In addition, two local finance people were allowed to attend. First, Mr. Turan, because he was a Vice President of the largest bank in Turkey, and spoke English, German, French, and Turkish. He would play the role of a Turkish Co- Host. His first obligation was to introduce, in the opening ceremony, the Turkish President, the Mayor of Istanbul, and other dignitaries who would welcome the Congress attendees to Turkey and the Congress. The two Turkish hosts would be with the Congress every minute of every day and night. Therefore, he was up and out of the house before Aykut even woke up. Father and son did not get a chance to say good-bye. And they would never have another chance.

As they approached the Palace entry, he quickly read through the program schedule:

TENTH ANNUAL WORLD ENTREPRENEURS CONGRESS CIRAGAN PALACE AND KEMPINSKI HOTEL ISTANBUL, TURKEY

PURPOSE: This annual congress is held to bring together the two members of Scientific World Entrepreneurism, the Inventors and the Patrons, such that their combined efforts can result in bringing positive benefits for all peoples of the world.

Monday, October 27, 2032

9:00 AM – Opening Ceremony in Room Sultan Osman
        President of Turkey
        Mayor of Istanbul
        Turkish Undersecretary of Economic Development
        Turkish President of the Chamber of Commerce
        President of the Association of World Entrepreneurs
10:00 AM - Scientific Presentations
        Room Sultan Mehmed – Robotics and Eubotics
        Room Sultan Suleyman – Telokinetics -Teloportation
        Room Sultan Mustafa – Artificial Intelligence
        Room Sultan Abdulhamid – Bio-Android-Technology

Lunch

1:30 PM – Scientific Presentations
        Room Sultan Mehmed – Atomic Chemistries
        Room Sultan Suleyman – Nanotechnology
        Room Sultan Mustafa – Chimeric Architecture
        Room Sultan Abdulhamid – Nuclear Physics
4:30 PM - Social Event – tour of Dolmabahce Palace
7:30 PM - Evening Dinner – Dolmabahce Palace

Tuesday, October, 28, 2032

9:00 AM – Scientific Presentations
        Room Sultan Mehmed – Telecommunications
        Room Sultan Suleyman – Micro-instrumentations
        Room Sultan Mustafa –Recyclable Energy Systems
        Room Sultan Abdulhamid – Oceans and Seas

Lunch

1:30 PM – Scientific Presentations
>Room Sultan Mehmed – Medicine/Pharmaceuticals
>Room Sultan Suleyman – Molecular Genetics/ Biochemistry
>Room Sultan Mustafa – Bio-Atomic Chemistries
>Room Sultan Abdulhamid – Plasmonies

4:00 PM – Social Event – Tour of Topkapi Palace
7:00 PM – Cocktails and Dinner – Topkapi Palace

Wednesday, October 29, 2032

9:00 AM – Room Sultan Osman- Special Presentations
>Dr. Lawrence Greensbourgh, Nobel Laureate in Medicine
>Dr. Elizabeth Rochester, Nobel Laureate in Chemistry

10:30 AM – Scientific Presentations
>Room Sultan Mehmed – Fourth Dimension Systems
>Room Sultan Suleyman – Fresh Water Chemistries
>Room Sultan Mustafa – Nanobots
>Room Sultan Abdulhamid – Telepathy

Lunch

2:00 PM – Room Osman – Business Meeting and Closing Ceremonies
3:00 PM – Social Event – Tour of Aga Sophia, Blue Mosque, And Grand Bazaar
7:30 PM – Cocktails and Dinner on Turkish Cruise Ship While Touring Up the Bosporus and Return to Kempinski Hotel

As Mr. Turan's car turned into the Palace grounds, he motioned to the driver that he needed a few more minutes to complete his scanning through the World Entrepreneurism Congress program. His chauffeur continued along the land side of the palace and parked in the south reserved special dignitaries' parking lot. He quickly looked back to the last section and glanced over the list of names and areas of funding for the Patrons:

Venture Capital firms – National Capital Ventures Association, Village Ventures, Foundry Group, Davidow Ventures, Highway Ventures..........

Hedge Funds – Amaranth Advisors, DE Shaw, Man Group, Marshall Wace, Soros Fund Management, Bridgewater Associates.............

Angel Investors – names of many affluent individuals and the specific areas of high technology that each wishes to invest in, please check with..........

Crowd Funding – names of many collectives or groups of people and the specific area of high technology that each group wishes to invest in, please check with ....

Alternative Asset Management – Credit Suisse, Goldman Sachs, Apollo Management, Morgan Stanley, American Capital, Fortress Management Group ......

Venture Capital and International Investments Banks – Major government and private banks in Africa, Asia, Europe, Caribbean, Islamic Conference, World Bank, Preferential Trade Areas Fund ....

After quickly finishing with the program, he hopped out of the car, walked around the building to the water side and entered the front door of the Ciragan Palace. He saw the many civilian and military police already in their appointed security posts and noticed the two coast guard patrol boats idling nearby. The security consisted of civilian police, military police and one commando unit. While walking up to the second floor he thought through what he had just read.

'With so many areas of science and technology being talked about, and so many major venture capital investment organizations listening, this will certainly be a super meeting. I hope that the many scientists and many patrons find love-love relationships such that high technology can keep sailing along.' And he smiled at his own cleverness.

He walked over to the registration desks and sought out key members of the Board of Directors of the Association of the World Entrepreneurs and introduced himself. "My name is Bulent Turan. I am the Vice President of İşbank, the largest bank in Turkey, and I am one of your two hosts. Mr. Metin Gursoy, who is Vice President of Ziraat Bank, second largest bank in Turkey, is the other host. He will be here shortly."

The tall bald headed, blue eyed, serious looking gentleman wearing Italian wire frame glasses responded, "Thank you. I am President of the WE and Co- Chairman for this 2032 Congress. My name is Dr. Borstan Yeagar. I arrived yesterday afternoon from the US and have been checking everything, meeting rooms, support rooms, audio-visuals, lunch and dinner arrangements, and logistics to the hotel and back, various associated locations, security, and so on. It all looks very good to me. However, I do have one immediate concern. We have heard that we may be targeted by some terrorists or crazy group of conservatives. Do you know anything about this?'

Mr. Turan replied, "Yes, we have heard such rumors, but we have no definite information. Currently we have almost 500 police and military patrolling and protecting the hotel and palace grounds, and this security will travel with us when we go to other locations nearby. That calculates out to be more than one security personnel for every two Congress participants. When we travel to the social locations, we will travel by bullet proof buses with both police and military providing security with the caravan. All streets that we will travel on and places that we will visit will be pre-cleared of traffic and people. Only in the Grand Bazaar, a gigantic ancient shopping mall, will the pre-screened shopkeepers be allowed to stay to provide service to the attendees so they can purchase gifts. Our precautions are at the same level as if we were hosting NATO,

OECD, OPEC, or any other major meeting of very important people, just like yourselves."

Dr. Yeagar looked Mr. Turan directly in the eyes, smiled, and thought to himself, 'I like this guy; I can see that we will certainly get along just fine. No BS.'

The two of them got into conversation about travel and weather; is Istanbul always so lovely and warm in late October? After a couple of minutes of chatting, a short, very round, but proud bearing fellow with white hair, long dark eyebrows, and wearing a silk black suit walked up to the two of them.

Mr. Turan said, "This is Mr. Metin Gursoy, my co-host. Metin Bey, this is Dr. Yeagar who is the Co-Chairman of the World Entrepreneurs Congress." Mr. Gursoy responded with, "Hoşgeldiniz;" Welcome to Turkey.

The two Turks had both been in the banking field in Turkey for more than twenty years so they knew each other very well. Mr. Gursoy was also a refined gentleman, comfortable with foreigners; so, while Dr. Yeagar and Mr. Gursoy started talking to get to know each other, Mr. Turan slipped into an adjacent room and quickly downed two kasar peynirli pogaça (rolled pastries filled with cheese) and two elmalı pogacha (rolled pastries filled with apples). He had a quick small glass of brown tea. Both father and son had never realized that they each had a sweet tooth. But Mr. Turan wanted to be certain that his stomach did not embarrass him in front of the Turkish President. This would be enough for now.

As 9:00 o'clock rolled around, the large auditorium on the first floor, Sultan Osman Room, was almost full. The Turkish dignitaries had arrived from Ankara, and Mr. Turan sat each of them comfortably at a long table on a raised stage at the front of the room. In chairs on the floor of the auditorium the scientists or inventors and promoters or patrons sat sort of separately as most of them did not know each other. Hopefully that would change during the next three days. Better of course would be for many inventor and patron happy marriages. That was a major purpose of these annual meetings.

Nearly on time, Mr. Turan stood up, waited for the audience to quiet, and said, "My name is Bülent Turan. I am co-host at this Tenth Annual

World Entrepreneurs Congress. The other host is Mr. Metin Gursoy, sitting at the other end of this table."

He motioned for Mr. Gursoy, who stood up and waved, although most of the audience could not tell if he was seated or standing.

"If either of us can be of help to you in any way during your short stay here at the Ciragan Palace in Istanbul, please let us know. Now I have the honor of introducing to you the President of the Republic of Turkey ....

After nearly an hour of introductions and welcomes, and a few announcements, no major changes in scheduling were given, the conferees adjourned to the second floor to listen to the beginning of the Scientific Presentations.

At 10:00 AM the four corner Sultan's rooms were full, and the first four areas of lectures and discussions began: Robotics, Telokinetics, Artificial Intelligence, and Bio-technology. The scientists who were working in these four areas, and who were chosen to talk about their research, began to sell their high-tech ideas to people who came here looking for high tech ideas. The morning sessions included talks from twenty- three different scientists.

Around noon time the attendees migrated into the dining room of the Kempinski Hotel for lunch. Bulent Turan and Metin Gursoy sat at a head table with several members of the W.E. Board of Directors.

Dr. Yeagar introduced everyone – "This is Mr. Bulent Turan and Mr. Metin Gursoy, the Turkish hosts of our Congress. Going around the table left to right are Dr. Janice Beers from Montreal, Dr. Peter Wells from San Diego, Dr. Olivetti Mendini from Milan, and Dr. Dominga Gonzalez from Madrid. And of course, I am Dr. Borstan Yeagar from Munich. We thank you and Turkey for hosting us for this meeting. All of us have heard the terrorist rumors. But looking around it seems to me that you have everything well under control."

"I certainly hope so," replied Mr. Turan. "As you know, we have meetings like yours in the Ciragan Palace, which require the ultimate in security, two or three times every year. So, our security people are very experienced. I only pray that they continue their perfect record of no troubles."

Dr. Wells asked, "Is it possible to see the Whirling Dervishes? I understand that it is very hypnotic and can even put you to sleep or in a trance. What do you know about them?"

Mr. Turan answered, "The Whirling Dervishes was founded in the 13th century by Mevlana Rumi. This became the Mevlevi Order and they wrote of tolerance, forgiveness, and enlightenment. They developed a dancing ritual called the Sema. During the Sema, the dancers swirl with one hand pointing toward God and one hand pointing toward the earth. When performed by adherents of the Order in a prayer trance to Allah, the soul is released from earthly ties and becomes free to move with other free spirits and souls. The word dervish means doorway to the heavenly world. A special Rumi music is integrated into the dancing."

Mr. Gursoy jumped in, "The Order began as only Muslim, but a person from any religion may seek enlightenment. One famous Rumi verse goes:

'Whoever you may be, come – even though you may be an infidel, a pagan, or a fire worshiper, come – our brotherhood is not one of despair even though, you may have broken your vows of repentance 100 times, come -

And Mr. Turan continued, "The Dervishes had a very powerful influence on the political, social and economic life of the Ottoman Empire because several of the Sultans were Sufis of the Mevlana Order. Today it has no major influence on the life of the common Turk. But it is still a highly respected religious order and is known throughout the world; just as you were aware of Mevlana. This year's ceremony begins in two weeks in Konya."

Dr. Wells gave him a big smile and a thank you node of his head.

Dr. Yeagar commented, "Most of we scientists are not very religious. But there are some of us who are developing very difficult high-tech ideas such as multiple-telepathy, waste-psychokinesis, and precognition. Perhaps we could benefit from learning the Mevlana ways. I will pass this idea along."

"May I ask how you pass these ideas along?" asked Mr. Gursoy.

"This is a fair question," responded Dr. Yeagar. "I remember back at the beginning of this century when we high tech scientist were trying to organize, sell our ideas, find promoters, patrons, or whatever you wanted to call them; people with money who might be willing to spend it on an idea which might or might not bring them some money in return – a risky gamble. A few years ago, we had two bright and enthusiastic young Czars of High Technology, Theodore O'Reilly in the USA and Leon Odilone in the European Union. We talked to both of them. They suggested expanding our scientific meetings to include potential patrons. Both gentlemen would help promote the idea to venture capital and other such organizations and also provide funds to help us start engagement relationships. The Association of World Entrepreneurs and our Congresses are one result of these efforts. High technology research monies have increased more than 500% during the past ten years. Today money is readily available if you have a good idea, an excellent scientific record which proves that you can do it, and a good idea for something creative and potentially profitable. Today marriage partners are available. Meetings such as this are critical in passing ideas along. We owe a very special thanks to these two very special young gentlemen who were suddenly removed from our battle for matching good ideas and solid money. Bless their souls."

"In the past you would read about a new high tech finding every month or two," added Dr. Wells. "Now you read about one every week. And in the near future you will be able to talk about a new high technological system entering the marketplace with new products every day of the week."

The conversation then turned to the 2028 World Cup in which both the USA and Turkey played in the semi-finals. Turkey beat Argentina, but Brazil beat the USA. In the finals, Brazil beat Turkey and the USA beat Argentina. So, the argument developed: - How could Turkey claim to be second and the USA third in the World when they did not play each other? In such tournaments there should be another match played between the second and third place winners to determine who was really second. They all agreed that it was time to change some peculiar ancient rule that **did** not allow proper hierarchal determinations.

26B

World Entrepreneurs – II

Monday and Tuesday of this week were a continuation of a Kurban Bayram, a religious holiday, so Turkish schools were not in session. Monday morning Aykut woke up and suddenly remembered yesterday's promise to himself to try to find out about any movement between Masyaf and Istanbul. He called his best Syrian friend and classmate, Asu Kalan. He invited Asu and his Syrian friend, Sargon Khalife, whose entire family was murdered earlier this year in Kadikoy. They would lunch at the Bebek Hotel Restaurant which was on the Bosporus about two miles north of the Ciragan Palace. The WE Congress area was already closed down for a mile in every direction so he took the northern entry route into Bebek.

By 1:30 PM, the three of them had settled into patio chairs at a table overlooking the Bosporus. They fell into an embarrassed silence as they watched an international container ship heading for the Mediterranean Sea and Europe, and a large oil tanker going in the other direction toward the Black Sea and Russia. After a few difficult moments, Aykut finally said, "Sargon, I hope you are doing better. I understand that you are receiving support from our people and the Turkish government. Just remember it is good to finish high school now, as you will get a better job someday, and you might even go to a university; why we have 21 universities here in Istanbul, and 15 are state universities which are not so expensive."

Sargon responded, "With friends like you and Asu, who are university bound, I have no choice but to study hard and try to keep up with you. Yes, I hope that I can do that. Not one of my family members, here or Syria, ever went to a university. I would go down in the Khalife family history books if I did that."

And he grinned. And his two buddies grinned back. He was a survivor. Sargon was slowly recovering from the tragic loss of his entire family in a single night. With the Turks helping, he had begun a new life. At least he had stopped crying half of the night and seeing his bloated mother floating above the old rough grey wooden floor. Fortunately, after he had entered the apartment that night, he passed out, psychologically. His mind went blank. And today he has almost no memory of seeing the other bloated family members lying all over the apartment floors and in beds. So, his mind has accepted the macabre death of his mother, but the other family members are just 'somewhere'.

Asu said, "I heard that on your big exam last week you got the highest grade in class. Is this true?"

Sargon just looked out into the water, blushed, and said nothing.

"And I understand that you have a couple of Turkish girls giving you the eye," added Aykut.

Again, Sargon said nothing. He was still shy around these two fast track young Turks.

After ordering some lunch and chatting for a while, Aykut commented, "I know that you don't want to talk about that night, but did you hear that your family was possibly killed by some kind of new poison which came from the Citadel of Masyaf?"

"I know." Sargon replied.

Asu and Aykut looked at each other in surprise. "You know?"

Sargon, now watching a ferry boat cross the waterway answered, "During the past couple of years, several village families in northern Syria have been killed like this. Everyone says it comes from Hashashin."

"Sargon," Aykut asked, "did you know that I recently visited the Citadel of Masyaf? I went inside and I downloaded information that supports the rumors that you hear. Some type of very deadly poison is being made there and being used to kill people's enemies. My American friends believe that it is being used to kill many people all over the world."

Sargon's eyes enlarged, "You went into the Citadel of Masyaf?"

Aykut saw the fear in Sargon's eyes and said, "Most of the Citadel has been completely renovated and is open to tourists. I went there with a Turkish tourism group and toured the fortress."

Sargon breathed a sigh of relief and said, 'You are very brave. And now you want me to find out more about this poison, don't you?"

Aykut just smiled. "You are the brave one. I am just trying to help. Today there is a big conference at the Çırağan Palace. My father is participating in the conference. My American friends think that someone will try to use one of those poisons to kill people during the conference. If you have any friends or contacts that you could talk to or ask about a Hashanshin poison and the Istanbul conference this week, please ask for information or help. I am afraid for my father's life."

"I will try."

Sargon's eyes met Aykut's and held for several moments. They exchanged smiles. Aykut just knew that this guy was going to make it in life; he wanted to help as much as he could. Aykut gave to Sargon his cell phone number and hoped. He had a feeling that Sargon would find out something, good or bad. And he did.

During that first day of the World Entrepreneurs Congress, the attendees had collected on the second-floor conference rooms of the Çırağan Palace to listen to the scientists talk about their high-tech research in Robotics and Eugotics, Telokinetics- Teleportation, Artificial Intelligence, Bio-Android-technology, Atom Chemistries, Nanotechnology, Architecture, and Nuclear Physics. There were seventy-one speakers trying to 'sell their wares'.

Near 4:30 PM, after the end of the afternoon presentations, the participants loaded into a dozen bullet proof buses and traveled the two miles south down the Bosporus to the land entrance to the Dolmabahçe Palace, the last palace of the Ottoman Sultans.

The Dolmabahce Palace was the Sultan's home as well as office and was built between 1843 and 1846 on reclaimed land on the west or European shore of the Bosporus. It was designed by Ottoman Armenian architects who combined Ottoman, Baroque, Rococo, and Neoclassic features. It is the largest palace in Turkey with 450,000 enclosed square feet and nearly one million square feet of immediately surrounding pools and gardens. It has over 300 rooms, 45 corridors, 6 hamams or large steam baths, and 70 toilets. It is surrounded on all three land sides by a 50-feet high five-foot thick stone wall.

The water side is adorned with a scalloped chain wall on a 2000-feet long wharf. A major entry is located on the water side just off of the large ball room. Another major entry is on the south land side of the palace. A few hundred people lived and worked in the palace. Those living here included the Sultan, the Sultana or Sultan's Mother, wives, children, five or six favorite concubines and servants. Ottoman officials and government workers at the Secretariat had their own separate quarters.

The palace is divided into three interconnected areas or wings separated by gardens. The south wing is the Mabeyn-i Humayun or Selamlik which was reserved for men only. The Muayede Salonu or the ceremonial ballroom is in the middle. And the largest wing is the Harem-i Humayun or Harem which was reserved for the Sultan, women, and children. The buildings are fully connected and movement from one area to another is accomplished only through interior security-controlled corridors and doors.

The busloads of congress attendees parked and unloaded outside the south gates of the palace. They entered through the 65 feet tall elaborately designed iron gates of the wall and went into the south gardens. The first view of this all- white marble palace was the spectacular South Façade fronting on the Selamlik. The groups of scientists and patrons walked for fifteen minutes through flower gardens and around several small pools to reach the front stairway and then climbed up to the second floor. They would tour the palace in groups of 25 to 30 people, each group with a single guide who spoke their language.

So more than twenty groups, one group at a time, climbed the marble stairway and entered the Medhal Entry of the Selamlik. This first palace unit had two connected buildings. The first building was the lower and the second building was the higher administrative center for the Ottoman Empire. Anyone wanting to see the Sultan or who had state affairs or business with the Empire was required to enter this first large single room, register and file a petition, perhaps he would come and go for several waiting days. Finally, his petition would be heard by one or more of the many Ottoman officials. Minor officials were in this first building, first, second, and third floors. Senior ranking officials were in the second building, second floor. The highest-ranking officials, including the Grand Vizier, second to the Sultan, and the Sultan, had offices on the third floor, overlooking the Bosporus, and close to the water side entry door to be able to directly greet special dignitaries.

The interior palace walls, 25 feet high, still contain many portraits and paintings of famous visitors and historical events. All the floors are wood parquet covered with large and famous red/crimson Hereke carpets. And the famous three level double horseshoe shaped Crystal Staircase connects the two buildings to the Selamlik. It has a single one-hundred-ton royal Baccarat Crystal chandelier hanging from above, plus the staircase has elaborate brass and light/dark mahogany wood carved designs. Each floor has two or three large salons and each salon has one of more Baccarat or Bohemian Crystal chandeliers hanging from the ceilings. With more than 500 windows, each with ceiling to floor red/crimson curtains which are so thick that when drawn, the sun is completely excluded. All ceilings contain large painted scenes of Ottoman life. More than 50 tons of gold and gold leaf decorates the walls, ceilings, and staircases. The feeling of great wealth oozes from every direction.

Each group from the World Entrepreneur Congress slowly walked from large to small salons, from waiting rooms to meeting rooms, from luxurious office suites to common multi-person offices to small single offices, from open corridors to closed/controlled corridors, from large stairways to small closed/enclosed ones. Yet all rooms were clothed in the same red/crimson and gold designs. It took more than one and a half hours to walk through the Selamlik (men's quarters).

Eventually each group entered the central three floor ballroom area where they would return and have their dinner later in the evening. They each looked up and around the elaborately decorated room. It was 60 feet high, 10,000 square feet of ball room floor with its beautifully carved ceiling and a 250-ton royal Baccarat chandelier hanging from the center. There were many associated rooms to each side which were hidden behind closed doors. They contained all the dining support facilities including 15 kitchens, food preparation, and wash rooms. Each food 'type' was prepared in its own preparation room.

Historically, this ballroom was designed to regularly provide royal dinners for the Sultan, his family, and several hundred guests. Because it was the only room in the palace where men and women were allowed to share the same air, physical security, no electronic cameras in those days, was strategically placed at all entryways and at key locations throughout the room. Tonight, both electronic and physical security would be employed in abundance.

After a few minutes of walking and looking around the ballroom, each group was slowly led into the Harem. During the time of the Empire, no adult males, except the Sultan and eunuchs, were allowed into this world of the family. The two upper floors of this wing of the palace housed several large salons and one or two floor apartments. The ground floor was for the service personnel for the entire Harem (women and children's section). Each apartment had its own small receiving salon on the third floor with a private stairway leading down to a private second floor bedroom area. The Valide Sultan, Sultan's Mother, had large and extensive accommodations; and all other apartments were assigned to one lady and her children until the age of twelve years. Large apartments were for each of the Sultan's wives and their children; only women who bore him children were officially married to him and had special status. The smaller apartments were temporally assigned to the Sultan's current favorite women.

As usual, the male members from each Congress group walked, looked, talked, and compared this unique life style. Most of them could not decide if this was a good arrangement or not. At least you would have your mother controlling the ladies and choosing which lady slept with you each night. That might be interesting. Surprises could be fun!

The Harem was much larger than the Selamlik, but the rooms were larger, so it took only an hour to tour through this third section of the Dolmabahce Palace. After almost more than 2-hours of continuous walking, everyone was dead tired. But this was anticipated. As the participants slowly exited the Palace from the furthermost small northern exit of the Selamlik, they turned right and walked toward the Bosporus. The 200 feet wide, 2000 feet long wharf between the Palace and the water was lined with many small circular tables and chairs. Tea, coffee, and a variety of cakes and pastries were just waiting, and 650 scientists and patrons had tired legs that needed resting and empty stomachs that needed filling.

Sitting with their backs to the Palace and looking across the Bosporus, a continental divide, the eastern-most European sun sat on the western-most Asian coastline. The red-orange Asian mountain side slowly changed to pink to gray to black. Hundreds of thousands of home, street, and traffic lights began popping up along the central waterway in the city of fifteen million people. The numerous oil tankers, container ships, and local ferries lit up as they traversed the water. Each attendee relaxed, brought his blood sugar back up to normal, let the caffeine wake up his body cells, and tried to digest what the Ottoman Empire really was all about. After all, it seemed that the 600 years of Ottoman science apparently was devoted basically to their military.

Near 7:30 PM, dinner was announced; so, they walked back toward the center of the Palace and entered through the ornate 25 feet tall door, just off of the Bosporus, into the gigantic Muayede Salonu. They would be treated to a seven- course dinner. Lunch had been six hours ago; they were ready to do justice to a once in a lifetime Ottoman royal style banquet.

Mr. Turan and Mr. Gursoy had decided to split up and circulate with different groups to try to spread their hosting around. The one hundred and thirty round tables were set with six chairs, so Mr. Turan decided to join a table near the middle of the room. He introduced himself. They each introduced themselves to him; and he quickly understood that this group was a mixture of scientists and promoters from four different countries. Good, he wanted to try to understand both potentially marriageable partners.

Each table setting had a small menu lying on a sixteen-inch diameter ceramic plate; it was inscribed with a Sultan's seal or official Ottoman signature in the center, four forks on the left, three knives on the right, and three spoons just above the plate; three crystal glasses for water, red and white wines were setting at the top of the plate near the tails of the spoons. Each piece of cutlery was solid silver, of a different size, and each was to use specifically for eating specific foods. The large engraved plate was not to eat from, but served as a place to put each dish or plate from each of the seven courses of food. One was not supposed to get the big plate dirty. You were to eat from it not on it.

One of the scientists at the table with Mr. Turan asked, "Now how will seven courses of food get to everyone in this gigantic room, and which silverware will we use to eat which food, and where will the dirty dishes go?"

Mr. Turan replied, "Do not worry. These chefs and waiters have performed this miracle many times. Look at the menu, where choices of servings are available, use you pencil and check one of them. As you can see, there are two waiters per table. They will make note of your choices, carry each serving to the table, gently explain which cutlery to use, and wait until you are finished. They will then carry out the dirty dishes, and a few minutes later return with your next serving. They will thus make several trips to the various kitchens and back."

The same scientist said, "Thank you. We scientists love a challenge. And for a few minutes I could see the possibility of trying to organize this coming and going a dozen times per hour. It certainly is not efficient. And two waiters per table would be a bit expensive, if I was paying for it, but I am not. So, I will shut up and just enjoy being treated as royalty for one night in my life."

Mr. Turan picked up his wine glass gave a "Şerefe", the Turkish cheers.

DOLMABAHCE SARAYI – DOLMABACHE PALACE YEMEK LISTESİ - MENU

Course 0 – Kırmızı veya Beyaz Şarap (Red or White Wine)
Ve (and) Cevizli Ekmek (Walnut Bread), Mısır Ekmek (Corn Bread), Çavdar Ekmek (Rye Bread). – continuously available

Course 1 – Mercimek Çorbası (Lentil Soup), veya (or) Kremalı Mantar Çorbası (Crème of Mushroom Soup) Salata

Course 2 – Meze (Appetizers): Kara Zeytin (Black Olives), Patlıcan (eggplant salad), Ahtapot (Octopus), Cevizli Biber (Walnut and Cumin in Green Pepper).

Course 3 – Arugula Salad (Roka Salad with Mini Tomatoes, Mushrooms, Olive Oil, and Lemon).

Course 4 – Kuzu Güveç (Lamb Casserole) veya (or) Kağıtta Bonfile (Oven Baked Steak) veya (or) Levrek (Grilled Sea Bass)

Course 5 – Baklava (Filo Dough with Sugar and Pistachios), Kadayıf (Shredded Rye Meal with Honey, and Walnuts)

Course 6 – Karışık Meyve (Mixed Fruit): Şeftali (Peaches), Kiraz (Cherries), Erik (Plums).

Course 7 – Türk Kahvesi (Turkish Coffee), Amerikan Kahve (percolated American Coffee), Çay (Brown Tea)

After everyone was seated, Dr. Borstan Yeagar stood up and, using a hand microphone, called everyone to silence. After a few moments, many participants were still enjoying their sudden affluence and toasting their table colleagues with their Turkish wines, Dr. Yeagar said, "If you do not quiet down, I will cancel the food for the evening and we will all go back to the hotel!"

And that brought forth the yells and calls for him to go by himself. But there was soon silence in the large ballroom. Not everyone was sure that he did not mean what he said, nor if he had the authority to do this. So rather than take chances they 'quieted down.'

Again, Dr. Yeagar spoke up, "Thank you very much. We have two very important guests who have joined us tonight. They wish to congratulate us on our efforts to bring forth new and better living systems into the world. Each would like only very few minutes of you time."

And a nice applause and patience prevailed.

"The first guest is Mr. Erdal Eren, Govenor of the Province of Marmara, of which Istanbul is a major part."

Mr. Eren, sitting at the same table as Dr. Yeagar, stood up, took the microphone, and extended his thanks, and mentioned that there were many excellent tourist sites close to Istanbul such as the Black Sea and the Belgrade Forest. He would be happy to accommodate if anyone wanted to stay a couple of extra days and see the Istanbul environs.

Next to say hello was Mr. Ertugrul Tasdemir, the Mayor of Istanbul. He also cut both his welcome and thank you to a couple of minutes, and invited everyone to return to Istanbul when they could spend all of their time site seeing; and he recommended that would require a minimum of a week.

When the two Turkish government officials were finished, Dr. Yeagar again took the microphone, stood up, and commented. Because there is no longer an Ottoman Sultan in Turkey, my friends declared me as the Sultan for the evening. Therefore, as this is my routine dining room and my normal evening dinner, I crown all of you as my very 'best' friends and declare that the drinking and eating begin. Ohps! I can see that the drinking has already begun."

Now the Co-Chairman of the Tenth Annual Program for the Association of the World Entrepreneurs was enthusiastically applauded; and all his 'best' friends, followed the new declaration.

Early that Monday evening Sargon telephoned Aykut. "Aykut, you are correct. My friends tell me that a Masyaf package was carried by a Syrian courier to Istanbul three days ago. It is not known what is in the package, nor where it is currently located, but I have my suspicions. This is not good."

Aykut replied, "Thank you very much, Sargon. I will talk to my American friends and let them talk to the Turkish authorities. I am afraid the Turkish police can do nothing more, and I don't want to get either of us into trouble."

Aykut decided to call his father first. He fast dialed his father who was thoroughly enjoying his 'royal' meal. "Dad, are you enjoying the evening?"

Father responded, "Everything is great, even the food."

And he laughed as he knew Aykut would certainly enjoy this meal also. He would try to remember to take some dessert home later.

"These foreigners are the nicest and most optimistic people that I have ever been around. I think that they do not know how to look backwards; they only see tomorrow. How are you doing?"

"Not good. Dad, I just talked to my Syrian friend and he told me that they think some kind of poisonous chemical was shipped from Masyaf to Istanbul last week. I am afraid that the World Entrepreneurs Congress is a target for this chemical. And I am afraid for you."

His father responded, "Yes, this is not good news. I don't know what to do. I will talk with Lieutenant Ileri, Head of Security for the Congress, ask him to tighten the security even more, and double check all the food. I do not know what else I can do. Have you talked with your American friends?

"No, but I will call them now. Be careful."

"If the Americans have any suggestions please let me know, and I will immediately try to implement them."

"Promise me that you will be extra careful." "I will be extra careful. And I love you."

They both hung up, and Aykut called Jamie. There was not time to call up a computer conference.

As Jamie answered he became elated that it was Aykut. "I am so happy to hear your voice. We haven't talked in a long time. How are you doing?"

Aykut responded in a state of panic, "Things are not good. In fact, things are very bad. As you know Istanbul is hosting the World Entrepreneurs Congress. It is being treated as a major international conference and the highest state of security is everywhere. But my Syrian friends have learned that a Syrian courier has brought some type of package from Masyaf to Istanbul. They do not know where it is in Istanbul. I am afraid it is designated to be used at the Congress. The world's best high technology scientists and people who sponsor their research are together in the same place at the same time. It is a perfect target for those conservative killers. Please tell your Uncle Dagda, have him tell his nephew the President of the USA to tell the President of Turkey to stop the Congress so my father will not get killed."

And he was running out of breath, so had to stop.

Jamie responded, "Slow down. Sit down for a moment and catch your breath. Is your father attending the Congress?"

"Yes, he is a Turkish host, he is there now, and of course he won't leave."

"I will talk with my Uncle Dagda immediately," Jamie answered. "But I don't know if the States can do anything more than your people are already doing. Remember, if this package contains Nano killer chemicals, there will probably be a few hours delay built into it. Even food tasters would not be helpful, unless the food is prepared and tasted hours in advance of the dinner serving. And I imagine most chefs would declare that all foods were always prepared immediately before serving. After I talk with Uncle Dagda, I will call you back and let you know what he says."

Aykut's breath was now under control, he said, "Thank you very much. Don't worry about the seven hours of time difference; I probably will not be able to sleep tonight anyway. If you have any ideas at any time, call. Bye for now."

"Don't panic. We are in the right, it will work out."

The Ottoman royal style banquet went smoothly, and everyone had returned to their beds in the Kempinski Hotel before midnight. So, Tuesday morning, most scientists and promoters were up, finished with breakfast, and waiting to hear from the talks from high technology speakers in the areas of Telecommunications, Micro-Instrumentations, Recyclable Energy Systems, and Oceans and Seas. Thirty-eight scientists were going to speak.

At noontime most participants returned to the Kempinski Hotel pool and patio areas for lunch, basked in the mild autumn sun for a while, and then returned to the second floor of the Ciragan Palace for the afternoon presentations which included twenty-nine speakers: Medicine/Pharmaceuticals, Molecular Genetics/Biochemistries, Bio-Atomic Chemistries, and Plasmonies.

By 4:30 PM most participants were now exhausted and ready for some outdoor social activity. Again, they were loaded into a dozen bullet proof buses for the 45-minute journey down the Bosporus, across the Galata Bridge, and into the old walled city of Constantinople now called Old Istanbul.

A 40 feet tall, 6 feet thick stone wall surrounds the entire old city. In addition, there is water just beyond the wall on three sides – the Marmara Sea on the south, Bosporus on the east, and the Golden Horn on the north.

The west side is the only land side. Here there are two of these stone walls with a one- mile gap between them. The city was conquered permanently only one time in 2000 years, and that was by the Ottoman Turks in 1453.

Before that time there were 500 churches, now there are 500 mosques. A total of 67 Byzantine Kings and then 55 Ottoman Sultans ruled until the bloodless demise of the Ottoman Dynasty at the beginning of the twentieth century led by a group known as the Young Turks. The Empire was no longer by the end of World War I. The Republic of Turkey was established in 1923 with its political and military capital in Ankara, 500 miles east.

After the Ottoman conquest the Turks built many large and famous buildings and areas inside the now Old Walled City of Istanbul. The participants of the Congress were going to tour four of these famous sites. The second day, they would spend dinner evening at the first palace of the Sultans, Topkapi Saray. The third day they would tour three other famous sites, Hagia Sophia, the Blue Mosque, and the Covered Bazaar. Fatih Sultan Mehmet, the Conqueror built this first palace on a hill top which offered a spectacular view of the crossroads of the Golden Horn, Bosporus, and the Marmara Sea.

The bullet proof buses climbed up the hill and entered the south or 60 feet tall elaborately designed gate in the third wall of the Topkapi Saray, Bab-ı Humayun or First Imperial Gate. The Palace is enclosed by 3 fifty feet tall, eight feet wide stone walls. It is a large garden palace with many connected buildings and four large courtyards, lovely multicolored flower gardens everywhere sporting their last colors of the year.

This first courtyard is more than fifty acres in size and is full of numerous multi-hundred-year old oak trees. The buses parked here as no vehicles were allowed further. The participants were organized into groups of fifty or sixty, matched with Palace guides, and directly entered through the next elaborately decorated gate, Bab-us Selam, or Gate of Salutations. Thus, they entered into the second courtyard.

As they entered Mr. Turan received a telephone call from his son.

Aykut asked, "Is everything under control? Has anything happened to arouse your suspicions, any problems? Are there any non-Congress participants hanging around the foreigners? You don't have as much protection outdoors in the many buildings and courtyards at Topkapi. Did you talk with the police?"

He knew that they would be outdoors all evening in a very large area with many small paths and big trees, easy to be hidden.

Mr. Turan replied, "Stop. Aykut. Nothing has happened. I don't see any strange suspicious people around us. There are police and army people, with big and small guns, everywhere. And yes, I talked with Lieutenant Ileri. I told him the Masyaf rumors, the courier and the unknown package of suspected poison; all possibly targeted for the Congress. He told me he is aware of these rumors and is following up on them. But so far, there is no evidence to support the rumors. He said they added more police in the kitchens to watch for anything suspicious concerning the foods."

"And how do you feel, Dad?"

"I am having a wonderful time. And now I need to catch up with my friends. I will be with them all right. I will again stay at the Kempinski Hotel tonight. If things go well, I will come home tomorrow night after the Bosporus cruise dinner."

"I talked with the Americans; they did not suggest any special security measures, except to call the Congress to an early closure. But I know you cannot do this."

Actually, Jamie had not been able to reach Uncle Dagda or Uncle Jonathan in the White House, so he had not returned his call to Aykut.

Aykut gave up and added, "OK. But you should be extra, extra careful, just for me. You don't have to eat all types of the food they give you. You could do with a little dieting."

"Look who is talking!"

And they each laughed and hung up. Aykut went back to his worries. And dad went back to his enjoyment.

—◦◦◦◦)◦(◦◦◦—

The second courtyard is about twenty-five acres with the Harem on the left or west side and ten very large kitchens each with a prominent chimney on the right or east side. The groups strolled slowly through the dormitory styled Harem which could sleep more than 200 women. A large fourth courtyard is located behind the Harem, between the outermost wall and the Harem connected buildings. It is a one-hundred-acre forest and gardens restricted to only the women, children, eunuchs, and the Sultan. All one hundred plus rooms and corridors of the Harem are elaborately decorated with the famous Iznik (Nicaea) ceramic tiles – walls, floors, and ceilings. The male members of the Congress took special note that the Sultan occupied three specially designed bedrooms, with much gold and blue ceramic tiles. However, only the largest bedroom contained a large royal bed. This was to only be used to continue the genetic legacy of Sultanship over several hundred years.

On the other side of the second courtyard, several of the ten large kitchens, which had daily cooked and served more than 2000 people, had now been turned into a large museum. The groups slowly walked through the numerous displays of hundreds of state and royal gifts to the many Sultans and the Empire, dressing gowns and turbans of each Sultan, large Chinese and Japanese porcelain vases from the other end of the Silk Road, elaborate jewelry made with gems of all varieties, and gold porcelain table settings with German lead crystal glasses.

Within the second courtyard were several other famous buildings. The Divan-ı Hümayun building housed the rooms of the Imperial Council where the Sultan met with the Grand Vizier, the Minister of State, twelve Council Members, and other leading officials of the Ottoman Empire. Nearby is the Adalet Kulesi, Tower of Justice building. As the title suggests it was the Supreme Court of Justice.

Adjacent to these buildings is a building containing the sword and shield, and the military dress of Mohammad, the Founder of Islam. On the wall of this building are calligraphy, in gold, of some of the famous sayings of Mohammad. The scientists found these 1400-year-old historical pieces fascinating, and they were much talked about during the evening dinner.

Nearby is the Hall of Campaign Pages which contains pieces of royal wardrobes, displays from the Royal Treasury such as elaborately designed weapons, each made with iron, gold, silver, and numerous gems.

At the back wall of the second courtyard and in the center of this wall is the elaborate gate called Bab-us Saadet, or the Gate of Felicity. In front of this gate the Sultan held many ceremonies and handed numerous prizes and awards. Immediately behind the gate was the third courtyard of some five acres which connected to the Harem on the west, the fourth courtyard on the north, and stone walls on the east. The first building is the Aza Odasi, or Audience Chamber, where the Sultan directly heard special petitions or entertained foreign Heads of State. Beyond this room the fourth courtyard was limited to the Sultan, page boys, eunuchs, and female servants. This was the garden home of the Sultan, his wives, children, and favorite female companions. All business beyond the Aza Odasi was personal. Within this courtyard are several famous small kiosks such as the Conqueror's Pavilion, the Bagdad Kiosk, and the Miniature Portrait Gallery.

When the Republic of Turkey was established, the Topkapi Palace was nationalized as a palace museum. Not like the Dolmabache Palace, all meals were catered to every person within their living quarters; there was no central dining area. So, the Turkish government built a large modern restaurant on the far north-east corner of the third courtyard. It was constructed on several terraces which overlooked the Bosporus, the Golden Horn and the Marmara Sea. As the Congress groups finished their long walking tour, they entered the restaurant, sat at long tables with twenty chairs each, read the menus on their plates, and chose from bar-b-q beef or chicken; all other food was standard hot breads, mixed vegetables, rice, potatoes, bottled water, small bottles of red or white wine, Turkish desserts and coffee or tea. This might have been the first palace of the Ottoman Sultan, but the meal was modern republic Turkish, even rather 'western'. Last night was the fantastic food; tonight, it was the fantastic sea and stars.

Again, by midnight everyone was sound asleep in their beds in the Kempinski Hotel.

26C

World Entrepreneurs III

THE THIRD AND LAST DAY of the Tenth World Entrepreneurs Congress began as usual. Many of the participants had learned that if they rose early, they could sit in Europe and watch the sun come up over Asia. Some people had found their way to the Kempinski Hotel terraces and gardens which directly overlook the Bosporus, sat on park benches and low garden walls, and had coffee and pastry breakfasts. The golden sun rise was marvelous, but the humidity was 99%, it was chilly, so jackets were necessary.

The Congress began at 9:00 AM in the first-floor auditorium, named Sultan Osman, the first Sultan of the Osmanlı Empire. The British created the English word Ottoman (because they transliterated from the Arab alphabet) to replace Osmanlı, which really means he who comes from Osman. Most other languages use a version of Osman when they study or discuss the 'Ottoman' Empire.

Two honorary speeches were to be given by two outstanding scientists in High Technology. Dr. Lawrence Greensbourgh, Nobel Laureate in Chemistry in 2016, who identified the protein toxin in the poison of the rattlesnake, isolated this molecule, determined the gene which produced it, injected this toxin gene into the spleen of rabbits such that the rabbits continuously made the toxin and thus produced an antibody to the toxin to be able to live. This new high technology methodology now provides a large quantity of inexpensive anti- serum for rattlesnake bites.

The second talk was to be given by Dr. Elizabeth Rochester, who won the Nobel Prize in Medicine in 2026. She identified several specific heat and electrical activity patterns in the brains of people prior to them developing the now common chronic ailments of Parkinson's and Alzheimer's diseases. Such early detection has allowed for early preventive therapy which delays these diseases by several years.

So, the attendees listened to the life stories and research approaches to the successful multi-year research efforts of two of the gods of high technology, Nobel Prize winners. Near 10:30 AM the attendees went up to the second floor and into the corner conference rooms and listened to the final series of scientific presentations: Fourth Dimension Systems, Fresh Water Chemistries, Nano- biotics, and Telepathy - from thirty-seven speakers.

At noon they had lunch in the Kempinski Hotel environs, and then returned to the Sultan Osman auditorium. First on the program was the business meeting. It was announced that there were 52 engagements, 29 marriages, and numerous flirtations of scientists and patrons during the three-day congress. The Tenth Annual World Entrepreneurs Congress was voted successful. The election of new officers was held. The Association of World Entrepreneurs did not have additional functions, no other meetings, no research journals, no research books, no direct monetary support of laboratory research or laboratory researchers. The single function was to bring together, once a year, inventors and sponsors. Next year it was confirmed that the annual meeting would be on October 7, 8, and 9, 2033, in a Hong Kong hotel to be established.

At 3:00 PM, the happy conferees again climbed into their bullet proof buses. Police and army units escorted them on a traffic free trip back into the Old Walled City. They would tour three world famous historical sites and later enjoy a dinner cruise on the Bosporus.

First, they stopped at the Hagia Sophia, located near the First Imperial Gate of the Topkapi Palace. Police and military had already cleared the area of people. This religious structure was built from 356 to 360 ADE as the Cathedral of Constantinople by the Roman and Greek rulers. The massive dome was considered the epitome of Byzantine architecture. It was the center of the Eastern Orthodox Church for the next one thousand years. After the conquest by the Ottoman Turks in 1453, the cathedral was converted into a mosque. The Christian bells, altars, iconostasis, and sacrificial vessels were removed. The Islamic mihrab, minber, and four external minarets were added. This structure was the central mosque for all Muslims in the world for the next five hundred years. However, Christians kept on referring to it as Aya Sofya (St. Sophia). In 1935, after the establishment of the Republic of Turkey, the structure was converted to a museum.

Today it is the only building in the world that has interior walls and ceilings, paintings and relics of both Christianity and Islam. There is a scene of Jesus in the dome which is surrounded by calligraphy of verses of the Koran. As the scientists looked up at the giant central dome, which was more than two hundred feet high, built 1,500 years ago, and the four smaller domes, studied the wall mosaics of the Eastern Orthodox Kings and Queens, marveled at the multicolored windows at all levels letting the sunshine through, many came to the same conclusion. Religions, like their followers, can become friends. But to current historical facts, Hagia Sophia is the only building in the world that has recognized two of the major religions both in the past and in the present. It even gave pause for the few 'non-believers' that maybe they should reconsider the future for their souls.

Next, they walked for ten minutes to the south and entered the Sultan Ahmed Mosque, or the Blue Mosque. The police and army had cleared the area and around the mosque. It is the second largest of more than 500 mosques in Istanbul and was built between 1609 and 1616 ADE, has four minarets, one on each corner, constructed of white marble, contains several hundred million famous Iznik blue (only) ceramic tiles, holds the tomb of Sultan Ahmed I, a madrasah (Islamic school), and a hospice (hospital/

clinics). Upon entering through the thirty feet tall elaborate north door, everyone placed plastic slippers on his feet, carried his shoes, and several tour guides led them into the back of the single 20,000 square feet room which has a large central dome and many smaller domes on each side. Two thousand people can pray at one time. All the domes and the walls are completely covered with blue tiles. The numerous small windows allowed for the setting sunlight to reflect a blue-red aura in the air. It is quite magical.

Every square foot of the floor is covered with red/crimson carpets; some are well over 500 square feet in size. During worship, all worshipers line up on lines in the carpets in a military fashion, face the multi-stepped mihrab, located in the southeast corner of the room, from where the Imam preaches. In this way the praying Muslims face Mecca during their prayers. Conferees were allowed only in the back half of the large room because there were people praying, near the mihrab, at all times. As they walked, they inspected the blue tiles, soft wool carpets, numerous chandeliers, many multicolored windows, and several smaller domes with extensively written calligraphy of verses from the Koran, they whispered to each other and compared the Hagia Sophia with the Blue Mosque, architecture and interiors. Selective religious services are held in the Hagia Sophia, but here there are prayer services five times every day. After a half an hour of looking and listening to some of the tour guides quietly telling about historical events associated with the building, they slowly left by the large door on the south side of the Mosque, removed and discarded their plastic slippers, and started toward the Covered Bazaar.

As the groups walked up another hill toward the center of the old city, Mr. Turan's cell phone rang. He thought, 'not know'. He saw it was Aykut and quickly answered, "Aykut, are there new problems?"

Aykut quickly replied, "How are things going, Father? Is everything all right? No problems?"

Mr. Turan answered, "Up to now everything has gone like clockwork. We are currently walking from the Ahmet Mosque toward the Grand Bazaar. We are on the open streets and very exposed. But most of the general populace has been removed from the area; the police and army are on guard and walking with us, so we feel secure. I think there will be no trouble. The bazaar is only another ten minutes of walking; and after shopping the buses will pick everyone up from one of the four major exits of the Bazaar. We will be delivered directly to the ships in the nearby Golden Horn wharf. The rest of the evening we will be on the dinner cruise ships. I know some of the military will also ride in the ships and there will be two military shore patrol boats escorting us up to the Black Sea; we return directly to the Ciragan Palace. Now did you talk with your American friends?"

"Yes, Jamie called. He had spoken with two of his uncles. But they also could not suggest something other than the security precautions which you are already taking. Only a few more hours and everyone will go home, and the risk will go with them. I wish they would leave now."

"If things continue with no problems, I will come home later tonight, after the dinner cruise. I know that you have school tomorrow, so go to bed at your usual time. I will wake you up early and I will tell you how these scientific conferences work. Is that all right?"

"Like do I have a choice? I will see you in the morning. I love you."

Dad returned, "Everything will be fine. And I love you."

The conferees continued walking up hill until they came upon a very large covered shopping center. As before, the police and army had already cleared the entry areas and the interior, except for shopkeepers of the Covered Bazaar or Grand Bazar, several names are used. The Grand Bazaar began as a small shopping area during the Byzantine era but increased manyfold in physical size and number of shops, and, also became roof covered in 1461 by Mehmet the Conqueror as he re-made his newly conquered capital. Today it is the oldest covered marketplace in the world. It is one floor high, has four major entry-exit gates, thirty-two narrow streets each covered with ceramic tiles (no motor vehicles allowed); all walls and dome shaped ceilings are also covered with multi-colored ceramic tiles. The Bazaar covers more than two square miles, has 1,100 shops, and attracts nearly one million tourists/shoppers each year. The shops sell gold jewelries, gems, porcelain ware, clothing, leather products, silk products, carpets, bedding, spices, special foods, and tourist collectables.

As the groups of congress attendees transformed into tourists and entered the main gate on the upper southwest corner of the complex, the Nuruosmaniye Gate, again they were re-organized into small groups of twenty to thirty and matched up with a tour guide who spoke their language. Because the Bazaar was organized into twenty-eight Hans (shopping districts), and most of the narrow streets had numerous small hills and valleys with many curves, it was very easy to get lost. Everyone was given a street map and warned; "**stay with your guide**"!!!!

And indeed, this uppermost entry gate was the most spectacular of entries. As you entered you looked down Aynacilar Street in the Cebeci Han. This street was about a block long and had more than fifty gold only jewelry shops along both sides, vivid red and blue ceramic tiles on the walls and floors and in the dome shaped ceiling. Throughout the mall all shops had large entry doors or windows that glittered with displays of golden jewelry containing precious and semi-precious stones, cups, vases, dinnerware, statues, hanging medallions, military armor and weapons, and more. Each Han specialized in certain crafts – clothing, carpets, special foods, used ancient books and pictures, Ottoman furniture, and more. The tourists were not told that under the Bazar was some of the gold reserves of Turkey which were sold at the local gold exchange elsewhere in the mall. With the well experienced Turkish guides, the six hundred plus scientists and promoters had no problems in depleting their billfolds/ purses and filling their hotel suitcases with presents for the entire family.

After another hour of walking, even though there were pastry shops dispersed through the Bazaar, everyone was intent on buying presents and saving their stomach exercise for the evening dinner cruise. Each guide was assigned to one of the main four gates and was told to bring his group to that gate. At these gates the buses picked them up and took them down to the waterfront, again. Indeed, all of the tourist-conferees carried full shopping bags onto their bus. Now everyone was truly ready to sit, drink, eat, and be merry on a cruise ship headed toward the Black Sea and Russia.

The two dinner cruise ships, *Octopus Nest* and *Dolphin Reach*, were waiting for the group at the famous Galata Bridge where the Golden Horn and the Bosporus intersected. The wharf area near the ships contained several police and military units in pre-established guard positions. Already on each of the ships were police and military guards, the ship's crew, and the dinner preparation teams. Each ship was preparing to cruise for three hours and feed more than three hundred people. The meal would be 100% fish, and sea food, plus the routine Turkish vegetables and breads. Each ship had a large lower level enclosed room and a large upper level open room for eating, talking, and watching the stars.

The scientists and patrons selected which ever ship they wanted, climbed aboard, sat at one of the six-person tables, and ordered their drinks for the evening. The conference was a success. Now everyone could relax and enjoy the Bosporus smells, views, and scenes of many famous old houses and palaces.

Bulent Turan and Metin Gursoy sat together on the *Dolphin Reach* and talked about the past three days.

Bulent spoke, "This has been the most fascinating days of my life. Each of these scientists seem to want to change a small piece of the world. One of them called it a legacy. While the promoters seem to focus on making money."

"Yes," agreed Metin. "They both need each other. But to me, when they get married, they can never live in the same house, maybe adjacent houses."

"They certainly cannot sleep in the same bed!"

They both had a good laugh. "Turks always sleep in the same bed with their wife, unless they can convince their wife that they are a Sultan. But who can afford additional wives? Not me!"

And another round of laughter filled the air. They had better slow down on drinking their raki. Raki is liquor from distilled grapes with a touch of anise. It is closer to a cognac than whisky in alcohol content. So, it is necessary to drink it slowly and eat appetizers, especially breads and white cheese. They knew this, but tonight they were very happy and perhaps a little careless. It had been a unique one-time experience. And everything had gone like clockwork.

They continued to compare experiences for the hour while dinner was being prepared in the kitchens which were located in the stern of the ship. Tonight, a guest simply entered into a serving area between the kitchens and large salon and helped himself. It was a fish and seafood evening. All fish were grilled or fried over 3 ten feet long charcoal grills. You could choose between, hamsi (sardines), levrek (seabass), palamut (halibut), çupra (seabream), lagos (grouper), lüfer (blue fish), tekir (red mullet), and lipari (mackerel). There were small servings of kalamar (squid), ahtapot (octopus), and karides (shrimp). Additional foods were the routine vegetables, salads, breads; Turkish desserts and fruits; plus, coffees and teas. Everything was placed on two long serving tables with heat lamps so one could help himself and eat as much and as often as he wanted all evening. There was even a four-tier cake for each ship. It was dark chocolate with white frosting and ten candles on top; they would be lit later. The cake was on a small table in the center of the lower-enclosed salon. The writing in chocolate frosting read – TEN SUCCESSFUL YEARS!

The music was comfortable, in fact just right. Everyone was very relaxed and enjoying many new friends. Only one accident happened. Near the Black Sea the *Octopus Nest* and a super oil tanker came too close together such that the turbulence and large waves from the tanker caused the *Octopus Nest* to jump and dip for several minutes. Several serving dishes filled with food and some glassware turned over and fell to the floor. A couple of small tables, with plates of food on them, turned over. The table with the four-tier cake upset and the four layers went rolling in different directions along the floor. One lady fell and hurt

her left shoulder; but with several doctors available, they quickly found a shoulder brace for her, and tied up her shoulder. She was right handed so it did not slow down her eating or celebrating. And there was plenty of food for all.

As they entered the Black Sea the feature attraction of the evening in each ship was belly dancing. Each ship had a team of three dancers who performed a variety of individual dances and several group dances. Then men were chosen at random by the dancers and came up and were 'taught' how to belly dance. The last event of the Congress appeared to be the belly dancing contest while sailing back down the Bosporus into Istanbul. Both ships arrived at the wharf in front of the Çıragan Palace, conferees disembarked, and most very happily found their way to their beds by 1:00 AM. High technology research did have its fun times.

But the highest of technology cannot yet restore dead people to life.

A Declaration of War

Near sunrise on Thursday morning, Aykut woke up to the screams of his Mother. He jumped out of bed, ran into his parent's bedroom, and found her standing and looking at the other side of their king-sized bed. She was screaming and sobbing. Aykut went to his Father's side of the bed and pulled the covers down. What he saw could best be described as a fat cylinder shaped blob of pink jelly. He looked at his screaming Mother; he looked again at this thing in the bed. And then he suddenly realized that this thing was his Father. And he screamed, "No! No! No! Please Allah don't let it be!"

And Aykut and Mother both fell to the floor and into each other's arms. All they could do was vent their loss for a wonderful man and a beautiful father. But Aykut knew that this was punishment from the Korrectorizer.

After several minutes of sobbing, suddenly Aykut wondered where his little sister Gul was, only to remember that she had spent the night at their cousins' home. But then, where was Amber his 'big' brother during all this commotion? He ran into his bed room where Amber usually slept in his own bed near Aykut's bed. All was quiet. And then he sudden realized that there was a balloon shaped blob in Amber's bed. NOOO!!!! He was his best friend!!

Aykut quickly ran to his cell phone, called their doctor, the police, and then called the USA.

It was 7:45 AM in Istanbul and 12:45 AM in Boston. But Jamie answered on the first ring. He had not been able to sleep because his mind was still focused on the Istanbul Congress.

Aykut asked, "Is this Ey'tuka?'

And Jamie immediately recognized Mo'ata's voice and said, "No this is Jamie and I am still afraid for you. I knew that you would call so I was waiting. It happened, didn't it?"

There were several moments of silence. Finally, Aykut said, "Yes and they took my Father and Amber too."

And he broke down in sobs for several more moments. Jamie was silent as he shared the death of the third of their fathers. And it all began with his Father's death which was only three years ago. They did not realize that they had stepped into a tornado. How was this going to end?

Finally, with a wet face and tears still running down his eyes, Aykut tried to say something but could not get it out.

Tear eyed Jamie uttered, "I am very sorry. What can we do?"

After a couple more minutes, Aykut brought his emotions partially under control and responded, "Please tell your uncles. Ask Uncle Dagda and the SAATO to come and assist in the investigation. Find out how this was done. Find the nanotech system that did this. Find the people that did this. And kill those people who killed my Father."

Jamie replied, "I will do it. We must find these people. They may do it again."

There did not seem to be much more to say. So finally, Jamie said, "Call me anytime that you want to talk, day or night. Later when you are ready, we will call a computer conference and think up a new plan to help the world eliminate them."

And they both hung up. The Four Colored Musketeers would indeed make a major contribution toward this, regardless of the cost.

Word circulated through to Uncle Dagda, Uncle Jackson, and Uncle Jonathan. Uncle Jonathan telephoned the Turkish President, Mr. Mehdi

Etiler, and permission was granted for Mr. Dagda Murphy and SAATO to join Mr. Doğan Kavlakoglu, the same MIT investigator that Mr. Murphy had worked with during the Kadikoy family murders. Mr. Murphy was working in Berlin, Germany, so he and Mr. Femer hopped onto their private jet, flew east, and landed at the Atatürk International Airport shortly after lunch on Thursday.

As they de-planed Mr. Kavlakoglu met them and spoke first, "Welcome to Turkey. Again, the circumstances are not pleasant. Let us go to the cars and we can talk on the way."

Mr. Murphy responded, "I am sorry about the situation. But thank you for allowing us to look over your shoulder during your investigation of these macabre deaths. If we can help in any way, you have only to ask."

Mr. Kavlakoglu looked Mr. Murphy directly in the eyes. "I must bring you up to date. During the past three hours, more morbid deaths have been found at the Kempinski Hotel. They were all attendees and participants at the World Entrepreneurs Congress which took place at the Ciragan Palace during the past three days. It ended last night. The number that I received just before you landed was 157 deaths and the counting was continuing. The news media is slowly discovering this massacre, and we are trying to control it. Apparently, the red phone lines, between our President and the Presidents of several countries, are getting hot. Most of the dead are foreigners."

Mr. Murphy looked at Mr. Femer: both acknowledged what they had suspected. It happened – probably the Korrectorizer!

So, the three bullet proof limousines carrying Mr. Murphy, Mr. Kavlakoglu, and their associates speeded toward the Kempinski Hotel. On route Mr. Kavlakoglu explained what he currently understood about the situation:

"This morning at the Kempinski Hotel, around 7:00 o'clock, wake up calls went out to several of the participants of the World Entrepreneurs Congress, which ended with a dinner cruise on the Bosporus late last evening. The Congress was considered to be very successful. Most of the room calls went unanswered. So, after more than a dozen or so went unanswered, the management sent security personnel to those rooms. Knocking on the doors brought no response. The Hotel's Director gave permission to the security personnel to use their pass cards and enter each room. They did. And in every room, they found the same situation. Lying in the bed, supposedly face up, was a weird looking bag of fluid. After pulling the covers completely off of the bed, a long oblong shaped pink blob, which apparently was at one time a person, was found. Obviously, the live guest of that room was not found. This bag of fluid had a very bad smell, so both doctors and city police were immediately called to come and help determine what it was."

"By then it was past 9:00 AM, many of the Congress attendees had not come down for breakfast, so more attendee-guest's rooms were checked; more of the same was found. As I said, the last call that I received just before your plane landed was at least 157 macabre deaths. Each had attended the Congress and gone on the dinner cruise last night. We have locked down the entire area of the Kempinski Hotel – Ciragan Palace, and the two cruise ships, the *Dolphin Reach* and *Octopus Nest*. We are currently talking with all service personnel who were working at the Hotel or Palace during the past three days, and all personnel involved with the ships and the dinner last night. We are going directly to the Hotel now. I will call for an immediate update from all three investigation teams currently in action."

Mr. Murphy asked, "Do you have any ideas how or why such a monstrous massacre would happen?"

"Ideas yes, but no solid evidence."

'I assume that this conference was treated similar to all of your major conferences with level ten security, police and army units, bullet proof buses, pre-cleared streets and touring areas, food tasters, and the other things that you are so competent at doing to protect super VIPs?"

"Absolutely,' answered Mr. Kavlakoglu. "For three days there was no hint of any problems. Officially the Congress adjourned yesterday afternoon. In the early evening most participants toured Hagia Sophia, Blue Mosque, and the Covered Bazaar. They were on the streets in the Old Walled City for several hours, no problems. And dinner last night was on two chartered dining ships named the *Octopus Nest* and *Dolphin Reach*. The ships simply went up the Bosporus, entered the Black Sea, and then returned to the pier in front of the Ciragan Palace. Both ships followed the same schedule, served the same foods which were grilled and fried fish and seafood, and routine vegetables, breads, desserts, coffee and tea. Last Monday evening they had a big Ottoman royal styled dinner in the

Dolmabahce Palace. Tuesday evening, they ate standard Turkish foods at the Topkapi Palace. But last night the ships were chartered from a famous company, the Blue Voyage Tours. The tour company was responsible for last night's dinner."

"If it is possible, may we also see these ships and talk with representatives of the charter company? And we would be pleased to test any of the foods or drinks that you consider to be suspicious of carrying a poison; you are calling these murders from a poison, I assume?"

"Yes, that is the best word to use. People understand that word. Mention of a nanotechnical molecular system could possibly create some panic. Fortunately, the news media is not my responsibility. I thank Allah."

Mr. Murphy followed, "Are the senior employees of the Blue Voyage Tours company under 'police control'?"

"Yes. Also, the senior employees of the three food catering companies are also under 'police control'."

And the two gentlemen smiled at each other. They were still on the same wave length again.

The cars arrived at the Kempinski Hotel near 2:30 PM. The group, with Mr. Kavlakoglu leading the way, started making the rounds by talking with on-site investigators and employees of the hotel. Later in the day they would talk with remaining 'living' Conferees, who had talked with their country's consulates, and obtained legal assistance and permission from their governments to answer questions. All interviews would be recorded in the presence of an international lawyer chosen by the consulate, and then they would be allowed to return home.

The rest of the afternoon was spent on the two ships, talking with the onsite investigators and interviewing all personnel who worked on the ships Wednesday night. Near midnight Mr. Murphy and his team were housed at a nearby hotel, and went directly to bed, terribly exhausted. Members of the Turkish investigation teams went home for the night.

At 9:30 the next morning Mr. Kavlakoglu, Mr. Murphy, and key members of their teams went to the offices of the Blue Voyage Tours. They spent most of the day talking with the police investigators, and interviewing

senior and even junior personnel, and carefully grilled the managers of the kitchens on each ship. In the afternoon they visited each of the three kitchens where all of the food was prepared that went to the two ships for the Wednesday night dinner voyage.

Arrangements were made to take samples of all foods and drinks for testing for poisons in the Turkish State Food Analytical Laboratories. And from certain foods that were considered extra suspicious, samples were sent to Dr. William Stronger at MIT in Boston. Dr. Stronger would search for any type of nanoproduct.

During the many interviews and analysis of the sequence of events, certain loopholes appeared, so certain team members returned to the Hotel, Palace, ships, and even re-checked certain shops in the Covered Bazaar. Again, everyone worked well into the evening and then dropped into their bed sometime after midnight.

At 9:00 AM on Saturday the six investigative teams composed of more than five hundred Istanbul and national police/investigators, army investigators, and the private teams of Mr. Kavlakoglu and Mr. Murphy, met in the conference room in the Istanbul Governer's House; Mr. Kavlakoglu began.

"Thank all of you for your intensive and long hours in this, the most difficult and morbid crime ever seen in Istanbul. During the past two days we have interviewed more than one thousand people, and we have a lot of information and data. Let us see if we can put this together and come up with some useful answers as to how, where, and when, possibly even why? Let us begin with Inspector Kazanci. Your team was responsible for checking out the Kempinski Hotel, Cıragan Palace, the surrounding environs, and interviewing all of the personnel."

Inspector Kazanci reported, "On the night of Wednesday, October 29, 2032, there were 713 guests staying at the Kempinski Hotel. 686 of them were registered with the World Entrepreneur Congress which took place on October 27, 28, and 29, 2032 in the next door Ciragan Palace. Most of the attendees of the Congress stayed at the Kempinski Hotel from October 26 through October 29. No tourists were even allowed into the Hotel during those days and nights, but there were several businessmen, both Turks and foreign, who we have interviewed. We do not consider them to be involved in the macabre massacre. There were also several wives of Conferees."

"Of the 686 participants staying at the Hotel on Wednesday night, October 29, 2032, 669 were foreigners from 32 different countries. And yes, we now have copies of passports and recorded interviews of each foreigner in attendance on the last day and night of the Congress. Many of them have already left for their homes."

"Thursday morning, October 30, 2032, we found 324 bloated bodies, in 307 rooms in the Kempinski Hotel. 319 of the bodies were thought to be foreigners; 5 were thought to be Turks. In an attempt to help develop some insight into the murders we counted the deaths per country. There was no pattern; most attendees were from the USA, Europe, Japan, and China; and most deaths were proportionally the same. In our opinion, there was no ethnic targeting involved."

Inspector Kazanci continued. "Each body was in the same exact state. They each looked like a plastic sack of pink morbid soup, gave off a horrible smell, and shaped like a sausage with red and brown blobs floating and moving inside. Each had two eye-like buttons floating in a head like area near the pillow end of the bed. Some of the sausage sacks had hair on that end. Miniature fingers could be observed on two arm-like projections, and miniature toes could also be seen on lower leg-like extensions. There was no major bleeding. However, one such 'body' was accidentally punctured by a hotel employee. That 'body' looked like a deflated balloon swimming in a pool of pink fluid; that smell was really terrible and overwhelming. It was a terrible macabre setting. We had to close off that entire floor."

"Forgive my description. I have several pictures which my associates are now handing out to you. As you can see, one cannot tell one body from another. At this point we can only assume that the body on the bed in a certain room belongs to the person who registered for that room and whose passport we are still retaining. No faces could be determined. No fingerprints could be taken. We did manage to obtain some skin samples and we are waiting for the DNA analysis to try to confirm which body belongs to which passport. We have no reason to suspect any switching of people and rooms. But we are not closing out such possibilities. It is my understanding that the bodies will only be released after some mechanism of identification has been worked out to the satisfaction of Turkish and international authorities. Is this correct?"

'That is my understanding also," replied Mr. Kavlakoglu. Mr. Murphy asked, "Could you perform optic retina scans." "No, we tried, but failed."

"Do you know how they died?" asked Mr. Murphy.

Mr. Kavlakoglu answered, "Most of the foreigners would not or could not sign for permission for autopsies. So those bodies will probably be released tomorrow. The 63 bodies which we were given permission to autopsy will require another day due to other bureaucratic and logistical problems. Probably the death certificates will read 'death due to an unidentifiable bone poison'. However, one pathologist has already informed me that there are no bones. They had dissolved or been digested by something. No bones, no body shape, no head. What a terrible way to die."

'Similar to ruptured kidneys, liver, stomach, intestine, spleen, colon, or digested lungs,' Mr. Murphy thought to himself. 'And now dissolved or digested bones. It is not possible to become more morbid or macabre.'

But he would be wrong.

"Any other information that you want to present now?" asked Mr. Kavlakoglu.

"We are working on a couple of other leads, but the data is not yet ready. Maybe after we hear the other information these leads will somehow fit into the emerging picture," responded Inspector Kazanci.

"Very good," said Mr. Kavlakoglu. "Inspector Keskinoglu, your team interviewed the foreigners. Did you learn anything useful from the interviews with the 'living' foreigners?"

Inspector Keskinoglu answered, "Of the 669 foreign participants, 319 foreigners were found dead, so 350 foreigners lived. We interviewed 347 living foreign attendees. The three Chinese participants were not allowed to talk with us, and they went directly back to China. However, we did make copies of their passports and escorted them directly onto their airplane. We had excellent cooperation from the other foreigners, even some suggestions as to why this happened."

"When comparing statements from the foreigners, there was little to help us understand what happened. Each of them did believe that the World Entrepreneurs were being targeted by someone. None believed this was an accident. They were very pleased with the meeting. All talked about how the entire meeting had gone so smoothly. And then suddenly they wake up to catch a plane to return home only to learn that half of their colleagues were murdered in such a macabre fashion."

"Of course, rumors had begun about the types of deaths. They were now becoming afraid about holding the Eleventh World Entrepreneurs Congress in Hong Kong next year. And many speculated that the killing agent was an unknown high-tech weapon system, possibly of nanotech origin."

"One interesting piece of data came out of the interviews with the foreigners. We made a list of which ship these foreigners were on Wednesday evening for the dinner cruise. Of the 347 'living' conferees, 342 were on *Octopus Nest*. If the groups were divided up reasonably equally, half on each ship, then most of the 324 participants who were killed must have been on the *Dolphin Reach*. So, we have sort of dabbed the *Octopus Nest* the 'living' ship and the *Dolphin Reach* the 'death' ship."

Mr. Murphy asked, "I assume you recorded what they ate, drank, who they partied with, how they partied, when they went to bed after docking and on and on. Were there any differences between the various conferees on the 'living' ship?"

"Very little, only minor differences," responded Inspector Keskinoglu. "Of course, what we need is to talk to the conferees on the other ship to determine what they ate, drank, and so on. But obviously we cannot do this."

Mr. Kavlakoglu added, "Are you saying that the deaths are related to something that was on the *Dolphin Reach,* the 'death' ship. How do you propose finding that cause?"

"We did identify two American conferees who were on the *Dolphin Reach* and lived. Comparing the interviews with them, and the interviews with the living from the Octopus Nest, we found no differences in their enjoying most food, drinks, and having a good time. We simply found no apparent dinner consumption differences between the two survivors of the 'death' ship and the dinner consumptions of the passengers on the 'living' ship."

"When these two Americans found out that they were the only survivors on the *Dolphin Reach*, they agreed to stay a few more days just in case some questions occurred that only they could answer. They are staying at the Kempinski Hotel. I have their cell phone numbers."

After a few moments of quiet, Mr. Kavlakoglu asked Inspector Atalay if he was ready?

Inspector Atalay began his report: "My team carefully inspected both ships, froze a sample of all cold drinks including water, wines, beers, raki, and whiskeys; and every type of food that was served; this included fresh and cooked foods such as fish, sea food, each type of vegetable, salads, desserts, coffees, and teas. We froze samples of all food additives such as salt, pepper, spices, catsup, mustard, mayonnaise and such. And we also took samples of the cooking oil, butter, and margarines for analysis. Samples of every food and drink have been sent to be laboratory analyzed for toxins or poisons. We are waiting for the results."

"We inspected and took these drink and food samples from both ships. We interviewed every employee on both ships and found no suspicious events that could have contributed to this terrible mass killing. We ruled out the heating and ventilation systems because all of the attendees walked onto the ship and walked off of the ship three hours later. And my understanding is that each went to the Hotel and up to his bed normally. No noticeable drug effects were observed. Besides, no ship's employee even became sick after working on the ship for four to five hours."

"Does anyone have any questions? If not let us continue," commanded Mr. Kavlakoglu. "Inspector Devrim, please give us your report on the security personnel."

"We also inspected both ships, the Kempinski Hotel, and the Ciragan Palace searching for anything that might be suspicious in these multiple murders," began Inspector Devrim. "We basically found nothing. We interviewed 53 security personnel in both the Hotel and Palace who were in senior positions of responsibility during the entire time of the World Entrepreneurs Congress. And we interviewed 31 civilian police and 24 military security personnel. They reported to us that they observed nothing unusual or suspicious on the days or nights of October 26, 27, 28, and 29."

After a few moments of pause, Mr. Kavlakoglu spoke up, "Inspector Cichek, what did your team learn from interviewing the Blue Voyage Tours personnel?"

Inspector Cichek said, "We talked with CEO, President, Senior Manager, and three junior level management people. The Senior Manager, Ms. Ayshe Yaprak was responsible for the entire Bosporus dinner tour.

She has held this position with the Blue Voyage Tours for the past 23 years, very experienced. They arranged for all of the food and drinks, and gave to us the names of the three food catering affiliates, Turkish Special Delights, Natural and Clean Foods of Turkey, and the Bosporus Meals, Incorporated. We went to each of these food caterers."

"As you know food catering is very common in Turkey. These people are generally extremely reliable. We interviewed the management and several employees at each place, inspected the kitchens, and found nothing unusual or suspicious. And we had the same result from talking with the management personnel of the Blue Voyage Tours. All these establishments have been providing services for many years. They are well known and reliable. I looked at the schedule books of the Blue Voyage Tours; they have provided the Bosporus dinner cruise for more than 11 five-star hotels in the past year alone. In conclusion, it is difficult to understand how these companies could have allowed any poison food or drink to be served."

Mr. Kavlakoglu returned, "I appreciate the positive reputation of these Turkish companies; but somehow, and it is probable, that something got into the food that killed 324 people! If these reputable companies prepared everything that went into the mouths of those 324 people, it must have occurred through the efforts of at least one of the kitchen personnel who prepared the food, or drinks. Don't forget, not one single member of the kitchen staff, in the company's kitchens or the ship's kitchens even got sick. Why?"

"What I am saying is that this macabre massacre is our fault, we Turks. We invited these people here. And we killed them. We cannot bring them back to life, but the bare minimum that we can do is to find their killers. Now, Mr. Inspector Cemal Cichek, take your team and go back to those reputable companies, interview every employee who prepared any food or drink that was placed on the dinner cruise ships for last Wednesday night. I want a recorded and signed interview statement of everyone working in the kitchens, even if they only filled the salt shakers. If you need 100 more investigators for you team, you now have them. And build the fear of Allah into these people. I want some positive results."

"Yes Sir!" came swiftly from the mouth of Inspector Cichek. Mr. Murphy spoke up. "May I ask something?"

"Of course," responded Mr. Kavlakoglu.

"When something is not there," he began, "and you think it should be there, then you may need to look for the thing which prevented that something from being there. By finding the preventive thing, you may find the original something."

"For example: Let us look at the statements concerning food consumption of those two Americans who survived on the 'death' ship, *Dolphin Reach*, and compare this with statements concerning the food consumption several of the people on the 'living' ship, *Octopus Nest*. Let us look for what is not on the list of all of the 'living' conferees. If there is a common thing, a food, not present, it may show us where something, a poison, may be present. Try it."

Mr. Kavlakoglu looked at Mr. Keskinoglu whose team interviewed the conferees. Mr. Keskinoglu quickly pulled up those files on his lap top. After ten minutes of comparing food consumption statements, they identified three foods which were not on any of the lists: shrimp, ketchup, and the chocolate cake with white frosting.

"Looking at the three foods, Mr. Murphy said, "I suggest you target these three foods, find out which caterer and which individual or individuals prepared those foods, and nail him to the wall."

"Mr. Cichek, did you hear that request? Then go and do it, now!" shouted Mr. Kavlakoglu.

Mr. Cichek and his team members got up, and immediately left to go to those caterer's kitchens, and do it.

Mr. Murphy spoke up again. "I have one more request. Can you please call the two American 'survivors' of the 'death' ship and confirm that indeed they did not eat the shrimp, use the ketchup, or eat the chocolate cake with white frosting, and why?"

Without waiting to be asked, Inspector Keskinoglu stood up, walked to a corner of the room, opened his cell phone and dialed. Five minutes later he sat back down with a smile on his face, and said, "One of the Americans did use the ketchup, so that food is OK. Neither ate the shrimp nor the cake. So those two foods are still suspect."

Inspector Devrim commented, "I may have some information that will help concerning the chocolate cake. While interviewing the security personnel who were on the *Octopus Nest*, the 'live' boat, they did mention an almost boating accident. Apparently, the *Octopus Nest* and a super oil tanker came too close together, large waves were generated, and several tables and dishes of food upset onto the tables and the floor. The cake was sitting on a small table in the center of the salon. It upset and the cake rolled on the floor, so it was discarded. No samples of this cake were available for us to analyze. What I am trying to say, it is possible that the chocolate cake with white frosting that was on the *Octopus Nest* was not eaten."

Mr. Kavlakoglu followed up, "So if both cakes on both ships had poison in them, and the cake was not eaten on the 'live' ship, but eaten on the 'death' ship, indeed it is possible that the cake is a major suspect."

Mr. Murphy asked, "Is it possible to check with the *Dolphin Reach* ship's captain to confirm the almost accident, and with the Food Director on board the *Dolphin Reach* to confirm that the cake was not eaten after this almost-accident but was thrown away. If this is all true, we need to obtain a piece of the cakes from both ships to test for poisons."

"Inspector Devrim, check with both ship's Captains. Inspector Atalay, find out if we have frozen samples of both cakes from both ships; make certain that they are tested for toxins or poisons. Inspector Balci, call Inspector Cichek, who is currently on his way to the caterer's kitchens, and update him on our new information and thoughts. Have him check even the ingredients used to make those cakes and the frostings. As soon as he has any information, tell him to report to us immediately. And we will meet again here in this room three hours from now, this evening at 7:30. I want everyone ready to re-review all of our findings tonight before we go home to bed. So, get ready. I want those killers."

Are echoes of the recent past reverberating in the Istanbul air?

"You can inform your colleagues to watch for a massive strike on high technology in a repeat location but water born. It will be an early Christmas present for our common enemy at a location where they do not even celebrate Christmas."

28

Counter Attack

IT REQUIRED SEVERAL DAYS BEFORE Aykut's Mother could completely remember and explain what happened on Wednesday evening, November 29, 2032. Mr. Turan had left the ship and his chauffeur brought him home around 10:45 PM. This was confirmed by the chauffeur. Mr. Turan had brought with him three pieces of chocolate cake with white frosting from the *Dolphin Reach*. He told his wife that they could all have a chocolate breakfast in the morning, he had already eaten his share. While the couple was getting ready for bed and having this conversation, Amber, reached onto the table, and in haste devoured two pieces of the cake. This was very unusual because Amber was a well-trained dog and never ever touched people food. So, he got a scolding was sent to bed, put the last piece of cake in the refrigerator and then they went to bed. The rest is already known.

[What was not known at that time was that all the uneaten cake from both ships was discarded into the Bosporus, somewhere near the end of the evening, by two of the kitchen workers. So, the one remaining piece of cake in the Turan's refrigerator was the source that was later used by Dr. Stronger to identify the presence of a Nano-killer in the white frosting on the chocolate cake. After three years of searching, the smoking gun came from Aykut's refrigerator.]

Several weeks after the macabre massacre in Istanbul Jamie initiated a computer conference of the Four Colored Musketeers.

He began, "Ey'tuka is present. Who else is present?"

In response he heard: Tsu'teye is present. Na'via is present. Mo'ata is present. Ey'tuka continued, "I am sorry from the bottom of my heart to Na'via and Mo'ata. I lost my Father and two of my best friends during the past three years. I still see them, hear them, talk to them, and cry for them. I don't think a boy ever totally recovers from losing good friends, or a father."

"I am very sorry also," said Tsu'teye. "Since my Father is one of those developing new high technology systems, I am afraid for him every day. If these people continue, I am certain he will be somewhere on the death list."

"Thank you," Mo'ata replied, "Only if one experiences the sudden loss of loved ones can one begin to understand the feeling of being half dead, and sometimes wishing one was totally dead."

Na'via added, "I want to thank you also for your cards and calls. It helps a lot to have reliable brothers like you guys. And it helps me because I have many older brothers and sisters who are teaching me to look forward. That is what you have to do Mo'ata – look forward."

"Na'via is right, Mo'ata," said Ey'tuka. "My big sisters and my three uncles have helped me a lot. And at least you have one big brother – Na'via is four months older than you."

And they all started laughing; that broke the tension, somewhat.

"So Na'via, my big brother, what are we going to do about these morbid killers?" asked Mo'ata.

Na'via responded," We should ask Ey'tuka that question. With his uncles he has a more complete picture than we do."

Ey'tuka said, "Yes, Uncle Dagda and I have talked several times. He has told me what this Presidential Commission is thinking. They believe that there is a group of international conservatives who want to stop change, especially changes resulting from high technology. Part of this involves simply trying to freeze the world as it is now because they like it, as is; and part of it is that they are afraid they may lose business and even see their industrial or commercial systems could become extinct in the near future. To accomplish slowing or stopping high technology they are purchasing different kinds of Nanotech weapons. So, there are certain nanotech companies that are selling their Nanotech weapons to anyone, and of course they lack the morals to follow up where and how they are used."

Tsu'Teye spoke, "This is the rationale they teach in socialist systems like in China. Capitalism will always fail. Why? Because. If you ever want to hang a capitalist, you can always find another capitalist to sell you a hanging rope. And just around the corner is another capitalist that will do the job for you, all for money of course."

And all four boys just groaned.

"I have an idea which I want to share with you guys," said Ey'tuka. "It is this – If low tech people can use high tech weapons or Nanotech systems against high tech people, then high tech people can us low tech weapons, written and spoken word, against low tech people. We have not had a world war for one hundred years. And the regional wars have always been less than ten years in duration. I don't know if the pen is mightier than the sword, but each decade the word controls more of the world than jet fighter airplanes."

"Today, because of verifiable peace and defense treaties, positive-positive foreign trade agreements, and international organizations which allow leaders of many countries to meet and try to solve their problems by talking; even many former enemies are talking with each other."

"In 1900 there were less than one hundred democracies in the world. In 2000 there were more than three hundred. Some of the new democracies were established because of guns, but most due to negotiations, words,"

"Why don't we start a campaign to inform the world about the possible dangers of Nanotech products. The Nanotech scientists will not appreciate it, but more than five hundred people have been brutally killed with Nanotech weapons obtained from some 'brother' Nanotech scientist. And many of those killed were Nanotech scientists or their brothers, high tech scientists. They should want strong controls put in place to prevent or control production of these killing machines."

Tsu'teye spoke up. "Ey'tuka is right. The Americans used atomic fusion technology to produce atom bombs and killed or mutilated several hundred thousand Japanese. But after that controls were put into place and today only a few countries have a deliverable atomic bomb. And atomic fusion technology is used by many countries as energy to produce electricity for cities, and for almost every large ship in most navies, such as frigates, destroyers, aircraft carriers, and submarines."

Mo'ata said, "I agree with Tsu'teye. If you want, maybe you could talk with your father about government controls and obtain his opinion. If he agrees maybe he will help us."

"But how do we do this?" asked Na'via.

"I have talked with my uncles about the how," responded Ey'tuka. "Because Uncle Jonathan and Uncle Jackson are in politics, officially they cannot help. But unofficially maybe Uncle Dagda might 'accidentally' leave copies of what the Commission has been doing and saying on my desk; he frequently uses my Father's desk, which is now my desk, when he stays with us. This weekend he has business in Boston so he will be with us for a couple of nights. I could use the information if I happen to see it on my desk. And I would only use the numbers and places, but no names or specific dates."

"I will write a paper, using this information, which I will give to my cousin Maria O'Hannessy who writes a column for the *New York Times*. Uncle Dagda has talked to her and explained the situation. She will rework my paper for her column and publish it in the Sunday editions of the *Times* in New York, Los Angeles, London, and Hong Kong."

"And Mo'ata, do you feel up to writing a personal experience about finding your father and dog, not only dead but in a very macabre state, and how you, your mother and little sister have tried to deal with it?"

Mo'ata thought for a few moments and finally responded, "Yes, if it will help catch those killers or their Nanotech weapon suppliers, I will do so."

"Excellent," Ey'tuka responded. "I have another good contact with the *Newsweek* magazine. But now, I have more information for you. Tomorrow the President's Commission will meet. They have evidence of a Nanotech system in the white frosting on the chocolate cake in the dinner that the participants ate on the ships on that terrible Wednesday night, last October 29. It was placed in two cakes on board two different ships. One of the ships had almost an accident by running into an oil tanker and in the process their cake was knocked onto the floor, so it was not eaten but thrown away. Everyone on this ship lived. The other ship sailed smoothly, the cake was eaten, and almost everyone died during the night - no cake, life; with cake, macabre death."

"And how did this Nanotech system get into the frosting? The chef that prepared the cakes and frosting was killed. He was found decapitated. One week prior his wife and two little girls disappeared. They were found dead and partially eaten by animals somewhere in the Syrian mountains."

"So, I guess in order to try to find the killers or the source of the Nano-tech- weapon, a Turkish commando team night-raided the Citadel of Masyaf and confiscated several vials of what was thought could be Nanotech weapons. Dr. Stronger at MIT has analyzed the contents of these vials. One vial contained a Nano-substance that matched the Nano-substance that was extracted from the white frosting of the chocolate cake."

"Now there is hard evidence to tie the Masyaf factory to the mass killings in Istanbul. This will be discussed by the Commission. They will then make recommendations to the American President."

Na'via asked, "We sent a sample of my father's blood to you for Dr. Stronger to analyze. Do you know what the results were?"

"Yes. There was a nanoproduct identified from your father's blood, but it did not match the one from the cake. If I understand correctly, a Nano-product prior to being placed in the body may be changed by the body such that when extracted from the body it may be different. I think that a body changes or metabolizes everything we put into it."

Na'via agreed. "My big brother and I discussed that. And I think you are right. We probably will not know if the two Nano-killers were the same or not. So, there may be at least two different Nano-killers. If so, does that mean there were two different production factories or two different sources for the one mass killing?"

And the Four Colored Musketeers continued talking for another hour and started making a list of low technology mechanisms that they could use to inform the public; it included on line systems such as twitter, face-book, various blogs, sail it, myspace, QWZ, spam mail. Mo'ata, in addition to writing a personal tragedy letter, will also develop a nanotech game with creatures depicting Nano- good-guys, Nano-bad-guys, Nano-politicians, Nano-good-drugs, Nano-bad-drugs, Nano-fast-drugs, Nano-delay-drugs.

On November 5, 2032, Presidential elections had been held throughout the United States. President Jonathan O'Reilly could not run for a third term, but he supported his party's candidate, Senator William Blackson, who won in a close race. Promises had been made to continue the programs began by President O'Reilly. On November 12, the last meeting of the Presidential Commission began at 9:00 AM in the second-floor conference room of the Department of Justice building on Mass Avenue in Washington, DC.

And it would be the last, because when a President leaves office his Commissions can be continued only if re-established by the new and incoming President. Attorney General and Chairman of the Commission, Jackson O'Reilly looked around the room and found every current appointee present. They knew this meeting was going to be an important one.

"Welcome," said Mr. Chairman. "I am certain that all of you have been reading about the recent morbid massacre in Istanbul. But what you do not yet know is that we have finally found a smoking gun. Mr. Murphy, would you please explain?"

Mr. Murphy began: "During the last week in October some of the world's best high technology scientists met with some of the world's promoters or supporters of the development of high technology. They met for three days at the Ciragan Palace on the Bosporus in Istanbul. The meeting went smoothly until the last night."

"On Wednesday, October 29, during an evening dinner cruise a nanotech 'killer' system was determined to be involved via one of the foods – a desert cake. One of the two cruise ships almost had a boating accident and their cake fell to the floor, was dirt contaminated, and apparently was discarded; all the conferees on this ship lived. The other ship had no travel troubles; most of the Conferees ate their clean cake and died during the night while asleep in their beds. The Nanotech system apparently dissolved or digested the chromosomal genes/DNA in body cells of those who ate the cake, but there was a five to six-hour delay in the action. Dr. Stronger, would you care to comment?"

"Yes," replied Dr. Stronger. "On October 31, we received eighty-four food samples taken from the two ships as Mr. Murphy just described. We analyzed them for any type of Nanotech product. We found one in the white frosting of the chocolate cake."

"On November 2, we received five vials apparently taken from a high-tech production facility in Syria. We analyzed the solutions in these vials using the same methodology as used for the Istanbul foods. We found in vial number three a Nano-tech product such as the one we found in the white frosting. My initial conclusion is that it is very probable that this Nanotech product caused the death of these 324 people and was produced or stored in the Syrian location."

"Allow me to give one last explanation of the mechanisms of these Nano- products. In the beginning, Dr. Jiang explained that the deaths in the chest and head area were due to an injection into the spinal cord which allowed Nano- carriers with iron atoms to reach certain areas of the brain. Using attached specific homing MoABs they short circuited specific areas and destroyed the regulatory controls of heart beat, breathing, vision, blood pressure, brain blood circulation, eye function, and so forth. Those were simple assassinations of individuals. I agree."

"Now they have advanced to a completely new Nano-system. They can attach models of the human stomach's own digestases, proteins which digest or melt what we eat, onto homing MoABs. Don't forget we do eat skeletal muscle (meat), heart, kidney, and liver; smooth muscle such as intestines; and fatty tissues such as brain. For such things as bone, dog and cat digestases could be used. So, in my opinion, they use our own digestive molecules as models to synthesize special digestases in a test tube, attach them to special homing MoABs, and now we have a new super Nano-killing system. They can: 1) inject this directly into the spinal cord or the veins of a person; 2) put it into the air such that it would be inhaled into the body; 3) or coat it with some synthetic material such that our stomach will not digest it when we eat or drink it, but it will be directly absorbed into the blood stream and go to its cell or tissue target. It is probably the latter design mechanism used in this orchestrated killing."

"The new super Nano-killing system would allow one to target any cell or tissue in the body via the air or mouth. And you could target large groups of people, even enemy armies. To prevent such an attack, one would have to either stop eating, drinking, or breathing. Very difficult!"

And there were no comments, only several moments of silence around the room.

"Thank you," replied Mr. Murphy. And he continued, "In addition, Dr. Stronger now has one Nanotech system used in these killings. So, he can begin to try to reproduce this set of molecules in an attempt to confirm his theories and more completely understand how they work. If he can do this, then I hope that we will be in a position to develop a defense against such systems. Am I correct, Dr. Stronger?"

"That is the direction we are going in my laboratory. But we will not be there tomorrow."

"Mr. O'Reilly spoke up, "We are prepared to wait no longer. We must act know because in two months we will have no authority to act. Plus, President O'Reilly was warned about the possibility of this attack, and failed to prevent it. So, he feels personally responsible for these many deaths. He has already started working with two of his long time close congressional friends, Mr. David Hempshire, House Majority Leader, and Mrs. Laura Greenstein, Chairman of the Senate Ways and Means Committee. They are preparing a bill to be presented to the Congress next week. The bill is entitled 'The War Against Macabre Deaths'. It is being designed to bring all people, laboratories, and factories in the Nano-sciences fields under a special set of government regulatory controls. Also, next week a worldwide media campaign will begin to make people aware of the extent of these macabre mass killings and the need for action."

"The President understands it is common for outgoing Presidents to just sit quietly and coast out the last couple of months in office. He plans to sprint during his last two months and I think he can convince enough members of Congress to join him. This is true especially with the 182 members who lost in the elections, will not return in January, and want to leave a more 'complete' legacy."

"The President feels that this slaughter of some of the world's best high technology minds was a declaration of war by certain conservative groups. He plans to initiate an immediate and harsh counterattack. So, he does not want from us 'should we go to war or not go to war', he has already decided to begin preparations for such a war now. He wants from us recommendations as to how and where we should strike, and when. This morning I want us to first discuss the situation, and then make a list of suggestions for countering and preventing these mass macabre killings around the world."

For the rest of the morning the President's Commission prepared a list of what they consider to be critical to trying to prevent and control the use of nanotechnology as weapons. Some of the ideas included:

- Set up a new Division of High Technology within the Department of Justice and the Department of Health and Human Services, and attach a Nanotechnology Control Committee within this new Division.
- Develop a worldwide data base of researchers and manufacturers of nanoproducts and the types of nanoproducts with which they are involved; recruit a committee of nanotech scientists and international lawyers to assist in these efforts.
- Perform unannounced in-house inspections of 'suspect' nanotech laboratories and factories.
- Monitor exports and imports of all nanoproducts similar to that of drugs, toxic, and radioactive chemicals.
- Develop a list of Nano-scientist suspects based upon their lifestyles, professional friends, or the type of nanoproducts that they are involved with researching or producing.
- Treat 'suspect' Nano-scientists similar as 'suspect' terrorists by monitoring their business and personal communications, monitoring business and personal finances, and regular unannounced inspections of the suspects' laboratories and factories.

The following Sunday in the *Times* Newspapers was found a column written by Maria O'Hennessy:

MACABRE DEATHS IN OUR OWN BEDS?

During the past five years more than five hundred people around the world died or were killed in a brutal macabre fashion, yet we were never completely informed by authorities. It is possible that they were killed by nanotechnology produced Nano-systems. As you know Nanotechnology is a very high technology science that puts atoms together to produce molecules such as Nano-drugs, Nano-machines, Nanocarriers, Nano-self-assembly factories, Nano-devices, Nano-electronic systems, Nano-physics systems, and on and on. Nanotechnology has moved mankind to another level of knowledge which should again raise our standard of living. With Nano-technology products we can now diagnose and cure diseases that were previously not curable. But as with all new super knowledge comes the possibility of misuse. That has also now happened.

During recent years someone has been using several types of Nano-systems to kill individual people in 2028, 2029, and 2030, families in 2032, and now large groups of people in 2033. Each person was killed while at home in his own bed, in a bed in a five-star hotel, or in a workplace. The types of death were heart stoppage, respiratory failure, rupture of carotid arteries in neck, brain failure, bleeding from optic nerve or eyes, bleeding from olfactory nerves or ears, intracranial bleeding in the brain, ruptured coronary arteries of heart, ruptured kidneys, ruptured liver, ruptured pyloric sphincter of the stomach, ruptured colon, ruptured spleen, dissolved lungs, bones, and total body cells. Morbid? Macabre?

These killings occurred in Mexico, Czech Republic, Brazil, Germany, Belgium, Sweden, USA, Libya, Spain, Turkey, South Africa, and the recent macabre massacre in Istanbul involved the deaths of citizens from 32 different countries. Men, women, and children have been killed. Many of the dead were experts involved in high technology fields. So, someone is using high technology systems to kill people who produce this technology. Ghastly? Disgustingly Repugnant? Morbid? Indeed Macabre!

What are the authorities doing to stop this? Ask your elected officials. Does your Congressman, Senator, Parliamentarian, or even local Governor or Mayor know about these killings? Why has it been kept a secret for so long?

Are we no longer safe in our own houses in our beds? Can we not sleep in a high security five-star hotel without fear of being murdered? Are our workplaces no longer safe? How can one protect himself or his family from such Nanotech weapons? Where are the controls to prevent the illicit manufacture and sale of these Nano-systems?

A few days after this article hit the newsstands people started asking these questions of their elected officials. A general foggy fear began to occur in many countries. And then the second article appeared in the *Newsweek* magazine by Anonymous:

SEE YOUR FAMILY MELTED – TRUE STORY

Two adult sisters were happily married, had prosperous working husbands, a comfortable life, and three little girls in elementary school. The two families lived in condos in the same building but on different floors, so the children played together continuously. On one recent Thursday morning, around 7:45 AM, one sister heard screams and crying coming from her sibling's apartment. She instructed her daughters to keep an eye on their little cousin who had spent the night at their home.

She used her spare keys to enter her sister's house. There was a terrible smell coming from the bedroom, so she went in that direction. She found her sister lying on the floor in the hallway. Her face was wet from crying and she had passed out. Mother went further and entered the master bedroom. The covers were pulled off of the bed and there on the sheets was a strange large tube-shaped pink jelly-like liquid thing that had stuff floating inside it and it was giving off that smell. She looked more closely and saw that the thing had a ball shaped structure near the headboard that had two button-like objects floating around. After a few moments she finally realized that that was her brother- in- law.

And then suddenly she heard the son sobbing over their large pet dog. She looked into the son's bedroom. Once again there was a small tube-shaped pink jelly-like liquid thing that had stuff floating inside lying on the dog's bed; and there was a small ball shaped thing near the head that had two-button like objects floating around.

By then the impatient little girls were knocking on the door to be let in. The Mother cracked the door open and the putrid smell shocked the little ones. Her explanation was that there was an accident and that she had to call the doctor immediately. This was serious and would they please go back home, prepare for school and leave at once after drinking a glass of milk? Even though the girls were not privy to the macabre sights, the smell was enough to deter them, and they immediately obeyed Mother's plea.

Both adult sisters and three little girls now have terrible memories that will never go away. One can only hope it doesn't affect the children's future capacity to adjust to change if or when they get married and have children. And how can their mother's older sister ever recover after losing her husband and their very special dog in one night? And the son lost his best friend in such a morbid way. – This is a true story. Anonymous

[And this nightmare would haunt Aykut for the rest of his life.]

Before Thanksgiving there was a new bill entitled 'The War Against Macabre Deaths' which was being talked about in both the United States of America House of Representatives and the Senate. It was being scheduled for a vote in both Houses immediately after the Thanksgiving weekend. If it passed money was already being identified to recruit several administrators and space was being set aside in both the Department of Justice and the Food and Drug Administration, located only a few blocks apart in DC. The counterattack on this nanotech war could begin before the O'Reilly administration left office. And if President William Blackson kept his word, these efforts would continue for at least four more years. Such is the way of democracy in the USA. The nanotech war would probably move forward at various paces in other democratic governments around the world.

On January 1, 2034, former President Jonathan O'Reilly received a bundle of twelve red roses and a Happy New Year card by special delivery. Who still remembered him enough to send to him flowers? He smiled as he opened the card and read:

IT HAS BEEN FUN – BUT NOW YOU ARE GONE.
WHO CAN I PLAY WITH?
THE KORRECTORIZER

29

Accelerated Battles?

ARLY IN FEBRUARY 2033, THE new President kept his promise and continued the new war against mass killing by high technology or nanotechnology systems. The new Division of High Technology was in full motion. Within this Division there was a new standing Committee of Nanotechnology Control which was responsible for establishing inquiry teams that would include nanotechnology scientists, selected high tech scientists, university science and Food and Drug administrators, and lawyers from the Department of Justice. Initially, they would focus on the 'suspected seven' and begin detailed inquiries into these scientists.

There was enough evidence on Mr. Boris Kukrynisky in Moscow, Russia, Dr. Frans Heinz in Munich, Germany, Dr. Mario in Buenos Aires, Argentina, Dr. James Walters in Ottawa, Canada, Dr. Chi Jiang in Los Angeles, USA, Dr. Jun Jiang in Berlin, Germany, and Dr. Cho Jiang in Nanjing, China, to initiate site visits for each. But the major problem was that most of these men were citizens of and living in a country other than the United States. Permission was given only from Canada and Germany to interview their people, Dr. Walters, Dr. Heinz, and Dr. Jun Jiang. And of course, Dr. Chi Jiang was an American citizen living in Los Angeles.

This Committee of Nanotechnology Control's first inquiry team was composed of five members who were to go to Ottawa, talk with Dr. Walters and some of his key people, look at his laboratories, and check his recent international travel and bank accounts. The team included one nanotechnology scientist, one high technology scientist in electronics, one FDA administrator, one DOJ administrator specialist in banking, and one lawyer specialist in international drug exchange.

The leader of the inquiry team was Dr. Maxine Javer, Professor of Nanotechnology at the University of Seattle, Seattle Washington. The team met privately in a small conference room at the University of Ottawa with Dr. Walters. Dr. Javer introduced each member of the team and explained, "Thank you for your time Dr. Walters. We are here under the authority of the USA Division of Nanotechnology Control and permission from the Canadian Food and Drug Regulation Agency. This is not an official investigation; nothing is being recorded; this is an official inquiry. You will be notified of the results of our inquiry in two-months."

"I am certain that you are aware of the recent series of single and mass murders occurring around the world in which nanotechnology is being held responsible. The USA has established a new executive Division to control production, international movement, and use of potential nanotech-weapons. We have read your very impressive curriculum vitae and congratulate you for your establishing this Canadian Center for Nanotechnology. In the fifteen years of its existence it already has reached the status of one of the best nanotechnology research institutes in the world. Today our inquiry will focus on your own personal research, the three private nanotech companies that are performing research by your previous and current post docs and students, and about your association with the Norte del Valle Cartel and one Wilbur Sanchez. Do you understand?"

Dr. Walters very nervously replied, "Yes. Do I need my lawyer?"

"That is up to you. As I said this is an official inquiry. It is not an official investigation. From today's inquiry we are requested to recommend an official investigation if we think a closer examination of your work is necessary."

Dr. Javer continued, "Now then, could you give us a brief description of your recent, say ten years, the current nanotechnology research, and where it is being carried out?"

"All right," responded Dr. Walters. "My research involves nanocarriers which transfer various types of metals into body cells using MoABs homers. The metals we are studying include iron, cobalt, nickel, copper, and zinc.

These five atoms are similar in atomic weights so they fit the nanotech molecules that we are working with, and they each affect biological cells in different ways. I have three students and one post doc studying this system here in my labs in the university center, and I have eight people working on metal nanocarriers in three private laboratories in the Ottawa area. I will give to you their names and the addresses if you want. You can go to these labs and talk with the researchers. We have nothing to hide."

"Maybe later; we understand that you have another laboratory in Bogota, Colombia. Can you please explain that connection?"

"Dr. Jose Sanchez was a student of mine for almost ten years. He received his MS, PhD, and worked with us as a post doc for two more years. Four years ago, he returned to Colombia and has set up the first nanotechnology laboratories for that country. He was an excellent student and is now my friend and I occasionally send to him research supplies that he cannot buy in Colombia. You can imagine what difficulties such a young man must have trying to perform high technology in a country where democracy is only occasionally used as a form of government."

"And yes, his father is Wilbur Sanchez who is involved with a Colombian drug cartel. I do not know if or how his father helps Dr. Sanchez in his laboratories, I do not ask. It is none of my business. In fact, I really do not want to know."

"Does Dr. Sanchez occasionally come and visit you here in Ottawa?

"Yes, he has returned to work here for a few days at a time, perhaps three or four times during the past couple of years. He simply does not have certain types of laboratory equipment for certain types of experiments. So, he comes here, performs the experiments, and then takes the new molecular constructs back with him. This is not a problem."

"Do you know what he does with or how he uses these new constructs?"

"If you are asking me, does he make nanotech-weapons, my answer is no. But I have never been to Bogota, or to his laboratories, nor have I tried to find out what he does with his final nanotechnological systems. Again, I consider that none of my business."

Dr. Javer asked, "What if he is making Nano-death weapons and is using your instruments and laboratory supplies to do so?"

Dr. Walters responded "As I said I think not, but I have never asked him such a question, because I do not believe he would do such a thing, even under pressure from his father."

"Besides, are American gun manufacturers liable for the more than two million men, women, and children killed with American guns during the past century and all over the world? Has gun technology moved from sling shots to guided missiles, from kill distances of a few feet to many miles, from killing one person to killing thousands with one shot? Is the American National Rifle Association just a fancy boy's club that only finances pro-gun politicians? Name one American gun manufacturer that has gone to court on murder charges. **I could go on and on!"**

Everything was very quiet for a couple of minutes. Then, finally, Dr. Javer, avoided the questions and asked, "Does any member of the inquiry team want to ask any questions?"

The DOJ banking specialist spoke, "Do you receive any money from Colombia for your consultation support of the Bogota laboratories?"

"No, I do not receive money from Colombia for consultation support," Dr. Walters answered.

"Then will you give your permission to allow us to examine your bank accounts over the past five years? How many Canadian, American, and offshore accounts do you have?"

"No. That is going too far. If you want to enter my booking systems, I will have to ask for my lawyer. Like most 'older' professors who have a university salary and private companies, my annual reports to the IRS should be enough for you to learn where my income originates. If you want more you will have go through my accountant and lawyer."

The inquiry of Professor and Director Dr. James Walters continued for the rest of the morning. The team next visited his three small company labs and talked with the researchers. Later in the day the inquiry team thanked him, and returned to their homes. Each took one week to perform additional research on Dr. Walters, trying to answer questions that he would not answer. Then they each wrote up their report and sent it to the team leader Dr. Javer. She wrote a final report, included the reports from each committee member, and made a general recommendation to the Nanotechnology Investigative Committee concerning Dr. Walters and his nanotechnology research.

[[The subsequent post inquiry research by inquiry team members revealed several suspicious areas that needed further investigation. The Bank of Colombia had a branch office in New York City. The university tuition and fees of all three of Dr. Walter's children were being paid out of three different accounts from this bank. Dr. Walters claimed all three children as dependents on his IRS filings but did not take education expenses for them. Mr. Wilbur Sanchez had visited Toronto three times in 2030, twice in 2031, and one time in 2032. Dr. Sanchez had entered and left the USA nine times in the past two years. Dr. Walters's private laboratories sent fifteen packages of 'laboratory supplies' to a postal address in Bogota during the past two years. Dr. Walters had visited Colombia once in 2030 and once in 2032. One offshore bank account in Dr. Walter's older son's name was found in Jamaica.]]

During the middle of February, 2033, the Division of High Technology's Committee of Nanotechnology Control organized its second inquiry team which went to Munich to talk with Dr. Frans Heinz, two Germans would be included on the team. The team was composed of two Nanotechnology scientists, one high technology scientist, one electronic engineer, one chemical engineer, one HHS official, one international banking specialist, two lawyers specializing in international corporate law and European Union corporate law. The leader of the inquiry team was Dr. Joseph Barkley, high technology scientist and Professor of Molecular and Biochemical Sciences at the University of Chicago.

The inquiry team met with Dr. Frans Heinz, and the CEO, CFO and several key administrative officials of the company Nano-Solar, LTD in the conference room of the company. Dr. Heinz is a Professor of the University of Munich, was Vice President for ten years and has been President for the past seven years of this multi-billion-dollar company. Before he joined them as President, Nano- Solar LTD focused on solar or heat energy activation of high tech and Nanotech-systems for use in transportation such as airplanes, trucks, cars, and ships. In recent years they added a large and rapidly expanding division to heat energy activation with Nanotech systems for digestion of biological materials to release molecular oxygen.

As the meeting began, Dr. Barkley introduced his inquiry team, Dr. Heinz introduced his High Tech and Nano-solar team; each team aligned along opposing sides of a twelve feet long conference table. Dr. Barkley was at one end, Dr. Heinz at the other. Dr Barkley first explained that their legal authority lay with the USA Division of Nanotechnology Control, Food and Drug Administration and the Department of Justice, and the German Ministry of Justice and Ministry of Commerce. This meeting was not an official investigation, but was only an official inquiry, no tape recorders. Within two months the inquiry team would send a report to him and to each German official government agency or department as required. Everyone would receive a letter telling them the results of the inquiry.

Dr. Barkley spoke, "Dr. Heinz, I know that you joined Nano-Solar LTD several years ago. Since then you have initiated some new research that seems to be really taking off. The Nano-solar stocks have increased 58% in the past two years alone. And your profit margin has almost doubled in the past five years. Can you give us an idea how you accomplished this?"

"It is very simple. It is all related to a new series of products that we have developed and are now starting to mass produce. Let me start at the beginning. Several years ago, one of my very bright graduate students discovered that if you placed the tail of a firefly on a leaf, the leaf degraded/digested fifty times faster than if the leaf degraded on its own. The light fluorescence comes from the light organ of the firefly and occurs by a simple protein enzyme, called luciferase. The protein luciferin is activated by luciferase and produces light and molecular oxygen. So, we now can manufacture Nano-systems that can produce oxygen to make environmentalists happy, or we can produce light/energy to make the organic products people happy. Several commercial systems now use it to enhance their manufacturing."

Dr. Barkley said, "I'm sorry, I can understand the environmentalists being happy with more oxygen being produced, but what is the connection to the organic people?"

"That is because this is the true secret at the bottom of the pot," replied Dr. Heinz. "And I have not told you that yet. Let me just say that the two luciferin/luciferase molecules can be linked to a wide variety of molecules to provide energy or light to stimulate these molecules. For example, linked to the proteins tropin or tropinomysin they can kill certain types of fungus, therefore are natural not synthetic pesticides."

"Linked to the protein starchase, they can digest plant starch to glucose to increase alcohol production seventy five percent faster. And linked to any of the stomach's digestases for digesting selected proteins or DNA, they can increase protein digestion or DNA digestion two hundred times faster. This increases the production of protein building block components, the twenty-four amino acids, which are used in vitamins and certain nutritional supplemented products."

And the two Nanotechnology scientists suddenly looked each other in the eye. The last two macabre mass murders could have been caused by something similar to the last described type of nanoproduct.

One of the nanotechnology scientists spoke up, "Can you link this 3-4 molecule complex to a MoAB to give it a homing capacity?"

"Of course," Dr. Heinz replied. "We do not do this. But we do manufacture these Nanotech systems in quantity, picogram quantity not just nanogram quantity. So, they can be attached or linked to any homing MoAB. There are two or maybe three companies that buy the Nanotech product from us and then add their own 'homers'.

The nanotechnology scientist followed up, "Can you design a nanoproduct that will digest bones?"

"Yes, we can. We just have to use some of the stomach protein digestive enzymes from dog or cat's stomachs, not human stomachs. Humans do not digest bones, dogs and cats do."

Again, the two Nanotechnology scientists exchanged glances.

"All right," said Dr. Barkley. "Does anyone want to tell us about sales, exports within the European Union or abroad, subcontractors, collaborators, steady customers, banks and other financial areas?"

The CEO responded, "We have two subcontractors, one in Nanking, China and one in Paris, France. We....

The CFO responded. "We use seven banks in Europe, four in Germany, two in Switzerland, and one in London. And we use one bank in Los Angeles, USA which handles most of our sales in North and South America, We....

The meeting continued until noon; they all had lunch in the executives dining room, and then spent the afternoon touring the three interconnected buildings which housed administration, research, and production units for a wide variety of high tech nanoproducts.

[[During the two weeks following the visit to Nano-Solar LTD and the interviewing of Dr. Heinz and his administrative colleagues, various members of the inquiry team attempted to follow up on certain difficult answers that they had received. Two components stood out. Nano-Solar LTD had two very steady customers who were suspect. One was Immuno-Central, Inc in Milano, Italy. Immuno-Central, Inc specialized in preparing homing MoABs, had Italian Mafia linkages, and controls the Perzoni Bank and Securities Exchange. Dr. Heinz's mother's expenses in the Munich nursing center are paid from an account in the Perzoni Bank and Securities Exchange, Munich branch. The other regular customer is a new private Ku Chong High Technology Center in Beijing, China. This Center is also associated with a mafia group called the Chinese Five Snakes. It has its own bank called the Fung Won Exchange Bank. Dr. Heinz's father's medical expenses are being paid for from an account the Fung Won Exchange Bank Berlin branch.]]

Dr. Chi Jiang, Dr. Jun Jiang, and Dr. Cho Jiang are fraternal, not identical triplets. They lived together until school age when their father, Xoa Jiang, separated them; Chi went to the USA for part of his education; Cho remained in China but was moved to Nanjing for his education; Jun went to Germany to be educated. So, the triplets are not as close as one would expect. Because the three are all partners and part of the management of the Jiang Nano-Control International, it was decided that all three brothers should be reviewed, one at a time, via a different inquiry team. Therefore, the Committee of Nanotechnology Control's first inquiry team for the Chinese brothers was composed of two nanotechnology scientists, two high technology scientists, one HHS official, one DOJ official, one official from the Department of Transportation, and one certified accountant specializing in China/USA imports/exports. They would talk to Dr. Chi

Jiang first as he was both a Chinese and American citizen, living in Los Angeles.

In the fourth week of January 2033, this third inquiry team sat in the conference room of the JNI factory in Silicon Ledge. Professor-Doctor Chi Jiang, by himself, met with them. He wanted to talk to the entire team in the morning; after lunch he had arranged for the appropriate researchers, production directors, and company officials to meet with the key members of the team. After Dr. Mathuson, inquiry team leader, a nanotechnology scientist from Columbia University, introduced each team member to Dr. Jiang, Dr. Mathuson began with the questions. "Can you please briefly summarize how you started your nanotechnology research, established your company, and in what direction your research and production efforts will go tomorrow?"

Dr. Jiang responded, "How long do I have, five minutes, five hours, or five days?"

And that brought a round of smiles and chuckles as Dr. Mathuson's face developed several shades of red.

"I can give you somewhere between five minutes and five hours. Is that reasonable?"

"I was educated in chemical engineering in New York City, a medical school in London, nanotechnology training in Boston and then nanomedicine in Los Angeles at the California Institute of Technology. So, I was 35 years of age before I took my first job as an Assistant Professor here in California. But I was there in the beginning of the science, that we now call nanotechnology, and the recognition of what such technology could do for improving human life. In other words, day one was basic research in nanotechnology, day two was commercial application of nanomedicine products. I took advantage of the situation and now live in both worlds."

"My lovely Irish wife died when my son was a small child. So today I have two loves, my sixteen-year old son and nanomedicine. I spend sixty hours in a six-day week in nanomedicine, and one full day with my son. And I am happy to see that he appears to have interest and skills in the nanotechnology direction."

"I try to spend most of my research time in the basic science of nanomedicine such as: developing molecules that can construct or repair damaged cell membranes and cellular organelles, working with communication molecules such as mini-hormones and micro-hormones, and trying to develop replacement aging tissues like retinal vision cells in the eye and acoustic cells in the ears. The eyes and the ears are the first body organs that deteriorate during aging. Because basic research does not bring in the money, and to help bridge the gap between basic and applied research, I built, with my brothers, the Jiang Nano-Control International. Both of my brothers have doctorates in chemical engineering, and nanotechnologies. The branch of JNI that you are sitting in is directly under my control. We do both basic research and applied research here. Some of my university students also find good research projects for their PhD studies.:

"Our two branch factories in China at Changzhou and Jincheng City are under control of my youngest brother, Cho. They are predominately factories which produce only nanoproducts that we think are marketable. And my second brother, Jun, lives between New York City, Berlin, and Jincheng City. He is basically responsible for marketing JNI nanoproducts, plus he has three import/export companies involved in chemicals and pharmaceuticals."

"The three of us get together every three years on Chinese New Year Day at our Grandfather's small castle northwest of Beijing near the Great Wall. Grandfather was a high ranking General of Chairman Mao Tse-Tung. It was his money that paid for the education of my father who became a physician in Beijing, paid for all of the advanced education for his three grandsons, and will pay for university expenses for my son, if he decides to go to the university. Chairman Mao endowed all of his senior generals. The Jiang endowment was substantial."

Dr. Mathuson asked, "Do you have regular JNI Board Meetings in which the three of you are together to consult on projects?"

"In the past we had difficulty agreeing on projects. Therefore, several years ago we established a Board of Directors for each Branch of JNI. My brothers are not on the Board of the Los Angeles Branch. And I am not on the Boards of the two Chinese Branches of JNI. Jun travels much but he comes by to see me a couple times a year. We spend two or three days discussing new nanotechnology, what nanoproducts might be ready for the market place next year versus several years from now. He uses this information to seek and establish markets. And I give to him ideas, even methodologies to take to Cho. I have occasionally even suggested nanoproducts would be difficult versus easy to turn over into mass production. So, we do manufacture select Nano-systems in these facilities; and Cho manufactures other Nano-systems in China."

'After lunch I will introduce the laboratory people on your inquiry team to the Directors of our three research divisions – Nano-repair, Nano-exchange, and Nano-communications. And you can talk with some of the students and workers if you wish. I will also take your office people to our CFO and the accounting, shipping, receiving, personnel, and anyone else that you want to talk with. We have nothing to hide. And I hope that you will say this in your final report."

One of the high technology team members asked, "Have you worked with nanocarriers?"

Dr. Jiang answered, "Yes, but not for several years. There is too much competition out there. There are now four or five types of nanocarriers being marketed by several companies. This makes the area of nanocarriers no longer interesting for me."

The other high technology team member asked, "Have you worked with attached or linked natural molecules. For example, a Nano-molecule linked to a protein digestase linked to a MoAB?"

"We are developing new methods of attachment or linkage of synthetic Nano-molecules to natural molecules. This needs a lot more research. I do have two students working on this type of methodology. When perfected, linking artificial and natural molecules should allow for a log leap advance in biology. Our bodies have 30,000 genes which code for near 100,000 natural protein molecules. We can synthesize an almost unlimited number of synthetic Nano- molecules. Using synthesized genes and natural genes we can combine the two. Combined Nano-synthetic and Nano-natural molecules would open the doors to creativity. Now that becomes really scary."

The inquiry team continued talking with Dr. Chi Jiang until noon and had a very nice catered sea food lunch in the conference room. Then the Director of Communications gave the entire team a tour of the factory, and left each team member with the appropriate employee of JNI so they could complete their inquiry. Each team member had left the JNI to start toward their home in the early evening hours; all members were Americans, but living on both coasts, so JNI chauffeured cars made several trips to Los Angeles International Airport.

[[Three weeks later Dr. Mathuson received reports from each of his inquiry team members. He was not really surprised that there were no major problems for Dr. Jiang; he appeared to be a hard-working scientist who was very productive, but they had doubts about his connections with his brothers. No problems in exports/imports, bank accounts, illegal employment, or with nanotechnology patents. But it was unanimous that Dr. Chi Jiang should remain under surveillance, and that Dr. Jun Jiang and Dr. Cho Jiang should be more thoroughly investigated.]]

From the previous President's Commission reports, seven men had been identified as suspects in the effort to solve the macabre killings. Three had been inquired and interviewed. However, Dr. Boris Kukrynisky was a Russian citizen and lived in Moscow, Dr. Mario Kemps was a citizen of Argentina and lived in Buenos Aires, Dr. Cho Jiang was a citizen of the Peoples Republic of China and lived in Nanjing, and Dr. Jun Jiang was a German citizen who was currently in China with no specific known date for returning. So, it would appear that the Division of High Technology's Committee of Nanotechnology Control was currently at a standstill until someone at a higher level of government could obtain for them access to any of these other suspects; or if Dr. Jun Jiang returned to New York City or Berlin.

So, the Committee of Nanotechnology continued to follow, collect, and document high tech and nanotech scientists, monitor their research, and watch for nanoproducts that had weapon-like capacities. While Mr. Dagda and his ISAAT had three candidates whom they would continue to monitor and quietly investigate; and of course, four more for whom they would continue to collect data and try to obtain access.

30

Family Honor

DURING THE SECOND WEEKEND OF February 2034, Li and his father drove up to Big Bear Lake in the Bernardino Mountains, an hour drive north and east of Los Angeles. There was a hot spell in southern California, 92°F; it was the last weekend of Li's mid-school year break, and Dr. Jiang had been giving the recent government review of his life serious thinking. They were to stay for a couple of days at the Big Bears Lodge on Big Bear Lake and perhaps do a little canoeing, fishing, and talking. Big Bears City was at 6,000 feet and a 45°F cool. Located in the mountains close to Los Angeles and San Bernardino it was popular winter and summer. The trout, catfish, and bass were really biting, according to the newspapers. The Christmas-New Year's crowd had completely disappeared. Snow had been light; the ski crowd had not yet arrived. They sort of had things to themselves, which is the way Dr. Jiang wanted it to be.

Going up the last few miles Li said, "The snow-covered pine trees are really beautiful, aren't they Dad?" It had snowed during the previous night.

Father answered, "Yes, it reminds me of my childhood in the mountains of Shijiazhuang, just west of Beijing where your grandfather's old castle is located. As children our father would take us up there each winter in February to celebrate the Chinese New Year. The nature was similar, steep, sharp rock mountains with many pine trees, and snow. There were no man-made paved roads, ski slopes, boat docks, heated and air-conditioned chateaus, or hundreds of people coming and going. Nature was beautiful, and empty of people. When I was there three years ago, it had not changed. I hope that it does not. I want to take you up there someday."

They drove into the front parking area of the Big Bears Lodge which resembled a Swiss Chateau with a series of dormers located on the third floor. Dad had reserved a three-room suite on the upper floor such that each evening those windows would provide a cool western sun descending into the cold blue lake. Just the current opposite effect of a red-hot sun setting over the San Pedro Channel off Los Angeles. They arrived around 7:15, went up to their room, quickly ordered dinner, and toasted (wine to cola) just as the setting sun began to enter the lake for the night. Father and son were both drifting in another world. Both had much to say, but could not yet put it into words, English or Chinese. For now, on to bed.

The next morning Dad asked, "What do you want to do, canoeing or fishing?"

"Both would be good," Li replied with a big smile. He would soon be sixteen, and was looking his Dad directly in the eye. After all, Dad was a full- blooded Chinese, son was half Chinese and half Irish. And Mother was a tall Irish woman. But he had been raised the Chinese way. Even when he now looked down on his Father, physically, he would never be able to alter his cultural ways. Chinese fathers were always first and correct.

They had hearty egg-bacon and pancake breakfasts, as it would be cold out there on the lake, in a canoe, trying to paddle, and to fish with gloved hands. They picked up their thermos jug of hot green tea, donned their parkas, walked down to the lake, rented a two-person canoe, placed their fishing rods and reels into the boat, purchased a small package of caddisflies and a pail of bloodworms to use as bait for fresh water trout. Both Dad and son were planning to catch enough trout to supply them with trout dinners all next week. The restaurant would do the cooking.

Li spoke up, "Do you want to wage ten dollars that I can catch more fish than you do?"

Dad answered, "I will give you ten dollars for every fish beyond what I catch. I catch one and you catch one hundred, I give you $999." And they both laughed. Li said, "Never happen!"

They launched the boat into the gun metal blue water with crisp sunshine filling the sky, but it was slowly disappearing under approaching dark clouds. Predictions were for scattered snow showers in late afternoon; so, the fishing must be accomplished with fast and furious efforts.

Dad suggested, "Let us go over to the north side as the mountains are taller and there is a good forest close to the water which should protect us from the winds as they come on during the afternoon."

They canoed over to Jacob's Cove, let the canoe drift, baited their hooks and tried their luck. After two hours of only a few nibbles, Li suggested, "Why don't we try a little further west toward Swivel's Island and troll."

They paddled for another half hour and as they approached the pencil shaped island they cast in opposing directions from the boat and slowly trolled along the mainland side. Within five minutes Dad caught a small trout. He had just re- baited and set out his troll line when Li hooked a near three-pounder.

Li looked at his Dad's fish, smiled, and said, "Maybe we should be betting on total pounds of fish instead of numbers"

"Just wait," was the response.

By 3:30 PM the winds out of the northwest had become vigorous. They had landed twelve trout, which was going to be more than enough. The white caps in the center of the lake were increasing in number and size, and they had to cut across the center to return to the lodge. So, they stopped fishing and headed back. Half way back a cold rain-snow began. The return trip took over an hour. They were dripping wet and totally exhausted. They docked their canoe, grabbed their fish, and ran for the lodge. As they entered their rooms the smell of smoking wood and the heat of a roaring fireplace hit them in the right place. Li hopped into the hot shower first. Dad ordered crackers and mixed nuts, plus a large tea pot of green tea. After Li finished, next he took his hot shower.

As Dad also put on a wool bathrobe, courtesy of the lodge, he walked into the salon and toward the blazing fire. He looked at the almost empty dish sitting on the table in front of Li, who sat tall in his wool bathrobe. The dish had been filled with nuts before he went in to take his shower. He commented, "I would have ordered double snacks if I knew that that lake turned you into a monkey."

Li replied, "I saved the cold fish for you. Be happy."

And he laughed. Dad just smiled. Teenagers were not born to be understood. But he was very proud of Li. He was becoming a tall, intelligent, gentle and super active young man. Li would make it in life.

And Dad continued, "As usual, weather never stops the Chinese. Five thousand years of living, migrating, and fighting on foot in mountains and snow. And today the 'modern' Republic of China has just crept from being a developing country to the lower level of a developed country, if you ignore the twenty five percent unemployment rate and the one dollar per day wages."

Li was not sure where Dad was going with this history lesson, but he knew better than to change the subject, yet.

"When my brothers and I were about five years old, before our father sent us to three different continents to school, we would see this horrendous poverty; this Chinese human tragedy was on every street corner. I wanted to do something to help my people. My brothers laughed at me and said that all the money in the world would not help one and a half billion people cross the river. I guess they were right."

"So, what did I do, I flew over the river to the Christian west, and learned about atoms and molecules. Yes, I have trained many young doctors, including Chinese students, and I have made a very significant contribution to the knowledge base of medicine. Already work like mine is producing diagnostic tests and drugs that can diagnose and cure diseases which were not detectable or were incurable only ten years ago. Now I ask you, how does that help the Chinese people living in Asia?"

Li said, "Dad, you may be a super scientist, but you are still not a god. Only a god can help one and a half billion people enter the modern world within a couple of generations. If you put together all of the best Chinese scientists, who are trained and working in 'western modern' countries where the best equipment, supplies, and openness to free knowledge is commonplace, you put them all to work, you would not raise the GDP 1% in mainland China. Now Taiwan does not count. It is not a Chinese country. It, just like Japan and Germany, were foreign little brothers of the current most powerful country on earth, the USA. They had tremendous assistance from outside. The Peoples Republic of China never had any rich brothers, and has always been surrounded by non-friends."

"You are right my son," Dad responded. "It would take a miracle, not just one mortal man like me. I guess the one regret that I have is that I did not stay there and try. But if I am totally honest with myself, I would have failed."

And suddenly Li changed the subject. He declared, "Guess what? Last week, in my Kung Fu martial arts group I became a level three instructor. And my teacher says that if I continue in the Five Animals Kung Fu, next year he will recommend me for the American Martial Arts Championship Festival. It is being held in New Orleans. That is a city I have never even flown over. Can I go if I qualify?"

Dad answered, "Of course, if you let me come along and cheer for you." "Maybe we can drink beers together on Bourbon Street. You can drink beer there at the age sixteen," Li slipped in.

Dad replied, "If you win, I will even buy the beers."

And the ice was finally broken such that they could unburden their troubled minds.

After another hour or so of small talk, Dad finally opened up his current nightmare. "I am sure that you heard about the recent visit to the JNI factory by a Federal governmental regulatory group. Because of the many mass murders during the past few years, and the difficulty in determining the cause of these murders, the previous government passed laws which established a new Division of High Technology that is now responsible for monitoring many types of high-tech research. They have a Committee of Nanotechnological Control which has several inquiry teams. These groups are interviewing scientists, and also reviewing their laboratories, research projects, and production products. They are making an inventory of goods and are watching nanotechnology. One of their inquiry teams spent all day, a couple of weeks ago, with us at Silicon Ledge. It was scary because I have never been so challenged before. I have nothing to hide. But just their presence made me start to doubt myself."

Li asked, "What do you mean, Dad?"

"It is not my specific research projects or our products that concern me. But my brothers take my ideas and sometimes steal my products. I do not know what they do with them. I have been at fault for not watching them more closely. But I am so busy that I do not like to travel just to check out my brothers. I should be able to trust them. But now I do not."

And Li knew he was talking about a possible relationship between the Chinese Branches of JNI and the macabre murders. And he knew it was time for his confession.

"Dad, I also have a fear of those many deaths and my uncles. I must tell you. I am sorry but I should have told you before. Several years ago, I met three boys my age from three other countries. We became friends and called ourselves the Four Colored Musketeers, because we each have a slightly different skin coloring. During the last couple of years, my American brother, whose father was one of those killed, has an uncle who is investigating these murders. The two of them talked and we learned that several JXW nanoproducts were used in helping cure people, thus the Jiang name came into the picture. I do not think any of the nanoproducts have killed people."

"While I was living with Uncle Jun in Nanking, I learned that JNI had factories in Changzhou, Jinchang, and in Masyaf, Syria. Did you know about the Masyaf factory?"

Astonished, Dad blurted out, "No, I did not."

"Since you never mentioned it, I thought that you didn't. Also, did you know that the Jinchang factory kidnaps slum people from the surrounding neighborhood and use them in experiments?"

Dad could not say anything, finally he said, "I suspected that my brothers were being less than honest with me when we discussed research and production methodology in those factories. But I never dreamed that anyone, let alone my own blood kin would do such things. Does the American government know about this?"

"Yes. And in the past few months my South African brother's father was so killed, and my Turkish brother's father was so killed. And my deepest fear is that our JNI nanoproducts could have done this." And he broke down crying.

His father went over to him, sat down on the arm of Li's chair, and held him close for several minutes. As his son was crying with guilt, he swore that he would have it out with his brothers next Friday, as that was the 2033 Chinese New Year day. All three of Jiang brothers would meet at grandfather's castle for two days.

———◦◦◦❊◦◦◦———

The following Thursday Chi Jiang flew to Beijing International Airport, rented a four-wheel-drive SUV, and drove for three hours through snow and ice to Shijiazhuang and then on up to Grandfather General Mei Jiang's old castle.

'Jun and Cho Jiang are already in China so they may have arrived earlier,' he thought.

As Chi approached the dark stone thirty room two story rectangular castle, two turrets, one on each corner, he saw smoke coming from all nine chimneys, so he thought that his brothers were probably here, and the villagers were working. The castle was surrounded by sharp mountains and dark forests; it was built as a hunting retreat for the two sons of Emperor Yuannian or Hong Xiuquan in the middle of the nineteenth century. It had always been a family- oriented castle and did not have the usual tall stone walls surrounding it. In addition, it had not been modernized; February New Years' Days required an effort from the local village, which received an annual retainer to maintain the castle; the villagers had just cleaned the building, arranged the beds, brought and prepared food, and lit all of the fireplaces. The two cars sitting outside the entry confirmed that his brothers were here. Both cars were covered with last night's snow, so he knew they had arrived a day or two ago.

He was not sure how to discuss the Syrian factory problem, but it was critical that it be discussed. As he stepped out of the car, both brothers came bounding out of the door to greet him. He was immediately suspicious. This was not normal.

Jun, always the more aggressive of the two brothers, was the first to reach Chi, gave him a big hug, and said, "Welcome to our common home. It is good that we return here regularly to renew contact with our family. It is the only common place remaining where our souls can meet."

Cho quickly followed, "Welcome home." And he also gave Chi a big hug.

Chi was rather shocked and all he could manage to say was, "Thank you. I also am happy to return to the house of our fathers. I only wish that Chinese New Year's Day could be in July, that way we would not have to live from fireplace to fireplace."

It brought forth some smiles as they knew Chi's life in southern California deprived his body of its anti-freeze molecules. The cold winter wind was really howling; and indeed, Chi was shivering already.

Jun grabbed Chi's suitcase and the brothers quickly went inside out of the wind, but with all the fireplaces blazing the temperature would not go above 65°F during the next couple of days.

They walked directly into the Great Room, two-floor high of open space, dark oak paneled, and a bright red-orange fire in the walk-in fireplace on the far wall. Chi immediately began to warm up. In the past this room had provided a nest for fifteen to twenty young Chinese lords to feast, party, whore, and celebrate, simply because they had family relationships to the current Chinese Emperor's family. On one wall hung numerous weapons used in war and hunting including the many types of bladed weapons such as the qiang (long spear), jian (long sword), ji (halberd), pi (double bladed spear), and the dao (saber). Another wall hung a group of weapons used in martial arts such as the balisong (butterfly knife), karambit (small curved knife), dagger (double edged knife), and pinyin (crescent moon shaped blades).

In two of the corners of the room stood man sized statues with full-scale eighteenth century body armor and war-helmets. Down the center of the room was a twenty-foot long table with benches which allowed unlimited feasting each night in order to celebrate the day's successful hunting. Hanging from the second level walls one could also see the hunting trophies, some more than one hundred years old. They included the heads of several deer with more than fifty- point antlers, wild boar, Chinese tiger, Siberian tiger, snow leopard, Tibetan wolves, and big ram Argali sheep. Indeed, it had been a hunters' castle-lodge for the privileged.

The three brothers walked through the great room to a small one floor tall meeting sized room with a blazing fireplace. It was nice and warm, almost cozy. It was also paneled with dark oak wood which was as old as the building itself. One of the villagers had taken Chi's suitcase up to a second-floor bedroom. All bedrooms were similar except for the gigantic Master bedroom, almost as large as the current conference room, but where only the original Jiang owner had slept, Grandfather General Mei Jiang. The General's spirit was still sleeping there, or so his male offspring thought. No other Jiang male had ever slept in the room.

One of the villagers brought three brass cups containing warmed red wine. After a couple sips of the tasty wine Chi began, "I am happy that we three at least get together once every three years. I think that we need to bring our families together here also. I doubt if I would even recognize my nephews and nieces walking down the street. I have not seen any of them in several years."

Jun said, "Chi is right. We should try to bring our families together often. Maybe we could rotate. One year in China, one year in Germany, and one year in the USA, California. That way the children could also see other cultures."

Cho responded, "My daughters are so stupid they would not know what culture was. Besides, women only need the one culture where they were raised. I have Chinese business friends who educated their daughters in Moscow and in Paris. I know."

"And now they can be proud of their highly productive daughters," Chi remarked.

"That is what you may think," said Cho. "One problem, both of the daughters are married, playing housewife, raising children, and living in their husband's culture. The fathers don't even see their daughters anymore. Where is a father supposed to live out his life if his daughters desert him for another culture? And naturally it would be a culture where the father does not even speak the language."

"And what if you don't have any daughters," Chi responded. "Just because you guys have daughters; I have to hope my son can find a girl he likes who becomes a daughter in law that I like." And he laughed.

"Remember the fun times when we were kids here in this old castle," Jun thought out loud. "I think it was our last visit in the summer before father sent us in different directions. We were playing up near Blackberry Hollow when the wild boar blasted out of the berry patch and headed directly for us. Chi and I climbed up two nearby pines, but Cho was in the open and couldn't make it to a tree, so he started running. What does our big brother, the hero do? He hops down from his tree, picks up a rock, steps out into the open, shouts at the pig, throws the rock at him, and hits him right on the nose. The pig didn't like it, changed directions, and headed toward Chi. And Chi just made a face at it and again hopped back up into his tree. That wild boar went right up the tree after you.

Remember he managed to rip your pants leg when you were at least twenty feet up the tree."

"That is because he was twenty feet long," Chi laughed.

Jun continued, "And Cho did not stop running until he reached the inside of the castle."

The only memories of their common childhood were between five and fifteen years of age, after which father, for reasons he did not explain to them, sent them to three different places to begin new lives to grow up. For the next couple of hours, they reminisced about those first years, and especially they pretended to be hunter, soldier, prince, and emperor in the forested mountains on bright summer days. As with all adults, such times are just memories, some to be remembered and some to be not-remembered.

Near 7:30 PM the villagers set one of the long tables with three benches in the Great Room and brought forth the venison steaks, baked potatoes and the few vegetables that were available in the mountain village in mid-winter. But the fresh dark bread and warm red wine allowed the meal to be special. The setting was unique and family oriented. A couple hours later the food was consumed but two jugs of wine remained. A villager set a basket of red apples on the table. They opened the second jug of red wine; and started the post dinner conference with red apples and wine.

Chi began, "We need to talk some business before we can no longer talk." And he held up his wine glass and gave a toast, "Chtob vse byli zdorovy." (Russian for - let everyone be healthy.)

Chi continued, "If you have not yet heard; the American government has a new Division of High Technology which has a Committee of Nanotechnology Control that has established several inquiry teams. These teams go out to selected nanotechnology laboratories and factories, interview scientists and workers, and are developing an inventory as to what type of research is being done in every location. An inquiry team came to the JNI at Silicon Ledge a couple of weeks ago and spent all day talking to everyone and making notes of research, production, finances, imports and exports, bank accounts, travel of key people, important visitors, and on and on. And they went back ten years examining our bookkeeping and finances. Now I was told that this was just an inquiry, not an investigation. From the inquiry, this team will recommend whether we should be investigated, officially, or not. Changzhou and Jincheng may be next."

"Don't worry about us," Cho replied. "We will not be touched."

Both Cho and Jun looked Chi directly in the eye, and seemed to say, so what? The air was getting cold, even in front of the sparkling fireplace.

After a few moments, Chi continued, "Both Changzhou and Jincheng are legally registered as factory branches of JNI. JNI is an American registered company. Therefore, the American Government can, by international law, appeal to the Chinese government to allow an investigation of both of these companies."

Cho just laughed. "If they do that, I will ask the Chinese government to nationalize both companies and they will no longer be branches of JNI. Our current exports are bringing a healthy profit which Beijing now understands to be a good thing. So, don't threaten me."

Chi turned to Jun and asked, "And what is your opinion of this?"

Jun said, "The only JNI that should concern you is the American JNI. You are the President, CEO, and Chairman of the Board of Directors. We are not even on the Board. We are simply major shareholders. And that burden can be lifted in one telephone call to New York's Wall Street. I agree with Cho. Do not be afraid of some new American government committee."

Chi answered, "I think I am beginning to understand. All right, I am certain that you are aware of the five hundred morbid killings around the world that is being blamed upon nanotechnology systems. The news media is even using the word Nano-weapons. Such publicity hurts both research funding and sales of nanotechnological products. Do either of you know anything about these killings?"

Jun looked at Cho and said, "In any killing with guns, single murders or massacres or wars, is the person that provides the guns and bullets charged with the killings? No. The person who does the actual shooting or the politician or general who orders the shooting is charged with murder or genocide. The factory that produces, sells, and delivers those guns, bullets, tanks, artillery, bombs and even the jets or missiles goes free. Killing of people is not the fault of weapons' manufacturers, regardless of the manufacturer."

Cho added, "Hundreds of years ago wars were fought with bows, arrows, and cutting weapons. Look around you on the walls. The blacksmiths hand-produced those weapons. But he was not charged with the murder of the people who were killed with his weapons. No. The blacksmith was a great and indispensable member of the family of the generals or warlords. He even moved from army to army, and was well paid. Without him they might not have adequate weapons technology to even hunt or fight. Hunting/killing weapons went from stone to copper to bronze to iron to steel swords and arrow heads. And then came along, via Chinese creation, gun power. Next, the numerous advanced modern explosive killing weapons of today. Never were the people who made any of those weapons accused of murder."

Jun continued, "Alfred Nobel invented dynamite, explosives that killed many, many people. Was he ever accused of murder? No. The gigantic profits that he made from selling his explosive 'killing' weapon are used today to give large monetary rewards to people, who are considered by a small group of Swedes, to be outstanding in generating new knowledge. Some of that new knowledge leads to the basis for new weapons."

Chi was beginning to understand that his brothers, whether involved in the Nanoweapons that were used in the macabre killings of so many people or not, they did not even consider that whoever supplied those weapons was guilty. So, he turned to a different approach.

"I have learned that in the two factories at Changzhou and Jincheng you are using humans to test various nanoproducts. And that these men, women, and children are not paid volunteers, but are homeless migrants and immigrants living in the slums near the factories, especially in Jincheng. Is this true?"

"No. This is not true," Cho replied. "We do not use children at either factory." And he and Jun started laughing.

Chi's face turned red, and he did not know what to say. These were his brothers and they were admitting, indirectly, that unknowing humans were part of the research testing in both Chinese factories. Again, as Cho and Jun were still smirking, but not saying anything, Chi decided to ask the big question.

"Is there a factory in Syria that is producing some of our nanotechnological systems?" he asked.

His brothers did not answer, but looked at the fire and continued smiling. They realized that their brother knew everything. They knew he had recently been on an American Presidential Commission to investigate these international killings, so he probably learned these things while on that Commission. Finally, Cho spoke, "The factory in Masyaf is not registered to anyone or any country. And it simply became necessary to test certain nanoproducts on men and women, and also on groups of people. So, we subcontracted these research efforts. And it is working out very well."

Chi really could not believe what he was hearing. He began thinking, 'My genetic brothers are killing people in order to test new Nano-systems. And this is justified because if those Nano-systems are finally used to kill 'normal' people, the killers will be the ones who use the weapons. The ones who produce the weapons will be innocent.'

This was too much to swallow in one bite. Chi stood up, gave both of his brothers a strange look, and went upstairs to bed. Later, he would deal with this problem in a different way.

The next morning Chi spent the entire morning hiking, by himself, up in the mountains above the castle. He visited all of his old favorite haunts. This was his most favorite place on earth. It was here he could think most clearly; and he did.

31

The End or The Beginning?

TWO DAYS AFTER THE CHINESE New Year's Day, Dagda Murphy was one of the first to know. All seven of the macabre murder suspects had been under continuous surveillance by ISAAT. Therefore Mr. Murphy knew that all three Jiang brothers were in their grandfather's mountain castle in Shijiazhuang, China. He had two of his people staying in the nearby village and following their daily activities. So, he was the first American to receive the news from China.

The electronic encrypted message was as follows:

1-XXX-1 - All three Jiang brothers dead. Chi Jiang found dead in his bed, heart stopped; no blood found anywhere. Jun Jiang found dead in his bed, head missing; no blood found anywhere. Cho Jiang found dead in his bed, head missing; no blood found anywhere. Speculation is that Chi killed his brothers, cut off their heads, and buried the heads somewhere in the mountains. He then took some type of poison which stopped his heart from beating. No third parties are thought to be involved: 1-000-1

How was Uncle Dagda going to break this news to Jamie and the Four Colored Musketeers? All four of their fathers had now been killed with some type of Nano-weapon. At least maybe with all the Jiang brothers now dead, hopefully the Korrectorizer was gone from the picture. Maybe the macabre killings would cease. Maybe.

At least there are four fatherless boys alive and trying to make the world a better place in which to survive.

www.ingramcontent.com/pod-product-compliance
Lightning Source LLC
Chambersburg PA
CBHW031615180726
48284CB00005B/1552